LOVE ON A DARE DUET

CARA MARSI

THE PAINTED LADY PRESS

A GROOM FOR CHRISTMAS

BY

CARA MARSI

When a young woman hires her hometown's former bad boy to be her pretend fiancé for the holidays, she finds she can't wrap up her feelings as easily as a Christmas gift.

New York jewelry designer Graceann Palmer has two days to find a fiancé to bring home to Pennsylvania for the holidays so her matchmaking mama will quit fixing her up with jerks. The Falcon, a motorcycle-riding, leather-clad former high school crush, helped her out once before. Maybe he'll do it again.

Jake Falco, man of many mysteries, is back in town on a mission—one the people of Spirit Lake most likely won't appreciate. When Graceann presents him with her crazy scheme, it gives him something he's always wanted—a chance to get to know Graceann. It also gives him the perfect opportunity to add fuel to his project of revenge.

But as Jake and Graceann grow closer, their engagement-of-convenience begins to feel like the real deal—until Jake's secrets are revealed.

Can a relationship that began with lies and secrets bloom like a rare Christmas rose into happily-ever-after?

CHAPTER ONE

"*I* have two days to find a fiancé." Ignoring the anxiety that tightened her stomach, Graceann Palmer dipped her fork into her apple pie à la mode and slipped the tasty treat into her mouth.

Her friend Kate sat next to her at the counter in the quaint fifties-era Spirit Lake Diner, located just outside the small Pennsylvania town of the same name. Kate grinned. "You could advertise online: *Fiancé wanted for Christmas. Good pay. Temporary position.*"

"Like I'd get a real upstanding guy that way," Graceann said.

Kate shot her a sympathetic smile. "Face it. You'll have to tell your family you lied."

Bing Crosby's *I'll Be Home for Christmas* flowed from the jukebox, mocking Graceann. Her lie had caught up with her. She would come home for Christmas, minus a made-up fiancé.

Graceann finished her pie and pushed the plate away. "Tell my family the truth and have my mom try to fix me up with someone like the dentist she invited to spend the holidays with us last year? Boring, conceited, and he couldn't keep his hands to himself. Yuck."

The door opened, bringing in a fresh round of cold, snowy late December air. Shivering, Graceann drew her sweater closer around her.

"I wouldn't mind finding *that* under my Christmas tree," Kate said.

Graceann followed her friend's gaze to the tall man who'd just entered the diner. Dressed all in black—black motorcycle boots, black jeans, black leather jacket—and walking with the lithe grace of a panther, he took a seat at the other end of the counter. She studied him while he studied the menu. He had classic "bad boy" written all over his features—sharp cheekbones, dark stubble on a square jaw, and midnight black hair tied into a ponytail. Long, tapered fingers held the menu.

Suddenly, he looked up. Clear blue eyes connected with hers. Recognition spiked through her and sent her pulse jumping like a kid on Christmas morning.

"The Falcon," she whispered.

"What?" Kate gasped. "You're right. It *is* The Falcon."

His full lips tilted in a slow, sexy grin, showing even white teeth. He nodded at them before turning his attention to the waitress. After he gave his order, he didn't look in their direction again.

Kate gripped Graceann's arm, her fingers digging into Graceann's flesh beneath the heavy sweater. "Wow. The Falcon. I heard he left town the day after his graduation from Spirit Lake High fourteen years ago and hasn't been heard from since."

"Wonder what he's doing back here," Graceann said. In school, she'd had a crush on The Falcon even though he was two years ahead of her. She'd never told anyone, not even Kate.

"He's a little scruffy," Kate said.

"Scruffy, my tush. He's hot."

Kate grabbed her arm again as Graceann lifted her coffee mug. Coffee sloshed over the sides onto the counter. Setting the mug down, Graceann gave her friend an exasperated look. "What?"

"I have it," Kate said. "Your fiancé."

"What are you talking about?"

"The Falcon. I'll bet he'll pretend to be your fiancé. After Zach bowed out, you said you'd be willing to pay someone. The Falcon always needed cash. Do it. Ask him."

"You're crazy. I haven't seen him in fourteen years. He could be a serial killer for all we know."

Kate shook her head. "He's not. We would have heard." She leaned closer. "You'll be at your grandmother's with the whole family. You'll be safe. Your grandmother is old-fashioned. She'll put you in separate rooms. It's not like he's a total stranger. Bring him to meet the family, pretend you're wildly in love. Your mom will quit trying to fix you up. After the holidays you won't ever have to see him again. Once you're back in New York, you can tell your family you broke the engagement. That's what you planned to do with Zach."

Graceann put a hand up. "This is the craziest idea you've ever had, and you've had plenty. I can't ask this guy to go along with my scheme. I'll have to resign myself to fending off another loser my mom pushes at me. She means well, but she won't accept that I'm not interested in marriage. After what Michael did, my whole family feels sorry for me. I don't want or need their pity."

"Michael was a jerk. He didn't deserve you. Listen to me, Graceann. Ask. The. Falcon. What could it hurt to at least ask?"

"His name is Jake, and I'll think about it."

"Don't wait too long. He'll be out of here and you'll have missed your chance."

Graceann sipped her coffee and stole glances at Jake Falco. Maybe Kate was right. Jake had always been nice to her and had even come to her aid once when the mean girls were harassing her. He might help her out now. At her grandmother's, they'd be surrounded by family. She wouldn't be alone with him. Her gut feelings were usually on target, so she'd learned to listen. She'd ignored her instincts with Michael and look how that had turned out. Something was telling her to go ahead and take a chance on Jake.

"I'll do it." She stood before she lost her nerve.

He raised his head as she approached. His eyes, blue as a bright winter sky, lit with awareness. He brazenly scanned her in the same way he used to check out some of the other girls in school, but never her.

Her heart pounded, the sound pulsing in her ears. She nearly turned to rush back to her stool, but desperation propelled her toward him.

"Graceann Palmer," he said when she reached him. His voice, deep, smoky, richer than she remembered, warmed her like well-aged whiskey.

The opening line she'd rehearsed dried in her throat. "Hello, Fal…Jake," she stammered.

He gestured to the stool next to him and threw her a sardonic smile. "Have a seat. Catch up on old times."

What was she doing? They were no longer in high school. This man was a stranger to her now. She sat down gingerly and glanced over at Kate. Her friend gave her the thumbs-up sign.

"So, Graceann Palmer," he said, turning in his stool to face her. "What have you been up to?"

Giddily flattered that he remembered her name, she found the words to answer him. "I moved to New York City." She smoothed a hand over her jeans, feeling as nervous as the awkward teen she'd once been. "I design jewelry."

He quirked an eyebrow. "Impressive. Did you design that necklace you're wearing?"

She raised her left hand to rub the large blue stone set in sterling silver and hanging from a silver chain. It was one of her favorites. "I did."

Uneasy under his intense gaze, she lowered her hand to rest it on her thigh.

"Not married?" he asked.

Her chest knotted with the familiar pain of betrayal. "Not married. What about you?"

"Nope. Never been."

Whew. She hadn't considered the possibility he'd be married. "Where do you live and what sort of work do you do?"

"I live here and there," he said with a shrug. "Some would say I don't work at all."

"Intriguing." She noted the age and well-worn dullness of his distressed leather jacket. Maybe Kate was right. He'd lived on the poor side of town when they were growing up. Maybe things hadn't improved since he'd lit out all those years ago.

The sounds of food sizzling on the griddle and silver clanking against glass filled the diner, but an uncomfortable silence settled between them. The pungent odor of hamburger and onions cooking roiled her already unsettled stomach.

"I'm surprised you recognized me," she said into the silence. "It's been fourteen years."

He studied her. When his glance dropped to her mouth, his eyes darkened. "How could I forget those beautiful green cat eyes of yours or those lips?" he said in a husky voice.

Stunned silent, she opened her mouth and snapped it shut. Up close, he carried the scent and the appearance of the outdoors —all hard muscles, bronzed skin and the aroma of clean, pine-scented air. She swallowed. It was easy to believe the rumors that had swirled around him in school, stories about the women he'd slept with. Not girls. Women. He was playing with her. He couldn't really be trying to seduce her. Unlike the insecure girl she'd been, she could now handle the likes of Jake Falco.

Graceann drew a deep breath and plunged in. "I have a proposition for you."

He quirked that eyebrow again. "Sounds interesting."

9

"It's not what you think."

He laughed. "What I'm thinking is very good."

Heat suffused her cheeks. "Clean out your mind. It's a business proposition."

"Too bad." He signaled the waitress for two cups of coffee, then re-settled onto his stool, his attention on Graceann. "Go on. I'm listening."

Covering her anxiety, she added cream to her coffee, stirred, then took too big a sip and choked as the liquid burned its way down her throat.

He patted her on her back until she waved him away. "I'm fine," she managed. Pushing aside her cup to let the drink cool, she locked her gaze with his. She would not let him intimidate her.

"I need a fiancé."

His lips tilted in amusement. "Are you asking me to marry you, Ms. Palmer?"

"No. I'm asking you to pretend we're engaged."

He lowered his gaze, stared into his coffee, then back to her. "Why would I do that?"

"I'll pay you five thousand dollars."

His features tightened. "You think I need money?"

"No! I'm the one who's desperate."

"I see." He smiled, but the smile didn't touch his eyes.

"Wait. That didn't come out right. I'm desperate because my pretend fiancé canceled out on me at the last minute and I need a substitute. Fast."

"Baby, I'm not a substitution for any man."

"No, I didn't mean—"

"Forget it." He studied her for a moment, then smiled thoughtfully and reached out to brush a strand of her hair off her face. His touch sent heat flowing like warmed honey through her veins. "Just know I'm the real thing, princess."

She pulled away. "Stop playing with me. This is strictly business. You come with me to my grandmother's house day after tomorrow. We stay through the holidays. We pretend we're in love. Everyone is happy. New Year's Day I pay you the five thousand. We go our separate ways."

Turning away, he sipped his coffee. Then he put down his cup and met her gaze. "Why would you need a fake fiancé? I would think you could have as many men as you wanted."

"Why is my business. What do you say? Or do you already have Christmas plans?"

A shadow seemed to flit across his face. "I have no plans."

She bit down on her lip. "Well?"

He glanced at her left hand again. "We'll need a ring."

Relief flooded her. *Yes!* He'd do it. She was safe from another terrible fix-up. "I made a ring. It's cubic zirconia, but it looks like the real thing."

He laughed. "You come prepared."

"A friend was going to act the part of my fiancé, but at the last minute he got an invitation to go to Santo Domingo with his new girlfriend."

"Not much of a friend."

"Zach would have stayed, but I told him not to worry about me. He really likes this new girl and I didn't want to wreck it for him. Zach had his heart broken a year ago and needs someone in his life."

"You're a good friend as well as beautiful." Giving her another of his sexy grins, he held out his hand to shake hers. "Well, Ms. Graceann Palmer, it's a deal. You've hired yourself a fiancé."

CHAPTER TWO

*J*ake shifted his garment bag to his other hand and picked up his duffel when the dark blue BMW with Graceann at the wheel drove into the parking lot of the Spirit Lake Diner. She pulled up and gave him a tentative smile. If possible, she was sexier than she was two days ago when he'd agreed to go along with her crazy plan. He had his reasons for agreeing to help her, but he wouldn't delve into them now.

He walked around to the passenger side, opened the back door, deposited his duffel on the floor, hung the garment bag, then got into the front seat. "A punctual woman," he said as he fastened his seatbelt. "First woman I've known to do that."

She pulled out of the parking lot and slid a glance at him. "How many women have you known?"

He chuckled at the way her face reddened. For all her innate sexuality, she still retained the innocence he remembered from all those years ago. "I've known a few."

"I'll bet you have."

"Are you being sarcastic, Ms. Palmer?"

"No, not at all. I'm sorry. I'm really grateful to you for helping me out like this."

He didn't want her gratitude. A kiss? He wouldn't refuse that, though. "Nice car," he said.

"It belongs to Zach. I don't own a car. Don't need one in New York City." She cleared her throat. "When we get close to my grandmother's I'll pull over and we can change places. They know I don't have a car so we'll tell them this is yours."

He shrugged. "Whatever." He settled into his seat and watched the countryside flash by like a Currier & Ives winter scene. The Poconos were beautiful this time of year with snow blanketing the mountains. There'd been times in the past fourteen years when he'd actually missed it here.

Between Christmas and New Year's the place would be swarming with skiers. He'd never been part of the ski crowd, never part of any crowd. Suited him just fine. He studied Graceann's profile. Her straight nose and firm chin hinted at a strength he suspected she didn't know she had. Concentrating on her driving, she flicked out her tongue to sweep along her top lip.

He shifted as his jeans got a little tighter. He wondered if she realized how damn sexy she was. She must have felt him watching because she glanced at him. "What are you looking at?"

"You, and it's a beautiful sight."

Her attention back on the winding road, she said, "Stop playing, Jake."

"Aren't we supposed to be in love? I'm in fiancé mode already."

"Save it for the family."

"Why don't you tell me what's going on? The truth. Since you hired me, I think I need to know why you're doing this and what I'm up against."

She gripped the steering wheel with her gloved hands and concentrated on the road. "It's like this. My mother thinks I need a man in my life. I've told her I'm not interested in marriage, but she won't believe me. Especially after what happened two years ago."

"What happened?"

She turned those big green eyes on him for a second, then focused back on the road. "I was in a relationship. He wasn't who I thought he was. It ended badly."

A twinge of guilt made Jake shift uneasily. He wasn't exactly who Graceann thought he was either.

"Anyway," she continued. "My family feels sorry for me. They were upset by what happened. My sister has a terrific husband and two wonderful kids, my parents have had a happy marriage for almost forty years. They, especially my mother, won't rest until I'm safely married."

"How is having a temporary fiancé going to help things? When the holidays are over, we go our separate ways."

"I'll tell them I broke the engagement. If they think I broke up with you, they'll stop feeling sorry for me because they'll know I'm in control of my life and perfectly happy on my own."

He sank into his seat, making himself more comfortable. "There's a flaw in your plan. I don't believe your family will let up on you. Are you going to hire a new fiancé every Christmas?"

She laughed, a clear, crystal sound that floated through the car and arrowed straight to the empty places in his heart.

"I know my family. My plan will work."

"Let's hope so. For your sake. Tell me about your family."

She visibly relaxed and he guessed she was more at ease talking about a safer subject.

"My dad is Mark," she began. "He's a retired engineer. He owned his own engineering firm. My mom is Angie. She, along with two friends, used to own a gift shop in town. My sister is Lorrie, a schoolteacher, but now a stay-at-home mom. She's six years older than I am so she was out of school when you started. Her husband is Andrew. He works for an insurance company. And there's Grandmom." Graceann's voice softened. "I grew up in Grandmom's house. We all lived with her. My parents still do. Grandmom's the greatest."

At her obvious love for her family, a familiar knot of regret and loss tightened in Jake's chest. He shoved it away, back deep inside him where it belonged.

A half hour later Graceann turned off the main road onto a smaller road, then pulled over. He recognized it as the driveway to Spirit Manor, the Palmer family mansion. Once, as a teenager, he'd taken his newly-restored motorcycle out for a test drive. Harry, the mechanic he did odd jobs for all through school, had given him the wreck of a bike two years before. Jake had lovingly restored it, and on a glorious spring day he'd ridden it to the outskirts of town where the wealthy people lived. He'd driven up to Spirit Manor to get a glimpse of Graceann's house. He still remembered the feeling of sitting on his bike and gazing at the large stone mansion, wondering what it would feel like to have a real family, with siblings, and loving parents.

He'd done all right for himself. The good people of Spirit Lake might have ignored him and brushed him aside as Falco trash, but that was their problem. Revenge was a bitch.

He and Graceann exchanged places, and he adjusted the seat and mirrors, put the car in gear and drove the rest of the way. The house, gray stone with a turret on one side, loomed ahead, peeking through the evergreens like an ancient ever-watchful sentinel. Jake rubbed his hand along his denim-clad thigh as anxiety wound through him. He shouldn't be nervous. He was only playing a part, something he was good at. He'd been acting, hiding his true self, for most of his life.

He pulled into the circular driveway in front of the impressive structure. The sculptured fountain with its marble carving of an Ancient Roman woman surrounded by fish spewing water was now covered and dry. He remembered admiring the fountain that long-ago spring day. The statue with her arms outstretched seemed to welcome all visitors. He'd wondered then if the flesh and blood family would welcome him as the marble woman seemed to. Would they welcome him now?

Next to him, Graceann let out a sigh. "Here we are. Curtain time."

He unfastened his seatbelt and leaned toward her. "Might as well start now." Framing her face between his hands, he touched his lips to hers. At first she stiffened, but he continued to press his lips against hers, drinking in her sweetness. Her lips softened and she let out a low moan. Surprised and pleased at her reaction, he deepened the kiss, slipping his tongue into her willing mouth. She slid her hands up his chest and pressed closer.

Suppressing a groan, he fought the desire to skim his hands over her ribcage to her chest. For a petite woman, she had magnificent breasts.

The sound of voices cut through his sensual haze. He reluctantly drew away. Graceann watched him with wonder in her incredible eyes. Her breathing was labored. He resisted a smile. This gig might be lots more interesting than he'd hoped.

"That was for practice, right?" She rubbed a finger over her lips and lowered her voice. "You really know how to play a part."

"You didn't like it?"

Her face pinked. "It doesn't matter what I like. This is a business deal."

"So you keep reminding me." He looked toward the steps where a group of people huddled watching them. "Your family?"

She looked over and groaned. "Do you think they saw us?"

"I'm sure they did. You stay there and I'll come around and open your door."

"I'm capable of opening my own door."

He touched the tip of her nose. "But we want to make a good impression, especially on your grandmother."

"Then maybe we'd better sit here for a little while," she said with a pointed glance at his lap.

He grinned. "See what you do to me?" When she rolled her eyes, he laughed. "Give me a minute or two."

"I'll get out first." She unfastened her seatbelt, opened the car door, and stepped out. With a wave to the group on the steps, she called out, "Hey, everybody. We're here."

Jake watched as her family ran down the steps to greet her. His lips still burned from their kiss. Damn! The woman could kiss.

After she'd been hugged by each member of her family, they looked toward him, and Jake knew it was show time. He looked down. Good to go. With a grimace, he left the car and walked toward the group. Graceann grabbed his hand and drew him forward. "Everyone, this is Jake Falco, my fiancé."

He could swear he heard a note of pride in her voice. He dismissed it as wishful thinking.

"Jake, this is my grandmother, Bea Palmer," she said, indicating a slender woman in her eighties with softly curling blonde hair and a twinkle in her blue eyes.

"So happy to meet you, Jake," her grandmother said, holding out her hand.

He took her hand, noting how fragile it felt, like a small bird. "Nice to meet you, Mrs. Palmer."

"Call me Grandmom."

In a rush, Graceann introduced him to her mother Angie, an older version of Graceann, who shook his hand and frowned. "Falco? Are you from around here?"

"Jake's from Brooklyn," Graceann said.

She quickly introduced him to the rest of the family—her dad Mark, who gave him a tight smile while he assessed Jake. Her sister Lorrie, a blonde who resembled their father, gave him a quick hug. Next came Lorrie's husband Andrew, a slim balding man, and their two kids, baby Christian and toddler Isabella. Jake's head swam with all the names. The love the Palmer family had for each other was palpable, filling the air. A pang of envy for all he'd missed tugged at his heart.

"Let's see the ring," Lorrie said, diverting his attention.

Graceann slipped off one black leather glove and held out her left hand. A huge stone glimmered in the weak sunlight. Smaller stones surrounded the main one. Graceann was a hell of a jewelry designer. He'd seen plenty of diamonds in his line of work, and if he didn't know any different, he'd think hers was the real deal.

The women gathered around ooohing and aaahing. Graceann's father looked at Jake and shrugged. Jake smiled.

"Let's go in," her dad said. When Jake moved to go to the car to get their luggage, her dad shooed him away, saying, "We'll get that later."

Graceann reached for Jake's hand as they climbed the marble steps. He leaned in to whisper in her ear. "Great ring. Could have fooled me."

"Thanks," she whispered. "Ready? Too late to back out now."

He squeezed her hand. "I'm not going anywhere."

*G*raceann stepped into her grandmother's large marble-floored foyer. Inhaling the sweetly sharp aroma of holly and evergreens, she glanced around, trying to picture the festively decorated space through Jake's eyes. The oversized potted poinsettia plants around the perimeter showcased the stately Christmas tree, lit by a myriad of twinkling white lights and festooned with multi-colored balls. The tree stood in the niche formed by the curving staircase and stretched from the floor to almost touch the two-story high ceiling. Memories of happy family Christmases flooded her, warming her all over.

But more was happening to her than joyous holiday memories. Jake's hand in hers had tingles running up her arm. And that kiss in the car even now warmed her like hundreds of burning Christmas candles. Maybe she'd made a mistake in hiring him as her pretend fiancé. It would take all her willpower to get through the holidays without wanting another kiss.

At least.

She stared at Jake, but couldn't read his expression. Vaguely disappointed he didn't seem to share her enthusiasm for the beautiful holiday decor, she forced a smile and turned to her grandmother. "Grandmom, the tree's more beautiful than usual, if possible."

"Thank you, dear. Your mother and Lorrie did most of it."

"I love it."

"We guys carried the tree in and set it up," Andrew, Lorrie's husband, said.

Lorrie patted his hand. "Of course you did."

Graceann laughed, letting go some of her tension.

"It is beautiful, Mrs. Palmer," Jake said at last, with a smile for the older woman.

"How nice of you to say, Jake. But please call me Grandmom." She touched Graceann's arm. "Let's go into the dining room. We're having a casual lunch."

The family moved almost as one toward the dining room at the right of the foyer. Graceann released Jake's hand and followed the others. Not hearing him behind her, she turned around.

He stood very still staring at the tree.

"Jake?"

He turned to her and blinked. Longing flashed in his eyes so quickly she wondered if she imagined it.

"We're having lunch now," she said.

He swept his arm out. "After you, princess."

Before he could take a step, the sound of barking, then the click of nails on the hardwood stairs heralded the arrival of her grandmother's Shih Tzu, Fluffy. Yapping loudly the dog ran right at Jake.

Jake stepped away from the animal. Fluffy continued yapping and running around Jake's feet.

"It's only Fluffy," Graceann said. "He won't hurt you."

"That's what they all say," he ground out. "I prefer cats."

Graceann widened her eyes. "You have cats? That's good to know in case anyone in the family asks."

He nodded and again tried to sidestep Fluffy. "I have two."

"Where are they?"

"With a friend."

"Fluffy, come in here," her grandmother called.

Jake let out an audible breath as the dog trotted into the dining room. "Let's eat," he said.

Frowning, Graceann led him into the other room where a table that could easily seat one dozen was set for lunch.

Jake leaned over to whisper in Graceann's ear. "This is a casual lunch? Is the whole town dropping by to eat?"

"This is Grandmom's idea of an informal meal," she whispered back.

When they were settled at the table laden with bowls of Greek salad and plates of cheese soufflé, along with baskets of crusty French bread, Jake picked up his fork and dipped it into his salad. Graceann, seated next to him, touched his arm.

He gave her a quizzical look, and she said, "We have to say grace."

"Sorry." He put down his fork.

"Mark," her grandmother said, with a nod toward Graceann's father.

The family bowed their heads. Graceann watched Jake through lowered lashes. He had bowed his head, too. He was trying to fit in. Good. Maybe things would work out.

"Lord, thank you for this food, and thank you for bringing Jake into our household and into Graceann's life. Now, dig in." Her dad winked at her.

She grabbed her water goblet and gulped, wishing she could wash away the guilt of deceiving her family as easily as she washed away the dryness in her throat. She hated lying to them.

After lunch, Jake brought their bags from the car. Graceann deposited hers in her room, then showed Jake to his room. She smiled as they headed to the other end of the long hallway. Leave it to Grandmom to put them as far apart as possible. As if a hallway would stop them if she and Jake were truly lovers.

"Here we are," she said when they'd reached the guest room

where Jake would spend the next nine days. She swung the door open. Carrying his garment bag and duffel, he followed her.

"Nice." His gaze swept the large room, done in various shades of blue. A queen-sized bed covered in a navy-blue comforter was set against the far wall under windows that looked out to the lake. Jake set his bags on the bed and moved the white curtains aside to peer out. "Great view. As a kid, I always wondered what it would be like to live here."

"You did?"

He turned from the windows. "Silly, huh?" He scanned her, and his eyes flashed with desire. "Maybe I just wondered what it would be like to be close to you."

He'd taken off his leather jacket, and the deep blue sweater he wore made his eyes bluer and emphasized the broadness of his muscled chest. His faded jeans hugged legs that went on forever. She wondered if he worked out, then licked her lips at the delicious image of Jake pumping iron.

"We're alone now," she said. "You can drop the act."

"Oh?" He stalked toward her, a predator after his prey. When he reached her, he touched her chin with his index finger, tilting her head until their eyes met. An unexpected sensual tension flared between them. "Maybe it's not an act."

Graceann forgot how to breathe.

Jake smiled and leaned in for a kiss.

Graceann lifted her hands instinctively to put space between them. "Jake. No. Really. I, uh—"

A furious yapping broke the moment. Jake stepped back, away from Fluffy's teeth snapping too close to Jake's ankles. "What is the matter with that dog?"

"He knows you don't like him." She suppressed a laugh at the sight of the tall, muscled Jake and the tiny barking dog. Or was it a laugh of relief?

"Down," he said to the little dog, who suddenly quieted and

sat silently watching Jake. "This is why I like cats. They don't bother you."

Graceann couldn't hold her laughter any longer. When she finally composed herself, she wiped away tears to find Jake staring at her, his features tight.

"You think it's funny this little monster keeps bothering me?"

She nodded. "I'm sorry, but it is."

His features relaxed and he chuckled "I guess so."

"Why don't you like dogs?"

"One bit me when I was ten. I had to go to the ER."

"That explains it." One mystery solved. "Would you like me to speak to Grandmom and have her quarantine Fluffy for the duration?"

"No, I can deal with a yappy dog. But thanks."

Her gaze went to his bags on the bed. "You should unpack, then we can go downstairs to join the rest of the family. Okay?"

He grinned. "You're the boss. I'm only the hired gun."

She rolled her eyes, making him laugh.

He nodded toward the windows. "I saw the dock out there. After I unpack, how about we take a walk to the lake?"

He wanted to be alone with her? The thought thrilled and scared her. Unable to find words, she nodded.

Her grandmother's voice calling Fluffy drifted to them from downstairs. With one last yap at Jake, the dog bolted out of the room.

"I'm glad he's gone," Jake said.

"You and Fluffy have nine days to learn to tolerate each other." She frowned. "I think it's going well with the family, don't you?"

"I'm not sure. Your mother thought I seemed familiar."

"My family wouldn't know you. My parents barely knew the kids in my high school class. They didn't know any of the kids in the other classes. And my sister was four years ahead of you. I think our secret is safe."

"Our families weren't exactly in the same social circles either."

She wondered at the tinge of bitterness in his voice.

"We need to work out some details if we're going to carry this off." He sat on the bed and patted the spot next to him.

Graceann sank onto the bed, being careful to sit as far from him as possible. The mattress dipped, the movement sliding her a little closer to him than she thought prudent. Amusement glinted in Jake's eyes as he watched her. She folded her hands demurely on her lap, trying to ignore the clean, outdoors scent of him, the way the beginnings of a stubble on his square jaw gave him the look of a pirate. The way her heart pounded.

Jake's mouth tilted in a mocking grin. "Afraid of me, princess?"

"Not on your life." She scooched over a little, away from him. "What do you want to talk about?"

"Your family is going to have a lot more questions about me. You told them I live in Brooklyn. No way do I have a Brooklyn accent."

She smoothed a hand over her jeans, gathering her thoughts. "I know. It was the first thing I could think of. Zach's from Brooklyn."

"You worked it all out with Zach, but not me? Never mind. Let's use Zach's information. What type of work does he do?"

"What do you do? We'll use that."

He shook his head. "We'll use Zach's."

She wondered if Jake was into something illegal. Her stomach churned at the thought. "Zach is a trader with a Wall Street firm," she said slowly.

Jake laughed. "I don't look like anyone's idea of a Wall Street trader."

She glanced down at his motorcycle boots. "I know. We'll say you repair and customize motorcycles."

"That'll work. When I was in school I restored an old motorcycle. Still have the thing. Do you think your parents will be happy their little princess is with a mechanic?"

"Stop calling me princess. You're over thinking everything. Just play the part."

He stood. "At least your parents will be relieved when you tell them you broke the engagement."

She stood, too. "My parents will accept any man I love if they think the guy will treat me right. They're not snobby."

He turned away from her. "I need to unpack." He unzipped his duffel and began to pull out T-shirts and sweaters. Going to the large dresser, he opened drawers and carefully set the garments inside.

With a glance at Graceann, he said, "I don't need help, but if you want to give me a hand, suit yourself." He nodded toward the garment bag.

Still musing over the abrupt change in conversation, Graceann grabbed the bag, hung it in the closet and began to empty it. Thoughtfully, she ran a hand over a white Egyptian cotton shirt with a designer label, then unpacked several other similar shirts in different colors, four pairs of black slacks, and several pairs of expensive jeans. When she pulled out a beautifully tailored gray suit sporting the label of a top designer, she blinked. A pricey collection for a man who didn't own up to having a regular job.

"Nice clothes," she said when she'd finished hanging them in the walk-in closet.

"I have a taste for the finer things."

"Where do you live, Jake?"

"Wherever it suits me." He didn't look at her.

"What about your cats?"

He turned to her with a cocky grin. "In good hands. Don't worry about them, princess."

Instead, the mischievous look he gave her told her she should be worried about *him*.

CHAPTER FOUR

*A*fter Jake unpacked, he and Graceann strolled along the wooden walkway to the dock behind her grandmother's house. Shivering with the cold, he dug his hands into the pockets of his leather jacket and inhaled the clean, crisp air, redolent with the scent of pine. His jacket wasn't heavy enough, but he'd been away so long he'd forgotten how brutal the winters could be here in the Poconos.

He glanced over at Graceann, walking next to him and bundled into a wool jacket, scarf and gloves. Their breaths mingled in the frosty air, a reminder of the kiss they would have shared in the bedroom if that pesky little dog hadn't appeared.

Graceann gave him a shaky smile. He made her nervous. Good. It meant she wasn't immune to him. Why that suddenly mattered he had no idea.

Reaching out, he took her hand. When she tried to pull away, he gripped it tighter and leaned over to whisper in her ear. "You never know who might be watching from the house. We have to put on a convincing show."

"All right, but don't take advantage of the situation."

"Who me? Take advantage?"

She laughed. The sound made his heart jump. He liked seeing her smile and hearing her laugh. Her carefree response shed a soft light into the dark places returning to Spirit Lake had reopened.

When they got to the dock, still holding hands, they stared out over the ice-crusted lake. "I used to love coming to the lake when I was a kid," he said. "Any troubles I had dissolved into the water, regardless of the time of year."

"What kind of troubles?" She looked up at him with luminous green eyes that reminded him of a brightly shining Christmas light. Calm, clear, innocent eyes. The kind that could look into and steal a man's soul.

He shrugged. "The usual kid stuff. Nothing serious." *Liar.*

She studied him before turning to gaze out over the water again. "It is pretty here. I miss it at times. In the summer I usually go to the Hamptons on weekends. Zach has a house there. But sometimes I come home and hang out here."

An unexpected stab of jealousy knifed Jake. "You and this Zach, you're close?"

With a nod, she turned back to him. "He and Kate are my best friends. Kate lives here but she comes up to New York to stay with me whenever she can. I usually stay with my parents when I come back, but I've been staying at Kate's place nearby the last few days. We wanted some girl time. Now that she has a boyfriend, I don't see her as much."

"You and Zach, were you ever…did you ever…?" He knew he sounded like an idiot, but he had to know.

"God, no. He's more like a brother to me. He lived in the apartment next door when I first moved to New York. He was a big help, showing me around the city. Why do you ask?"

He shrugged. He couldn't explain what he didn't understand himself, but the thought of her with another man clenched his gut.

"Zach was going to pretend to be your fiancé?" he asked. "Don't your parents know him?"

"They never met him. The few times they came to New York to see me, Zach was away. That's why he would have been perfect as my fiancé, but I think you'll work out just fine," she said with a smile.

Returning her smile, he slid his arm around her waist and pulled her against him. When she started to protest, he said, "Our audience, remember?"

"Now I know you're taking advantage of the situation."

"Always. But you're paying me and I always give my customers their money's worth."

Quiet, she stared out over the lake again, but didn't pull away.

"Why doesn't a woman like you have a boyfriend or a husband?" he asked.

She lifted a wide-eyed gaze to his. "What do you mean, a woman like me?"

"Smart, sexy, stunning. I should think you'd be fighting the men off."

She swallowed. "Me? Stunning?"

"You don't see it, do you?"

"Let's drop that line of conversation. You can tell *me* something though."

"Maybe."

"Did you like being called The Falcon?"

"Sometimes." Graceann came from a loving, supportive family. She wouldn't understand the ugliness and shame of his upbringing.

"Does anyone call you that now?"

"Nope." Forcing a smile, he tried to relax and turned his attention back to the still lake.

"Not real forthcoming with information, are you?"

"Depends on who's asking."

"Are your parents still alive?" she asked.

He stiffened. "They died a few years ago, within months of each other. They were living in Florida."

"I'm sorry to hear that. They couldn't have been more than—fifty or so? Was it an accident? Were they in the hospital?"

He felt the weight of her curiosity, but continued to stare out over the lake. "No." He wasn't about to tell her the sordid details of their passing.

An owl hooted in the wind, making him shiver inside.

"You must be freezing in that coat," she said, so gently it nearly ripped a hole in his hardened heart. "Let's go back in," she said quietly. "I could use a cup of hot chocolate."

Grateful beyond words that she hadn't pursued the subject, he followed her into the house, his thoughts a tumble. Somehow he had to change his game plan, find a way to keep Graceann off-guard so she wouldn't ask so many questions.

<><><>

Later that day, Graceann, her mother and her sister worked together in the kitchen preparing dinner. Her grandmother had given her cook and housekeeper time off so they could spend the holidays with their own families.

The other adults sat in the adjacent great room talking, watching a football game, drinking, and nibbling on appetizers. Tomorrow was Christmas Eve and the house would be a bustle of activity for a few days, but today was laid-back, a time to chill out.

"How did you and Jake meet? You've been so secretive about him." Her sister Lorrie glanced at Graceann then went back to slicing vegetables for the salad.

Their mother slid the chicken breasts into the oven, then washed her hands.

Graceann looked around the large white recently renovated kitchen that opened into the great room, or family room, before turning her attention to her mother and sister. "Why are we in here cooking while the men sit around? What is this, the nineteenth century?"

"Stop trying to change the subject." Lorrie pinned Graceann with her eyes. "How did you and Jake meet?"

"I want to know, too." Her mother grabbed a stool next to the center island and settled onto it. She reached out and plucked a few grape tomatoes from the dish in front of Lorrie and popped one into her mouth.

Graceann set down the paring knife she was using to peel the potatoes. She inhaled the tangy scents of lemon and rosemary rising from the chicken. The signature cinnamon cake Grandmom had baked earlier cooled on the counter. Its aroma mingled with the lemon and rosemary, sweetening the air.

"We met at the Hamptons this past May. Jake's friends owned a house next to my friend Zach's." The lie rolled easily, too easily, off her tongue. A knot of guilt and anxiety tightened in her chest. She hoped her dad hadn't asked Jake the same question. Desperate, she really hadn't thought this whole thing through before presenting Jake with her proposition.

Lorrie set down her own knife. "Hamptons, huh? Jake doesn't look like the Hamptons type." She grinned. "He sure is sexy though."

"Lorrie, you're a married woman and a mother," their mom said.

"Please, Mom." Lorrie rolled her eyes. "Like you never noticed any good-looking guys after you met Daddy."

Shaking her head, Graceann went back to peeling the potatoes.

"Despite his long hair and that black leather, Jake seems nice enough," her mother said.

The tone in her voice made Graceann stop peeling and wait for the "but" she knew would come.

"But," her mom continued, "he repairs motorcycles? With

your education and your background, are you sure he's the man you want to spend your life with?"

Graceann dropped her paring knife. It clanked onto the granite counter. "Mom, you sound so snobby. That's not like you."

"Seriously, Graceann," Lorrie said. "Hunky as he is, Jake's a little rough around the edges. Not your type at all."

Graceann gripped the edge of the counter. "Remember how you all loved Michael, the Wall Street wizard with the fancy car and clothes, the penthouse in Manhattan? How'd he turn out?" She could feel her temper rising. "A snazzy resume and a lot of stuff don't make a guy my type. Besides, how do you know what my type is?"

"Wow, we hit a nerve," Lorrie said.

"We're not being snobs, dear." Her mom reached across the counter and touched Graceann's hand. "We only want you to be happy."

"I am happy."

Lorrie went back to her slicing. "Well, it's obvious you and Jake are in love, but...I just hope it all works out for you."

Graceann stilled. She and Jake in love? They weren't *that* good at acting. Trying to digest Lorrie's words, she went back to peeling potatoes.

Her mother cleared her throat. "I saw Steven Craig a few weeks ago."

"I haven't seen Steven in years," Graceann said, concentrating on peeling and chopping. "How is he?"

"He left Philadelphia. Didn't like the city. He's decided to stay on the East Coast. He said he liked it here in the Poconos the times he visited with you so he's setting up a law office nearby in Harmony and bought a house there. He asked about you, and even gave me his phone number to give to you."

"Nice to know he's doing well, but I'm not interested in calling him." Finished with the potatoes, Graceann walked over to the cabinets and pulled out a large pot, then went to the sink and began filling the pot with water.

"I always liked Steven and hoped you and he would get together permanently someday," her mother said.

Her mind only half on what her mother was saying, Graceann continued to fill the pot. "Steven and I dated off-and-on those two years in college. We parted friends."

"He's spending the holidays alone. His parents are in Europe."

The implication behind her mother's words penetrated Graceann's brain. A shiver of apprehension, cold as the water streaming into the pot, ran up her spine. She set down the pot, turned off the faucet and faced her mother.

"Mom, what are you trying to say?" Graceann pressed back against the hard edge of the sink. Maybe it would give her strength for what she feared her mother was about to admit.

Her mom fidgeted, then, with a sheepish grin, said, "I invited him to spend Christmas with us and stay for a few days."

"You didn't!"

"Really, Mom," Lorrie said. "This is a family Christmas and Graceann brought her new fiancé. How do you think Jake will feel when one of Graceann's old boyfriends shows up?"

Graceann threw her sister a smile of gratitude, then turned to her mother. "You knew I was bringing someone home. Why did you invite Steven? When did you invite him?"

"You said you were dating someone," her mother said, a note of exasperation in her voice. "Suddenly you're engaged. I'd already invited Steven."

"Lorrie's right. Everyone will be uncomfortable. Un-invite Steven."

Her mother stood, a stubborn look Graceann recognized all too well on her face. "I will not un-invite Steven. That's very uncharitable of both of you. The poor man was planning to spend Christmas alone. He's an old friend. Inviting him was the least I could do. I'm sure Graceann and Jake will handle it."

Graceann stared at the ceiling in frustration. Things were bad enough with her trying to pass Jake off as her fiancé. Now Steven, who'd at one time begged Graceann to marry him, would be their guest. This time, her matchmaking mama had gone too far.

CHAPTER FIVE

*M*ark Palmer strolled into the kitchen. "How's everything going in here? Do you need any help?" Frowning, he glanced from one woman to the other.

"We're fine, Dad." Lorrie's words broke the tension that hovered in the air.

"I came in for beer for me and Andrew and a club soda for Jake." He turned to Graceann. "Is Jake a recovering alcoholic?"

Hell if I know. She almost blurted the words out loud. "Why do you ask?"

Her dad shrugged. "He said he didn't drink. Young men these days usually drink too much, if you ask me."

Graceann struggled to keep the surprise from registering on her face. She wouldn't have taken Jake Falco, The Falcon, for a non-drinker. The guys he'd hung out with at school were reputed to be big partiers, but she hadn't known Jake well and didn't know if he drank. Maybe he'd given up drinking since then. "He's not a recovering alcoholic." She crossed her fingers behind her back and hoped she was telling the truth. "He just doesn't like alcohol."

"Strange." Her dad walked to the large stainless side-by-side refrigerator and pulled out two bottles of beer. "I'll be back for the club soda in a minute."

"I'll bring in the soda," Graceann said.

As he started to exit the room, he turned around and chuckled. "Isabella and Fluffy are both taken with your fiancé."

Some of her tension dissipated, and Graceann laughed. "Isabella and Fluffy the wonder dog? This I have to see."

When her father left the room, Lorrie grabbed Graceann's arm, stopping her on her way to the refrigerator.

"Why didn't you tell us Jake's name or anything about him before you got here? All you'd ever say is you were dating someone. What are you hiding?"

Graceann forced a smile. "I'm not hiding anything. We had a whirlwind romance, and we've just gotten engaged. I'm still trying to get used to the idea. I wanted to keep him my secret a little longer. And I was afraid if I told you too much about him, I'd jinx our relationship. I talked constantly about Michael and look what happened." That excuse sounded lame even to her ears. She'd lied to them about dating someone, and she'd only hatched this crazy scheme with Zach three weeks ago. She wasn't even sure she'd have given them Zach's real name when he met them.

Anxious to escape the kitchen and the women's thoughtful gazes, she filled a glass with ice, poured a bottle of club soda over it, added a wedge of lime, and carried it to the other room.

The great room, comfortably furnished with two brown leather love seats and a matching sofa facing them, oversized tables and plush chairs, the hardwood floors covered with Oriental rugs, was her favorite room. A Christmas tree, smaller than the one in the entry hall, was set by the bay windows. The family would gather around that tree Christmas morning to open their gifts.

The picture that greeted her as she entered pushed aside her anger and anxiety about Steven. Jake was bouncing a laughing Isabella on his knee and Fluffy sat at his feet staring up at him.

Jake might be a bit rough, he might be mysterious, but he had a way with children, and maybe dogs. He liked cats. There were reassuring depths to him she hadn't begun to fathom.

He looked up and their gazes caught. The air around them thickened. Andrew, Lorrie's husband, yelled at something on the TV, breaking the spell. Fluffy stood and barked at Jake. The sounds made baby Christian, asleep in his infant seat, stir, but he didn't waken.

"Here's your drink," she said to Jake. "I'll take Isabella."

She placed his drink on the table in front of him and he held out the toddler to her. Inhaling Isabella's sweet scent, she pressed the little girl close. Isabella's blonde curls tickled Graceann's face. She'd always wanted children, wanted it all—the loyal, faithful, loving husband, the house filled with laughter. Pets. But after Michael she didn't know if she could trust another man enough to open her heart.

Fluffy was in full yap mode now. Jake sipped his drink and warily watched the dog.

"Fluffy, leave that poor man alone and come over here," Grandmom said. With one last yap, Fluffy trotted over to Grandmom and settled at her feet.

Smiling, her grandmother looked toward Graceann. "Isabella looks good on you." With a pointed look at Jake, she said, "You and Jake will have beautiful children."

Jake choked on his drink. "I'm fine," he managed when Graceann started toward him. "Drink went down the wrong way." He wouldn't meet her gaze.

"Fluffy likes you, Jake," Grandmom said. "I've never seen my dog so fascinated with anyone."

"I'm not sure 'like' is the right word. I'm more of a cat person, and I think Fluffy knows it," Jake said.

"You and Graceann must get a dog and a cat after you're married," Grandmom said as if issuing a royal decree. She picked up a glass with her favorite drink, scotch on the rocks, and sipped, then looked at Graceann. "Will you live in New York?"

"We haven't decided yet," Graceann said quickly, catching Jake's eye.

"I will live anywhere Graceann wants," he put in amiably. "After all, my role in life is to make her happy."

Grandmom beamed. "How nice."

Her father and brother-in-law shot Jake incredulous looks.

The man was enjoying overplaying the devoted fiancé too much. Graceann intended to have a little talk with him later. She set down the squirming Isabella, who ran to her father. Then with a last warning look at Jake, Graceann went back to the kitchen.

Later that night, after the rest of the family had gone to bed, Graceann and Jake sat alone in the great room. A Hallmark Christmas movie played on TV. It was one Graceann had seen several times. "I love this movie," she said. "I'm a sucker for Christmas romance movies."

Jake slid his arm along the back of the love seat to her shoulders, then pulled her close. His muscled thigh pressed against hers and sent desire shooting through her. Although she found herself powerfully attracted to him, she tried to move away. Being this close to Jake was too emotionally dangerous.

He held her tighter. "Where do you think you're going?"

She turned to him, their faces a whisper apart. Words dried in her throat. She licked her lips. If she leaned forward even a little, she could kiss him. She straightened. "Everyone's in bed now. You can relax the act."

"What if someone has insomnia and decides to join us? We have to keep up appearances."

"Let's just watch the movie." She deliberately focused back on the TV, but barely registered what was on the screen. Jake was too darn distracting.

He chuckled but didn't release her. "I remember when this movie was shot. A friend of mine worked on it."

She turned to him. "You know someone in Hollywood? Really? Who?"

"No one you've ever heard of."

"Oh." Although she really would have liked to pursue the subject further, to delve into discovering Jake Falco, the man, she had to remind herself they had only a business deal. There was no need to get personal.

When the commercial came on, she pulled back and faced him. "We need to coordinate some things." *And I need to tell you my mother invited my ex-boyfriend to spend Christmas with us.*

He studied her with those cool, clear baby blues, making her shift uncomfortably. When he looked at her mouth, intention in his eyes, she scooted to the other end of the love seat.

"Do I make you nervous, Ms. Palmer?" Laughter tinged his voice.

"No."

"Liar."

"Let's talk business." She folded her arms across her chest.

"You're on."

"Did you tell anyone how we met?"

He shook his head. "Didn't come up."

"Here's the story. We met this past May in the Hamptons. I was staying at Zach's house and you were next door at a friend's. We'll call your friend Joe in case anyone asks. You and I have been together ever since."

"I don't have a friend named Joe." He shot her a wicked grin and slid closer. "At least I moved in on you fast." He took a strand of her hair and twirled it around his finger. "I like that. When I see what I want, I take it. I'd never wait too long to make you mine."

At his words, her pulse jumped. "Get serious."

"I am serious."

The man was an accomplished seducer. Yet, there'd been sincerity in his expression and his voice.

"Never mind that," she said. "That's our story and we're sticking to it."

He laughed softly.

She tilted her head and studied him. "Are you a recovering alcoholic?"

His features tightened as his lips thinned. "Why do you ask?"

"You don't drink."

Jake lowered his gaze and she thought he wouldn't answer. At last he turned to her with hooded eyes. "My parents drank enough for two lifetimes and lost their health before forty, their lives before fifty-five. I have no desire to be like them."

She touched his hand where it rested on the cushion. "I'm sorry, Jake. I didn't know."

He grasped her hand, holding it tight. Longing flared up deep inside her. The glow from the TV and the table lamp cast a pale light that emphasized his sculpted cheekbones and full lips. She wanted to stroke his face, hold him close and comfort him, to loosen his hair and slide her fingers through the thickness.

"What are you thinking about?" he asked in a quiet voice. He lifted her hand and turned it over to kiss her palm, then closed her fingers as if he wanted her to hold onto his kiss.

"I'm thinking how sad your childhood must have been." *And how I want to hold you.*

"I survived." He moved away, his gaze still on hers. "I'll tell you something I've never told anyone."

"Okay."

"That time when I was ten and the dog bit me?"

Graceann nodded.

"A neighbor took me to the ER and stayed with me because my parents were passed out drunk in the house."

She put a hand to her throat. "That's awful."

"It was a long time ago. But I've never been comfortable around dogs after that. Too many bad memories."

"Jake," she whispered. Pity for what he'd gone through mingled with pleasure that he trusted her enough to open his heart. "I'm so sorry."

A door opened and closed somewhere upstairs, making her jump.

"Someone might be coming," Jake said. "Let's make this real."

Before she could respond, he'd tugged her into his arms and his lips were on hers, soft, hot, seductive. Everything faded—the TV, the sounds of the house settling around them, the scents of holly and evergreen. She wound her arms around his neck and melted into him as he deepened the kiss and slipped his tongue into her mouth.

He reclined, bringing her with him until she lay on top of him. She fit nicely against the hard contours of his body. Her blood felt scorching enough to liquefy her bones. He cradled the back of her head and massaged her scalp as they kissed.

Lost in Jake's passion, his touch, the longing she felt for him, Graceann was barely aware of soft shuffling nearby. The loud sound of a throat clearing finally sliced through her erotic stupor.

Graceann disengaged herself from Jake and twisted her head to look behind her. Lorrie, dressed in pajamas and robe, stood in the doorway, looking contrite. Graceann quickly sat up and straightened her clothes while Jake did the same.

Lorrie grimaced. "I'm sorry. Truly. I came down to get Christian a bottle."

Graceann smoothed a hand over her hair. "You could have used the back stairs to go into the kitchen." She should be grateful Lorrie had interrupted them. Instead, she felt…frustrated.

"I didn't think."

"Dogs and sisters," Jake muttered. "Can't catch a break."

Lorrie frowned. "What?"

"Nothing." Graceann threw Jake a quelling look. "It's time for us to go to bed anyway."

He cocked an eyebrow. "Bed?"

"Alone. We're in my grandmother's house."

Lorrie laughed. "Do what you want. I'll never tell."

Graceann stood. "Goodnight, Jake, Lorrie. See you in the morning."

"Goodnight, sweetheart," Jake said.

Graceann felt him watch her as she walked away. Her insides churned and her legs felt rubbery. Clearly, being alone with Jake Falco was perilous to her self-control.

CHAPTER SIX

*Y*awning, Jake staggered into the kitchen, moving like Frankenstein's monster, which was how he felt every morning until he'd had his first hit of caffeine. After a fitful night with erotic images of Graceann dominating his dreams, he'd given up the fight and gotten out of bed.

The kitchen was deserted at seven o'clock and the house tomb-quiet. Never up this early except when he was on a shoot, he made a beeline for the large single-cup coffee maker perched on the gray granite counter. Heavy white mugs were arranged around the machine. After brewing the strongest cup he could, he took it to the center island and settled onto one of the stools.

Dim sunlight streamed through the opened blinds, bathing the stainless appliances and gleaming white cabinets. A new day, a clean day to wipe away old memories and start fresh. Guilt and coffee mixed an unsettling brew in him. Maybe he should have been upfront with Graceann from the start and told her his real reason for coming back to Spirit Lake. If he was completely honest with himself, he'd admit some perverse part of him wanted her to accept the man he was now, not her distant memory of a wild guy with a bad rep. Acceptance hadn't come for him in Spirit Lake and he expected it never would. Not with what he had in mind.

Sipping his coffee, his thoughts returned to Graceann, where they had been all night. He wanted her. Had from the first moment he'd spotted her in the diner. No use trying to deny it. He'd wanted her in school too, but she'd been too young, untouchable. But this wasn't high school, and he'd agreed to go along with her charade to get close to her. There were other reasons. Reasons he would keep quiet about for a little longer.

As if he'd conjured her up, Graceann stepped into the room. She froze in the doorway when she saw him. Like a man starved for the sight of his woman, he devoured her with his gaze. Dressed in jeans and a long-sleeved shirt, her dark hair caught in a messy ponytail, her fresh-faced sexuality stirred a yearning in him he'd long ago buried.

He couldn't resist. "Good morning, princess." Teasing her was too much fun. It also masked his growing feelings for her.

He could swear she growled.

"Not a morning person, I see." He chuckled.

"No." She padded to the coffee maker on feet encased in Indian moccasins and fixed herself a cup, then sat across from him at the counter.

With her hands wrapped around the mug, she took a long sip, then let out a contented sigh as she set the mug down. "The first cup of the day is the best."

"Agreed."

She drank a little more before she fixed him with those sultry bedroom eyes that appeared even larger behind the lenses of her stylish glasses.

"You look good in glasses," he said.

"No, I don't. I always wear my contacts."

"Trust me. You're sexy as hell in those glasses and with that mussed, just-had-sex-hair."

She waved a hand. "Don't go there, Jake. We need to talk. About last night."

"What about it? I was kinda having fun."

"That can't happen again. No more kissing when we're alone."

He grinned. "You liked it."

"That's not the point." She frowned, as if trying to seem severe, but only succeeded in being adorable.

"It's exactly the point." He reached for her hand, but she pulled it out of reach, shaking her head.

Her stubbornness made her even sexier. Damn, he had it bad.

"No more kissing," she repeated in a firm voice. "And why are you up so early?"

"Same reason as you, I suppose."

"*I* couldn't sleep."

"Neither could I." He smiled and leaned closer. "I dreamt of you and what I'd like to do with you."

"I didn't dream about you. And stop with the seductive talk."

"You're a terrible liar." He shot her a wicked grin. "You think I'm seductive?"

She shook her head, clearly not prepared to answer, and drank more coffee. As she sipped, her gaze went to his right forearm, bared by the T-shirt he wore. Frowning, she set down her mug. "Is that a tattoo of a falcon?"

He ran his hand over the tattoo. "I've had it a long time. Got it the week before I graduated high school."

"So you *did* like being called The Falcon."

"Falcons are predators. I got this to remind me that someday I'd crush my enemies."

"That's harsh." She settled back onto her stool, as far away from him as she could manage.

Jake could swear the temperature in the room dropped a few degrees. So Graceann wasn't an eye-for-an-eye sort of woman. No surprises there.

"I felt harsh back then. Don't worry, princess. I've mellowed since. The falcon now tells me to soar, to follow my own path, that I'm the only one responsible for my life."

"That sounds better." She met his gaze again. "Exactly what path do you follow? What type of work do you do?"

"I need more coffee." He ambled over to the coffee maker and brewed another cup, his back to her. "I've done lots of things in my life. I've been a waiter, a house painter. I write a little." All true.

"What have you written?"

"Nothing you would have heard of." Coffee done, he carried his full mug back to the counter and sat. "Forget about me. Tonight is Christmas Eve. What are the plans? I need to know what I'm facing so I can make a good impression on your family."

She rubbed a tapered index finger along the gray and silver granite. He liked that she wore light pink nail polish on her short nails and not the dragon-lady red so many women in his world favored.

"I have to go into town today," she said, lifting her eyes. "I want to get a few gifts for the family. I want you to go with me. We have to keep up appearances."

He held out his hands. "Hey, I've been doing my part. Engaged couples can't keep their hands to themselves. I'm only doing what's expected, but you seem to have an issue with that."

"You really are impossible."

"But you like it." He grinned over the rim of his mug.

She laughed. "You keep believing that."

He studied her. In the early morning sunlight, she appeared younger, more innocent. Most of the women he'd known in the past had been hardened by life. And many of the women he met in his line of work now were overly aggressive, coarsened by their lifestyles, as if they'd left their softer selves in another life. "Don't ever change, Graceann."

"What does that mean?"

"Always stay sweet."

Her eyes widened in surprise and she swallowed. "Let's get off that subject. It's agreed, we go into town today?"

"Sure. I should probably pick up a few gifts for your family from me."

"You don't have to do that."

"I want to."

She smiled. "That would be nice. Tonight the whole family, except Grandmom and the children, will go to Midnight Mass. You'll be expected to go."

His chest tightened. "I haven't been in a church since my First Communion."

"Your family didn't go to church?"

"Nope. We didn't much celebrate Christmas either."

She reached out and touched his hand where it rested on the counter. "That's too bad. I think church and the holidays are good for kids."

He turned his hand over to grasp hers, holding it tight. He felt a surge of triumph when she didn't try to pull away. "You're probably right, but we weren't like your family."

"I know you have no siblings, but what about other family? Grandparents, cousins, aunts?"

The loneliness he'd learned years ago to keep at bay threatened to break through. He beat it back. "No one." He shook his head. "My dad was from Pittsburgh. He was estranged from his family. I think my mom was originally from down in Delaware. She never talked about her family."

Sadness softened Graceann's eyes. "I can't imagine not being close to my family. I love them all so much."

"I know you do, and they're good people, but maybe you need to separate from them a little."

"What do you mean?" She pulled her hand free.

"You're thirty years old. I don't get this whole subterfuge you're putting on. Tell them the truth. You have a right to live your life the way you want. They can't control you."

"I don't want to hurt them. And you have no right to tell me how to handle my family."

"I don't mean to upset you, but you've got to break the ties sometime. Or at least loosen them."

She opened her mouth to speak when footsteps cut into the tense atmosphere. They turned toward the doorway leading to the back stairs.

Rubbing her eyes, Lorrie, dressed in the same pajamas and robe she'd had on late last night when she'd interrupted them in the great room, sauntered in. "Hey, you two." She headed for the coffee maker. While her coffee brewed, she turned to them. "You're up early." She grinned. "Or maybe you haven't been to sleep yet."

"Lorrie, that's crude," Graceann said.

Jake smiled at Graceann's indignation. Her combination of sexy and naïve shot a dose of desire through him, and he shifted in his seat.

"I'm sorry," Lorrie said. "That *was* crude. Blame it on sleep deprivation. Christian is teething. You'll see what I mean when you have your own kids."

When she turned away to fix her coffee, Jake glanced at Graceann. Her face had flushed a becoming shade of pink.

He saluted her with his mug. Her face got pinker.

Cradling her coffee mug, Lorrie settled onto one of the stools around the counter. She sipped, then set down her cup and said to Graceann, "Did you tell Jake about Steven?"

"I was about to when you came in."

"Steven?" He shifted his gaze from one woman to the other.

Graceann rubbed a hand along the counter top as if lost in thought, then met his eyes. "Steven is an old boyfriend from college. He's moved to this area and Mom invited him to spend Christmas with us and stay a few days."

Jake managed to keep his expression neutral as a twinge of hurt settled in his chest. He wondered if Graceann's mother had invited the other guy after she'd met Jake because she wasn't happy with her daughter's choice of fiancé. He was only playing a part, he reminded himself. If he and Graceann really were in love, her family would know the whole truth about him. They might approve. Anyway, what her family thought of him wouldn't matter. Only Graceann would matter. Yet, a part of him wanted acceptance from her family, fake fiancé or no.

Graceann gave him an embarrassed smile. "I'm sorry, Jake. Lorrie and I both told Mom she shouldn't have done that, but Mom's stubborn."

"And she has her own agenda," he said. "She evidently likes this other guy."

"I don't care what her agenda is," Graceann said. "You're my fiancé and that's all there is to it." As if she'd realized what she'd said, she clamped her mouth shut.

"Jake, don't worry about our mother," Lorrie said.

"I'm not, but I hope to get her to like me."

"She will," Graceann said. "Daddy seems to like you."

"Maybe," he said with a shrug.

Graceann took a large swig of coffee and set down the mug, then stood. "I need to get dressed. Meet me downstairs in an hour and we'll head for town?"

"Sure thing, boss," he said. "And wear your glasses today." When she shot him a puzzled look, he smiled and said, "Please."

Graceann shook her head as she walked from the room. The graceful sway of her hips sent blood rushing to his lower regions. He needed more coffee, but with Lorrie there, he had to stay put for a while or risk exposing his burgeoning lust for Graceann.

<><><>

Jake parked the BMW on Main Street and hopped out. He walked around to the other side to open the door for Graceann, but she'd already exited and waited for him on the sidewalk. He locked the car with the remote key. "Nice car. I ought to get one."

"Do you have a car?" she asked, cocking her head toward him.

"I have a Maserati."

She laughed. "You would."

He laughed with her. He'd learned a long time ago how effective it could be to tell the truth in jest.

"Where to first, princess?"

She pointed down the street. "The wine store is two blocks away. I want to get Daddy his favorite wine. I could have gotten it in New York, but I didn't want to carry it all the way here."

As they walked, Jake scanned the street, lined with upscale boutiques and restaurants, a far cry from the dingy shops he remembered. Spirit Lake had rebuilt itself into a trendy mountain town. The mouth-watering aroma of tomato and basil from the pizza place mingled with the scent of sizzling beef from the Asian restaurant, giving him hunger pangs.

Green and red lights hung across the narrow street, and red foil stars swung on the streetlamps. Even the other shoppers carried a festive air as they went about their business. The town had never looked this clean and happy when he was growing up here.

Bells rung by Salvation Army volunteers on both sides of the street added to the holiday atmosphere. When they passed the Salvation Army kettle, Jake pulled a twenty-dollar bill from his wallet and dropped it into the kettle.

"That's awfully generous," Graceann said.

"Not really. I know what it's like to be on the receiving end of charity."

The softness in her gaze touched his heart. He didn't want her pity. He took her hand in his. "Let's go. Lead the way."

At the shop, she chose her wine and headed to the counter. Jake perused the shelves, selecting a few bottles, and followed her.

She glanced at the wine in his cart. "I've never heard of that brand."

"It's a boutique winery in Napa Valley," he said. "I'm surprised to find it here. A buddy and his wife own the winery. I thought a few bottles would make good gifts for your dad and Andrew."

"You know people who own a winery, but you don't drink? And you know someone who works on movies?"

"I get around."

She frowned but didn't say anything more.

An hour later, they'd bought toys for Isabella and Christian, scarves for Graceann's mom, sister, and grandmother. Strolling to the car, they passed a boutique of high-end women's clothing.

Jake grabbed Graceann's hand. "Let's go in here. I want to buy you a gift."

"You don't have to give me anything."

"I can't have your family think I didn't give you a Christmas gift."

"The engagement ring is my gift."

She looked so serious and so gorgeous as she stood there arguing with him, her dark brown hair spread out over the shoulders of her olive-green jacket. The scarf around her neck, in shades of green, changed her eyes to the deep color of holly leaves. She'd worn her glasses, as he'd asked. When she'd come downstairs ready for their shopping trip wearing them, pleasure had stirred in him.

He pulled her into the store. "Don't argue. I'm your fiancé and I'm buying you a gift."

The saleswoman showed them dresses and purses as they wandered through the small, elegant shop. Jake shook his head at each selection. "I want something special for my fiancé."

A mannequin wearing a delicate shawl of pale green silk shot with gold thread caught his eye. "Can we see that wrap?"

The saleswoman hurried to take it off the mannequin, then

handed it to Jake. He pulled the soft fabric through his hands, then turned to Graceann. "You said your parents are having a big New Year's Eve party. This shawl matches your eyes. Maybe you can wear it to the party."

Graceann's eyes lit up as she fingered the gauzy wrap.

"Try it on," the saleswoman said.

Jake laid it over Graceann's shoulders. The green did indeed bring out her eyes.

"It's gorgeous," Graceann said, running a hand over the fabric.

"It's yours." Jake turned to the beaming saleswoman. "We'll take it. Can you gift wrap it?"

With a nod, the woman hurried away, the shawl in her arms.

"Thank you, Jake," Graceann said.

Her smile sent his heart into a tailspin. She parted her full pink lips, inviting his kiss. He bent and brushed his lips over hers. "You're welcome, sweetheart."

"I need a gift for you," she said.

"I don't want anything."

"But you won't have anything to unwrap tomorrow morning."

"That's nothing new. I'll tell your family you've given me the greatest gift of all—you've agreed to be my wife."

"That's corny."

He touched the tip of her nose. "Your family will love it."

Later, juggling packages, they exited the shop. Jake stopped at the door of a doggie boutique. "Maybe we should get a gift for Fluffy. A muzzle would be perfect."

Graceann laughed. "The little yapper would find a way to tear it off." When they passed a stationary store, Graceann stopped. "I know what to get you for Christmas."

"I don't want anything from you."

She handed him her packages. "I'm getting you something anyway. You stay here. I'll be right out."

Fifteen minutes later, carrying a small, wrapped package and smiling like the cat that swallowed the proverbial canary or two, she came out of the shop. "I'm ready."

She took a few of the packages from him before they continued their walk. Jake couldn't remember the last time he'd felt this happy, this carefree. Graceann did that for him. He never wanted the day to end.

A familiar looking figure hurrying along the opposite sidewalk made Jake stop and stare.

"What is it?" Graceann asked.

He squinted. "Is that Ryan Nelson? What happened to him? He looks like hell." The scrawny man coughed as he held the collar of his coat close and turned a corner out of sight. Jake met Graceann's gaze. "His father was mayor when we were in school. Didn't Nelson go to Princeton?"

She shook her head. "He lost his scholarship when he got arrested for dealing drugs. He's been to rehab many times, but he can't seem to stop using."

Jake released a breath, feeling a smidgen of his old bitterness float away. He'd not been part of Nelson's rich, fast crowd in school, but he'd known about the guy's run-ins with the law, problems his influential father had smoothed away. Jake and his friends had gotten blamed for some of the stunts Nelson and his crowd had pulled. The town was only too eager to believe the worst of the guys from the bad side of town. Looked like Nelson's shenanigans had finally caught up with him. Jake had expected to feel a flash of triumph, but he felt only pity.

"Jake? Are you okay?" Graceann tugged on his arm.

He smiled down at her. "I'm fine. Better than I've been for a while."

They'd walked a little way when it was Graceann's turn to freeze and halt in mid-stride.

"What is it?" he asked.

"Steven," she whispered. "Shoot."

A dark-haired guy of average height, his hair cut military short, and wearing an expensive-looking camel overcoat, hurried over to them.

"Graceann," he said when he reached them. "Sweetheart."

He bent as if to kiss her, but she stepped back to press closer to Jake. "Hello, Steven."

His light gray eyes roved over her, insolent and possessive. Jake wanted to grab the guy by the throat.

"Your mother invited me for Christmas," the guy said.

"I know." Graceann turned to Jake. "Steven Craig. Jake Falco. My fiancé."

"I heard you'd gotten engaged." Steven dismissed Jake with cold eyes.

Jake smirked. "Always good to meet *old* friends of my fiancée's."

Steven's features tightened. "When's the wedding?"

"Six months," Graceann said.

"Three months," Jake said at the same time.

Jake and Graceann stared at each other.

"Sorry, darling," Jake said. "I know you need six months to plan, but I can't wait that long."

She stood on tiptoe and kissed him lightly on the lips, then turned to Steven.

"We need to go," she said. "See you tomorrow."

Steven scowled, and Jake laughed as he and Graceann strolled away.

"Nice guy," Jake said.

When they reached the car he unlocked it with the remote key. They stuffed the packages in the truck and he opened the passenger door for Graceann, then slid into the driver's seat. As they drove away, he said, "How did someone as classy and sweet as you get mixed up with a jerk like that?" He sounded like a real fiancé, a jealous one. He really was beginning to live the part.

"Steven's not so bad when you get to know him. We dated

off-and-on for a few years. He didn't want to be exclusive, and that was okay with me. Not many guys asked me out, but Steven always had a string of girlfriends. When he was between girlfriends, he'd date me."

"You put up with that? And what was wrong with the guys you went to college with? If you were mine, I'd never let you go." Damn! He couldn't believe he'd said that. He had to stop this!

"Oh," she said, clearly startled.

He didn't have to see her to know she'd blushed.

"I don't know why I put up with him," she said slowly, recovering from her moment of surprise. "Maybe I didn't care enough."

"Baby, whatever the reason, you've got to learn to stand up for yourself."

"I've learned. Since I've been in New York I've become independent and I can take up for myself. I couldn't run my business if I didn't know how to negotiate with my suppliers and customers. I wouldn't put up with a guy like Steven now."

"But you're afraid to tell your family to let you live your life on your terms."

She sighed. "I know, but I'm working on that. Jake, please don't tell me what to do."

He hated the bitterness that rose in him. "Forget it."

Tension rode in the car with them all the way back to the house. Jake had enjoyed being alone with Graceann, enjoyed spending time with her in town. Until he and his big mouth had ruined the day. He needed to remember his place in her life.

He was just the temporary help.

CHAPTER SEVEN

*I*t had started to snow while they were at church. Graceann couldn't remember the last time she'd felt so peaceful. Giving a contented sigh, she stared out the windshield at the gently falling flakes as Jake maneuvered the BMW through the narrow streets on their way back to the house. Lorrie, Andrew and Graceann's parents rode in front of them in Lorrie's minivan.

"It's so beautiful with the Christmas lights reflecting on the pure white snow," Graceann said. "It's a silent, magical picture."

Jake chuckled. "Feeling poetic, are you?"

She laughed. "A little. I get carried away during the holidays. We couldn't ask for a more beautiful Christmas Eve. Or rather Christmas morning." She reached over to increase the volume on the car's radio. "Listen. It's Bing Crosby singing *White Christmas.*" She clapped her hands. "No one does that song better than he does."

"You really love Christmas."

"It's my favorite holiday. Isn't it yours?"

"It never was." His voice thickened. "Until now."

Graceann stared at his strong profile with his hawk-like nose and proud chin. His words and the huskiness of his voice sent her temperature soaring and she loosened her scarf. She wanted to tell him he could drop the act because they were alone. But he'd sounded so sincere. And for a little while she wanted to believe the fantasy that she and Jake really were a couple in love.

"It's been awhile since I've seen snow," he said, his attention on the road that was swiftly becoming slippery. "I've almost forgotten how to drive in the stuff."

"It's not cold where you live?"

"I try to follow the sun."

Enigmatic as always, she thought, as she snuggled down into the soft leather seat. She would allow nothing to mar the peace and contentment she felt at the moment. "Church was nice, wasn't it?"

"I enjoyed the service, to my surprise. The choir was great."

He reached across the car's console and took her hand in his. His touch warmed her through her wool gloves, and with another contented sigh, she scrunched farther down in her seat and looked out the side window, watching the soft snowflakes float around them. Jake had seemed enthralled at church, interested in everything around him. The clothes he'd chosen to wear reflected the importance he'd attached to this night, which pleased her. He wore his black leather jacket, but he'd dressed in black slacks and a white shirt instead of his usual jeans and sweater. And rather than boots, he wore black shoes that looked like fine Italian leather. Others in the church had shot curious stares his way, and she wondered if any of them recognized him as the infamous Falcon. Thankfully, unlike most times, her parents didn't stay to talk to the other parishioners. With the lateness of the hour, her parents had merely waved and exchanged Christmas greetings with their friends.

She'd been proud to be seen with Jake. Truth be told, she felt good whenever she was with him no matter how he dressed. That thought came out of nowhere and sent her head spinning. What, if anything, was going on between them?

Determined to tuck away her uncomfortable thoughts, she slid him a glance. She'd dwell on things later. "Aren't you cold in that leather jacket?"

"A little, but I'm a big boy. I can handle it."

"Those nice shoes you're wearing will get ruined in this weather."

"Don't worry about it. They're only shoes."

He seemed to take everything in stride and didn't obsess over his appearance like some men she knew. But then most men didn't have the innate confidence of Jake Falco.

Graceann glanced at the car's digital clock as they pulled into Grandmom's driveway. Two o'clock. She yawned.

"Tired?" Jake released her hand and turned off the ignition.

"I am. Isabella will have all of us up in a few hours. She's three now so Santa's real to her. She doesn't understand about letting grownups sleep."

He laughed. "I don't need a lot of sleep. But let's get you to bed."

When they got inside the quiet house, everyone said their goodnights in hushed tones. The others trooped softly upstairs, but Jake held back. Graceann, with a foot on the bottom step, gave him a questioning look.

"I'll stay down here for a while. I'm not sleepy." He grinned. "But I am hungry. I thought I might have some of that delicious fried chicken your grandmother made for dinner tonight."

"Okay. See you in a few hours."

A half hour later Graceann lay in bed, wide-awake. She hadn't heard Jake come upstairs. She needed to sleep, but wanted to be with him even more. Refusing to examine why, she slid out of bed and slipped a thick robe over her short nightgown.

She pulled the robe's sash tight and jammed her feet into slippers, then padded down the back stairs to the kitchen where a dim light glowed. Jake sat at the center counter, a plate of cold chicken in front of him. A large glass of water was set next to the plate. He'd taken off his jacket and rolled up the sleeves of his shirt, exposing muscled arms with a sprinkling of fine dark hairs. The light caught his falcon tattoo, seeming to make its wings flutter. Christmas carols, the volume low, played on the radio.

He'd loosened his hair, and the thick midnight black strands flowed to his shoulders. Her throat went dry and her heart thumped, drowning out the sounds of the music.

He looked up. His blue eyes lit with awareness, sharpening her own awareness of him. Hot-cold shivers slid down her arms.

"What are you doing up?" he asked, his voice soft and husky.

"I couldn't sleep." She moved into the room and went to the cabinet to get a glass, then filled the glass with water and sat across from him. "This is nice." She scanned the dimly-lit kitchen. "Serene. The Christmas music is the perfect touch."

"I never enjoyed Christmas carols before. I thought they were corny. But I don't feel that way now. They go with the peacefulness here. You're lucky to have such a loving family."

"I know." She locked gazes with him. "Jake, even though we started out with a business arrangement, I'm glad you're here. And I'm glad we could give you a good Christmas. I hope it's one you'll always remember."

"I'll always remember it. And you." His voice softened and he looked away. She wondered if he could be uncomfortable. The Falcon, uncomfortable? That was a new one.

When he turned back to her, his full lips tilted in a teasing grin. He was again the cocky, confident guy she'd come to know. "We both seem to have trouble sleeping lately."

"It's the holidays. Lots going on." She wrapped her hands around the glass but didn't drink.

"Baby, it's a lot more than the holidays keeping us awake. I have a cure for what ails us—Falco's never-fail insomnia remedy."

"I'm sure you have many satisfied customers," she said primly, but she couldn't stop the smile that broke free. She took a long swig of water, moistening her dust-dry throat. Too bad the liquid couldn't extinguish the desire crackling in her like a yuletide fire.

"I think you'd enjoy what I have in mind."

Her gaze swept him. *Oh, yes. I know I would.* "Let's not go there," she said instead. She might not be as experienced as Jake, but she wasn't inexperienced, as he seemed to think. While it wasn't her usual style, a certain amount of primness seemed to be the only thing keeping her safe these days. Somehow during their short time together, she needed to refrain from proving herself otherwise. But could she manage?

His grin widened, and he pushed the plate of chicken toward her. "Have something to eat."

She shook her head. "Not hungry."

"Your grandmother makes some mean chicken." He took another leg from the plate and bit into it, then wiped his mouth with his napkin.

"Grandmom's a good cook."

Finished with the leg, he wiped his mouth again and set the plate aside. "What about you? Can you cook?"

"When I have to."

"You'd be surprised at the women I know who couldn't boil water if their lives depended on it."

She raised an eyebrow. "What kind of women do you know?"

He laughed. "I don't kiss and tell, Ms. Palmer."

Heat spread over her chest, up her neck, to her face. Of course, he wasn't the kind of guy who boasted about his conquests. Avoiding eye contact, she ran her fingers over the rivulets of water on her glass.

"Not wearing your engagement ring?" he asked.

She raised her gaze to his. "I don't wear jewelry to bed."

He grinned. "What else don't you wear to bed?"

"Stop it, Jake."

He held his hands up in surrender. "I promise to be good, or at least to behave. You won't let me be as good as I can be."

The teasing note in his voice told her he wouldn't try very hard to behave, and that thought sent a hot curl of excitement through her. She wanted him to misbehave. There was no use denying it. Getting to know him, the real Jake Falco, was more exciting than her memories of him. She wanted him.

"The ring you designed is beautiful," he said, breaking into her thoughts. "You're very talented."

With effort, she pushed aside her lustful ramblings, at least for the moment. "Thanks." Finished with her water, she slid the empty glass away.

"How did you start designing jewelry?"

"I've always been artistic. Get that from my mother's mother. I taught myself to work with gems and metals. I earned extra spending money at college making and selling jewelry. Knowing what I wanted to do, I took some business courses in school and made a strategic plan. When I graduated, I took the money Grandmom and my parents gave me for a graduation gift, got an efficiency apartment in the East Village, joined an artistic co-op where I could sell my jewelry, and here I am."

"You're one smart lady." He studied her. "Business must be good if you can afford to pay me." He grinned. "And to think I cut my fee for you."

She couldn't help smiling. "My business is growing. At first, my parents gave me a monthly stipend, but now I support myself." She shrugged. "I'm not exactly living the high life, but I'm saving money, building a reputation and gaining more customers all the time." Leaning closer, she said, "And I can afford to pay you."

He sipped his water and watched her over the rim of the glass, then set down the glass. "You should be proud of your success. Your family should be proud of you."

"I am and they are."

"Good," he said with a smile.

They stared at each other. Yearning pulsed deep inside in her, making her suck in a breath.

Until she recognized the song playing on the radio, *Grandma Got Run Over by a Reindeer*. Nerves and the comical lyrics made Graceann shake her head and laugh. Jake joined her.

When the song ended, she pushed up from the stool. "On that note, I guess I'd better go back to bed."

"Me, too. Let me get rid of this empty plate." Jake scraped the leftover chicken bits into the garbage compacter and rinsed the plate before putting it into the dishwasher, then he turned to Graceann. "After you."

He followed her up the stairs, so close she inhaled his woodsy masculine scent. With him so close and she clad only in her nightclothes, excitement began to mount in her.

When they reached her room, she pushed the door open and turned to him. The dim hall light reflected in his eyes, eyes that held desire and something that made her breath hitch.

"I'll see you later." She took a step back into the room.

"I'd better come in with you, in case there's a bogeyman hiding under your bed." He followed her and quietly closed the door.

Then he pulled her into his arms. Up close and personal. She leaned into him, seeking his heat, and splayed her hands on his chest. The steady beat of his heart vibrated through her. "I think the only thing I need to fear is the man standing before me."

"Are you afraid of me?"

"I'm afraid of what you make me feel."

"How do I make you feel?"

She licked her lips. "Like I want and need something that's just out of reach."

"It's not out of reach, Graceann." He took her lips in a crushing kiss that shattered any control she still had. She opened her mouth, giving him entry, kissing him with a wild abandon she'd never felt before. With a low, guttural groan, she wound her arms around his neck and pressed close, melding her body to his strong frame. She tunneled unsteady hands through his hair. It was as silky and thick as it looked.

He kissed the corners of her mouth and the curve of her throat. Needy cries erupted from deep inside her. As he kissed his way to her chest, his fingers fumbled with the sash on her robe. It fell open and he slid his hands inside and up her ribcage to cup her breasts. Her nipples puckered and her breasts strained against the thin satin of her nightgown. He caressed her breasts, pushing them together, then kissed the hollow between them.

Graceann threw back her head, willingly giving him whatever he wanted. He backed her up against the wall. His hands spanned her waist and he feasted on one breast and then the other through the soft material.

Fisting her hands through his hair, she drew him closer. His erection pressed against her stomach. When he cupped her buttocks and lifted her, she wrapped her legs around his waist. Her body on fire, she cried out. His kiss swallowed her moans.

He ended the kiss and rested his forehead on hers, his breathing harsh. "You're amazing. What am I going to do about you?"

She slid down him and pulled away. "Make love to me, Jake. I need you."

A door slammed somewhere in the house. She tried to ignore it. All that mattered now was her and Jake and her fierce desire for him.

He released a tortured breath. "I want you, Graceann. So much. But I won't take advantage of you."

She cupped his face between her hands. "You're not taking advantage."

"You've lived a sheltered life. You always have. I'm not the kind of guy you're used to. Hell, I'm not the kind of guy you deserve."

"Don't sell yourself short, Jake. You're exactly what I need."

He brushed a whisper-soft kiss on her lips. "It's been a long day and you're tired. After a few hours of sleep you'll feel differently. Goodnight, princess."

With that, he slipped out the door.

Graceann sank onto her bed. Who would have thought? The Falcon was a gentleman. Of all times to show his chivalrous side, he had to pick tonight. She sighed and touched her breasts. They were tight and hot, pushing against the confining nightgown.

For sure, she wouldn't sleep, not now.

CHAPTER EIGHT

A child's loud squeal jolted Graceann awake. Groaning, she burrowed deeper into her covers. Isabella was up and sounded determined to go downstairs to see what Santa brought her.

Graceann opened her eyes slowly. Her eyelids felt like sandpaper. She rolled over and glanced at the small nightstand clock. Barely seven! With another groan, she put her pillow over her head. She'd gotten to sleep less than three hours ago. A high-pitched shriek along with the sounds of footsteps and hushed voices in the hallway told her she'd get no more sleep this morning. Besides, she wanted to watch Isabella open her gifts.

She threw aside the covers, slid out of bed and sat on the edge with her feet on the floor, blinking to adjust to the weak sunlight sneaking through the blinds. Her eyes watered. If just the slight bit of sunlight bothered her, she was in for a hell of a day.

There was another reason the day might be a tad awkward. The memory of Jake and his kisses and caresses early this morning cut through the cobwebs in her brain. Those kisses! His lips and hands touching her, fondling her breasts. What had gotten into her? What about preserving Jake's image of her? What had happened to her common sense, to their "business" arrangement?

She'd had a sexual relationship with Michael, and had enjoyed it. But whatever desire she'd felt for him was a pale imitation of the real passion, of the wildness, Jake incited in her.

Edgy and agitated, she jumped out of bed and headed to her attached bathroom. She needed to splash cold water on her face. A little while later, dressed in jeans, a sweater, and her favorite moccasins, she opened her bedroom door. And came face-to-face with Jake.

"Merry Christmas, princess. I was about to knock."

"Merry Christmas to you, too," she said, her voice low and breathy.

He scanned her face, stopping at her mouth, then his gaze dropped lower before meeting her eyes again. "Did you sleep at all?" His voice was gravelly, as if he hadn't slept either.

"A little. What about you?"

He brushed his thumb over her cheekbone. "Not much. I couldn't stop thinking about you."

Her whole body was instantly on fire. She wanted to pull him into her room and make wild love, but that was her libido talking. She needed to get a grip. Laughter and Isabella's excited cries provided Graceann a much-needed distraction.

"We'd better go down," she said.

Jake stepped back. "Yeah."

They found the family in the great room gathered around the tree. Grandmom, a mug of coffee in hand, sat on one of the loveseats. The others relaxed on the sofa and watched Isabella pull gifts from underneath the tree. Baby Christian slept in Lorrie's arms, oblivious to the tumult.

As Jake and Graceann headed to a small table set with coffee and bagels, Fluffy came running into the room, yapping at Jake.

"Fluffy, stop it," Grandmom said. "Come over here."

With one last bark, the dog trotted over to Grandmom and sat at her feet.

Jake's features relaxed and he let out an audible sigh. After Graceann and Jake each poured a cup of coffee and slathered bagels with cream cheese, they settled onto the other loveseat.

When Isabella lifted a new baby doll from a box, she squealed, then holding the doll, she ran over to Jake and waved it.

Laughing, he set his mug on the coffee table and picked up the little girl, settling her on his lap. "What a nice doll," he said. "Will you let me play with it some time?"

With a solemn expression, Isabella shook her head and clutched her doll tighter. When she began to squirm, Jake set her down, and she ran back to the tree and more gifts.

As Isabella, then the others, opened their gifts, Graceann slid a glance at Jake. She'd never seen him smile so much. His smile lit up his face and eyes, making him look younger and vulnerable. A little bit more of her heart melted.

The women liked the scarves she and Jake gave them. The wine Jake gave to her father and brother-in-law was a big hit, too.

"I know the owners of that winery," Jake said.

Andrew's eyebrows rose. "Sweet!"

The whole family seemed to have accepted Jake. Except her mom, who gave Jake tight-lipped looks that made Graceann's chest clench with annoyance. Graceann was giving her mother what she wanted and she still wasn't happy. Reminding herself her engagement to Jake was a farce, Graceann took calming breaths. The fake engagement had started to feel like the real deal.

"Open your gift from Jake," Lorrie urged.

Graceann got up from the loveseat and grabbed the gold foil-wrapped package with the green silk shawl from under the tree. She opened it slowly, drawing out the suspense for the others, then held it up for the rest to see, pretending to be surprised.

"It's beautiful," Lorrie said. "It's so you. Try it on."

"It's lovely," Grandmom said with a smile for Jake. "Jake has wonderful taste."

"Let me put it on you." Jake stood, took the wrap from Graceann and draped it over her shoulders, lifting her hair off her neck. He brushed his hands up her arms as he bent to softly kiss her nape.

Jake was certainly playing his part. Her skin tingled where he touched, and his hot breath on the back of her neck sent delicious shivers along her spine. "Thank you for the gift," she said softly.

The others, except for Graceann's mother, watched, grinning. A hot flush spread over Graceann's face.

"Open your gift, Jake," she said quickly. She picked up a package wrapped in silver with a red bow and handed it to him.

When he'd unwrapped it and pulled out the leather-bound journal she'd given him, he looked at her with amazement, then gave her a wide smile. "Thank you."

"You said you like to write. I'm hoping now you'll find the incentive."

"I will." He kissed her long and hard.

Her breathing ragged, she finally pulled away. She could feel her mother's steady gaze. Graceann's face burned hotter and she knew she must be as red as the brightest Christmas bulb. She needed to tell Jake to tone it down. Like he'd listen.

When they'd finished opening the gifts and eaten more bagels, Graceann and Jake went upstairs to shower and dress. At the door to her room, Jake cupped her shoulders and turned her toward him. He leaned down and gave her a slow, sweet kiss, running his tongue over the seam of her lips until she opened to him.

After long, lust-filled minutes, they separated. Graceann gazed into his eyes. "What are you doing, Jake?"

"I'm kissing you. What does it feel like?"

"I've told you we don't have to put on an act when we're

alone. I'm beginning to think you're enjoying this way too much."

He skimmed fingers over her lips. "I am enjoying it. A lot. And, baby, it stopped being an act a long time ago."

"You didn't want me earlier today. You walked away."

"I'm not good for you, but that doesn't stop me from wanting you."

Frowning, she stepped back, fighting the adrenaline rush of excitement his words provoked. "I need to get changed." She slipped into her room and shut the door, wishing she could lock out her growing hunger for him as easily.

Graceann took extra time with her appearance, telling herself she wanted to look especially nice for Christmas. "Who are you kidding?" she asked her reflection before heading downstairs. "You're doing this to excite Jake."

Her bad girl self was coming out to play. She'd dressed in a black wool pencil skirt and green silk blouse and she put on a pair of earrings that looked like miniature green Christmas balls. Kate had given them to her last year. Walking carefully on her black suede stilettos, she held the handrail as she made her way down the stairs to the living room. What would Jake say if he knew she was wearing a red thong?

The men were already there, drinks in hand, snacking on appetizers. She could use a drink herself. They wouldn't have lunch today because they'd have an early, big dinner. As she entered the room, her attention focused solely on Jake, listening intently to something Andrew was saying.

Jake looked delicious as always. Today he wore a tan shirt, unbuttoned at the throat to expose a scattering of fine dark hairs, and black slacks. His hair was neatly tied back with a leather cord in his usual ponytail.

He turned. The pure masculine appreciation in his sapphire eyes stole her breath. Everything else faded as they stared at each other.

68

She smiled. Mission accomplished.

"Graceann," her dad said, distracting her from Jake and her lustful thoughts. "Come in and have a glass of this Pinot Grigio Jake gave me. It's some of the best I've tasted."

She walked into the room on legs that wobbled like jelly. Looking at Jake had her hormones revved up like a train speeding toward derailment. It seemed her plan to excite him had managed to get both of them worked up—and they still had an entire evening to get through.

She took the proffered glass of white wine from her father and sat on the loveseat next to Jake. "Where are the kids?" she asked Andrew.

"Both sleeping, thank God. Isabella wore herself out."

Jake laughed. "That's what Christmas is all about, the kids."

Graceann sipped the wine. Her father was right. The wine was wonderful. Strange that Jake, who didn't drink alcohol, would know the owner of a winery that made such a premium wine like this. She took another sip and slanted a glance at Jake. He smiled. She gathered he hadn't had a childhood filled with fond memories, yet he seemed relaxed and happy here with her family. Feeling more relaxed herself, she settled into her seat.

"Where are the others?" she asked.

"Your grandmother's napping," her father said. "Your mother and Lorrie are in the kitchen. They say they need to start dinner, but I suspect they're drinking wine and trying to escape from the rest of us."

The shrill ring of the doorbell disturbed the calm. Graceann looked at the clock over the mantle. Twelve. She groaned inwardly. Steven was here.

Graceann started to get up, but Lorrie came from the kitchen at the back of the house and hurried to the door, her heels clicking on the marble floor of the foyer. Their mother was close behind her.

Graceann heard the door open, then Lorrie saying, "Merry Christmas, Steven. Nice to see you again."

"Steven! Merry Christmas," her mother said, more animated than Graceann had heard her in the past few days.

Suppressing the urge to roll her eyes, Graceann looked at Jake. His mouth had set into a thin line. Then Steven, holding several wrapped packages, and followed by the two women, stepped into the room. "Merry Christmas, everyone." Dressed in a black overcoat brushed with snow, he looked around the room, arrogance and confidence in every line of his body.

He set his packages on a nearby table and walked over to Graceann. Bending, he placed a kiss on her cheek.

"Merry Christmas, Graceann. You look fantastic."

She hadn't dressed for him. She'd dressed for Jake. She had the uncomfortable feeling Steven was the Grinch, come to steal her Christmas spirit.

Ignoring Jake, Steven greeted the others. He slipped off his overcoat and handed it to Lorrie. Dressed in a dark blue suit Graceann suspected cost a few thousand dollars, a snowy white shirt, the cuffs sporting gold cufflinks, and a blue striped tie that perfectly complemented his suit, he was the picture of a successful lawyer.

Graceann slid closer to Jake. She preferred Jake's natural sexiness to Steven's polished fashion-magazine look.

"Steven, you remember Jake," she said.

Forced to openly acknowledge Jake, Steven looked over. "How's it going, Falco?"

"Couldn't be better." Jake put his arm around Graceann's shoulders.

After a half hour of awkward conversation, the women excused themselves to go into the kitchen to prepare dinner. Eager to escape Steven's possessive stares, Graceann didn't complain about the women doing all the cooking.

Her mom had put the turkey in the oven earlier and had

prepared the green bean casserole the day before. Lorrie made her signature dish of scalloped potatoes while Graceann set about making the cranberry stuffing, which they cooked separately from the turkey. Christmas songs played on the radio, bathing the room in cheerfulness. The holiday spirit didn't reach Graceann, however. She seethed over her mother's meddling. Steven's presence had put a damper on her Christmas joy.

"Need any help?" Jake poked his head into the kitchen.

"Can you make mac and cheese?" Lorrie asked. "Isabella loves it and she won't eat any of what we're cooking."

He grinned. "I make a mean mac and cheese. Point me to the ingredients."

As if someone flipped on a bright Christmas light, Graceann's melancholy mood lifted. Smiling at Jake, she set about putting the ingredients out for him.

Working side-by-side with Jake, the Christmas music held new meaning. Contentment settled over her, and her body seemed to melt with his nearness. As if he could read her thoughts, he looked over and gave her an intimate smile.

Graceann noticed her mom stealing looks at Jake. Why couldn't her mother see what a great guy he was?

Damn, she was thinking like a woman in love.

No, that couldn't be.

She smoothed a hand down her body-hugging skirt. She wasn't in love with Jake. In lust maybe, but not love. The Christmas music, the scents of cinnamon and pine, the bright decorations, had all put her in a romantic bubble that would burst like an icy water balloon once the holidays were over. What was she *thinking*, wanting to seduce Jake into sleeping with her?

"How's it going in here?" Steven, glass of wine in hand, strolled into the room.

Graceann bristled. "We're good. Everything's under control."

Beside her, she felt Jake stiffen.

"Kitchen duty, Falco?" Steven asked with a jeer.

"Best place in the house, surrounded by beautiful women," Jake said.

Lorrie snickered. Graceann smiled. Her mother, a confused look on her face, stared at the two men. Her mom should have expected this, having inviting Steven when Jake was there.

The men faced off like two bucks, antlers ready, preparing to fight to the death. *Have a Holly, Jolly Christmas* played on the radio. Graceann wanted to put her head in her hands and groan. Her mother might have started the ball rolling, but she herself had given it a huge push downhill, dressing to entice Jake.

Clearly, Steven thought she'd done it for him.

A holly, jolly Christmas indeed.

CHAPTER NINE

Graceann was determined to enjoy their Christmas dinner and not let Steven's presence interfere. He sat across from her, and much as she tried to ignore him, she felt his hot stares. Jake and he paid no attention to each other. If the others at the table noticed, they didn't show it and kept up a lively conversation in between bites of mouth-watering food and sips of luscious wine. When Jake took her hand in his under the table, Graceann threw him a grateful smile and began to relax. Jake understood how Steven's being there upset her.

Afterward, Jake cajoled the men into cleaning up while the women rested. Now, seated on the sofa in the great room, Graceann slipped off her heels, put her feet up on the coffee table and sipped coffee. Grandmom, a glass of red wine in hand, sat on one of the loveseats. Lorrie relaxed next to Graceann, and their mother sat in a plush chair near the fireplace. Isabella and Christian were once again asleep upstairs.

Christmas music played softly in the background, an accompaniment to the sharp crackle of the fire in the fieldstone hearth fireplace. The scents of bayberry and cinnamon from candles set strategically throughout the room wafted over them. Graceann sighed. She felt full, satisfied…happy.

Her grandmother glanced toward the kitchen where the men worked, then nodded at Graceann. "That Jake of yours is a good man."

Lorrie chuckled. "Anyone who can get Daddy and Andrew to clean the kitchen is a keeper."

Graceann smiled. "None of them seemed to mind, except Steven." She shook her head, wondering if Steven had recently gotten so arrogant, or if he'd always been that way and she hadn't noticed.

Her mother snorted. "Steven is our guest. He should be in here with his coffee, not stuck in the kitchen. I'm sure he didn't expect to work for his meal."

"For God's sake, Mom, get over it," Lorrie said.

"Jake's a guest, too," Graceann said. "He doesn't mind cleaning up."

Her mom put up a hand. "I stand corrected, although we are providing room and board."

Before Graceann could respond, her mother met her gaze, adding, "Jake seems devoted to you, and I want you to be happy. But I pictured you with a man who's more…who's in a more professional line of work."

Jake, devoted to her? She barely heard the rest of her mother's speech. Jake was a hell of an actor if he'd convinced her mother he loved Graceann. He'd told Graceann he wanted her, and she knew his desire was no act. The realization both thrilled and scared her. But love and lust weren't the same, and this felt like more than lust.

Her mother was staring at her, expecting an answer.

Graceann blinked. "Professional? What does that have to do with whether a man will make a good husband?"

"Graceann's right," her grandmother said.

"I agree," Lorrie said with a nod.

A contrite look swept over her mother's face. "I only want you to be happy, Graceann."

"I know, Mom."

Grandmom set her wine glass on the table and rubbed her upper arms.

"Are you cold?" Graceann asked her.

"A little."

"Where's your sweater?"

"On my bed."

Graceann pushed up from the sofa. "I'll get it for you."

She trotted up the stairs and went into Grandmom's room, the largest bedroom in the sprawling house. She found the sweater on the bed and grabbed it, then left and closed the door behind her. As she walked down the hall, she heard footsteps on the stairs and Steven came into view.

He hurried toward her. "Good. You're alone." He gripped her shoulders and backed her against the wall, standing close, too close. His wine-laced breath fanned her cheeks as she held the sweater against her chest like a barrier. She tried to squirm free but he refused to let her go.

"What do you want, Steven? I need to get this sweater to my grandmother."

"Graceann, I know things didn't work out between us, but I'd like to give us another chance. Of all the women I've dated, you're still the one I want to spend the rest of my life with. You'd be a great asset to my career and a great mother to my children. Why do you think I moved here? I figured you'd want to live close to your family once we were married."

"Married? You're delusional, Steven. I'm engaged to someone else. You asked me to marry you once and I said no. I thought we parted as friends."

"Friends?" Steven's gray eyes bored into hers. "That guy you're engaged to isn't our kind, Graceann. He's rough, crude. A woman like you needs someone like me, a man with polish who appreciates money and all it can buy, a man who can give you a comfortable life."

She put a hand on his chest and felt his muscles tense. "None of this is your business. Don't ruin our friendship with all this possessiveness, Steven. Now let go of me. I need to get back downstairs."

"Damn it, Graceann—"

"You heard the lady. Get your hands off her."

Graceann gasped. She hadn't heard Jake come upstairs. She peered around Steven. Jake stood nearby, his body tense, poised for a fight. The look on his face was one of controlled fury.

Muttering another curse, Steven released her and slithered back a few steps. Hands out, palms extended, he faced Jake. "Hey, man, I didn't mean anything by it. The lady and I had a thing going once. She's looking so hot tonight. Can't blame me for trying."

"Get the hell away from my fiancée before I forget I'm in her grandmother's house," Jake snarled.

With a black look at Graceann, as if this were all *her* fault, Steven skirted past Jake and down the stairs.

"Are you okay?" Jake asked, turning to her.

"I'm fine. He doesn't scare me." She clutched her grandmother's sweater tighter against her chest and shook her head. "Was he always a jerk and I never noticed until now?"

Jake stepped closer and brushed strands of hair back from her face. "I think he was always a jerk but you were too sweet to notice."

The intensity in his eyes made her breathing go shallow. "I'm not that sweet, Jake."

"I think you're very sweet." His voice softened. "And delicious."

Her breathing stopped.

He smiled and moved back. "Let's go for a walk to the dock. I think we both need a break. Time to put things back in perspective. Bundle up. I don't want you to be cold."

I could never be cold around you. If anything, I'm overheated. The words pushed into her mind and made her blush. "A walk sounds great. After I bring Grandmom's sweater to her."

Fifteen minutes later, wearing her knee-high boots and bundled into a long coat, scarf and gloves, Graceann strolled beside Jake over the wooden walkway to the dock. He wore his black leather jacket, but had borrowed gloves and a brightly colored striped scarf from Andrew.

"The scarf suits you," she said.

Grinning, he looked down at her. "Really? I don't see myself as a striped scarf kind of guy."

She laughed and grabbed his hand. It felt right to hold onto him.

"Your brother-in-law strikes me as an uptight sort," Jake said. "What's he doing with a scarf like this?"

"Lorrie gave it to him. Andrew is the button-down type. Even though he's a great guy, I think Lorrie would like him to be a little more exciting."

They'd reached the dock and, still holding hands, stood near the edge and looked over the water. Broken bits of ice floated in the inky blackness. The snow had stopped and clouds smudged the sky, letting the moon peek through. She inhaled the clean, crisp, pine-laced air.

Jake squeezed her hand. "What kind of guy do you want, Ms. Palmer? A buttoned-down insurance type like Andrew or someone with a little danger?"

Staring out over the water, she formulated her answer before she turned to look up at him. "I want a decent guy who doesn't lie to me, who treats me with respect, and who won't cheat. And who totally loves me."

"That's a tall order," he said quietly. "Most guys I know couldn't live up to that."

"I won't settle for anything less."

"And you shouldn't. You deserve the best." His gaze locked with hers. "You don't want a guy who lies, yet you're not being truthful with your family about me." His voice had softened.

"I know it's hypocritical. Believe me, I feel guilty." She blew out a breath and watched as it frosted in the air. "I'm in too deep with this whole scheme and I don't know how to get out of it."

"Easy. Tell them the truth."

"Do you always tell the truth?" she asked, meeting his gaze again.

His mouth set in a tight line and he glanced out over the water. "Not always."

There he was, being secretive again. Jake had more layers than Grandmom's six-layer coconut cake. Graceann suspected that, unlike her grandmother's cake, Jake's layers wouldn't be so sweet. The thought gave her an unexpected thrill. What had he asked her? Something about danger?

"Tell me about your bad relationship that ended two years ago, the reason you came up with this charade." Jake's words hovered in the night air.

"Why do you want to know?"

He gripped her shoulders and pulled her around to face him, then held her in the circle of his arms. "A man hurt you, and it wasn't Steven. You say you don't want to get married but you concocted this whole lie for your family. Tell me about the man behind this."

When she shivered, he gathered her closer. Held in Jake's arms, Graceann felt secure and safe. She didn't want to think what that meant. The holidays would be over soon and they'd go their separate ways. The thought of not seeing him again sent an arrow of regret through her.

Taking a calming breath, she lifted her face to meet his eyes. "His name was Michael, and I fell head over heels for him the first time I met him. He was handsome, smart, witty, polished.

He drove a Lamborghini and dressed in designer clothes. He completely swept me off my feet."

Jake stiffened. If she didn't know better she'd think he was jealous.

"You're not as superficial as that, Graceann. There had to be more to this guy. What type work did he do?"

"He was a financial wizard who worked on Wall Street. In fact, Zach introduced us. Zach thought we'd be good together. He didn't know the real Michael either."

"Who was the real Michael?"

"A serial cheater and pathological liar. Michael lied even when he didn't have to. Because of his looks and his money, he had women chasing him all the time. He rarely said no to them."

Remnants of the pain Michael had caused her twisted like a knife in her chest. She'd gotten over him, yet his betrayal had cut her deeply.

"Don't blame yourself." Jake kissed the top of her head. "Go on. I know there's more."

"There is. He asked me to marry him. I was so excited and happy. My family loved him. My mom was over the moon. I sometimes wonder which impressed her more, Michael's resume or the three-carat diamond he gave me. It wasn't long after we became engaged that I had a visitor to my table at a craft show." She chewed her lip. "And everything fell apart."

"A visitor?"

"A beautiful woman. She told me a jarring story."

Graceann blinked back tears at the memory. "I didn't believe her. I got someone to watch my table and I went outside to confront her with her lies. She told me everything—about Michael's other girlfriends, of which there were many, the way he spent money on them. She said he was marrying me because I was respectable and from a good family. I'd be an asset to his climb up the career ladder." Graceann grimaced. "Not the only time I've heard that one."

Remembered humiliation rolled through her and she rested her hands on Jake's upper arms, as if bracing herself to be pummeled anew by the devastating news she'd learned that day. "I defended him until I couldn't, until she hit me with the worst of it."

Jake hugged her close. "It's okay, Graceann. You don't have to tell me any more if it hurts too much."

Swiping at tears, she stepped back. "I want to tell you. This woman, her name was Kristin, was Michael's common-law wife. She lived in New Jersey with his two kids."

"He had kids and a woman stashed away in Jersey?" Anger radiated from Jake, so strong it hung between them like a black storm cloud.

Graceann nodded. "She said she loved Michael. They'd been high school sweethearts. When she got pregnant at eighteen, he refused to marry her. They lived together and had another child. But he still wouldn't marry her."

"Yet she stayed with him?" Jake asked.

"She said she loved him."

"That's not love. That's a lack of self-respect."

"I agree." Graceann gripped his arms again. "Michael had told her I was malleable, that he could do whatever he wanted after we were married and I wouldn't question him. So he would continue to support her and the kids while married to me. What a fool I was. But Michael was wrong about one thing. I'm not malleable and I wasn't about to stay with him."

"Baby, I'm sorry." Jake gathered her to him.

His heart beat strong and steady under her cheek, comforting and safe. Funny that The Falcon could make her feel so protected.

She pulled away and looked up at him. He watched her with eyes filled with understanding. "I'm okay now. I broke up with him right away. But I really feel sorry for Kristin and I think about her from time to time. I hope she comes to her senses and leaves that jerk."

Jake chuckled and brushed a light kiss on Graceann's lips. "Only you could worry about your ex-boyfriend's mistress. Proof of your sweetness and your adorableness. Don't ever change."

"Jake, I keep telling you I'm not really that sweet."

"Baby, you don't get it. You're the whole package—smart, caring, beautiful, and hot as hell."

He pressed his lips to hers in an urgent kiss that electrified every part of her body and touched something deep in her soul. His kiss coaxed and teased, urging her to give more, to give herself completely. An ache built between her thighs as she wound her arms around his neck and melted into him, opening her mouth to his hot invasion, letting him know she was his for the taking.

Consumed by her need, she moaned deep in her throat as her hands fumbled with the leather cord holding back his hair. She untied the cord and dropped it, then tunneled her fingers through his hair, craving naked skin next to naked skin, his hair brushing her bare chest.

He rained kisses along her neck. Then, cupping her face, he stared into her eyes. "I want you, Graceann."

Her heart pounded. "Jake, I—"

"Graceann! Jake! Come quick!" Her father's harried voice reached them and they pulled apart.

"Something's wrong," she said, her emotions an untidy mix of fear, frustration, and relief. True, she wanted Jake, but what did she really know about him?

All she knew was she was grateful for the strong, solid grip of his hand as he held hers while they ran to the house where her father waited by the back door, a worried look on his face. The sound of approaching sirens pierced the night air.

"What's wrong?" Graceann asked.

"It's your grandmother. We think she's having a heart attack."

CHAPTER TEN

*A*t six the next morning, Graceann and Jake trudged wearily up the walk to her grandmother's house after spending the night at the hospital. Graceann's parents were still with Grandmom.

As they slipped through the door and walked into the foyer, Lorrie, who'd stayed home with Andrew, Steven, and the kids, ran down the stairs. "You two look exhausted. Go upstairs and rest. We'll keep the kids quiet." She released a deep breath. "Thank God Grandmom's going to be okay."

Graceann rubbed a hand over her face. Her muscles screamed with fatigue. "I'm so glad it was only indigestion, but when you're in your late eighties the doctors can't take any chances."

"When are Mom and Dad bringing her home?"

"The hospital said they'd release her about noon."

Fluffy ran down the stairs, quiet for a change, and looked around. He began to whimper. Graceann bent to scratch him behind the ears. "You miss her, don't you, Fluffy? She'll be home soon."

"Come with me, Fluffy," Lorrie said. "I have a treat for you in the kitchen." The dog obediently followed her.

Graceann stood and Jake put his arm around her shoulders. "That dog must really miss your grandmother. He didn't try to bite me."

"He doesn't try to bite you."

"Yes, he does. The dog hates me."

She laughed. "No, he doesn't."

He gave her shoulder a gentle squeeze. "You see the good in everyone, even an annoying little dog." He grinned down at her as she smothered a yawn. "It's been a rough night. You need to rest."

"So do you."

"Don't worry about me. I wasn't an emotional ball of nerves until the good news came. Let's get you upstairs for some quality sleep."

When they reached her bedroom door, Jake took her in his arms and kissed her tenderly. She pulled away and skimmed a finger down his face. "Thanks for staying with me at the hospital. You didn't have to. I could have come home with Mom, Dad, and Grandmom."

He smiled. "How would it look if your fiancé selfishly abandoned you at the hospital?"

"Once you commit to a role, you really live the part, don't you?"

He silenced her with another soft kiss. "When I'm hired for a job I always deliver. Now get in there and get some sleep."

Graceann watched him as he strode with his customary lithe grace along the hallway to his room. Jake Falco was a very complex and caring guy once you looked under the surface. Smiling, she slipped into her room.

Nightgown on, she was ready to sink into her bed when a light knock sounded at her door. Heart thumping in anticipation of seeing Jake, she threw on her robe and opened the door. Her heart tumbled with disappointment when she saw Steven standing there.

She pulled her robe tighter. "What is it, Steven? I'm getting ready to take a nap."

"May I come in?"

Unsmiling, she gave him a level look. "No."

"I won't touch you. I promise. I need to say something."

With a sigh of resignation, she let him in, but was careful to keep the door open. Arms folded across her chest, she said, "Okay, start talking."

He smoothed a hand over his short hair. "I still love you, Graceann. I want to marry you. Your family wants that, too. Drop this jerk you're with and come back to me."

She took a step away. "You're the jerk, Steven. I can't believe we were even friends. I'm with Jake and it's where I want to be." As she said the words, she knew they were true. She wanted to be with Jake.

Steven grasped her shoulders. "You belong with me. You belong *to* me."

Breathing heavily, she jerked free and flung an arm toward the door. "Get out of my room and get out of this house. Now."

He stood there with a calculating expression on his hardened face.

"If you don't leave this minute, I'm going to scream. Jake and Andrew are here and they'll come running."

He backed toward the door. "I won't give up. That long-haired grease monkey isn't for you."

"Jake's twice the man you'll ever be. Get out."

His eyes like thunder clouds, Steven stormed out of her room and down the hall to his room.

She closed her door, leaned against it, and pressed a hand to her quaking belly. Funny how she once thought she might be in love with Steven. Everything about him paled in comparison to Jake. Jake liked to tease her but he was never mean. She couldn't see him acting as boorishly as Steven. Her mother had inadvertently done Jake a favor by inviting Steven. She'd allowed Graceann, and hopefully the rest of the family, to see Jake had something Steven didn't—depth and character.

As she slipped into bed, the realization hit her that she thought of Jake as a real fiancé. When had that happened? Before she could figure it out, she drifted off to sleep dreaming of Jake.

Later, the sound of voices woke Graceann. Yawning, she rolled over and looked at the clock. One. She'd slept for over five hours. That was enough. She'd never get back to sleep anyway.

She took a quick shower, pulled her hair into a ponytail, threw on a sweater and jeans—and her glasses—shoved her feet into her comfy moccasins, then headed down the back stairs. When she entered the kitchen, she found Lorrie, Andrew, and Jake seated around the center counter drinking coffee.

Like a heat-seeking missile, she zeroed in on Jake. He threw her a smile that lit up his face and made her throat go dry. "After-noon, sunshine," he said, getting up from his stool and walking slowly toward her. He took her hand and pulled her to a stool. "Sit. I'll get you a cup of coffee. Do you want anything to eat? Lorrie makes a mean pumpkin bread."

"Thanks, Jake," Lorrie said. "I'm glad you like my pumpkin bread." A blush spread over her face.

Andrew shot his wife a narrow-eyed look that made Graceann stifle a grin.

"I love Lorrie's pumpkin bread," Graceann said, starting to rise from her stool.

Jake shook his head. "You stay there, princess, and I'll wait on you."

Lorrie sighed. "Jake, you spoil her."

He chuckled. "And I intend to keep doing it."

Graceann widened her eyes at Jake. He winked at her, then strolled to the coffeemaker. She wondered when she'd lost control of the situation.

"Steven left in a hurry," Lorrie said. "Did you have anything to do with that?"

Graceann shrugged and feigned innocence. "I guess he thought with everything going on now, it would be best for him to leave." She frowned when Jake nearly knocked over the pitcher with the creamer. What happened was between her and Steven. Wasn't it?

If Jake knew anything, he wasn't saying.

Then neither was she. "Is Grandmom home yet?" she asked her sister.

Lorrie nodded. "They got in about a half hour ago. They're all resting. Even Fluffy. He won't leave Grandmom's side. Other than being tired, she seems back to her old self."

"That's good."

As Graceann was finishing her third cup of coffee and her second piece of pumpkin bread, a loud wail coming from the second floor shattered the silence.

"Isabella," Lorrie said, pushing away from the counter. "She's going to wake everyone. I hoped she'd sleep longer. All the Christmas excitement, I guess."

"Stay here," Andrew said to Lorrie. "I'll get Isabella." He jumped up and jogged to the stairs.

Lorrie sank back onto her stool as her look of gratitude followed Andrew from the room and up the stairs.

Graceann cradled her mug and inhaled the sweet aroma of hazelnut. "Jake and I can take Izzie off your hands for a while to give you a break."

"Sure," Jake said. "Why not? Would you mind if we took her outside to build a snowman?"

Lorrie looked at them as if they'd morphed into two of Santa's more unlikely elves. "Do you know what you're saying? She's a handful."

Jake chuckled. "She won't be a problem." He looked toward Graceann. "Right, sweetheart?"

She gave him her sweetest smile. "That's right, *darling*."

<><><>

Dressed for the outdoors, Jake waited by the front door with Graceann for Lorrie to bring Isabella. Graceann leaned in to whisper to him. "You were really laying it on thick back there in the kitchen."

She looked so adorably self-righteous with her eyes flashing. He suppressed a laugh, knowing even a smile would get him a punch in the arm. Giving her what he hoped was an innocent look, he said, "I want to spoil you, *sweetheart*."

"I'm not you're sweetheart, *angel*."

"Who says you're not?"

Before Graceann could answer, Lorrie came down the stairs holding a bundled-up Isabella. When she got to the bottom step, she let the little girl down. Isabella waddled over to Graceann and held out her arms. Laughing, Graceann picked her up. "You can barely move in all these clothes, sweetie." She kissed Isabella on her cheek.

"I don't want her to catch cold," Lorrie said.

"She can't move enough to catch a snowflake," Graceann said.

Lorrie shrugged.

Jake opened the door. "Let's go build that snowman."

Later, a giggling Isabella helped Jake and Graceann roll a huge snowball into place for the base of the snowman. The little girl was covered with snow. "You look like a snowman yourself," Jake said. Isabella giggled louder.

Graceann knelt to brush snow off Isabella's coat and adjust the little girl's hat. At the picture of maternal love, Jake reeled with unexpected longing. Fragments of memories rose in him like spirits arising from a mist—his mother adjusting his hat in the same way Graceann fixed Isabella's; his mother holding him against her chest in a tender embrace. When he was small, his mom always wore rose-scented perfume. Even now the scent of roses reminded him of her. He had so few memories of loving times with his mother. Too soon, the roses were replaced by the stench of alcohol.

Uneasy with his painful trip down memory lane, Jake gathered snow and molded it between his hands until he had a perfectly formed ball. Today was a time for fun, the kind of fun he barely remembered with his own parents. He readied his arm for the pitch.

Finished with the little girl's hat, Graceann stood. Her eyes grew wide when she saw the snowball. "Oh, no, you don't," she said, laughing. She scooped up a clump of snow to throw at him, but he was too fast. His snowball hit her in the shoulder.

Before he could throw another one, she quickly formed a ball and threw it, hitting him in the arm.

Laughing, Isabella danced around them. "Me, me!" she shouted.

"Over here, Izzie," Graceann said. "Girls against the guy."

"I'm outnumbered," Jake said in mock fright.

The intense snowball fight was the most fun Jake had had in more years than he could remember. His leather jacket was covered with snow, but he didn't care. He deliberately took a very long time making each snowball to give the females, especially Isabella, ample time to pummel him.

Graceann and Isabella's laughter tinkled in the clear air, a happy, carefree sound that shot an unfamiliar feeling of joy to his heart. With a saucy smile for him, Graceann handed Isabella a perfectly formed snowball to throw. His chest tightened. Graceann had never looked sweeter than she did at this moment, with her thick hair flying around her face and her cheeks pink from the cold. Her full lips—.

He had no more time to think as Isabella's snowball hit him in the heart. Clutching his chest, Jake fell onto the snow. Isabella squealed with delight. The females high-fived each other.

Jake's laughter joined theirs. No matter what happened between him and Graceann, this Christmas with the Palmer family would go down as his happiest ever. A tinge of sorrow wrapped around him with the realization of all he'd missed in his life. Real families had fun together. Real families loved each other.

Graceann signaled him the fight was over and stooped to pick up the little girl. "You're tired, aren't you, sweetie?" Isabella wound her arms around Graceann's neck and snuggled close.

As Jake stood, Graceann raised her gaze to his. Something passed between them then, something vibrant and pulsing and filled with promise. His breathing slowed. A vision of him and Graceann together, of her holding their child, wavered before him. He couldn't move, couldn't look away.

"We'd better go in," Graceann said.

The moment was lost. Shaking his head, he said, "Take Isabella in then come back out. We haven't finished yet. We promised her a snowman."

Dusk was settling around them as they finished building their snowman. Graceann and Jake stood back and studied their work. They'd dressed their creation in an old fedora and a red scarf Lorrie had found in the house.

"Looks damn good," he said. "That's one of the handsomest snowmen I've ever seen. We need to take his picture."

"We're artists," Graceann said.

He turned to her. "You're the artist. You're the one who designed him. I'm the laborer following your orders. Very few people could do what you do with jewelry. Or with snowmen."

Smiling, she took a bow. "Thank you, Jake."

Her smile chipped away a little more of the wall around his heart. "I like your family." His words came out unbidden. "I always figured close families were dull, but your family's cool. I didn't believe parents and siblings could love each other. But you all do."

She slipped off a glove and reached out to touch his face. "Oh, Jake."

He wanted to take her into his arms and never let her go. But he didn't want her pity. Deliberately breaking their tender connection, he stepped back and gave her a wicked grin. Her gaze traveled to the arm he held at his side. A huge snowball rested in the palm of his gloved hand.

"Oh, no." She began to run away.

The snowball hit the middle of her back, then he tackled her. They rolled on the soft snow-packed ground together. When they'd settled, she lay on her back with him on top of her. He propped himself up on his elbows.

Her pupils were dilated. "No fair," she said. "I wasn't ready to fight." Her words came out on a husky breath.

"Are you ready for this?"

He took her sweet lips in a kiss that poured out his need for her, a need that grew stronger every day. She wrapped her arms around his neck and pulled him down. He slid his tongue along her lips. She opened to him. She tasted of coffee and mint. His body on fire, he wondered why the snow around them didn't melt.

When his hard erection pressed against her stomach, she moaned into his mouth. Her passion fueled his hunger. He kissed her harder and deeper, as if he could devour her.

"Dinner's ready, you two!" Lorrie's high-pitched voice coming from the opened front door was the most unwelcome sound he'd heard in a long while.

Jake slowly pulled away and stared down at Graceann. Happiness and desire flashed in her eyes. "You are amazing," he whispered.

"So are you." She cupped his face. "You're wonderful."

He froze. Him, wonderful? "You've been out in the cold too long."

<><><>

Dinner was an informal affair around the kitchen counter. Lorrie had taken a tray of food up to their grandmother. After they'd had their coffee and dessert, Graceann stood and pushed her stool away. "Is it okay for Grandmom to have dessert? She loves apple pie."

Her mother nodded. "The doctor said she can eat anything but to watch her portions. And she can't have coffee for a while."

"Good," Graceann said. "I'll bring dessert and tea to her. I haven't seen her since she got back from the hospital."

Graceann knocked softly on her grandmother's door, then pushed it open. The older woman was sitting up in bed watching TV. Her tray with the empty dinner dishes was on the nightstand. Fluffy was curled up close to her. The dog lifted its head when Graceann opened the door, then with a yawn, went back to sleep.

A fire snapped in the fireplace, heating the room and filling it with the acrid aroma of burning wood. Sweet memories stole over Graceann. She and Lorrie used to sit on either side of Grandmom on the bed while she read to them as a fire crackled in the hearth. Smiling, she walked into the room.

Grandmom returned her smile and muted the TV. Graceann set the dessert plate and the tea mug on the tray next to the dinner dishes, then leaned over to give her grandmother a hug.

"You look good, Grandmom." She settled onto the bed and held one of her grandmother's hands.

"I do not look good." The older woman touched her hair with her free hand. "I have bed head."

Graceann laughed. "So you have a little bed head. You're still beautiful."

Her grandmother's face lit in another smile. "You always know the right thing to say. Where's that handsome fiancé of yours? I watched out the window as you two built the snowman." She gave her a sly grin. "I saw the snowball fight, too."

Had her grandmother seen them kiss? Graceann's face felt hot and she knew she blushed. "You shouldn't have been out of bed."

Grandmom waved a hand. "I'm fine. Everyone coddles me." She shifted, and Graceann fluffed her pillow behind her. Settling back, the older woman studied Graceann. "I like Jake very much." She stroked Fluffy's head. "Fluffy likes him, too."

"I'm not sure 'like' is the right word for what Fluffy feels toward Jake."

"I know my dog. He's a good judge of character. He likes Jake. So, did you and Jake set a date yet?"

Graceann looked toward the window as guilt choked her.

"What is it, child?" her grandmother asked. "Something's bothering you."

Graceann faced her grandmother and kissed her on the cheek. Grandmom's skin felt paper-thin. Swiping at a tear, Graceann took a steadying breath. "I was afraid we'd lost you. I don't know what we'd do without you."

Grandmom snorted. "I plan to live to 100 or beyond. By the time I go, you'll be glad to be rid of me. But there's something else bothering you. 'Fess up."

Graceann blew out a breath. "I was afraid you'd die not knowing the truth about Jake and me. I don't know if I could have lived with that guilt."

"What are you trying to say?" Grandmom's brow furrowed.

"If I tell you something, promise you won't tell anyone, especially Mom and Daddy." She squeezed her grandmother's hand.

"That depends on what it is."

"Promise me. Please."

"I promise since it clearly means so much to you."

She rubbed her grandmother's hand, gathering her thoughts, then raised her gaze. "Jake and I aren't engaged. I hired him to be my pretend fiancé through the holidays."

When Grandmom stared at her without saying a word, dread settled like a tight knot in Graceann's chest.

"Why would you do that?" her grandmother asked at last.

"You know how Mom is always trying to fix me up with some guy. Look at how she invited Steven here. She feels sorry for me and she won't listen when I tell her I'm over Michael and I'm doing fine on my own."

"Your mother means well. She and your father want you to be happy."

"I know. But I am happy. I have my work, which I love. I have friends. I have New York City. I have an active social life."

"Your parents want to see you settled like your sister, with a dependable family man like Andrew."

"Lorrie's happy, and I'm happy for her. Maybe I'll get married someday, but I'm in no hurry." The snap of the fire caught her attention and she looked over. She watched the blaze flicker and sputter as her words tumbled out, as wavering and unsteady as the flames. "I'm not sure I want to get married, but I do want children. I'd have to get married to have them. That's the way I was raised. Why can't Mom accept that I'm capable of finding my own man and living my own life?" She turned back to her grandmother.

"I understand, dear. I want to see you happy, too. And I'd like more great-grandchildren before I go."

Graceann kissed the older woman's cheek again. "I know, but please let me do what I want in my own time and my own way."

"Who is Jake, really?" her grandmother asked.

"I went to school with him. He was a couple of years ahead of me. I—I'm paying him to act the part of my fiancé."

Grandmom raised an eyebrow. "Paying him?"

"It sounds tawdry when you say it like that, but it's strictly a business arrangement."

"I see." She sank into a thoughtful pause. "Does Jake really repair motorcycles?"

Graceann chewed her lip. "I don't know what type work he does."

Grandmom raised both eyebrows this time. "You don't know what he does, yet you trust him enough to bring him into my house, to meet the family?"

"I do trust him." The words slipped out. "He's a decent man."

"And you're in love with him."

Her grandmother's quiet words jolted Graceann. "No, I'm not. I like him, that's all."

"Child." She smiled and patted Graceann's hand. "I've been around a long time. I recognize when two people are in love. Jake loves you, too. I watched you together outside building the snowman, chasing each other. You're in love."

"Don't say that. Please. After the holidays, I'll pay Jake and he'll go back to wherever he lives and I'll never see him again." Sadness tightened the knot in her chest.

"I don't believe that's what you want. You want him to stay."

"I admit I've gotten close to him these last few days, and I might miss him a little, but life goes on and I'll move onto other things and so will he."

The older woman studied her. "Whatever you say, dear. I promise not to breathe a word to your parents, but how will you handle Jake's exit from your life?"

"I'll tell them I broke up with him. That he didn't want to break up but I decided he wasn't the guy I wanted to marry after all. They'll stop feeling sorry for me because of Michael and realize I'm in control of my life. Then Mom will quit trying to marry me off to guys like the dentist who couldn't keep his hands to himself." She shuddered. "Or the guy who called his mother five times during our dinner date. And she'll quit inviting Steven to spend family time with us."

Grandmom laughed. "You don't know your mother. Nothing will deter her in her quest to see both her girls happily married."

Stubbornly, Graceann shook her head. "My plan will work. I know it will. Remember your promise."

"Something tells me things won't work out exactly as you've planned," her grandmother said. "Life has a way of throwing us curves."

CHAPTER ELEVEN

The next morning Graceann sat in the kitchen having a breakfast of English muffin, jam and coffee. All except her mom and Jake were there. Isabella held court from her highchair, getting more cereal on her than in her. Graceann let her gaze linger on her niece and sister. In between sips of coffee, Lorrie wiped the milk off Isabella's face and tried, but failed, to keep her highchair tray clean. Graceann smiled at the homey picture her sister presented.

Footsteps on the back stairs snatched her attention and she focused on the doorway. Jake, dressed in a sweater, jeans, boots, and his leather jacket strode in and deposited his duffel bag on the floor. She and Jake hadn't had a chance to be alone again last night. But her sleeping hours had been filled with erotic dreams of him. She'd woken in a state of frustration, her body tight with need.

Seeing him dressed for the outdoors and carrying his duffel, Graceann's heart sank. He was leaving.

"Where are you going?" she asked him.

"Morning to you, too," he said with a smile. He looked around at the others. "Morning, everyone."

The others mumbled their greetings.

Fluffy, at his food bowl, looked up, then ran at Jake and began barking.

"Fluffy, stop it," her dad said.

With one more bark at Jake, Fluffy trotted back to his food.

"You're leaving?" Lorrie asked with a frown.

Jake met Graceann's gaze. "Work called. I need to go away for a few days. I've ordered a car. I have time to grab a cup of coffee first."

"I'll make one for you," Grandmom said. "It'll be ready in a minute."

He smiled at her. "Thanks." Then he turned to Graceann. "Can we talk? In private?"

Nodding, Graceann rose.

Jake held Graceann's elbow and led her into the entry hall, far enough from the kitchen so no one could hear them.

Once they were alone, she pulled free, and rubbing her arms, faced him. "Why are you leaving now, of all times? I'm paying you to be here for the entire holiday." Her voice came out harsher than she'd intended, but she couldn't let him know she didn't care about the holiday or what she was paying him. She'd grown close to him these last few days and she didn't want him to go.

He smoothed a hand over his hair. "I know. I wouldn't go if it wasn't important. I'll only be away a few days. Something came up." His expression sobered. "I never intended to take your money."

She stepped back. "You didn't?"

"No, but that's not important now."

"I think it is. But we'll discuss it later because the most important thing at the moment is my mom's New Year's Eve party. I need you here for that."

"I'll be back in plenty of time. I promise." He pulled her to him and looked deeply into her eyes. "Money or no money, I never go back on my word. Trust me. Please."

She'd told her grandmother she trusted Jake. Yet, apprehension settled like a ball of ice in her chest. If Jake walked away and never came back, the humiliation would haunt her for years. And her mom would never stop trying to marry her off to some jerk. She stared into his face as he held her gaze.

"All right, but where are you going?" she asked.

"Not far. I'll be in the area. I'm not at liberty to say much now, but I'll tell you all about it as soon as I can."

"You're not into anything illegal, are you?"

He flinched as if hit. "Do you have so little faith in me?"

Knowing she'd hurt him and suddenly realizing it was because of her own fear of being hurt by him, she touched his arm in apology. The leather of his jacket was smoother and softer than it looked. This was no ordinary motorcycle jacket, but something much more expensive. Another mystery. She shoved the realization aside. She needed Jake to return for New Year's Eve.

"I've gotten to know you well," she said quietly. "And I don't believe you'd be into something illegal, but you've got to admit you're awfully mysterious."

"I'm not hiding anything dark. I swear to that. I like to keep things close to my chest. And I'm a tad superstitious. I don't want to jinx something by talking about it."

She studied him. She would take him at his word. What choice did she have? "Better drink that coffee before your ride gets here."

As she followed him back to the kitchen, she told herself everything would be okay. But the apprehension that lay heavy in her chest wouldn't melt.

<><><>

Jake settled into the luxurious back seat of the town car. Nervousness had him feeling like a green kid just out of film school. He hadn't expected his partner to find potential backers so soon. They'd pitched the original story arc, and that's what the backers were interested in. After spending time with Graceann and her family, Jake knew he had to make adjustments to his story. He had ideas percolating in his mind, ideas he believed made the story better. He needed to sell it to his partner along with the backers.

Hard as he tried to focus on the upcoming meeting, his thoughts kept winding back to Graceann. Maybe he should have been upfront with her from the beginning. Yet, he held back. First, she'd offered him money. Now, she thought he might be into something illegal. She still couldn't separate him from the mixed-up kid he'd been. He'd left that kid behind the day he'd hopped on his chopper carrying the money he'd earned from his after-school job, money he'd hidden from his parents, and made his way cross-country.

Each day he spent with Graceann made him more deter-mined to show her the real man behind the laid-back façade. He'd known his share of women who wanted him only because of his connections in the industry, who didn't care to delve too deeply into Jake Falco. He wanted so much more from Graceann.

The picturesque countryside rolled past. It should have soothed, but it didn't. His mind was awhirl, filled with Graceann and the dilemma in which he found himself. He needed to focus. This meeting was too important to blow. Forcing his thoughts back to the meeting, he rehearsed his pitch.

<><><>

She missed him. And she was annoyed. Tomorrow was New Year's Eve, and Jake hadn't returned. As much as Graceann tried to deny it, the minute Jake left three days ago, a void had opened in her heart. He'd begun to mean much more to her than a fiancé-of-convenience.

The thought scared her to death.

Standing at the counter in the butler's pantry, she completed the mindless task of polishing one of Grandmom's silver tea services. They wouldn't be using it at the New Year's Eve party, but her mom had insisted on polishing it so she could display it on one of the two sideboards in the dining room. The housekeeper had polished the smaller silver set before she took off for the holidays, but Graceann's mother had changed her mind and decided she wanted to use the larger one.

The more Graceann thought of Jake and how much she missed him, the harder she rubbed the sugar bowl. If it were a genie's lamp, the genie would have been out by now and she'd have her three wishes. She could use a little magic to bring Jake back soon, before the party, before she went crazy with missing him.

Where was he? He'd called her every day, though they were rushed calls to say hello. She always heard others speaking in the background, but Jake didn't offer where he was. Damn cell phones. Much as she loved them, a person could be calling from anywhere in the world.

Jake had called her every night, too, as she was getting ready for bed. Those calls were longer, with enough sexual innuendos and tension bouncing between them to melt her phone.

Giving the sugar bowl a few last wipes, she set it back on the tray, her thoughts still on Jake. She needed time alone without silver bowls and party-obsessed mothers. And she needed to discuss her fears and her growing feelings for Jake with someone. She couldn't talk to Lorrie without divulging her deception. Kate was still in Philadelphia with her boyfriend's family but promised to be at the party tomorrow. She'd talked with Kate a few times by phone since the holidays began, but there were some things that needed saying in person. Her confusion about Jake was one of those things.

"Graceann, are you finished yet?" Her mother's voice startled her.

"Be right out." Straightening, she mustered her courage to face her mom, or rather Angie Palmer, drill sergeant. Yesterday, a cleaning crew had given the house a good going-over. But her perfectionist mom had enlisted everyone in the family to help with extra cleaning and arranging and rearranging the furniture to accommodate the eighty people expected at the party. The Palmer family's New Year's Eve party had grown through the years from a quiet gathering of friends to a catered, elegant event.

As much as Graceann loved the annual party, the days leading up to it were always fraught with tension as her mom made everyone around her crazy with her insistence on perfection. Even Grandmom had gone into hiding, taking Fluffy with her.

Graceann found her mother bent over the center counter in the kitchen, intently entering notes into her tablet. Her mom kept copious notes on each year's party. "What's up, Mom?"

"The catering people will be here any minute." Her mom didn't look up. "I need help directing them to where I want the tables set up. Your father and Andrew went to the hardware store hours ago to get some tools. I don't know what kind of tools they needed so desperately they had to run out now."

Graceann suppressed a grin. She knew her dad and Andrew had wanted an excuse to escape. She didn't blame them. "Stop worrying, Mom. Your party is a success every year. This year will be the same. Everything will work out. It always does."

The doorbell rang, making both women jump. "That must be the caterers with the tables," her mom said.

"I'll get the door." Graceann hurried out.

She flung open the front door and gasped. Jake stood there, looking a little tired, with a few days' growth of stubble on his face. She'd never seen a more beautiful sight.

"You're back." Her words tumbled out on a shaky breath.

He stepped inside and gathered her to him, holding her tight.

"God, I missed you," he whispered. He buried his face in her hair.

She clung to him, inhaling his pine-laced scent of the outdoors. He'd come back to her.

He kissed her throat and worked his way up to her mouth. "I can't believe how much I missed you," he said against her lips. Then his lips captured hers in a kiss that told her the truth of his words.

She opened to him, giving herself freely. She didn't care who saw them, didn't care that Jake might guess how much he was coming to mean to her. All she cared about was that he was here, now, with her.

"Graceann, is that the tables?" Her mother's voice shattered the moment.

Graceann and Jake pulled apart.

Angie walked into the foyer. "Jake, you're back. Just in time. We need all the help we can get."

A confused expression on his face, Jake looked at Graceann. She laughed. "You'll probably wish you'd stayed away a little longer. We're in full party mode."

He put his arm around her waist. "I couldn't stay away longer. I had to get back to you."

"Tell me when they come with the tables. I'll be in the kitchen." Angie made a quick exit.

Graceann smiled at Jake. "If you value your sanity, do whatever Mom tells you."

"That sounds ominous," he said with a laugh.

"It is. How did your, uh, business meeting go?"

"Good. Probably could have been better. They didn't show their cards so I couldn't get a read on what they're thinking."

"You want to tell me about it?"

"I want to tell you, but I can't yet. Still unsure of things and I don't want to jinx myself. I will tell you soon. I promise. If I don't get backing for my project, there won't be much to tell anyway."

Disappointment worked its way through her. She trusted Jake, but he didn't seem to trust her enough to tell her where he'd been for the last three days. Backing? Project? What kind of business was he in?

The doorbell rang again and she had no more time to dwell on Jake's reason for being away. While the catering crew delivered the tables, Lorrie came downstairs after having put the kids down for their naps. Her dad and Andrew strolled in a little later. They admitted they'd stopped at the local pub while out.

Lorrie sidled up to Andrew and said, "Coward."

The next hours were spent in a flurry of activity. The men put up New Year's party decorations while the women directed the caterers to set up the tables and rearrange the furniture again. As they worked, Graceann's mother floated around like a butterfly on steroids. Finally the tables were placed to her satisfaction and covered with white linen tablecloths. Tomorrow morning the florist would bring the flower arrangements for all the rooms on the first floor.

After dinner and some TV watching the family called it an early night. Jake followed Graceann up the stairs. They hadn't had a chance to talk since he'd gotten back. They stopped at the door to her room, and he took her into his arms and held her close. Feeling secure and peaceful, she rested her head on his chest.

"Your mother is a whirlwind, isn't she?" he said.

"When it comes to her New Year's Eve party, yes."

"Do you think she likes me any better now that Steven is gone?"

"She likes you." She pulled back to look at him. "She recruited you to help out with the party preparations." Graceann chuckled. "She only lets family touch those decorations. Does it matter to you what she thinks?"

He shrugged. "A little. But I understand if she can't accept me. I'm not exactly marriage material."

She placed a finger over his lips. "Don't sell yourself short. You can't fool me. You're a dependable guy."

He blinked and looked at her with hooded eyes. Then his lips tilted in a teasing grin. "I must be a better actor than I thought. See you in the morning."

She nodded, then watched as he walked down the hall with the lithe grace that always caused her heart to thump a little louder.

A half hour later, she'd showered and put on her nightgown. As she brushed out her hair in front of the mirror, she felt restless, needy. Her body thrummed with pent-up energy. She stopped brushing in mid-stroke and stared at her reflection. She knew what she wanted, what she had to do.

CHAPTER TWELVE

*G*raceann knocked on Jake's bedroom door. He opened it and peered out. When he saw her, his face broke into a smile and he opened the door wider, beckoning her in.

"To what do I owe this pleasure?" he asked when she'd slipped inside.

She licked her lips as her hungry gaze scanned him. His hair was pulled back as usual but damp as if he'd just gotten out of the shower and he was clean-shaven. Dressed only in his jeans, his chest bare, his masculine beauty made her breath hitch. His broad chest with taut, sharply defined muscles and a scattering of black hairs tapered to six-pack abs. She followed the line of hair leading past the waistband of his jeans. Her mouth went dry.

Jake closed the door and leaned against it. The glint in his eyes made her take a step back. Maybe she should have thought this whole thing through.

"Graceann, what are you doing here?"

She pulled the sash on her robe tighter, as if she could rein in her desire for him. "I, uh, I couldn't sleep."

"There's a lot of that going around." He moved closer. "Is there something you want?"

"Yes," she managed.

"Is this what you want?" He skimmed his fingers down her throat, along her chest to the hollow between her breasts.

"Yes." The word floated out on a whisper.

Liquid fire raced through her veins when he loosened the sash on her robe and slipped it off her. She stood before him clad only in her short, sheer nightgown and a red thong.

He drew her close. "You're sure?"

"Surer than I've ever been about anything." She reached out a hand to cup the curve of his jaw. "I want you, Jake."

His lips met hers, hard and demanding. This time there was no gentleness, no hesitation. His kiss told her how much he wanted her. She wound her arms around his neck and twined her tongue with his in an erotic dance.

Still kissing her, he slipped her nightgown off her shoulders. She dropped her arms to let the soft silk slide down her body.

He stepped back, his breathing labored. "A thong? I would have expected demure white panties. Damn, you're sexy as hell and full of surprises."

"I've got more surprises in store for you."

"I can't wait." With a husky laugh, he stepped close again. His hands massaged and caressed her breasts as his mouth and tongue continued to assault her senses, driving her deeper and deeper into a pleasure-filled paradise where nothing existed but Jake.

He fisted his hand in her hair and tipped back her head, exposing her throat to his urgent kisses. Nipping and licking, he strung a line of hot kisses down her throat and chest to her breasts. He gently released her and knelt before her to slide her thong down her legs. She stepped out of the tiny piece of silk and kicked it aside. Pulling her closer, he kissed her stomach and dipped his tongue into her navel.

Graceann dug her fingers into Jake's shoulders, not sure her legs could hold her. Desire pulsed through her, making her tremble. She felt no worry, no anxiety, just a deep-seated need for this man. She wanted to melt into him, to become a part of him. Like a rare Christmas rose, Jake had slowly and seductively opened her to her full passion. Her newfound sexual boldness filled her with a mixture of delight and anxiety. She didn't question her feelings, but let them roll through her, blotting out all thought but the sensations his touch aroused.

He stood and took her hand, leading her to the bed. He yanked the comforter aside. With a sigh, she sank onto the firm mattress. The soft cotton sheets cooled her heated flesh.

"Take off your clothes," she whispered.

He quickly shed his clothes until he stood before her, an Adonis come to claim his woman.

"You're beautiful," she breathed, as her gaze drank in his long legs, firm thighs and his erection—hard, thick, magnificent.

He stared down at her with smoldering eyes, tempting and seductive as a moon-kissed night. "I've wanted you for so long."

She held out her arms. "Love me, Jake."

Then he was on the bed beside her, holding her close. Her breasts pressed against his muscled chest. She'd dreamed of him like this, dreamed of feeling his naked skin against hers. She loosened the strip of leather that held back his hair, tossing the leather aside. His hair fell in silky disarray around his face, as she'd imagined. She squirmed at the sudden rush of warmth to her lower abdomen.

He took her lips again in a deep, drugging kiss. She reveled in his possession, in his masculine strength. Pressing her onto her back, he kissed a scorching trail down her body, scraping his teeth against her skin, licking where he'd kissed, his hair a seductive curtain teasing her sensitized flesh. When he kissed her mound, she grabbed handfuls of the sheets, writhing under him.

He didn't linger, but continued his carnal trip, kissing her inner thighs, running his hands down her calves. When he got to her ankles, he raised one of her legs and kissed the arch of her foot. The delicious feelings that stole over her ratcheted up her desire.

Then he worked his way back up her body with maddening slowness, worshiping her with his talented hands and mouth, driving her little-by-little toward the edge.

When he slipped a finger into her wet folds, she arched up, releasing a low growl of pleasure. He slipped in another finger, massaging her nub with his thumb. He kissed her as his fingers thrust in and out.

Her climax built like flaming waves crashing over her in a wild crescendo. She gripped the sheets harder as she came apart.

He gathered her trembling body in his arms and held her close until she stilled. "You okay?"

"Never better," she croaked out.

Laughing softly, he slipped from the bed and walked to his duffel bag on the floor by his closet. Graceann touched her breasts, rolling the puckered nipples between her fingers as her gaze followed him. He was a god, with his long back that tapered to a slim waist and firm buttocks. His thick black hair skimmed his shoulders, swaying enticingly.

He pulled something out of his duffel, then turned around, holding a box of condoms. He walked back, opening it to pull one out, then tossed the box onto the floor.

"You were confident," she teased.

He grinned wickedly. "I may not have been a boy scout, but I believe in being prepared."

He sat on the bed, pulled on protection, then took her into his arms again.

As they faced each other, a surge of heat shot through her. She smoothed a hand over the firm, smooth planes of his chest and slid one of her legs over his. His penis jerked against her thigh. She basked in his masculine scent of spice and soap.

His lips took hers in a fevered kiss. She moaned softly, her body boneless, on fire. She'd waited her whole life for this man, for this sensation of falling into his arms, of giving herself freely —body and soul.

He rolled her over and settled his hard-muscled body between her legs. His features were tight, his eyes dark. His hair swung around his face. "Graceann," he whispered in a voice harsh with need.

Then he thrust inside her, hard and fast, going deep. Gasping, she arched her hips and met his every thrust. She closed her eyes, letting the raw sensations of Jake's body claiming hers override all thought. There was no yesterday, no tomorrow. There was only now.

"Look at me," he growled.

What she saw in his eyes made her shudder with desire and hope. Lust was there, but so were other emotions—hunger, need, vulnerability—emotions that made her heart pump so fast she feared it might shoot out of her chest.

He threw back his head and plunged deeper into her, harder and faster. A raging firestorm built inside her. She wrapped her legs around his hips, wanting to fuse her body with his as the storm possessed her, taking her closer and closer to the precipice.

His skin was damp against hers. Nothing but the sheen of sweat separated them. Fire inflamed her every cell, burning out of control. She was all raw need, wanting only to taste Jake, to consume him. Her climax hit her with explosive force, and she came apart again. She clung to Jake as he drove his hips harder and harder, then shuddered with his own climax.

Spent, they lay entwined in each other's arms. Finally, the coolness of the room made her shiver. They slipped between the sheets and pulled the comforter over them.

He took her into his arms again and kissed her gently on the lips. "That was incredible. You're okay?"

She touched his face. "That was beyond incredible. I want to do it again."

He laughed. "Again? Give me a little time, sweetheart, then I'm all yours."

She snuggled close. "Promise?"

"Promise."

<><><>

Jake stirred, then opened his eyes. The first light of dawn infused the bedroom in pale gray shadows. The memory of his night with Graceann brought him awake. He propped himself on his elbow and watched her as she slept next to him. Her chest rose and fell with her gentle breathing.

Her sable-colored hair spread over the pillow, and her long black lashes feathered her soft cheeks. The faint jasmine and sandalwood scent of her perfume mixed with the primitive scent of their lovemaking and tightened his body with a rush of desire. She looked sweet and innocent. Last night had proved, to his delighted surprise, she was far from innocent. Beneath her classy exterior beat the heart of a tigress, a hot, sexy woman with passion, imagination and a willingness to do whatever he wanted. She was unlike any woman he'd ever known.

He lay back down as guilt sucker-punched him in the gut. He should have told her the truth from the beginning, told her the real reason he'd come back to Spirit Lake. Fool that he was, he'd figured he could walk away from her without a backward glance. Graceann Palmer wasn't a woman a man walked away from with his soul intact. She was a forever kind of woman, but he'd never been a forever kind of man.

Jake rubbed a hand over his face. He was a love 'em and leave 'em type. Although, the past year he'd been so immersed in his writing and his various projects he hadn't time to love or leave any woman. Besides, love had little to do with his previous relationships. Yearning pounded through him, almost a physical ache, a longing to be the kind of man Graceann needed, maybe the kind of man he needed to be.

Guilt rose up again. Once he knew if they had backing for the project, he'd tell Graceann everything. His conscience eased a little. If she knew the truth, would she want him for himself, or for his public persona? She had to want him for who he truly was, without all the trappings. Anxiety settled in his chest again.

Beside him, Graceann slid closer, nestling her body against his. He turned on his side and looked at her. She opened her big green eyes, and he was lost.

"Morning," she whispered.

"Morning, princess." He leaned over her and kissed her softly.

She brushed hair back from his face. "I never knew long hair on a guy could be such a turn-on."

He chuckled and cupped her firm butt, pulling her closer. His burgeoning erection pressed against her soft skin. "Is that the only part of me that turns you on?"

"You have many fine, uh, qualities that turn me on."

"I never knew such a sweet princess could be so wild in bed."

Her sultry grin shot a fresh round of desire through him. "My days of being a sweet princess are over. You've turned me into a bad one." She wound a strand of his hair around her finger. "I like being a bad princess."

"Baby, I'm ready. Have your way with me."

CHAPTER THIRTEEN

That evening Graceann turned slowly in front of the full-length mirror in her room. She'd worn this body-hugging sleeveless black dress with the deep V-shaped neckline many times. It was one of her favorites. But tonight, she looked different. More vibrant, sexier. Her skin seemed to glow. Smiling, she ran a finger over her bottom lip, remembering Jake's mouth on hers, his teeth nipping her there.

They'd been so busy all day with party preparations that she and Jake had only had time to snatch a few minutes together. But while they worked getting the house as perfect as her mother demanded, she was aware of Jake whenever he was near. When they passed each other, they touched. She needed the physical contact or she'd go mad. And from the way he looked at her, he felt the same. For the first time ever, her mother's stress barely registered. Graceann's mind was focused solely on Jake.

With a sigh, she walked over to her dresser and picked up her dangling peridot earrings, a college graduation gift from her parents. They and the matching necklace would complement the green silk shawl Jake had given her.

She'd hooked the earrings through her ears and reached for

the necklace when a soft knock sounded at the door. Anticipating Jake, her pulse jumped. She opened the door to him.

"Wow, you look amazing," she said.

Wearing a charcoal gray suit, striped tie, snowy white shirt, and his black hair slicked back, he could have stepped from the pages of a men's fashion magazine. No one would think Jake unpolished tonight. Not that she cared. She wanted to devour him.

His eyes lit as his gaze made a slow, sexually-charged journey down her body and back to her face. "You look gorgeous...and hot."

"I'll show you hot." She grabbed him by his tie and pulled him into the room, then shoved the door closed and pulled his face down to hers. Gripping his shoulders, she kissed him with all the passion and wildness he'd unleashed in her. With a guttural moan, he cupped her buttocks and pressed her close until she felt his hard erection against her stomach.

Finally, breathing heavily, they pulled apart.

"Damn," he said, his voice shaky. "Let's stay here."

She laughed. "I wish, but we need to show up at the party. I'm almost ready. I have to put on my necklace."

"Let me do it." He followed her to the dresser, then picked up the large pear-shaped peridot stone surrounded by diamonds and strung on a delicate gold chain.

She faced the mirror with Jake behind her, lifted her heavy hair, and bent her head forward. He carefully clasped the pendant around her neck then planted a tender kiss on her nape. She released her hair to swing over her shoulders and down her back.

Their eyes met in the mirror. The desire that sparked from his set her body on fire. She leaned against his broad chest.

He wrapped one arm around her waist and pulled her closer. With his free hand, he touched the pendant, rubbing the stone. "This is pretty, but you deserve emeralds and diamonds."

"Emeralds?"

"To match your eyes." Slowly, deliberately, he dragged his fingers down her chest to the neckline of her dress. He caressed the swell of her breasts, spilling out from her lacy push-up bra. When he slipped a hand inside to massage one breast, her nipples tightened and she groaned softly.

She watched in the mirror as he fondled her. Her lips were parted and her eyes were passion-glazed. She looked like the star of her own sexual fantasy. But this was no fantasy. This was so much better.

"I can't wait to get you out of these clothes and make you mine again," he whispered.

"I can't either," she said in a husky voice.

He pulled away and turned her to face him. "We'd better get down there now because if we stay here one minute longer, we won't show up for the party."

With a smile, Graceann grabbed the green wrap from the bed. Jake slipped it over her shoulders, kissing each shoulder before covering it with the silk.

Holding hands, they left the room and walked down the stairs just as Kate and her boyfriend arrived. Kate's eyes slid from surprise to suspicion as she watched Graceann and Jake descend the stairs.

When they reached the bottom, the women hugged. Graceann turned to Kate's date and smiled. "Happy New Year, Brian."

He gave her a quick hug. "Happy New Year to you, too."

Graceann grabbed Jake's hand and drew him forward. "Jake, you know Kate. This is her friend Brian."

Kate hugged Jake. "Nice to see you again."

"You, too," he said.

As the men shook hands, they seemed to size each other up. Graceann hid her grin. Men were no different from women, checking out the competition. Jake had nothing to worry about. No other man could compare to him.

"Let's get this party started." Kate turned to Brian. "Would you mind getting me a glass of white wine?"

"Sure, sweetheart."

Jake nodded toward Graceann. "Do you want some wine, too?"

"Thank you. White is fine."

"The bar is this way," Jake said to Brian.

As the men headed toward the great room, Kate grabbed Graceann's arm and pulled her into the living room, away from the other arriving guests.

The string quartet Graceann's mother hired began to tune their instruments in a corner of the room.

Kate gave them an annoyed look and motioned to Graceann to follow her into the corner farthest away from the music.

"What?" Graceann asked once they were huddled together.

"Don't play innocent. What is going on between you and The Falcon?"

Graceann brushed hair back from her face, then met her friend's gaze. "It's Jake, and nothing's going on. We're still pretending to be engaged."

Kate put her hand on her hip and shot Graceann a look filled with disbelief. "If that's acting, I'll buy you each a ticket to Hollywood. My God, woman, you're in love with the guy. How the heck did that happen?"

Graceann took a step back. "I'm not in love with him. In lust maybe, but that's all it is."

"Girlfriend, you are in denial. You've fallen in love with The Falcon."

"No, I haven't."

Kate's eyes grew wider. "Oh. My. God. You've slept with him!" She moved closer and looked around. No one else had come into the room. In a conspiratorial whisper, she asked, "What's he like?"

Graceann bristled. "I never kiss and tell."

"Ah-ha! You admit you slept with him."

"I admit nothing."

Kate's expression turned serious and she put a hand on Graceann's arm. "What do you know about him? He looks like the same Falcon to me. You're risking your heart again. What happens when Jake rides out of town?"

"I won't get hurt." The lie stuck in her chest. She'd fallen hard for Jake. When they parted he'd take a huge chunk of her heart with him.

"What kind of work does he do?" Kate asked. "Where does he live?"

"I don't know."

Kate dug her fingers into Graceann's arm, making Graceann wince. "Didn't you learn anything from Michael? I'm sorry I talked you into hiring him to be your fake fiancé. I have a feeling this won't end well. Please be careful."

"I can take care of myself." Despite her words, anxiety took a firm hold in Graceann's heart. Kate had voiced the doubts Graceann had been ignoring.

Her thoughts were interrupted as guests, holding plates of food and goblets of wine, drifted into the room. Jake and Brian came back, each holding two glasses. Jake had a glass of wine for her and a club soda with a twist of lime for himself. When he handed Graceann her drink, his fingers lingered over hers.

"Happy New Year, baby," he said, his voice a low rasp.

<><><>

By ten-thirty the party was in full swing. Jake stood in the great room sipping on his club soda, taking a welcome respite from all the mingling and mixing. Smiling at the carefree picture Graceann and Lorrie presented as they talked and laughed across the room with some of their friends, he inhaled the aroma of pinecones and apple pie that wafted throughout the house. After this holiday, those scents would always bring bittersweet thoughts of love and family, two things that might always be missing from his life. When the stink of gin drifted to him from the bar, his stomach clenched with painful memories of Christmases in the Falco household. He moved to a spot farther away from the bar and drank deeply of his club soda, as if he could wash away the memories that never left him.

He'd made polite conversation with many of the party guests. Some of them had looked at him in puzzlement, as if they might know him. He wondered if they recognized him from the years he'd lived there or if they'd heard of him through his films. He dismissed that last thought. Only the most dedicated film buffs knew his work. He smiled. If things went the way he hoped, that might all be about to change.

Although he was good at mingling, he'd never enjoyed forced gaiety. The New Year's joy here tonight seemed genuine. The holiday parties he'd attended the last few years were glitzy events in over-decorated houses, where most of the guests attended to see and be seen. They were cold affairs lacking the old-fashioned good cheer he'd found with Graceann's family and friends.

His heart seemed to stick in his throat as he watched Graceann laugh at something Lorrie said. Graceann was hot, but more importantly, she possessed a refreshing charm he didn't think existed in many females these days. She looked happy, had looked that way all evening. He liked to think he'd put that smile on her face. Their lovemaking had been special, something he would always treasure.

Happiness. The word came out of nowhere and burst through him like New Year's fireworks. He looked at the others gathered in small groups in the room. People enjoying each other's company. Like the sun breaking through dark clouds, he saw it all clearly now. This was what normal people did. They liked each other, were glad to be together. Accustomed to being around dealmakers and dating women who wanted him for his connections, he'd forgotten how regular people acted. Even Graceann's mother, despite driving everyone crazy with the preparations, only wanted her guests to enjoy themselves.

It had been too long since anything in his life seemed real. He'd gotten so cynical.

Graceann belonged in this world with these decent people who had deep roots. The demands of his work dictated he move around, and he had invested too much sweat equity to stop. A thought edged into his mind, stilling him. Maybe if he had a woman like Graceann waiting for him, he'd have a reason to stay in one place.

"If it isn't Jake Falco." The slurred voice at Jake's elbow jerked him from his melancholy thoughts.

Jake turned his head to meet the cloudy gray eyes of Chad Wentworth, star quarterback when Jake was in school. He'd noticed Chad earlier but had avoided him. Chad and his fellow jocks had done all they could to make life hell for Jake and his friends.

Looking at the overweight, fleshy-faced Wentworth, Jake felt nothing. Before this holiday with Graceann, he might have sneered at Wentworth, or let his anger about his treatment at the guy's hands take hold.

"Wentworth," Jake said. "What are you up to nowadays? Still playing football?"

The guy guzzled some of the beer from the bottle he held, then released a bitter laugh. "Do I look like I play football?" He patted his protruding belly. "I run my dad's hardware store here in town. I haven't seen you since graduation. Where have you been?"

"Los Angeles."

"Doing what?" Wentworth stumbled slightly and Jake reached out to steady him.

Resisting the urge to wrinkle his nose at the overwhelming stench of beer emanating from Wentworth, Jake said, "I'm doing odd jobs out in L.A. Mostly house painting." He fought back the temptation to gloat a little. He hated to lie, but he'd be damned if he'd tell this jerk the truth that Graceann and her family didn't yet know.

"Not made much of yourself, I see," Wentworth said in a smug voice.

Jake shrugged. Let the guy believe what he wanted. Jake owed him nothing.

An overweight, heavily made-up woman, vaguely familiar, walked up to them. She took the beer bottle out of Wentworth's hand and set it on a nearby tray for empty glasses. "You've had enough. We need to leave."

"This here's the little wife," Wentworth said to Jake. "You remember Tiffany, don't you?"

She looked at Jake then, and recognition hit him like a bullet between the eyes. "Tiffany Johnson," he said. She'd been head cheerleader, the sexiest, most popular girl in school, and he'd wanted her. She'd seduced him one memorable night as they sat in her Mustang. Then she'd laughed about it with her friends, mocking Jake. The hurt had stayed with him for years.

"Jake Falco?" She scanned him with brown eyes he used to think beautiful. "You're looking good. Real good."

"Thanks." He signaled the bartender for another club soda. He wished Wentworth and his wife would leave.

The three of them stood in awkward silence for a moment. Then Tiffany took her husband's arm and pulled him away. "Nice seeing you again, Jake." They marched out.

Jake sighed with relief. To think as a kid he'd wasted anger and hurt on those two.

He sensed someone's stare and raised his gaze to find Graceann smiling at him from across the room. With a graceful sway of hips, she headed his way. Her smile and her sweetness knocked down the last bit of wall protecting his heart. Later, he'd figure out how to reconstruct the barrier he'd so painstakingly built since childhood.

Tonight belonged to Graceann.

<><><>

Finally, midnight approached. Graceann stood in the great room with most of the other guests. They'd crowded into the room ready to watch the ball descend on Times Square signaling the New Year.

Holding a flute of champagne, she nervously looked around for Jake. He'd had a phone call twenty minutes ago and disappeared. More mystery from him. The anxiety that had balled in her chest when she'd talked to Kate earlier returned full force as she wondered what secrets he kept.

She looked at the time on the TV screen. Eleven fifty-six. She wanted a New Year's kiss from Jake, but that wouldn't happen if he didn't get back soon. They hadn't much more time together.

This year's Christmas celebrations would be etched on her mind forever because of Jake. He'd made this whole holiday new, fresh, and exciting. She saw everything through his eyes—the special love her family felt for each other, the way they unselfishly cared about each other. She even saw more clearly why her parents wanted her to find a good man, a man to spend her life with. They wanted her to have what they'd found.

She would never have believed Jake could be a family man, but he'd shown her a softer side of him she suspected he kept hidden from most others. They would split up in a few days to go their separate ways. A part of her heart broke at the thought. She wanted to beg him to stay with her. She couldn't. They had a business agreement. That's all it was. The spirit of the holiday had gotten to her. Once she was back in New York, this whole interlude with Jake would be another pleasant memory.

She almost believed it.

She felt someone move to stand behind her. Inhaling Jake's unique scent of soap and spice, she smiled and turned around. Her heart did a little flip.

He'd loosened his tie, taken off his jacket and rolled up his sleeves. Every cell in her body went on alert.

He slipped his arm around her waist and drew her close. "I missed you," he whispered.

She noticed her sister and some of the other guests watching them. Lorrie gave her a knowing smile and held up her champagne flute in salute. Graceann snuggled closer to Jake and returned her sister's smile.

"Everything okay?" Graceann asked.

"Couldn't be better." He gave her a wide grin.

THAT PHONE CALL seemed to have lightened his mood, but hers dropped several notches. He still wasn't sharing anything in his life beyond their fake relationship, reinforcing that after he left, he'd be gone for good.

She glanced away as the crowd around them started chanting. "Ten. Nine. Eight. Seven. Six. Five. Four. Three. Two. One. *Happy New Year!*"

Jake turned her around to face him. He took the champagne flute from her and set it on a nearby table. Then he pulled her into his arms. "Happy New Year, sweetheart."

"Happy New Year, Jake."

He kissed her hard and deep with an urgency that matched her hunger for him and made her forget her fears of a minute ago. Her body stirred in response.

"Hey, you two, break it up." Lorrie's laughing voice came from behind Graceann. "Others want to wish you Happy New Year, too."

A hot flush spread up Graceann's neck and she reluctantly

pulled away from Jake. Then everyone kissed and hugged them, intruding on their little bubble.

<><><>

JAKE DIDN'T THINK the guests would ever leave. He wanted to be alone with Graceann, wanted to hold her, to make love to her. He needed her.

That phone call earlier had brought the news he'd hoped for. Finally, he had something he felt comfortable sharing with her, and he would. He never thought he'd want to share his life with a woman.

Until Graceann.

At three o'clock in the morning, the last of the guests left. Graceann's grandmother had gone to bed hours ago. Graceann's mother began to clear away dirty plates until her husband stopped her. "We're all tired. Let's get to bed. The caterers will be back later today to clean up."

"Yeah, Mom, let it go," Lorrie said.

As the others headed up the stairs, Lorrie looked back at Graceann and Jake standing in the foyer. "You two coming up?"

"In a little while," Graceann said.

When the others disappeared upstairs, Jake gathered Graceann into his arms. "I never thought we'd be alone."

She wound her arms around his neck. "I didn't either. I want you, Jake. Now."

Her words and the softness in her eyes were almost his undoing. He would leave her soon.

He couldn't.

Maybe he didn't have to. That phone call changed everything.

Feeling more hopeful than he had in a long time, he cupped

her face between his hands. "I want to give you a proper New Year's celebration and make slow love to you all night. We'll make our own fireworks."

She stood on tiptoe and kissed him. "That's what I want, too."

CHAPTER FOURTEEN

Graceann took Jake's hand as they ran up the stairs. When he saw the deserted hallway, he breathed a sigh of relief. Outside Graceann's room, he gripped her shoulders and turned her to face him. "I'm coming in."

"I know."

They slipped through her door and Jake closed it with his foot. He backed her up against the wall and braced his hands above her head. She licked her lips and raised her gaze to his. Desire and longing sparked from her eyes. She'd never looked more beautiful and desirable. At that moment he wanted nothing more than to make love to her, to hold her close forever, to cherish her, to protect her.

He slid his hand beneath the silky mass of her hair and cupped the back of her head, then kissed her with a hunger only she could ease. She pressed close and kissed him back with an urgency that filled him with masculine pride and wrapped around his heart. He was so hard he thought his cock would burst through the zipper of his pants. Hell, he'd been hard most of the night with wanting her.

But it was more.

He needed her.

She gasped when he slipped her dress off her shoulders and massaged her breasts through the lace covering them. Still kissing her, he reached behind her to unclasp her bra, freeing her breasts. Her incredible breasts.

Her hands slid up his chest to wind around his neck, and she loosened the cord holding his hair, freeing it to fall around his shoulders. With a sigh, she tunneled her fingers through it.

He left her full, soft lips to rain kisses down the smooth column of her throat. Clutching his shoulders, she threw back her head. That she gave herself so freely to him knocked down more of the barriers around his heart. He wanted to absorb her into his very soul, to love her so completely she'd never want another man.

He bent to suckle one puckered nipple then the other. He caressed her breasts again, pressing them together and flicking his tongue along her deep cleavage.

He picked her up and felt her body tremble as he carried her to the bed, then deposited her onto the white comforter. With her dress bunched around her waist and her perfect breasts bared, she was a fiery temptress who'd captured his heart so completely he knew a life without her would be empty. Only Graceann could make him whole.

She gave him a sultry look from lowered lashes, and like a man possessed, all thoughts fled except his fierce need to have her. He stripped off his clothes, throwing them aside, then joined her on the bed.

He made quick work of her shoes, dress, and thong. When he bent his head to suckle the hard peak of one full, heavy breast, she rubbed herself against him. He kept up his erotic assault, kissing and massaging her sensitive breasts. Intoxicated by her willing body, he felt ready to explode. Through sheer force of will he controlled himself. All he cared about now was her pleasure. Moaning deeply, she fisted her hand in his hair, and he knew she was on the brink. Her trust, her complete surrender to him, filled him with a yearning so strong it frightened him. There was no going back. He'd always belong to her. Crying out his name, she stiffened, then fell apart in shuddering waves.

He held her quivering body until she stilled. "Jake," she said again on a hoarse whisper.

Her mixture of strength and vulnerability bound him to her like ropes of velvet holding him a willing prisoner. He gladly relinquished his body and soul. The softness and trust in her gaze touched his core, healing some of the hurt and pain he'd hidden for so long.

"Graceann." He touched her face in wonder that this slip of a woman could so entrance him and make him want her in a way that was in turn painful and awesome. He'd lived so long afraid to love. Her faith in him was rapidly breaking down the last of the wall he'd erected around his heart.

Succumbing to her spell and his powerful need, he slowly kissed his way down her body, nipping and licking her smooth, hot skin. She arched her hips in frank invitation. When he kissed her trimmed thatch of dark hair, she keened, low and deep.

He slipped his fingers into her wetness. She was so ready for him. He stroked the sensitive nub between her legs and spread her folds. When he dipped his tongue inside her sultry heat she wound her fingers into his hair and opened wider.

He drove his tongue deep, tasting her essence. She whispered his name on a tortured breath. Delighting in taking her higher and higher, he sucked and kissed. His need for her built, his loins tightened, and he drove harder and deeper, tasting her, loving her. Screaming her pleasure, she pulled on his hair as she exploded around him.

Making his way back up her body, he kissed her breasts, her

throat, her sweet, inviting lips. She opened to him, her ravenous tongue dueling with his, her pliant body eager for him. He couldn't wait any longer. He grabbed a condom from the pocket of his pants and pulled it over his cock.

Pressing her into the mattress, he settled himself over her and drove into her. This was where he belonged, with her. He thrust hard and deep. She wrapped her legs around his hips and met his every stroke as he drove his hips against hers, submerged in her heat, his body on fire, every nerve in him aching for her love.

He kissed her feverishly, urgently as he pounded into her. Her fingers dug into his back and she arched her hips to take in more of him. Making guttural sounds, she began to tremble and raked her fingernails into his skin. Her body shook as her orgasm built. She grew still, then shuddered, crying out her pleasure.

Before she had a chance to recover, he rolled over, taking her with him, his cock still sheathed in her softness. Her breathing ragged, her eyes green as rich, dark emeralds, she straddled him.

Her long, thick hair swung around her face and over her breasts. She rode him hard and fast, her face tight with need. He filled his hands with her breasts and arched to meet her. She threw back her head, and with one long, drawn-out shudder, she climaxed again.

Only then did he allow himself the release he so desperately needed. He gripped her waist with his hands and let his orgasm roll over him in wild waves. He bit his lip, suppressing his cry. Finally, he lay still. Graceann collapsed on top of him.

He stroked her sweat-sheened back as she buried her face in his neck. After long minutes, she pulled away to look down at him.

"Wow!"

He laughed and pressed her against him again. Jake felt content, satisfied. He'd come home.

When their breathing returned to normal, Graceann rolled

off him. Facing each other, inches apart, he smoothed hair back from her face and twirled strands of the silky softness between his fingers. "Liked that, did you?"

"The best start ever to a new year," she said with a soft laugh. "Do you think anyone heard us?"

"Probably."

"Oh, God."

He chuckled. "Don't worry. We're supposed to be engaged."

Her features tensed. "Jake, it's almost over."

He placed a finger over her lips. "Don't talk about it. We have today."

Her throat worked as she swallowed. "We have to talk about it. We leave tomorrow. You said you don't want my money. Why did you take the job if you didn't want the money?"

His chest tightened and he twisted onto his back. With effort, he pulled his heart into the locked box where he'd kept it all these years, hiding it away from the foolish thoughts he'd had in the throes of passion. He'd never known real love, wasn't sure what it felt like. He didn't know if he was capable of giving Graceann the kind of love she needed and deserved.

"I used to see you in school," he finally said. "I would look at you, at how sweet, innocent, and kind you were, and I wondered what it would be like to be part of your life. When you asked me to help you with this charade, I took it as my chance to see how the other side lives."

"Oh, Jake." She moved closer, and propping herself on one elbow, stroked a finger down his arm. Every nerve in his body responded. He wanted to claim her again, to never leave her.

"What if I want to keep seeing you?" she asked, a hesitant note in her voice.

He turned to face her. "We've had a great time, Graceann, but reality looks a lot different than these past nine days. You might not want me when you go back to the real world."

"I'll want you, Jake. I'll always want you."

The hurt in her eyes aimed straight for his heart. Oh, hell, he was tired of being noble. Yes, she deserved the best of everything, but he couldn't let her go. Hope rushed through him. Maybe he was selling himself short, and her, too. Things were looking up for him. His career was on an upward spiral. He had a lot to be proud of, a lot to offer her. The tension and fear that were always present began to squeeze out his hope, but he fought it back. For Graceann, he'd let love into his heart.

She drew circles on his chest with her finger. "Where will you go now?"

"Home."

"Where's home?"

"My base is Los Angeles, but I'm seldom there." He grabbed her hand to stop her from drawing the lazy circles. "If you keep doing that, I won't be able to think, let alone talk, and we need to talk."

Her eyes, large and trusting, looked deeply into his. "We do need to talk."

He rubbed his thumb along her cheekbone. "Graceann, this Christmas with your family has been the best I've ever spent," he began. "I'll always be grateful to you for giving me that gift."

"Thank you for saying that." Her eyes glistened. With tears? "Was it hard growing up the way you did, with both parents alcoholics? Did they always drink?"

Startled by her abrupt change of subject, he rolled onto his back again. "My childhood was like scenes from a dark and dreary Swedish film. My dad drank from as long back as I can remember. My mom didn't at first. I have some good memories of her caring for me, watching out for me. I think she began drinking to keep Dad company. I believe she really loved him and she felt if she drank along with him, she'd show her love."

"Codependency. That's sad and kind of sick."

"Yeah, it is. That's what love does to people."

"No, it doesn't, not to most. Is that why you're afraid to love?"

He sucked in an unsteady breath. "I'm not afraid. I'm realistic."

"You've never had a real Christmas?"

"Not since I was very little."

"Jake, I'm so sorry."

He turned and took her into his arms. "I don't want your pity."

"What do you want?"

"You."

They drew out their lovemaking, taking each other tenderly, as if they both knew it might be their last time together. He worshipped her body, imprinting every curve and hollow, every sigh and smile, onto his mind.

Spent, they lay in each other's arms. Finally, Jake took a deep breath and pulled free. He rolled onto his back and stared at the ceiling. The softness of dawn filtered into the room. The dawn of a new day. Of a new year. And new resolutions. "Graceann, you need to know the truth about me. I'm a filmmaker and a screenwriter with a fair amount of success."

When she didn't react, he looked down at her. She was fast asleep. He smiled and gathered her to him. "Happy New Year, love."

He would tell her later, as soon as she woke.

They were awakened by a loud knocking at the bedroom door. Jolted upright, Jake looked at the clock. Nine. His head throbbed. They'd only gotten to sleep a few hours ago.

Next to him, Graceann shot up and gave him a questioning look. Another more insistent knock had her out of bed. She threw on her robe and cautiously opened the door a crack to peer out.

"Mom!"

Shit. Jake pulled the covers up to his chin.

"I know Jake's with you," her mother said. "Your father and I want to see both of you, now, in your father's office."

"What's going on?" Graceann asked.

"Come down please and we'll talk."

Graceann closed the door and faced Jake. "Daddy never calls a meeting in his office unless it's something very serious."

CHAPTER FIFTEEN

ake and Graceann dressed hurriedly. She pulled on yoga pants and a long-sleeved top. Jake slipped on his pants and shirt and hurried off to his room to change. Confused thoughts jumbled through Graceann's head as they met up together in the hallway, Jake now wearing jeans and a sweater, then ran down the stairs to her father's office. Her parents thought she and Jake were engaged, so she doubted they were upset because they'd slept together. It had to be something else, something very bad.

"I hope it's not Grandmom again," Graceann huffed, slightly out of breath.

When they got to the office door, Jake took her hand. "Whatever it is, I'm with you."

Graceann managed a smile. With Jake by her side she could face whatever her parents sent her way.

Feeling much stronger, she held his hand as they walked in, closing the door behind them. Her dad was standing in front of his massive walnut desk, his features tense. Her mother stood by the window, nervously rubbing her hands together.

"What is it, Daddy?" Graceann released Jake's hand and crossed her arms over her midriff to hide her trembling.

Her father ignored her and directed an anger-filled gaze at Jake. "You came into our home, accepted our hospitality, and all along you were using us. How were you going to portray us in the movie? As country bumpkins fooled by the big shot Hollywood producer?"

Jake stepped back as if punched. "It wasn't like that. I can explain."

Frowning, Graceann looked from Jake to her father. "What are you talking about, Daddy?"

Her father leaned against the desk, as if his legs could no longer support him, and grasped the edges with white-knuckled hands. "Max Stewart stopped by last night for a short while on his way to another event."

"Max Stewart?" Graceann said.

"Editor of the *Spirit Lake Times*."

"What does that have to do with us?" she asked.

"Max heard about your engagement. He told me one of his reporters would call me this morning for a comment. They plan to run a story in tomorrow's paper. I assumed they were going to do a fluff piece. I just hung up with the reporter. They're not writing a segment for the society page, but for the front page."

Beside her, she felt Jake stiffen.

"I don't understand," she said.

"What don't you understand?" Her father stepped away from the desk. "You don't understand why we'd be upset that you lied to us about your fiancé?"

Her mother left the window and came to stand next to her husband. "Graceann, how could you keep something like this from us?"

"How did the newspaper editor know about Jake?" Only she, Kate, and Jake knew. And why would the newspaper care that she'd hired a fake fiancé? She was going to be sick. This wasn't going the way she'd planned at all.

"How did the newspaper get hold of the story?" Jake asked.

Her father looked at Jake. "Your producer friends hung around town for a while and they like to talk."

"Producer friends?" Graceann turned to Jake, but he ignored her, his attention on her father.

"What did the reporter say?" Jake asked in a tight voice.

"I think you know," her father answered. "He wanted a comment on how I felt about my daughter marrying Jake Falco, Hollywood screenwriter, producer, and actor who was in town scouting locations for his latest film, a scathing depiction of Spirit Lake and its citizens."

"It's not what it seems," Jake said.

Lightheaded and nauseous, Graceann grabbed Jake's arm, forcing him to meet her gaze. "What's he talking about?" Her voice came out thin and shaking.

"I planned to tell you, Graceann," he said. "They had no right to leak that. We haven't signed the contract yet. What they said about the movie is bogus. Yes, I'm here to scout locations but the movie won't show Spirit Lake in a bad light. Not anymore. You've got to believe me."

"Believe you? You're a screenwriter, a producer? An actor, for God's sake. You're making a movie here? And you never bothered to tell me?" Anger slammed into her and she fought a new wave of nausea.

"You didn't know about this?" her father asked.

Graceann pulled air through her lungs and shifted her attention to her parents. "No, Daddy, I didn't."

"You thought your fiancé repaired motorcycles?" her mom asked in an incredulous voice.

Guilt mixed with Graceann's anger. "I knew he didn't fix motorcycles. I wasn't sure what he did."

"You don't know what type work your fiancé does?" her mom echoed.

Her dad rubbed a hand over his forehead and sat on the edge of the desk, his face pale. "One of you explain what the hell is going on."

"We need to tell them everything." Jake reached out to grab one of Graceann's hands.

She jerked away. "Don't touch me." The shock that flashed across his face cut into her heart. She'd hurt him, but he'd lied to her, or rather he'd kept the truth about himself from her. She'd lied to her family.

Karma was a bitch.

She twisted her ring, her faux engagement ring, around her finger, and focused on the opposite wall. Isabella's framed drawings in clashing crayon colors were hung there. The wildly mixed colors in the drawings matched her thoughts—mixed-up, chaotic, confused. She turned her gaze to her parents' bewildered ones. "Jake's not my fiancé. I—I hired him to play the part."

Her mother gasped and put her hand to her mouth. Her father sat straighter, his body rigid. If looks could wound, she'd be maimed now, along with Jake.

"Why. Would. You. Do. That?" her father said between gritted teeth.

Soft footsteps sounded outside, then a light knock on the door. Before anyone could respond, Grandmom came into the room and stopped, her gaze shifting among the others.

"Something wrong? I heard raised voices," Grandmom said.

"Jake is not Graceann's fiancé," her mother said. "She lied to us. And that's not the only lie."

Head shaking, Grandmom turned to Graceann. "I told you, child, that you needed to tell your parents the truth."

"You knew, Mom, and you didn't say anything?" Graceann's father's voice rose several octaves as he faced his mother.

"Settle down, Mark, and let the girl talk." Her grandmother

sank into a leather chair next to the desk and looked expectantly at Graceann.

Her parents turned anxious looks Graceann's way, too. "What possessed you to hire a fiancé?" her father asked.

Graceann continued to twist the ring around her finger. It dug into her flesh but she didn't care. She welcomed the pain. Physical pain was preferable to this gut-wrenching audience with her parents. "I thought if I had a fiancé, Mom would quit trying to fix me up with some guy."

Her mom bristled. "You're blaming me?"

"No, Mom, no. Of course not." God, she was handling this badly. She felt like a six-year-old getting a scolding. But she wasn't a child. She was a grown woman and she'd take responsibility for her actions. Beside her, Jake stood unmoving, only his ragged breathing a testimony to his raw emotions.

"I only want you to meet a nice man and settle down," her mother said.

"I know, but I can find my own guys." Graceann was surprised at the calmness in her voice. "Besides I don't want to get married, at least not for a while. I only want you to let me live my life and not try to arrange it for me."

"We're not trying to arrange your life," her dad said. "This is the craziest thing you've ever done. How long were you planning to keep up this false engagement?"

"After the holidays, I planned to tell you Jake and I broke up, that I didn't love him and it was my decision. I figured if you thought I was finally over Michael and in control of my life, you'd let me live it my own way."

"Graceann, how could you fool us like this?" Tears shone in her mother's eyes, twisting the knife of guilt deeper into Graceann.

"I'm sorry. I didn't mean to hurt you."

"But you *have* hurt us and disappointed us." Her father turned his angry gaze to Jake. "Did you think you'd get more fodder for your movie by living with us, observing us, mocking us?"

"My movie had nothing to do with my going along with Graceann's, uh—charade," Jake said in a harsh voice. "I knew Graceann from school. I wanted to help her."

Notching her chin up, Graceann looked at Jake. "Were you making fun of us all? What role would I play in your little movie?"

Hurt flashed across his features. But he wasn't the man she'd thought he was. It had happened to her again. Kate was right. She'd learned nothing from the debacle with Michael.

"We've gotten close these last few days," Jake said, his voice low. "Have I acted in any way like I'm making fun of you, or using you?"

"No, but you're an actor."

He stepped closer. She dropped her hands to her sides, but didn't move away.

"I never acted with you, Graceann. Not once. When I wrote the script, a lot of my bitterness toward this town and its treatment of me and my family came out. I hadn't intended that to happen, but it did. My original pitch was that the movie would be *Footloose* meets *Shaun of the Dead*. That's no longer the case. The revised version will show Spirit Lake as a decent place with good people."

"I have a hard time believing that," Graceann said.

"I don't know what to believe," her mother said.

Her father cleared his throat. The others looked at him. "Let me get this straight. You hired this man you barely know to come into our house?"

Graceann blinked back tears. "I did know Jake, sort of."

Her father waved a hand in dismissal at Jake. "I think you'd better leave, young man."

"I'll leave, sir." Jake nodded to her grandmother. "I'm sorry, Mrs. Palmer." He switched his gaze to her parents. "Mr. and Mrs.

Palmer, I meant no ill-will toward any of you. You treated me like a member of the family and I'll always be grateful." Without looking at Graceann, he strode out of the room.

"I can't fathom you had the audacity to bring a stranger into our home, Graceann," her father said. "I never knew you to be the reckless type."

Grandmom stood. "I think we all need to take a little time to breathe."

"I'm going to talk to Jake." Graceann slipped out of the room. The beginnings of a throbbing headache pounded her, but she needed answers—now.

She found him in his room packing. "Jake," she said from the doorway.

He turned to her with stormy blue eyes. "Come to make sure I'm not stealing the silver?"

She walked closer. "You wouldn't do that."

"Tell that to your parents. I saw the looks they gave me. The fine, upstanding people of Spirit Lake used to look at my family that way. That judgment of me based on my parents is why I couldn't wait to put this town behind me."

"You told me you held no hard feelings about this town. You lied. You do want revenge. You wrote a movie that will give you that."

He threw the shirt he held onto the bed and met her eyes. "I thought I learned a long time ago not to waste my energy on revenge. Apparently I was wrong. When I wrote the original script, my pent-up anger and bitterness came out, and it did show this town in a bad way. Now that I've gotten to know you and your family, I recognize the goodness of the people here, their kindness."

"Spare me."

His features tightened. "Think what you will. I'm revising the script. It's now *Twilight* meets *Shaun of the Dead,* a zombie teen love story." He smoothed a hand over his hair. "When I pitched it the other day to my partner and the backers, I was afraid they'd reject the new story arc. That phone call last night was my partner telling me we had the backing. This is the break we've been waiting for."

When she remained silent, he went back to tossing clothes into his duffel.

She fought tears. She was happy for his success, but he'd not been honest with her. He hadn't trusted her. How could she have been so wrong about him? "Why didn't you tell me what you do? A screenwriter and producer? That's something to be proud of. You know how I feel about men who lie, about men who have hidden lives."

He didn't look at her, but continued packing. "I didn't lie to you. I just didn't tell you everything."

"Omitting is lying."

He turned then and walked slowly toward her. When he reached her, he cupped her shoulders, his gaze intense. She knew she should step back from him, but she didn't want to. She wanted this whole nightmare to go away.

"If you knew the truth, would it have made a difference?" he asked. "Would you have treated me differently?"

"Yes. No. I don't know what you mean."

Disappointment washed over his features and he released her. "I guess you don't."

She scrubbed a hand over her face. "Why did you agree to my fake fiancé scheme?"

He leaned against the dresser with his arms folded across his chest. His relaxed stance belied the tension evident in every taut line of his body. "I was going to tell you the truth, even brag a little, that first day in the diner, but then you offered me money, and I figured you thought I was a loser, like most everyone else in this town."

"I never thought of you as a loser."

"Didn't you? You had a schoolgirl vision of me, maybe even a crush. I'm not that pseudo bad-boy. I never was. I didn't do half the things I was accused of." His gaze held hers. "Admit you liked the excitement of being with The Falcon."

Truth be told, at first she had pegged him as someone who'd never pulled up from his poor beginnings. And yes, she'd always found his bad-boy persona exciting.

Her legs felt wobbly and she sat on the edge of the bed. "The newspaper reporter said you're an actor, too. When we made love, was that acting? Did you mean all those things you said, all you did?"

His features softened and he came to sit beside her. Touching her chin with his fingers, he waited until she looked at him. "I meant every word, every kiss. Making love to you was the most real thing I've ever done."

She pulled free of his scorching touch. Her instincts told her Jake Falco was a decent and caring person, that she'd gotten to know the real man. But she wasn't a good judge of men. "You haven't answered my question. Why did you agree to go along with my plan, especially if you didn't need the money?"

He drew a deep breath and glanced away. "I used to see your family around town. I thought you couldn't be real, that families weren't kind and considerate toward each other. I wanted to prove to myself deep down that you were no different from my family. But I've learned your family is real and loving and good. Even now, with your parents angry at you, it's obvious they love you very much."

When he turned back to her, she read unhappiness in his eyes, but something else, something that made her pulse jump.

"And I wanted to know the woman you've become," he said. "No matter what's happened, how much of a mess we've made of things, I'll never regret getting to know you, Graceann."

Before she knew what was happening, he brushed his lips over hers, sweetly and gently, then pulled away. "I'll always treasure the time we spent together, making love with you, laughing with you."

She pressed a hand to her unsettled stomach. "You could have gotten to know me and my family and still told me the truth about what you do."

"Yeah, I could have. But I can be stubborn. I wanted you to accept me, the real me, Jake Falco, the guy I am, the guy I've always been, someone from a small town who's worked hard and paid his dues. I wanted you to want me, not some hot-shot Hollywood type. And maybe I wanted to see how a normal family spends Christmas."

"How did you end up in Hollywood?" she asked.

He shrugged. "I took all the money I'd saved from my after-school job, jumped on that old, restored motorcycle and started driving west. I slept in shelters in the cities and outdoors in the rural areas. Got to L.A., found a hovel of an apartment, did whatever work came my way—painting houses, waiting tables. And I wrote every spare minute. Through my restaurant job, I made good contacts in the industry and got a few acting gigs in low-budget indies. A producer I met liked one of my screenplays and bought it. And that's my story."

"You make it sound so easy."

His lips tilted in a wry smile. "It took me eight years to become an overnight success, but I was lucky."

"And talented."

"That, too, I guess." He rose from the bed and finished filling his duffel, then zipped it closed with a finality that stung her heart. He was leaving and she'd never see him again. He hadn't trusted her. He'd withheld the truth. He had a hidden life, like Michael. She couldn't accept that.

Fluffy ran into the room and began barking at Jake. With a wry smile, he said, "I won't miss that dog."

"Fluffy, get out of here," she said. To her surprise, the dog obeyed and trotted out of the room. She wanted to ask Jake if he'd miss her, but she couldn't.

"I called a car," he said. "It should be here any minute."

She stood, rubbing her arms. "Where will you go?"

"To my condo in Bremer first, then Los Angeles. I have reservations on a flight out tomorrow morning."

"You have a condo in the next town?" A new rush of anger hit her. "Another *secret*."

"I bought it a month ago so I'd have a place to stay while shooting the movie." He picked up his duffel and garment bag, then dropped them on the floor.

He was by her side in an instant. Pulling her against him, he kissed her hard, almost brutally. She stiffened, resisting him, then melted and returned his kiss. His lips softened and he moaned low in his throat. She opened to him, wanting to recapture the oneness they'd had when they'd made love.

He ended the kiss and held her at arm's length, his breathing ragged. "Come with me."

"To California?"

He nodded. "Let's see where this thing between us is going. I can afford to take care of you."

Every nerve in her body screamed for her to go with him, but pride had her backing away. Hands clenched at her sides, she all but hissed. "*See* where 'this thing between us is going'? You can *afford* me? I have a life here and I can take care of myself. I've been doing it for a while now."

"Graceann—"

She looked him right in the eye. Enough was enough. "It's best you leave."

<><><>

Graceann lay face down on her bed. She'd cried until she had no more tears left. She'd hurt her family with her lies, maybe even

142

hurt Jake. He'd hurt her. He hadn't trusted her enough to tell her the truth. Now he was gone.

Deep in her heart she believed he couldn't have been acting when they made love. She'd seen the passion and tenderness in his eyes, felt it in his kisses and his touch. Their lovemaking had been magical. He'd wanted her to want the real him. He had to care for her, at least a little. But he had a funny way of showing it, with his talk about "this thing between us." For her it was a lot more than a "thing."

Jake was no better than Michael, hiding the truth. No, Jake wasn't anything like Michael. Michael had never been tender. His passion had been polished, that of a man more interested in impressing a woman than in making her feel loved. He was the one who'd been playing a part throughout their affair, not Jake. And when she'd confronted Michael with the truth, he'd shown no remorse, and couldn't figure out why she wouldn't want to be with him, why she didn't care about his money and influence. Jake was no Michael.

Rolling over, she stared at the ceiling. This whole ordeal had taught her a hard lesson. The adage, "Honesty is the best policy," sprang to mind.

Brushing hair away from her face, she sat up. Her cell phone lay on the nightstand. She grabbed it and clicked on her photos, wanting to see Jake's face. Slowly, fighting tears, she scanned through the pictures she'd taken during the holiday. There they were—she and Jake and Isabella standing proudly by the snowman. She and Jake in front of the Christmas tree in the foyer, in the kitchen preparing Christmas dinner, with Kate and Brian at the party. In each picture Jake was smiling. He looked happy. That wasn't acting, she was sure of it. She believed he had loved being with her and her family, that they had helped him see the people and the town in a new, better light.

Setting down the phone, she stood and smoothed her palms

down the sides of her pants. She had to get on with her life, but first she had to face her family.

The others were in the great room. When Graceann entered, all conversation stopped. They turned and stared at her. She met her sister's gaze. Lorrie blinked and averted her eyes.

"I'll make you something to eat," her mom said, rising from the sofa.

"Sit, Mom. I have something I need to say to all of you." Graceann clasped her hands in front of her, willing calmness into her voice. "I realize now it was foolish and hurtful of me to deceive you. I was thinking only of myself and not what it would do to you."

"Let's put the whole thing behind us," her father said.

Graceann shook her head. "No. I have to say this. I know you love me and I love you. Seeing you this Christmas through Jake's eyes made me realize how very lucky I am to have you." She met her mother's gaze. "Mom, I know you only want what's best for me. And I adore you for it. But I'm able to take care of myself. Please let me live my life on my own terms. Have faith that you raised me right and I know what I'm doing."

Her mother swiped at tears. "I know, dear. It's not always easy to let go, but I'm trying."

"I didn't realize what Mom's matchmaking was doing to you." Lorrie shot a wry smile at her mother. "Sorry, Mom, but you did push some real jerks at Graceann."

Her words provoked soft laughter from the others.

"Are we okay now?" Graceann asked. "I'll live my life my way?"

"We trust you'll do what's right," her dad said. "But don't expect us to stop worrying about you."

Graceann smiled. "I know. And that's okay." She drew a steadying breath. "I have one more thing I need to say."

The others sat quietly, waiting.

"I Googled Jake. He really is an up and comer in Hollywood.

He produces and writes indie movies, little-known but well-reviewed. I guess that's why we hadn't heard of him. I may need to go to California. Jake and I have to settle things between us."

"Is that wise? To go after him?" her mother asked. "You should make him chase you."

"This isn't a game, Mom. Not anymore. I'm taking the initiative from now on."

"That's my granddaughter," Grandmom said.

"And my little sister," Lorrie said. "I always knew you were feisty."

Graceann laughed as relief flooded her. Her family understood. They'd support her in whatever she decided.

The doorbell rang, the sound puncturing the quiet and making Graceann jump.

"I'll get it," her dad said.

He hurried out to the entry hall, the rubber soles of his sneakers slapping against the marble floor. The door opened, then her father's voice rang out.

"What are you doing back here?"

CHAPTER SIXTEEN

*H*er heart thudding, Graceann hurried out to the entry hall.

Jake stood on the front step. The stubborn set of his jaw shouted his determination as he faced her father. "Please let me in. I have to see Graceann."

"I don't know if she wants to see you," her father said in a raspy voice.

Graceann understood what her father was doing...he was trying to protect her until she was ready to face Jake. "It's okay, Daddy. I'll talk to him."

Like a balloon pricked with a needle, the fight seemed to leave Jake and he visibly relaxed.

"You're sure?" her father asked.

She nodded.

"Use my office." He turned away without another word, leaving her alone with Jake.

Graceann motioned for Jake to come in. He slipped through the door and shut it behind him. "What are you doing here?" she asked.

"I have to talk to you." He stepped closer. "To explain."

She clenched her hands at her sides, fighting the urge to reach out and touch his stubbled face, to skim her fingers over his full lips. But she wouldn't make this easy for him.

"Please, Graceann, I really need to talk to you."

She turned and strode to the office, not looking to see if he followed, but she heard his soft footsteps close behind. When they got into the other room, she closed the door and went to stand in front of her father's desk. She folded her arms across her chest, as protection from her chaotic emotions.

Jake stood by the door, as if wary of coming too close to her.

"Why did you come back?" she asked.

"I got to my condo and I knew I couldn't walk away from you, not until I had your forgiveness, and maybe a lot more. I threw my bags in my condo, and the driver brought me back here."

He massaged his temple. "Hell, Graceann, I never meant any of this to happen. Please forgive me. I should have told you from the beginning. I was wrong. I should never have agreed to this fiancé charade. Because of me you were humiliated in front of your family."

She gave him a slight smile. "I humiliated myself."

He walked to one of the windows and opened the blinds to stare out, his back to her. Her hungry gaze devoured him. She'd hear him out before she decided if she could forgive him.

Finally, he turned to face her again. "I bungled things badly earlier when I asked you to come to California with me. I was being selfish, wanting to spend more time with you, but not considering you have a life and a career here. I didn't tell you the truth about me, yet I expected you to drop everything and come with me across the country. Some arrogance, huh?"

"Yeah, you were being a little selfish." Her soft voice tempered her words.

His lips tilted in a slight smile. "That's me. Selfish and stubborn. It's not the first time I've done something stupid, and it won't be the last."

She leaned against the edge of the desk. "Is that why you came back—to apologize?"

"That and more. At first, I didn't think the truth about me and what I do would matter. I was playing a role for you and your family." He held her gaze. "My role became real as I found myself falling in love with you. Once I realized how I felt about you, I told myself I wasn't capable of loving anyone and that you deserved better than what I could give you."

Love? Had she heard right?

"I was in denial about my feelings, and I hurt you," he continued, interrupting her thoughts. "The truth hit me on the drive to Bremer. I was more scared of losing you than I was of loving you."

She lowered her gaze as joy wound through her. They still had issues to resolve, but... She picked up a paperweight she'd given her father for Christmas one year. Graceann smiled. She'd been eight and had saved her allowance to buy him something special. A bright yellow flower was trapped inside the thick glass. The petals were opened, as if the bloom was grasping at freedom. Like the flower, Graceann had been trapped by her need to please her parents, her fear of expressing her feelings to them. Unlike the blossom, she was free now. Jake, despite his secrets, had helped free her.

Setting down the paperweight, she met his gaze.

He gave her a tender smile. Her heart stumbled when he smiled like that.

"Will you forgive me, Graceann? Will you give us a chance?"

"I'm trying to understand, Jake. You said you wanted me to care for the real you, and not some hot-shot Hollywood type. I get that now, although I still feel betrayed that you didn't trust me with the truth."

When he started to walk toward her, she held up a hand. "I

have more I need to say. I believe you about the movie—that you won't show Spirit Lake in a bad way."

His features softened. "Thanks for that at least."

Drawing a deep breath, she continued. "You were right about me, partially right. I did misjudge you when I asked you to be my pretend fiancé. I assumed you were down on your luck. And truthfully, I was excited at the thought of getting close to The Falcon, the mystery guy of Spirit Lake High. But then I got to know you and everything changed."

"How?" His intense gaze pinned her.

She straightened and clasped her hands in front of her. "I liked what I saw. It didn't matter what type work you did. I realized you're a loving, good-hearted guy."

He gave her a self-deprecating smile. "Are you sure you're talking about me?"

She laughed. "Yes, I'm talking about you, Jake Falco. I Googled you, you know."

"Find anything interesting?"

She exhaled slowly, feeling her tense muscles begin to relax. "I learned you're an up-and-coming indie film producer and screenwriter."

"Who no one's heard of."

"Not yet. I think all that's about to change. There's a lot of buzz about your new zombie film."

"From your lips to God's ears." He moved closer until inches separated them, then he took one of her hands in his. "You haven't said if you'll forgive me."

She wanted to forgive him. She hadn't been honest with her family and they'd forgiven her. She couldn't do less. Her breathing shallow, she nodded. "I do forgive you. We have issues of trust, both of us, but we can work through it."

He squeezed her hand. "I can't let you go, Graceann. I tried to be the hero who would set you free so you could find love with someone worthy of you. I'm no hero. I want you for myself. No matter that you deserve someone better than me, I can't imagine a life without you in it. I'll do my best to make you happy."

"Make me happy?" Anticipation made her heart beat a quick tempo.

"I'm not saying this right. My feelings for you scare the crap out of me. I've never been in love before."

"Maybe you should just say you love me. Is that so hard?"

"I thought I said that."

"You didn't, not in so many words."

Cupping her face between his hands, he said, "I love you, Graceann Palmer. I think I've loved you since that first day in the diner, maybe even before that, but I didn't have the courage to admit it until now."

She smiled. "I love you, too, Jake Falco."

"I know."

With a short laugh, she stepped back and wound her arms around his waist. "Arrogant, as always, I see."

"Not really. I was petrified you wouldn't forgive me and would send me packing." He skimmed a finger over her lips. "I heard you tell Steven I'm twice the man he is. And I knew you wouldn't have given yourself so freely to me if you didn't love me. That's who you are. And that's one of the many things I love about you."

He kissed her softly, as if wanting to savor her. When the kiss ended, he gave her a long, searching look from eyes that sparkled with love. "I never believed in love before you, never thought I was capable of it. You opened my eyes and my heart. I love you more than I thought it was possible to love anyone. Marry me, Graceann. Start a life and a family with me. All those things I told myself I didn't want, but deep down I craved. I want them all now, with you, only you." His voice softened to a husky whisper. "Please say yes."

They still had issues. She barely knew him, yet her heart leapt for joy at his words. She wanted him, needed him, in her life.

"Yes, I'll marry you."

"You will?"

The sound of her laughter floated through the room as joy filled her heart. "I just said I would."

He gathered her to him and crushed her lips against his in a kiss that poured out his love and branded her as his. She clung to him, eager and hungry for the man she would love forever.

When the kiss ended, she pulled away, her breathing ragged, and stroked his face. "Santa brought me the best gift ever. My very own groom for Christmas."

EPILOGUE

Two years later

Snuggling closer to her husband, Graceann took Jake's hand in hers as they rode in the back of the limo. The darkening city of Los Angeles, decked out for Christmas, blurred past, casting a colorful collage of white, green, and red lights on the tinted windows. Graceann sighed and squeezed Jake's hand.

"Happy?" he asked, smiling down at her.

"Delirious." She returned his smile.

He patted her seven-months pregnant belly. "How's little Jake doing?"

"I think he's calmer than I am about attending his first Hollywood premiere."

"You'll do fine. The paparazzi love you. The camera loves you. I love you." He brushed a whisper soft kiss on her lips. "You weren't nervous last week at the worldwide premiere in Spirit Lake."

"That was more of a hometown event, no red carpet, and there were only a few photographers. And you and your movie were a big hit. I don't believe the town's ever had that kind of excitement." Jake had rented out the largest movie theater in town and invited the townspeople. True to his word, Jake's romantic comedy zombie movie, *Night of the Loving Dead*, showed Spirit Lake and its people in a good light.

"Maybe we'll have the world premiere of my next movie there again."

She shot him a wry smile. "And maybe I won't be big as a house. My first Hollywood premiere and I'm huge." She smoothed a hand over the skirt of her red silk gown.

Jake leaned closer and trailed fingers along her cleavage, exposed by the low-cut neckline. "You get more beautiful every day. Pregnancy agrees with you."

Married one year ago on the afternoon of Christmas Eve in the church at Spirit Lake, Jake never failed to excite her. Even now, pregnant and riding in the back of a limo, she wanted him.

"You look amazing in that dress," he said. "But I can't wait to get you out of it."

"You look amazing in that tux, and I can't wait to get you out of it."

He laughed and tucked her arm through his. "I hope there are many more children in our future. And many more movie premieres." A note of nervousness had crept into his voice.

"There will be, for both. I want lots of children with you. And you'll make more hit movies. You're a talented writer and a savvy producer."

He lifted her hand and kissed it. "You'd compliment me no matter what because you love me."

"I love you so much my heart is ready to burst. But I wasn't merely giving you a compliment. The movie really is great. You're already getting glowing reviews, and not just from your adoring wife."

Blinking back tears of happiness, she looked at her left hand resting on her belly. The emerald stone in her engagement ring twinkled in the soft overhead lighting. She turned her hand, letting the light catch the facets of the large gem. Jake had had a jeweler friend make the emerald and diamond ring, an exact copy of the faux engagement ring she'd made. The jeweler was so impressed with her design, he'd hired her as a designer for his shop on Rodeo Drive. Thanks to Jake's contacts in the movie industry, she had a thriving jewelry business of her own. The female lead in Jake's movie wore jewelry designed by Graceann.

With a contented sigh, Graceann turned her attention back to the cityscape unfolding before her. Her family rode in the limo behind them. Christmas Eve was in a few days. Kate and Zach were flying in tomorrow to spend the holidays with them. Graceann hoped her two best friends could be civil to each other on the long flight. She loved them dearly but whenever they were in the same room, sparks flew.

She and Jake would celebrate their wedding anniversary and the holidays with her family and her two friends. The house they'd bought in the Hollywood Hills was big enough to accommodate everyone. Graceann's studio was in a small cottage on the sprawling grounds.

Grandmom had left Fluffy home with a friend, thinking it best to protect the little dog from Jake's cats, Sasha and Tasha. The cats were bigger than the dog and wouldn't take kindly to sharing space with him.

Graceann's whole family, including her mother, loved Jake. She glanced at her handsome husband, so striking in his tuxedo. No one loved Jake more than she did.

In the past year they'd given each other the life Graceann had always envisioned and the family life Jake had never dared to dream he could have.

The limo pulled up to the theater. A crowd waited behind the velvet ropes. When the driver opened the car door for them, flashbulbs went off. Jake got out first, then reached for Graceann's hand to help her out. She slipped her arm through his as they walked along the red carpet, smiling for the fans lined up to watch.

As they passed a group of teenage girls, one said, "He's so dreamy."

"He's hot," said another.

Jake leaned down and kissed Graceann lightly on the lips. "And he's so in love with his wife. I love you, my Christmas bride."

"And I love you, my Christmas groom."

THE END

WEDDED ON A DARE

By

CARA MARSI

When a struggling actress takes a role as the glamorous temporary wife of a wealthy playboy, she finds love doesn't always come on cue.

Struggling actress Kate Carluccio showed up for her wedding but her groom bowed out without warning. He absconded not only with her heart, but also her parents' life savings. Her confidence shaken, Kate's determined to find a way to restore her parents' money. Then she's offered the role of a lifetime: step out of her colorful high-top sneakers and into the glammed-up role of socialite wife to a shallow, annoying playboy. If only Kate wasn't also secretly attracted to him, the one-and-a-half million dollars he offers with his proposal of a marriage-of-convenience might be easier to accept.

Breathtakingly handsome, super rich, and sophisticated with a bad boy vibe, Zach Lyon is a tabloid favorite. He may be a vice-president at his father's company, but up until now he's just played a supporting role. But when he discovers two executives are conspiring to force his dad out and take over the company, Zach decides it's time to step into the spotlight. What better way than to take a glamorous new wife to Las Vegas to spend the Christmas holiday at the home of one of the conspiring executives?

As the curtain rises on the eclectic house party, Kate and Zach play their roles against the backdrop of schemers and snobs, while hiding deep secrets of their own. Can Kate pretend to love Zach without revealing the true depth of her attraction? Can Zach prove to his father he has the stability to go from understudy to leading man? They may have wedded on a dare, but with the stage set for romance, their marriage-of-convenience might just turn into a marriage-to-last-a-lifetime.

CHAPTER ONE

"*Y*ou're crazy if you think I'll marry you." Kate Carluccio slammed her glass of iced tea on the table and jumped up, almost knocking over her chair. Liquid splashed on her hand, its coldness welcome in the December heat of the Hollywood Hills.

"Why won't you marry me?" Zach Lyon, arrogant, wealthy playboy, pushed up from his chair and faced her, confusion in his grass-green eyes.

Uncomfortable under his steady scrutiny, Kate fidgeted from one foot to the other. "I'm sure you're not used to a woman turning you down, but I don't like you."

"You've made your dislike crystal clear over the years."

"The feeling is mutual. I doubt our marrying will make you like me any better either."

"I wouldn't say that."

Kate gripped the back of her chair and took measured breaths, fighting for composure after the shock of his proposal. Afternoon sunlight caressed her face and filtered onto the lattice-covered patio of Graceann and Jake Falco's house. The brightness gilded the white wrought iron furniture with a golden patina and made the drink in Kate's cut-glass tumbler sparkle. Multi-colored Christmas lights strung around the sliding doors leading into the house gave the area a festive flair. The twinkling lights and late-day sunshine reflected her best friend's life now, joyful and glittering. Kate wanted the love and happiness Graceann had found, but she wouldn't have it with Zach.

"I know plenty of married people who don't like each other." Zach moved closer until they were a whisper apart. "Afraid you'll fall in love with me?"

"As if." His seductive scent of citrus and male made her traitorous body sway toward him. She clutched the chair tighter.

Kate had disliked Zach from the first day she met him, when her childhood friend, Graceann Palmer Falco, moved from their small town in the Pocono Mountains to Manhattan. Zach, Graceann's new Manhattan neighbor, became her good friend.

With Graceann married to the love of her life, Jake Falco—actor, screenwriter, director, producer—Zach and Kate, frequent visitors to the Falco's sprawling house in the Hollywood Hills, were forced together.

"I dare you to marry me." Zach's voice and eyes held a challenge.

Kate put a hand on her hip. "You're a jerk, Lyon." Growing up with two older brothers, Kate had never met a dare she didn't like. Until now.

Zach's features softened, giving him a vulnerability she found appealing, too appealing. "I don't like begging a woman, Carluccio. I'm out of options. My terms are generous. We can help each other. Hear me out."

Shaking her head to dislodge Zach's proposition from her mind, Kate turned to go into the house. He grasped her arm, stopping her. She stiffened and fixed him with a narrow-eyed glare over her shoulder.

He released her and brushed a hand over his short dark blond hair. The setting sun glinted on the golden stubble on his chin.

The image of the hip young man-about-town, Zach wore designer jeans that probably cost more than her annual income. His long legs went on forever, and his pale blue shirt, untucked, stretched over his broad chest. Kate battled against the twinge in her stomach provoked by his sexy masculinity.

Relaxing his stance, he stepped back. "I don't mean to come on so strong. Graceann suggested you after she couldn't find another actress to take the role. She trusts you and didn't believe a stranger would be as dependable. She thinks our getting married will solve both our problems."

"Graceann needs to mind her own business." Kate clamped a hand over her mouth. Her friend would never do anything to hurt her.

Zach blew out a breath. "Sit down. Please. We'll discuss this like two rational people."

"When have we ever been rational with each other?" Giving him what she hoped was a cutting glare, Kate sat at the table. The idea of a marriage-of-convenience intrigued her. After the hurt Brian inflicted, a business arrangement suited her. She wished the man proposing the wild plan was other than Zach Lyon.

"Okay, I'll listen." She folded her arms across her chest.

Teresa, the Falco maid, came out to the patio with a fresh pitcher of tea.

Kate put her hand over her glass. "No, thanks, Teresa."

Zach nodded at Teresa. "Thanks," he said when she refreshed his glass.

Alone again, Kate focused on Zach. "Talk. I'll give you five minutes."

Setting down his glass, he leaned closer. "I know what happened with Brian. That's rough, to leave you at the altar and take your parents' money."

Kate pressed her lips together, fighting the anger, hurt, and worry. Her fiancé had humiliated her in front of her friends and family and run off with a large chunk of her parents' money, and much more from all the people who'd invested in his bogus scheme. A year later, the shame and pain lingered. Her parents assured her she wasn't at fault, but guilt over what had happened to them kept her up at night.

"So, you know the sordid details." Bitterness crept into her voice. "How does my marrying you help you? And, more importantly, how does it help me?"

He moved back in his seat, picked up his glass, drank, then set the glass down. When their eyes met again, his were shadowed.

The sadness in his eyes told Kate things might not be so perfect in Zach's privileged world.

"My relationship with my father has always been...difficult," he said. "I've disappointed him on many levels. He needs my help now, and I can't ignore it."

"I knew you had problems with your dad, but didn't know the details. Graceann told me you lost your mother and brother when you were eight."

"That was a long time ago." Zach drummed his fingers on the table top and hesitated, as if gathering his words. "Here's the deal. I'm a vice president in my dad's company, Star Ventures. We make military equipment, mostly mine-resistant armor for military vehicles. My title is symbolic. My dad's choice, not mine. I want a more active role in the day-to-day operations. I have some ideas I think will take us forward. Dad dismisses anything I say."

Glancing away, he stared at a spot above Kate.

"Why won't he listen to you?" she asked.

Zach's eyes met hers. "He knows my reputation and doesn't think I'll ever settle down enough to run Star Ventures. There's more. I've learned two of his top executives are conspiring against Dad, trying to prod him to retire and give control of the company to one of them, another V-P, a guy about my age." Zach released an audible breath. "I have it on good authority they're also embezzling."

Kate held out both hands. "Your dad's considering turning over his company to someone not in the family? Someone who might be embezzling?"

"You got it."

"That's tough, but he can do anything he wants with it."

Anger and hurt flashed over Zach's face. "His potential successor, Tripp Hunter, is married with a baby on the way. Dad thinks Hunter's a good family man, stable and mature, who will run the business the way Dad wants. Hunter is far from the paragon of virtue he portrays, but he puts on a convincing act."

Kate trailed a finger down the condensation on her glass. "Everyone is an actor. This sounds like a movie plot. Do you have proof about the conspiracy and the embezzling?"

"Not yet, but I will."

"I gather your dad believes the gossip rags about you." Kate's face heated. She sure believed the stories, which was one reason she didn't like Zach.

He nodded. "I need to convince him I'm not that guy."

His features tight, Zach ran a hand over his hair. Kate wondered what he would look like with longer hair she could slip her fingers through and ruffle. A tingle of excitement told her he'd be even sexier.

She pushed her thoughts from hottie Zach to his crazy plan. "You're offering me the role of your wife because you think marriage will make your dad believe you've settled down?"

He grinned. "That's it. Graceann tells me you're a gifted actor but haven't really put your talent to use, even though you went to one of the best acting schools in the country."

"What I do with my *talent* is my business." Her stomach clenched with the doubts and insecurities that had plagued her since childhood.

He held up a hand. "Sorry. I didn't mean to upset you. Let's get back to my plan. If Hunter wanted to bring the business forward, I wouldn't be so concerned. Hunter and his partner in crime, our CFO, will use the corporation as their personal bank and run it into the ground. My dad is only sixty. I'm afraid retirement, then seeing his beloved company destroyed, will kill him."

Zach chugged the rest of his drink and plunked the glass onto the table. "I tried to tell Dad my suspicions, but he cut me off. It might be a while before I get the proof I need, but I can't wait that long. The others are making their move. I need to force Dad to listen to me before it's too late."

"Why not hire a fake girlfriend or fiancée? Why not pretend to be married, at least until you wrest the company from the bad guys?"

"Dad wouldn't take a girlfriend or fiancée seriously. Only marriage, a real one, will convince him I'm no longer a player. He'll have someone check that the marriage is legal. The ones conspiring against him could investigate also. Everything has to be on the up and up. Unless Dad finds proof my marriage is real, he won't believe I've settled down."

Kate leveled her gaze at him. "I can understand why your dad would be skeptical. You're in the tabloids a lot, hot young Manhattan rich guy, always with a model or actress on your arm."

"Don't believe everything you read in those rags or hear on the gossip shows."

"What about all the girls I saw going in and out of your apartment when I visited Graceann?"

"You were watching me?"

His slow sexy grin made her face burn. She wrapped a hand around her half-empty glass and glanced away.

"Don't flatter yourself," she managed, turning back to him.

He waved a hand. "None of that matters. Take my offer. Help me, and help yourself."

She settled more comfortably in her chair. "Tell me how your nutty scheme helps me."

He rested his arms on the table and leaned in. "Stay married to me until I'm sure the company is safe, and I'll pay you one and a half million dollars."

"What?" She slapped the side of her head. "My ears must be clogged. Did you say one and a half million dollars?"

"Sure did. You can pay your parents back and have money for yourself. I'll pay your taxes. You'll have enough to finance a move to Manhattan or L.A. and support yourself while you go on auditions."

Anxiety and hope twisted a knot in Kate's chest. Her parents would have their money. She could use her portion to take acting lessons, get serious about finding decent roles. She could also fail as an actor and suffer public humiliation.

Kate stood and paced the length of the flagstone patio. She stopped and braced her hands on the stone railing, staring out at the splendor spread before her. The setting sun streaked the sky in shades of purple and gold. Sunsets in the West truly were spectacular. In the distance, purple-hazed mountains thrust toward scudding clouds. The sweet scent of roses and other flowers wafted from the extensive gardens below them. She breathed deeply, in and out, willing peace to her jumbled nerves.

More composed, she pivoted to face Zach and rested her hip against the railing. "We'll eventually get divorced. Won't that affect your relationship with your dad?"

Zach closed the distance between them. "Once things are settled and I have a more active role, with him still CEO, he'll trust me. My dad sacrificed everything, even his family, for that company. He can't lose it."

Zach rubbed the back of his neck, his gaze on Kate intense. "Another thing. We have to do this soon."

She drew in a breath. "Define soon."

"Within days."

Her chest tightened. "Days?"

"The company CFO has invited my dad, Hunter, his wife,

and me to spend the Christmas holiday at his ranch outside Las Vegas. I want to bring my new wife to the gathering."

A stress headache pulsed behind Kate's right temple. "A house party with people I don't know? Acting like someone I'm not?"

"You don't think your acting skills are good enough to convince others we're married?"

She bristled. "My acting skills are excellent." If she said it enough times, maybe she'd believe it.

"Prove it. Take my offer."

The force of Zach's stare made her head pound harder. She could do this, the ultimate dare. She swept her tongue over her lips. His eyes darkened, provoking an answering awareness in her, an awareness she didn't want or need. "This would be strictly business, right?"

"Yes."

"No sex?"

His lips curved into another of his smiles that sparked flashes of heat through her.

"If that's what you want," he said.

She lifted her chin. "Those are my terms, or else no deal."

He reached out and twisted strands of her hair around his finger. "You're welcome to change your mind any time."

"No way."

He laughed in that deep-throated way her traitorous body found so appealing.

She had lost her mind. She held out her hand. "Deal."

CHAPTER TWO

*Z*ach exhaled a relieved breath and stepped back, away from the temptation of Kate's full, pink lips, from the heady sweetness of her flowery perfume. Fantasies about her long, curling black hair spread on his pillow had given him erotic dreams for years. He wanted to see her golden-brown eyes filled with desire for him.

From the day he'd met Kate, he'd waged a battle against his attraction to her. An artsy type who didn't take herself seriously, she dressed in her uniform of jeans and high-top sneakers, so unlike the glamorous women he pursued. He suspected she didn't realize the power of her own beauty. He liked that about her. A man could build a family and a life with a woman like Kate, and that's what scared him to death.

Zach usually dated woman impressed with his money, cars, Manhattan apartment, and expensive clothes. None of that seemed to matter to Kate. He feared she saw through his trappings of wealth to the frightened eight-year-old boy whose world had been shredded when his mother died.

But Kate had agreed to his hastily-thought-out plan. He had

to have lost all semblance of sanity to come up with such a nutty idea. Desperation would do that to people, and it had certainly done it to him.

"Zach?" Her voice pulled him from his musings.

"Let's go in and give Graceann and Jake the good news," he said.

"I would hardly call it good news."

Ignoring her jibe, he went to the sliding glass doors and glanced into the living room. Soft lights from strategically placed lamps gave the area a sense of warmth and charm, fitting for the caring people who lived here.

Graceann and Jake's toddler, JP, ran into the room, Graceann in hot pursuit. "Get back here, Jake Palmer Falco," Graceann called out to the baby.

Zach grinned at the homey scene. Yearning wrapped around him. Deep down, he craved what Jake and Graceann had—a loving marriage, children. He wanted to give his children the kind of childhood he wished he'd had. He didn't know if he was capable of a lasting relationship, or even if he deserved one.

"What are you waiting for?" Impatience colored Kate's voice. "You've gotten awfully quiet. Rethinking things?"

He faced her. "Have a lot on my mind. The deal's still on. Thanks for agreeing. It will work out, Kate, don't worry." He scanned her, taking in her T-shirt stretched across full breasts. The shirt had a picture of Spock and Captain Kirk. No doubt bought at one of the thrift shops she frequented. Her torn jeans hugged her small, slim frame, and her pink high-top sneakers were unlaced. When she wasn't wearing a T-shirt, jeans, and sneakers, Kate wore long, flowing skirts and body-hugging tops, but always the high-tops. He wondered why she worked so hard to hide her beauty.

"You need a new wardrobe." He regretted the words as soon as they were out. Her face reddened, and she tightened her lips.

"Now you're going to tell me how to dress?" she spat out. "The deal is off."

He squeezed the bridge of his nose between his fingers and prayed for the right words. "Not trying to tell you what to wear, but if we're going to pull this off, you have to project the image of the type woman I'd marry."

Fixing him with a frosty glare, she tapped her foot. Damn, he'd done it again, opened his mouth and stuck his foot in. She was stunning, her lush chest moving with her rapid breathing, and her eyes sparking gold fire. If he told her how beautiful she looked when angry, he had no doubt she'd haul off and hit him.

"What does that mean—the *type woman* you'd marry?" Her jaw tight, she enunciated each word carefully.

He held up his hands. "No insult intended. You have a unique way of dressing that suits you. My father would expect me to marry someone like the women I'm usually linked with. He's got to believe this marriage is real in every way. I'll buy you a wardrobe to fit your role. Think of the clothes as costumes for a stage play in which you're the star. You're an actor. You can pull that off."

Kate chewed her thumbnail, her head down. Finally, she looked up. "I'll consider this an acting job. I'll give the clothes back to the wardrobe department, you, when this is over. I don't want anything from you except what's in our contract."

"Agreed. And one more thing, Kate. I need you to be fully committed. You can't call off the deal every time I annoy you." He grinned. "I may annoy you a lot."

She held up a hand. "Okay. Enough said."

* * *

ZACH SLID OPEN the door and Kate stalked into the house. She had to be nuts to go along with this charade. The money would help her parents. She would do it for them. For her penance, she'd marry Zach and put on a hell of a show for his dad and his co-workers. She'd figure out a way to put the acting creds on her resume.

Graceann, heavily pregnant and holding JP, smiled at them. "How'd it go?"

With a wry smile and a shrug, Kate said, "I'm doing it."

Frowning, Graceann glanced from one to the other. "You both look like you've lost your best friend. Come into the kitchen and we'll discuss."

"You two go," Zach said. "I think you need to talk."

As the women headed to the kitchen, Jake came into the room.

"Daddy!" JP held out his arms to his father.

Laughing, Jake took the child from Graceann, then bent to plant a brief kiss on her lips.

"How's the shoot going?" Graceann asked.

"It could go smoother. Tell you about it later." He grinned at Kate. "I hear a wedding might be in your future."

She flared her nostrils. "A business arrangement."

"Like ours was a business arrangement," Jake said, his attention on his wife.

The look of love that passed between Jake and Graceann pushed Kate's longing for love and family to the surface. She forced her thoughts away.

Graceann touched Jake's arm. "Not quite." With a teasing grin, she turned to Kate. "Maybe you and Zach will fall in love like Jake and me."

"Bite your tongue," Kate said.

Zach shook his head. "This is strictly business."

Jake grinned. "We know how that goes."

Laughing, Graceann hooked her arm through Kate's. "Let's go in the kitchen for some girl talk. Teresa left dinner warming up. We'll eat in about a half hour."

Jake bounced his son in his arms and kissed the baby's cheek. "Let's go outside with Uncle Zach and leave Mommy and Aunt Kate alone."

"*T*alk to me." With effort, Graceann settled her pregnant body onto a high stool at the kitchen island and shifted her attention to Kate. "From the expression on your face, you'd think the world is about to end. It can't be that bad."

She poured two glasses of lemonade from the pitcher on the island and handed a glass to Kate.

"I'm crazy to agree to this. I don't even like Zach." Kate tucked loose strands of her hair behind her ear and sipped her drink.

"I've never understood your dislike for each other," Graceann said. "Whenever you're in the same room, the tension is thick as grease paint."

Kate waved a hand. "Zach is a money-obsessed playboy."

"You're my best friends. Zach puts on a show to hide his feelings. He's a lot deeper than you or anyone knows. Without his help when I moved to New York City, I might have turned tail and run back to Spirit Lake. He's a caring guy, but he has issues."

"Father issues, but he wouldn't elaborate."

"When he gets more comfortable with you, he'll open up.

He's shared things with me, but I don't think he wants me talking about him."

"I'm not sure I want to get to know the *real* Zach Lyon. I'm fine with having only business between us."

With a sly smile, Graceann said, "You're the one who dared me to hire Jake as my fiancé. And you can see how that turned out. Maybe you and Zach will find you don't dislike each other as much as you think."

"Never!"

Chuckling, Graceann sipped her lemonade.

"He wants to buy me new clothes, to fit the image of the kind of woman the great Zach Lyon would marry," Kate said.

"We can go shopping. I know some great places where you can get the latest styles." Graceann patted her belly. "I can't shop for designer clothes now, but I can live vicariously through you. It'll be fun."

"Lots of fun." Despite the sarcasm that crept into her voice, Kate blinked back unexpected tears. "My parents lost their money because I brought Brian into our lives. I have to do this for them."

"Sweetie, your parents don't blame you. No one does. Brian fooled us all with his con. If Jake and I weren't setting up a household and getting used to being new parents, we would have invested in Brian's scam, too."

Kate tightened her hand around her glass. "Brian was a rat bastard, but he did me a favor. He opened my eyes to the deceitfulness all men are capable of. No man will ever again hurt me."

Graceann patted Kate's arm. "You'll meet someone decent who will appreciate the warm, wonderful woman you are."

"Puhleeze. I don't want a man. Not anymore." Kate smiled and held up her glass. "To Zach, my non-husband, and to a mutually satisfying business deal."

"Business has a way of becoming personal," Graceann said softly.

"There will never be anything personal between Zach and me."

CHAPTER FOUR

*K*ate smoothed a hand down the soft ivory silk of her cocktail-length dress with the scoop neckline —her wedding gown—and studied herself in the mirror. Graceann had taken her shopping at her favorite boutique, where Kate found her dress, the first one she tried on. Turning slowly, careful in her gold stiletto sandals, Kate barely recognized the stranger staring back at her, the stylish stranger.

With reluctance, she'd allowed one of Beverly Hill's top stylists to cut her long hair to shoulder length and add layers and deep auburn highlights to the black strands. Kate fluffed her hair and smiled, liking the way it curled softly around her face and highlighted her eyes, made bigger by the expert makeup applied by a celebrity makeup artist.

Peering closer, for the first time Kate saw a resemblance to her mother, a great beauty and former model, in whose shadow Kate continued to live. Much as she loved her mother, there remained the pain of not being good enough. Kate had carved out her own style, uniquely different from her mother's elegance.

Willing herself to relax, Kate rubbed a finger over the large blue topaz gem on a gold chain around her neck, her borrowed and blue. The one-of-a-kind design set in gold filigree was one of Graceann's newest creations. Kate's gown, her something new, with her gold hoop earrings, her something old, completed her nod to tradition.

She gave her reflection a self-deprecating grin, appreciating the irony. No matter what she wore, this wedding and marriage would never be traditional. She should have worn her high-top pink sneakers. Or her gold ones.

A knock on the door, then Graceann called, "Ready? Time to leave for City Hall."

"I'm ready. Come in."

Graceann entered and stopped, her eyes wide. "You've always been beautiful, Kate, but today you're spectacular."

"Stop it. Flattery is not required."

"I mean it." Graceann moved into the room and reached out to touch Kate's hair. "Your hair is gorgeous. You should keep it this length. It brings out your amazing eyes."

"Enough with the compliments."

"You need to learn to accept them," Graceann said.

"My mom gets enough for the both of us. I'm not her."

"You're dazzling in your own right. Embrace and celebrate your differences. I know you don't think you can compete with her, which is why you try to hide your beauty."

"My mother's great. I love her," Kate said.

"I know you do. Both your parents are loving, terrific people."

"Mom and Dad have always tried to bolster my self-esteem, but..." Kate let the thought drop. No difficult remembrances today. "Let's do this thing."

An hour later, Kate paced the hallway outside the judge's chambers. The towering Christmas tree at the end of the hall reached to the ceiling. The tree's blinking white lights, beacons of gaiety, mocked her. People bustled back and forth, a palpable holiday excitement reaching into every corner of the long hall. She wanted to shout, "Bah Humbug!"

This was so not how she'd pictured her wedding. She'd dreamed of a ceremony at her family's church in Spirit Lake, followed by an intimate reception at the town's pricey hotel. Her dream almost came true, except for one tiny detail—her groom had other plans that day.

Reality bumped up against her fantasy. Eight days before Christmas, she waited at Los Angeles City Hall for her groom, a sexy playboy she barely tolerated. They'd signed their marriage contract, drawn up by Jake's lawyer, yesterday. She and Zach concocted a background for Kate as a socialite, and a reason as to why they'd married so quickly.

Too wired to sit, Kate had elected to walk the hall. She glanced at the wall clock. Zach was late. Maybe he'd gotten cold feet. Her stomach dropped. No, please, not a second time. Her guilt over what Brian had done to her parents, and her desire to help them, put her in this position. She locked her knees. She would not run, although every instinct she possessed urged her to hightail it out of there.

The whoosh of the elevator doors made her whirl around. Zach stepped out. She sucked in a breath. The fit of his dark gray suit screamed custom made. The white of his shirt dazzled, and his tie in muted shades of gray and purple complemented his suit.

It hurt to admit it, but Zach Lyon was one hunk. The appreciative glances from some of the nearby women confirmed his appeal.

Zach's gaze connected with hers. Something arced between them, hot and crackling, like fireworks on New Year's Eve.

His arrogant smile knocked Kate back to Earth.

"About time you showed up," she said when he reached her. "I figured you'd chickened out."

He adjusted the cuffs on his snowy white shirt. His gold cufflinks twinkled in the sunlight streaming through the high windows. "I never renege on a deal." He touched her chin with his fingers until her gaze met his. "Were you hoping I wouldn't show?"

She jerked free. "I wouldn't care, but we have a deal."

A smile tugged at the corners of his mouth. "I think you care more than you want to admit."

Before she could shoot back a sharp retort, the door to the judge's chambers opened. A frowning Graceann beckoned to them.

"The judge is waiting. Are you two coming in?"

Kate pressed a hand to her stomach. "Showtime."

* * *

ZACH HAD NEVER WANTED MARRIAGE, but the gone-in-a-blink ritual made him feel…cheated. When he'd stepped out of the elevator at City Hall, he'd zeroed in on Kate with laser-like focus. Everything around him disappeared. Only Kate remained, elegant and sexy in her silk dress, with her soft cloud of raven hair framing her high-cheekboned face. Her beauty and a large dose of guilt had made his breath lodge in his throat. She should have been waiting to walk down the aisle with a man she loved. He hoped this contract between them wouldn't interfere with her finding her own true happiness.

Glass of wine in hand and seated on a comfortable chaise in Graceann and Jake's bright sunroom, Zach imagined himself on a movie set filled with beautiful people playing their parts. Not the wedding reception he would have imagined. The word awkward came to mind.

Kate and Graceann talked quietly at the tile-topped table as the maid carried in a ceramic bowl of salad, followed by the cook with a steaming pan of enchiladas. The maid poured Kate wine

180

from the bottle on the table, and poured Graceann another sparkling water.

"Come eat, Zach," Graceann called.

Throwing aside his musings, he pushed up from his chair and took a seat at the table.

Jake, finished putting JP to bed, entered the room. His gaze immediately sought out Graceann. The love shining from his eyes as he looked at his pregnant wife stirred something in Zach, a craving he refused to acknowledge. He was happy for the other couple. Life seemed to have something different planned for him.

Zach's attention went to Kate, his new wife. Kate Carluccio Lyon. His wife only until he secured the company for his dad and took his place in it. The thought provoked a surprising hit of melancholy.

With more control at the company, he could persuade his dad to expand beyond government contracts. More diversity would keep them viable. Hopefully, with the extra money he could give additional support to those poor kids in Nicaragua. The kids depended on him and his charitable organization to make their lives better.

He looked up to meet Kate's brown eyes. Bedroom eyes that wreaked havoc on his libido.

CHAPTER FIVE

*A*fter a quick breakfast and hurried good-byes to Graceann and Jake the next morning, Zach and Kate took a hired car to LAX for the short flight to Las Vegas. Dressed in expensive dark-washed skinny jeans, white silk top, and high-heeled black ankle boots, her newly-cut hair floating over her shoulders, Kate felt like an actor in a play. Or a fashion wannabe. Or a celebrity famous for being famous. Once at their destination, she'd put her acting classes to use with an Oscar-worthy performance as a loving newlywed and socialite.

She twisted the plain gold wedding band on her finger. A married woman now, but she didn't feel married.

She stole a glance at Zach, her husband, seated next to her in the car. His strong profile with his straight nose and firm chin spoke of a man who knew what he wanted and went after it. According to the gossip rags and TV shows, Zach didn't have to work too hard for whatever he wanted. Born to wealth, he led a charmed life surrounded by beautiful people. No wonder she and Zach had never gotten along. A little voice whispered she'd never given him a chance. His means and privilege had turned her off from the beginning and she'd never looked beyond that to the man. Yet, she'd always found him appealing, and had fought against the attraction.

Kate didn't care about money. She longed for contentment, a place in the world, and the confidence to take her acting career to the next level. That confidence had so far proved elusive.

Zach caught her watching him. His eyes, dark in the muted light of the car's interior, stared at her with an intensity that unnerved. An ache she didn't understand started in her chest and wound its way lower. She clasped her hands on her lap, protection from the sudden urge to run her fingers over his sharp cheekbones and full lips. With his looks, he could have made his fortune as a model or an actor.

"See something you like?" he drawled. His deep voice sent a thrill through her as much as she tried to deny it.

Kate arched an eyebrow. "Not much."

He laughed. "Get used to being around me, *wife*." He leaned close and cradled her face between his hands. "We *are* newlyweds. We should rehearse."

She narrowed her eyes and pulled free. "Don't even think it, buster. You take advantage of the situation and you won't be able to walk for a week."

"Ouch. You really are something."

"You'd better remember that."

"Oh, I will, but you remember when we're with the others over this holiday, we need to put on a believable show."

She slid away from him and folded her arms across her chest. "I'm a good actor. I'll play my part in front of our audience. But when we're alone, you keep your hands to yourself."

"Whatever you say."

His too-easy acceptance not to touch her when they were alone shot warning signals through her.

* * *

SETTLED in the first-class cabin of the commercial jet, glass of champagne in hand, Kate felt disembodied from her true self. The coach passengers filed in and Kate averted her eyes. She always flew economy, and never liked walking past the first-class section with everyone comfortable in their roomy leather seats, a gauntlet to remind the coach passengers they were somehow inferior.

She handed her empty champagne flute to the attendant and leaned against the soft seat. It had been a rushed couple of days and she needed to rest.

"Wake up. We're landing."

Kate jerked awake to a grinning Zach.

"Have a good sleep?" he asked.

"I can't believe I slept the whole flight."

"Sure did. You snored too."

"I didn't!"

"You didn't. But you nestled against my shoulder the whole time."

She put a hand to her mouth. "I'm sorry."

"Don't be. I liked it."

Embarrassment burned through her, and she stared out the window.

A young man named Skylar, their host's chauffer, picked them up at the airport in a limo. Kate settled into the backseat next to Zach. As they drove out of the airport toward the suburbs, the sun-drenched landscape with hazy mountains in the distance unfurled like a movie trailer before them. She twisted in her seat to stare back at the needle of the Stratosphere at the end of the Strip, piercing the blue sky, a reminder of another era.

She'd been to Vegas once with Graceann, on spring break from college. Kate couldn't remember much about that trip. They'd done a lot of drinking and partying. A world away from the life she'd stumbled into now—contract marriage to a man she didn't like, new expensive wardrobe, on their way to a ranch outside Las Vegas for an acting gig with real-world consequences. She wondered when she'd wake from this dream.

The limo smoothly ate up the miles through the desert and toward the mountains. After about fifty minutes, they pulled up to a high ornate iron gate. The driver punched keys on the box affixed to the gate, and the doors swung open to allow the car to slide through. The long drive lined with palm trees led to a circular driveway. Kate gasped at the sprawling house that stood majestically before them. Despite its size, the Spanish style mansion, with its red-tiled roof and arched windows, had a homey, welcoming vibe. Tiny white lights sparkled from the palm trees surrounding it. The driver pulled the car to a stop in front of marble steps. He walked around to her side and opened the door to help her out. She exited to the soothing sound of tinkling water from the marble fountain set in the center of the drive.

She turned to Zach, who'd climbed out of the car after her. "They call this a ranch?"

Grinning, he shrugged. "They do keep horses on the property."

"I guess it's a ranch then."

As the driver hauled their suitcases out of the trunk, Zach cupped her elbow.

"Ready for act one?" he asked.

Her attention on the house, she could only nod.

He leaned down to whisper in her ear. "Close your mouth. You're supposed to be from a wealthy family. Houses like this are common for you."

"For Kate Lyon, but not Kate Carluccio."

The front door opened. Zach bent and kissed her on the lips.

Too shocked to protest, Kate stood still. Zach's lips moved gently over hers, seducing with tenderness. As if another woman invaded her body, Kate wound her arms around his neck and returned his kiss. He tasted of coffee and mint and desire.

Damn, the man could kiss.

"Hey, you two, I know you're newlyweds, but we'll have none of that."

At the teasing male voice, Kate and Zach drew apart. Zach stared at her, an expression of wonder on his face, before he turned to the middle-aged, heavyset man by the open door.

"Come in and meet the others." With the appearance of an over-indulged aristocrat, the man waved them up the steps.

Zach slipped his arm around Kate's waist. "Break a leg, Mrs. Lyon."

CHAPTER SIX

*W*ith Zach's hand on the small of her back, they headed up the wide steps. Kate forced a smile, doing her best to act like the wealthy sophisticate she wasn't. *Focus, Kate, focus.* But she couldn't concentrate with her mind a jumble of conflicting emotions.

Zach had kissed her. And what a kiss! She could swear her toes curled.

They reached the older man who waited for them. She shivered at the calculating assessment in the man's small eyes as he studied her. Here stood a powerful man used to crushing others to get what he wanted.

Zach kept his hand on her back. "Carlisle, this is my wife. Kate, this is Carlisle Morgan, the company CFO and our host."

Kate almost looked around for Zach's wife. Right, *she* was his wife. His kiss had unsettled her more than she thought.

"Hello, Mr. Morgan." Her voice sounded an octave lower. "Thank you for inviting us to your stunning home."

Morgan shook her hand, holding it a little longer than necessary. "Please call me Carlisle." He released her and grinned at

Zach. "I can see why you had a quickie marriage. She's too beautiful to let her get away."

Beside her, Zach stiffened. "I agree Kate's beautiful, but that's not the only reason I married her. She's kind-hearted and smart. And she's good for me."

Kate blinked. When had she entered an alternate universe? Zach giving her compliments? He didn't even like her. Maybe she'd been wrong about that.

"Of course." Morgan's lips twisted, giving him a smarmy expression that made her want to retch.

"Let's go in," he said.

They stepped into a marble-floored entry hall with an ornate wrought-iron-railed staircase to the second floor. Next to it were stairs leading down. Afternoon sunlight streamed through the large Paladin style windows at the top of the stairs, gilding the floor with gold and pink. Morgan led them to a room on the left where a fire flickered in the baroque fireplace. A fire in Las Vegas? Sure, it was December, but it was warm. Maybe the Morgans liked the thought of a snowy, cold, traditional Christmas. Or maybe they were all about over-the-top opulence to impress others. And they called this a ranch.

A blonde-haired middle-aged woman, her hair perfectly coiffed in what Kate thought of as "anchor woman hair," rose from a chair by the fire as they approached. Her smile held no warmth, and her blue eyes reminded Kate of ice chips. A quiver ran along Kate's spine.

"Welcome to our home," the woman said.

Morgan nodded to his wife. "Gloria, you know Zach. This is his wife, Kate."

Gloria acknowledged Kate with a tepid smile, then she leaned in and gave Zach an air kiss. "Please sit." She gestured toward the grouping of sofas, love seats, and chairs in a pale green silk-like fabric, arranged in front of the fireplace. Other smaller seating groups were scattered around the room, a decorator's idea of hominess. Unlike the welcoming vibe of the outside, there was nothing friendly about the cavernous room.

"What would you like to drink?" Gloria asked. "We're waiting for the others."

"I'll have a bourbon," Zach said.

Kate jerked her head toward him. Bourbon? Seriously? She'd been in Zach's company numerous times. Despite his sophisticated veneer, he usually drank beer, and not always craft, but some of the "good ole boy" stuff.

"Kate? What would you like?" Gloria asked.

Kate smiled at their frosty hostess. "Sherry, please."

She suppressed a grin at Zach's surprised stare. Two could play this game. If Zach wanted to impress their hosts by drinking bourbon, she would drink sherry, something she'd had only once in her life.

Gloria gave the drink order to a butler who stood nearby. Kate hadn't noticed him enter.

Two young women bustled into the room. The older one, a clone of Gloria, but with softer, smooth, long hair, zeroed in on Zach, ignoring everyone else.

The other woman, younger, her expression open and friendly, with light brown hair artfully streaked with blonde highlights, smiled at Kate. Her gray eyes sparkled in welcome.

"Henry," the blonde woman said to the butler without looking at him. "Bring me some champagne."

"Very well, madam." He turned to the younger woman. "You, Miss Juliette?"

"White wine for me, please."

Bowing, Henry left the room.

"Zach, darling, how wonderful to see you again." The one who'd demanded champagne, her voice smoky, floated toward Zach. Her knee length silk skirt swayed when she walked, and her open-toed patent leather stilettos showed off long, slim legs.

She wrapped her arms around Zach and kissed him full on the mouth.

Crap! She's kissing my husband. Kate's anxiety mixed with jealousy that came out of nowhere like a desert dust storm.

Zach back-stepped away from the woman and grabbed Kate's hand, bringing her closer to his side. "Ava, this is my wife. Kate, this is Ava Morgan, Carlisle and Gloria's daughter."

Ava's blue eyes, as chilling as her mother's, scanned Kate. Smirking, she said, "Hello, Zach's wife."

Kate started to put out her hand to shake Ava's, then drew back at the other woman's remark. To regain equal footing, she gave the woman a curt nod. "Hello, Carlisle's daughter."

Beside her, Zach coughed.

"Hey, Zach. Cool you're spending the holidays with us." The younger woman, whom the butler had called Juliette, approached them. She hugged Zach, then turned to Kate, hand outstretched. "I'm Juliette. I'm excited to meet the woman who snagged Zach. He's a keeper."

Smiling, Kate shook Juliette's hand. The young woman's firm handshake, genuine smile, and warm gray eyes told Kate she had a friend in this cold place.

Henry came into the room wheeling a cart with the drinks. Morgan gestured toward the fireplace. "Let's sit by the fire."

Like children following a teacher, the group trailed after their host and took seats at the grouping around the fireplace.

When they were settled, drinks in hand, the fire crackling, Kate began to relax. She told herself the next week with this crowd wouldn't be so bad. She had Zach to guide her, and friendly Juliette. She felt someone's stare and turned to find Ava's wintry eyes on her. A warning the next week might be as bad as Kate feared?

Gloria smoothed her tweed skirt over her knees. "We have a lot planned for everyone this week. Tomorrow night we're all invited to Mel Ableman's Christmas party at his casino."

Kate widened her eyes. Mel Ableman was one of the wealthiest men in the world, a billionaire with casinos and hotels in every corner of the globe. His two hotels in Las Vegas were the most expensive in the city, their décor like small versions of the palace at Versailles. Too gaudy for her.

Gloria focused her attention on Kate, waiting for a response. With a smile, Kate said, "The party sounds wonderful."

Kate sipped her sherry and almost gagged at the sweetness. She remembered why she didn't like sherry.

"You did bring a gown, didn't you?" Ava's voice dripped with condescension.

"Of course." Thank God Zach had warned her she'd need some formal clothes.

Gloria took dainty sips from her glass of wine. "I hope you brought more than one gown, Kate. We're hosting our annual Christmas Eve gala here."

"I did." Kate forced herself to endure another sip of sherry before she blurted out something inappropriate, like *What is it with you women and gowns?*

Zach laid his hand on top of hers where she'd rested it on her thigh. The heat of his touch warmed her more than the sherry. She tossed back her drink. Sweet or not, she needed the liquid sustenance.

"When do you expect my dad, Carlisle?" Zach asked.

Carlisle looked at his gold Rolex. "Your dad and Elle are flying in with Tripp and Missy on the company jet. My driver just left to pick them up."

Zach tightened his hand over Kate's. She glanced at him. He tossed back his bourbon, his jaw clenched. Zach wanted to wrest the company away from Morgan and this Tripp guy. He couldn't be happy Tripp and his dad were traveling together. And who was Elle?

Morgan stood and grabbed the crystal decanter of sherry from the cart Henry had placed in front of them and poured

Kate another glass. Setting down the sherry, he picked up a decanter of bourbon and held it out to Zach, who nodded. When Morgan had refilled Zach's glass and his own, he sank into his chair.

"I love your outfit, Kate," Juliette said, breaking the tension.

Kate smiled. "Thanks." The designer clothes and shoes were so not what Kate was used to. Her preference ran to "Bohemian chic," as Graceann called it. Or "gamer style," with her no-name jeans and Converse sneakers. Kate was acting a part, she reminded herself. Her sleek new appearance was her costume. Shorter hair and sophisticated clothes were a small price to pay for one and a half million dollars. She could play this role for a week.

CHAPTER SEVEN

They sat before the fire for another ninety minutes, making small talk and nibbling on appetizers served by a maid. Playing her part of the happy newlywed, Kate's face hurt from smiling. Other than Juliette and Zach, she felt lost in the desert with rattlers nipping at her heels.

When the doorbell chimed, Kate breathed a relieved sigh. Something to break the boredom of forced conversation with people who couldn't be less interested in what she had to say. The sound of the front door opening, followed by the murmur of voices, made everyone turn to the doorway.

Henry, surrounded by two women and two men, stood at the living room entrance.

"Mr. and Mrs. Hunter," Henry announced. "Mr. Lyon and Miss Pickett."

Morgan chuckled and stood, striding toward the group. "Don't be so formal, Henry. We know who they are."

The others by the fire stood too, their attention on the newcomers.

A handsome sixtyish man, dressed in pressed khakis and a yellow sweater that shouted *country club*, moved away from the group. Tall and slim, his dark hair sprinkled with gray, his erect posture and build reminded Kate of Zach.

A thirty-something man of average height, with thinning dark hair and wearing a black overcoat hustled into the room, followed by a red-haired woman, slightly shorter than the man, wrapped in a full-length mink coat.

Seriously? Fur? In this weather? Even if she could afford it, Kate would never wear fur. Fur looked best on the animals it belonged to.

"Hey, Carlisle." The younger man held out his hand to Morgan.

They shook hands, then Morgan smiled at the older man and shook his hand. "Welcome, Greg."

"Thanks for inviting us, Carlisle. I always like coming here," said a soft female voice.

Kate looked around to see who'd uttered the words. The fourth person in the group, a woman of about fifty, her pale blonde hair in a severe short style, and dressed in a dark blue suit and sensible black flats, moved from behind Henry and smiled shyly at Morgan.

He ignored her and nodded at the men. "Have a smooth flight?"

Kate smiled at the sweet-sounding woman, hoping to take off some of the edge of Morgan's snub. The woman smiled back.

The younger man waved a hand and laughed. "Great flight. Flying private means not putting up with crying babies and coach riffraff."

Eyes narrowed, Kate studied him—no doubt the infamous Tripp. She guessed the fur-swathed woman was his wife. Kate stiffened. She so did not like this Tripp person. Zach, standing next to her, touched her hand and leaned close to whisper in her ear. "Let it go, Kate. Tripp's a jackass."

The fur-swaddled woman gave her husband a simpering smile. "Now, Tripp, we'll be parents soon."

His thin lips curled in a sneer. "Our nannies will handle the kids, and they sure won't fly in first-class with us."

The woman's face reddened. She looked at Morgan. "Thank you for inviting us. You and Gloria." The grin she gave Gloria reminded Kate of a little girl in school desperately trying to curry favor with the teacher.

"We're glad you and Tripp could make it out here for the holidays, Missy." Gloria's wide smile for Missy made Kate wonder about the woman's coldness toward her.

Tripp and Missy handed their coats to the waiting Henry. Without the concealing fur, Missy's very pregnant belly was on full display.

A twinge of sympathy hit Kate. Poor Missy, pregnant, and with an arrogant jerk for a husband.

Zach took Kate's hand as the group approached. Kate plastered a smile on her face, prepared to meet her new father-in-law.

"Dad. Elle. This is my wife. Kate, my father, Greg Lyon, and his executive assistant Elle Pickett."

She must be imagining things. Zach sounded proud to introduce her to his father.

The elder Lyon's pale blue eyes seemed to miss nothing as he scanned her.

Kate had the overwhelming urge to curtsy. "Nice to meet you, Mr. Lyon." She didn't feel nice at all.

While the elder Mr. Lyon stood silently, Elle grabbed Kate to her in a gentle hug. Releasing Kate, she smiled, her gray eyes soft. "I'm so happy to meet you. We're all in a bit of a shock at Zach's sudden marriage."

Greg Lyon cleared his throat and nodded at Kate, his narrowed eyes communicating his displeasure. "Never thought he'd settle down. I don't understand the suddenness."

Zach drew Kate close and placed a tender kiss on her hair. "Kate and I have been friends for years. One day, we looked at each other and realized we wanted to be more than friends.

Once I knew how much I loved her, why wait to make her mine?"

"Why, indeed," his dad said.

Surely no love lost between father and son.

Greg grunted and sauntered to the cart to pour himself a bourbon. He didn't ask Elle if she wanted a drink.

Zach turned to the younger couple, who stood nearby. "Missy, Tripp, my wife, Kate."

"Nice to meet you," Missy murmured, not making eye contact. She stood behind her husband. Kate wondered if the woman walked three steps behind him at all times.

Gloria, Ava, and Juliette surrounded Missy, all chattering at once. Kate felt like the shy little girl she'd been, ignored by the cool girls in school.

Tripp's eyes trailed down Kate, stopping at her chest. She clenched a fist at her side, fighting the urge to slap the smirk off his face.

"Zach, dude, lucky you with such a hot wife."

Zach squeezed Kate's hand. "You're right. I'm lucky to have her."

Kate smiled. Her acting coaches would be proud of her façade of friendliness. "I'm always happy to meet Zach's friends."

Tripp laughed. "Not sure about the *friends* part." He punched Zach's shoulder. "Right, dude?"

Zach glared at him. Kate stepped away from all that testosterone.

"Dinner is served," Henry announced, saving them all from whatever appeared to be going down between Zach and Tripp.

When Tripp held out his arm for Kate, she couldn't refuse. With a sigh and a glance at Zach, she headed into the dining room with Tripp.

She'd be eating with a nest of vipers.

CHAPTER EIGHT

*K*ate settled back in her chair at the long dining table, pressed a palm to her full stomach, and suppressed the urge to groan at the sheer pleasure of the decadent food she'd consumed. She smiled at Gloria. "That meal was amazing. I'll need to hit the gym hard after this holiday."

Filled with South African lobster tail, tender filet mignon, assorted vegetables, and fresh-baked bread, plus Crème Brûlée and Irish coffee, she'd probably waddle from the table. If she could even stand after the copious amounts of wine she'd drunk. If this crowd was as bad as Zach said, she suspected she'd have to indulge in lots of wine to handle the Morgans and their merry band of cutthroats.

Across from her, Zach laughed. "You'll be fine." He lifted his cup of Irish coffee to Gloria. "My compliments to your cook."

Murmurs of appreciation for the cook and the food rounded the table.

Finally, time for bed. Kate could relax and be herself. Being "on" all day had zapped her energy. They said goodnight to their hosts, then along with Tripp and Missy, followed Henry up the sweeping staircase to the bedrooms. He showed Tripp and Missy into the first room along the wide hallway, then led Kate and Zach to a room at the other end.

"Thanks, Henry." Kate gave the butler her friendliest smile to make up for the slight from the other couple, who never looked at the man.

"Good night, Henry," Zach said.

The smiling butler ushered them into their room. Bowing, he left and closed the door behind him.

Kate gasped at her first glimpse of the luxurious suite. They stood in a small sitting room furnished with a modern sofa in a smooth white fabric, and flanked by a chair upholstered in a bright flower motif. A glass-topped table rested on a small, white area rug in front of the sofa. Through a doorway off the sitting room, she spotted the bedroom, dominated by a four-poster king-size bed covered in white. A slow burn started at her neck. She would not think about Zach and that bed.

"Wow," she said. "This is something out of *Lifestyles of the Rich and Famous.*"

"It's okay."

Hand on hip, she turned to him and rolled her eyes. "I guess you're used to this kind of living."

"Don't hold it against me." His eyes teased.

She relaxed a little. "As awesome as this whole mansion is, there are other things more important."

He stepped closer. She inhaled his clean scent of citrus.

"Like those causes you're always involved with?" he said. "The animal rights groups, the kids' groups?"

Kate thrust out her chin. "I consider helping others to be more important than the pursuit of money." *Gag.* She sounded so self-righteous.

A shadow passed over his face, then he grinned and touched the tip of her nose. "You'll never be rich with that attitude."

She back-stepped, putting distance between herself and the too-appealing Zach. "Maybe I'm rich in ways you could never imagine. What I've never liked about you is your love of money and the acquisition of it."

"You really don't know me at all."

She started to give him a snarky quip, then closed her mouth. Over these past few days she'd seen a different Zach than the one she thought she knew. She wouldn't tell him that, not yet.

His eyes lit, and he reached out and touched strands of her hair, winding them around his finger. "I like your new style, but I liked it long, too."

Her breathing hitched as they stared at each other. This was Zach, she reminded herself. She didn't like him, never had. The memory of the kiss they'd shared earlier, never far from her mind, thrust forward.

She slid away. "Don't get any ideas, mister. Do you want to toss a coin to see who takes the bed and who sleeps on the sofa?"

His arm on his middle section, he bowed. "The bed is all yours, milady."

Shaking her head at his shenanigans, she ambled toward the bedroom. And froze in the doorway. One step over the threshold, and she'd be floating in a calming ocean, all blues, whites, and greens. The white silk comforter was turned down, and the hot pink silk pajamas she'd bought on Rodeo Drive were laid out on top, pops of color in the seascape. Four fluffy oversized blue and green pillows were arranged on the bed, in the casual way only a decorator could pull off.

A small loveseat upholstered in a nubby pale green fabric stood at the end of the bed. Kate meandered around the room, running her fingers over the satiny wood of a white dresser and two high white bureaus set against walls covered in pale blue wallpaper that looked like silk. She'd wandered onto the set of a 1930's romantic comedy where the furniture was white and glamorous. She half expected to see an old-fashioned white rotary telephone on one of the night tables that flanked the bed.

You're not in Kansas anymore, Kate. Or the Poconos either.

She spied the bathroom through an open door off the bedroom. She hurried over and paused at the lavishness before her. "After this, I'll be too spoiled to go back to my little Spirit Lake apartment." She could live happily ever after in the bathroom. White marble with flecks of gold and blue covered the walls and floor. A bathtub, big enough for two, sat against one wall. Next to it, the shower, which could easily fit two or more, was enclosed in frameless glass doors. Erotic scenes filled her mind—Zach and her in the tub, drinking champagne; in the shower having hot sex. She fanned herself with her hand.

Focus, Kate, focus. Her gaze wandered the rest of the ornate room. A marble-topped console with two sinks and an oversized mirror took over one wall. A marble table with a lighted mirror like a professional makeup artist would use was set into a corner. "These people sure like their marble," she muttered.

She peeked into a small room off to the side that held the toilet. On a trip to the Caribbean with Brian, they'd stayed at a luxury hotel with a similar bathroom. But this bathroom in the Morgans' house was tons better than that one. Kate stepped out of the bathroom before its awesomeness overwhelmed her senses.

The sounds of the TV in the other room intruded on her private dreams of lovemaking in the shower and sexy body massages with scented oil. She shut the bedroom door, closing out the noise, closing out Zach. An unwelcome kernel of regret opened in her, and she lowered herself onto the loveseat. Zach's chivalry in letting her take the bed didn't surprise her. Through the years, he'd teased her or ignored her, but he'd never been mean. She should have been kinder to him, especially seeing the way his dad treated him, but Zach's playboy reputation touched a nerve with her.

If she were completely honest with herself, fear had a lot to do with her dislike of Zach. Not fear that he'd hurt her, but that her traitorous body wanted him, had always wanted him. And that couldn't be, not now, not ever. They were too different. She'd never be comfortable in his world, and she didn't want to be. After Brian, her heart was off-limits to any man.

Zach, star of her sexual fantasies, threatened to take over her mind. Forcing her thoughts to a more mundane thread, she headed toward the walk-in closet, where her clothes hung next to Zach's, put there by the maid. Her thoughts took another dangerous turn. She wondered what life would be like if she and Zach shared a closet permanently.

"You've had too much wine, Kate. Stop with the thoughts." She found her purse on a shelf and slid her cell phone out to check the time. Past midnight. She had to get some sleep. But how much sleep would she get with Zach in the next room?

Kate undressed and slipped on the hot pink pajamas. The silk against her bare skin was so utterly sensual, she wanted to moan. So different from the oversized T's she usually wore to bed.

When she heard the light knock on the door separating the bedroom from the sitting room, she stilled. Another knock. "What do you want?" she called out.

"My clothes are in there. I need to use the bathroom and change for bed," Zach answered.

"Oh, right." She opened the door to him.

The first few buttons on his shirt were undone, the vee showing off a smattering of golden hairs. His rolled-up sleeves accentuated his muscled forearms covered in the same light hairs. He looked sexy and downright adorable. Her mouth went dry.

Zach's gaze, sensual as the fabric that covered her, made a leisurely sweep of her body. The gleam that lit his green eyes kindled an answering spark in her. Arms folded across her chest in a vain attempt to ward off the erotic temptations that surfaced, she stepped back to let him enter.

"Some of your clothes are in the closet," she said. "And I saw more of them in that bureau over there." She pointed toward the bureau set against the far wall.

He didn't move, only stood and stared at her mouth. Did she

have food there? She resisted the urge to touch her lips and find out.

Zach reached out and flicked a finger at the corner of her mouth. At his touch, she melted like ice cream dropped on a hot Nevada sidewalk.

His lips tilted in a sexy grin. "You had a dab of Crème Brûlée."

Without thinking, she licked her lips. Wrong move. Zach didn't bother to hide the desire that darkened his eyes.

Kate needed to get hold of the situation. "While you change, I'll check the linen closet for blankets for the sofa. You can use one of the pillows from the bed."

"Let's hope the staff doesn't figure out we're not sharing a bed," he said.

"So what if they do? This marriage is a business deal. Don't dare think it will ever be anything else."

He laughed, a husky sound that shot warmth through her and made her want to do something crazy, like tear up their contract and throw herself in his arms.

With a tempting grin, he said, "I'll be out of your way quickly."

"I have to ask you something first." She needed answers and she'd rather talk to him while he was fully clothed, for the sake of her suddenly overactive libido.

"Sure. What is it?"

She grabbed her silk robe from the loveseat and slipped it on, tying the sash tightly. Zach, arms folded, leaned against the bathroom doorframe.

"Gloria doesn't seem to like me," Kate said. "The chill coming from her was frostier than a Poconos snowstorm. She just met me. I don't understand it."

He straightened and rubbed a hand over his eyes. "I think I know. This could take a while. You might want to sit."

Kate perched on the edge of the bed.

"Remember when I was supposed to be Graceann's pretend fiancé?"

"And terrific friend that you are, you reneged on your agreement."

"Not my finest moment. But I'm glad it all worked out for Graceann."

Kate tilted her head and studied him. "I remember. A woman broke your heart, and some new woman invited you to the Dominican Republic or someplace for the holidays. Graceann felt sorry for you."

He nodded. "I'd been dating a model and thought I might be falling in love. She ditched me for a guy twice her age with more money than I'll ever see. I've since realized my ego was more wounded than my heart."

With a sheepish grin, he said, "I hate to admit it, but the new woman in my life was Ava Morgan. I spent the holidays with her and her family in a house they rented in Santo Domingo."

Kate jumped up. "I *knew* you and Ava had had a *thing*. It's obvious from the way she wraps herself around you every chance she gets."

"Jealous?"

Kate wanted to wipe the grin off his face. "No."

"Our *thing* lasted about six months. I knew right away she wasn't for me, but it took a while to extricate myself from her grasp. Her parents pushed us to make it permanent. Gloria still resents me for breaking it off with Ava." He shrugged. "So when I bring a wife around, she's not real happy."

"And neither is Ava."

He pushed away from the doorframe and waved his hand to take in the room. "All the trappings of wealth are here, but I've long suspected Morgan is teetering on bankruptcy. I hired a PI to delve into his finances. Gloria and Carlisle are desperate to marry their daughters off to money. They would have loved to have Ava marry into my family's money."

"So, Carlisle has a financial incentive to raid your dad's company."

"You're smart."

"I know."

He laughed. "Figured you'd say that. Anything else you want to know?"

When she shook her head, he opened one of the bureau drawers and rummaged through to pull out boxers and a T-shirt. "Toothbrushes and toothpaste in the bathroom?"

"Yes."

While he was in the bathroom, Kate searched the linen closet for bedding for Zach. She found a soft blue blanket and took that along with a pillow from the bed and set them on the sofa in the sitting room.

While she waited for Zach, she sat on the loveseat by the bed, turned on the TV that rested on her dresser, and idly flipped through the channels. She decided on a show about renovating houses. The couple on the screen went into spasms of delight over their design choices. Although not in the mood for TV, she had to keep her mind from conjuring up images of Zach in those short boxers. Of Zach naked. Of running her fingers along his muscled chest. She'd been too long without a man.

Finally, he emerged, clad in trim navy boxers and a white t-shirt that stretched across his firm chest. Not fair.

"Goodnight," he said.

"Goodnight." She stood. "I put some bedclothes in the other room. You should be comfortable."

"Thanks." He didn't move. His eyes darkened and fastened on her mouth.

She swallowed around her suddenly dust-dry throat. "Uh-uh, I have something else I wanted to say."

"Shoot."

"I'm sorry about your father. He wasn't very nice to you."

Zach's features tightened. "I'm used to that from him, but I didn't like the way he treated you."

"I didn't mind. Elle seems friendly."

"She's a good person. Been with Dad since before my mom died. Dad couldn't run the company without her. I think Elle's in love with him, but he doesn't see her that way."

Kate grinned. "They need my matchmaking services."

Zach invaded her space. She held her ground.

"No. Leave it alone," he said.

"I'm a successful matchmaker. I fixed up my brother Dave with his wife, and they're very happy. And I got Graceann and Jake together. All it took was a little dare."

"No matchmaking. Keep to the plan. Okay?"

Kate sidled away from him. "We'll see." Before he had a chance to respond, she said, "What will happen to Elle if your dad loses the company?"

"She'll be let go. I hope she's got some savings. I'll do everything I can to make sure Elle and the other employees don't lose their jobs."

"You've got your work cut out for you, going by the characters here." She touched fingers to her lips. "I'm sorry. I shouldn't have said such a catty thing."

"I share your assessment of them. Don't worry. I'd better get to my bed. Sweet dreams, Kate."

You, too. She mouthed the words as he walked away.

CHAPTER NINE

*Z*ach punched his pillow and scrunched down into the sofa, but sleep eluded him. The past forty-eight hours had caught up with him. He had a wife, the sexy, alluring reason for his insomnia. He should have hired an unknown actress for the part, a woman he didn't find so wildly attractive.

Kate had a raw, natural beauty that made his pulse race. No other woman threatened his self-control like her. To hold her at arm's length, over the years, he sparred with her whenever he was in her company. Other times, he pretended to ignore her. A psychiatrist would have a field day with that.

Kate trusted too easily, which was why that bastard of an ex-fiancé could break her heart. She deserved better. Someone better than Zach Lyon with his trust issues.

He'd learned early most people hid dark secrets. Charming to your face while twisting the knife in your back. Like the ones trying to oust his dad. He should walk away and let the chips fall where they may. Zach had given up on winning the old man's love. Yet, he didn't want his father to lose the company he'd worked so hard to build.

With a groan of frustration, Zach fluffed his pillow and

turned to his side, then adjusted the blanket around his neck, keeping out the draft from the air conditioner. His mind wouldn't shut up. He wondered if he'd get any sleep this night.

Faint moonlight peeked past the shades and gilded the room. The quiet settled around him. He began to relax, but the squeak of the mattress in the bedroom brought him fully awake. Erotic images of Kate filled him.

For this role, she'd transformed into a sleek sophisticate, a fitting wife for the prestigious Lyon clan. Kate, with her unruly black curls, innate kindness, and laughing brown eyes flecked with gold, made him yearn for something more than money and power. He suspected Kate would like the real man he kept hidden, the man who craved love and acceptance.

She'd never have a chance to see that man and his vulnerabilities.

He punched his pillow again, fighting his desire to go into the other room, to take Kate into his arms and bury his face in her flower-scented hair, to hold her close.

With pictures of Kate drifting through his consciousness, Zach finally fell to sleep.

* * *

SUNLIGHT PUSHED through the drapes in the bedroom and teased Kate's eyes open. Stretching, she sighed, loving the sensation of the sun's warmth on her face. Fully awake now, she picked up her phone on the night table. Only eight. Groaning, she set down the phone and closed her eyes, hoping to catch a few more zzz's after a restless night. Zach had populated her dreams with images of his full, sexy lips doing naughty things to her. Her body stirred in places she preferred not to think about. She shifted uncomfortably, trying to dislodge the desire that whipped through her.

A loud knock on the outer door to the hall had her scrambling to sit up. What the…?

"Mr. and Mrs. Lyon. Breakfast," called a female voice.

At the soft rap on the bedroom door, Kate flew out of bed and grabbed her silk robe from the loveseat. Tying the robe, she opened to Zach, clad in his t-shirt and boxers and holding the pillow and blanket he'd used on the sofa.

"The maid is outside with breakfast," he said softly. "We can't let her know I slept on the sofa."

"Let me have those and go let in the maid."

"Yes, ma'am." He saluted her.

At a second knock on the outer door, Zach shouted, "Just a minute."

Kate closed the bedroom door and threw Zach's blanket and pillow in the closet. She headed into the bathroom. She came out to another rap on the bedroom door and opened it.

"Breakfast is in the sitting room," Zach said. "I need to use the bathroom, then I'll join you." His gaze drifted over her.

She tightened the sash on her robe and went into the other room. A white cloth draped over the table in front of the sofa. The table was set with carafes, delicate china cups, and plates covered with silver lids. She sat on the sofa and poured cups of coffee for her and Zach.

He came into the room and sat on the flowered chair facing her. "Morning, Princess."

Kate glared at him and poured cream in her coffee. Cradling the cup, she sipped and released a contented sigh. Nothing tasted as good as that first sip of coffee in the morning.

Zach, a bemused expression on his face, watched her. "Not a morning person, I see." He removed the silver lids covering the food to show perfectly scrambled eggs, bacon, and grilled tomatoes. A separate plate held buttered toast. Kate's stomach voiced its hunger with a loud growl. Zach chuckled. She shot him another glare, provoking a grin from him.

They ate in silence. When Kate finished, she settled back, her hands wrapped around her coffee cup. "We need to talk."

Eyebrows raised, Zach looked up from pouring himself coffee. Setting the carafe down, he stirred cream into his drink. "You don't waste time. Talk about what?"

"I need to know some things so I can play my role."

He drank his coffee and studied her. Setting down the cup, he asked, "What do you want to know?"

She pushed her empty cup away and leaned forward, her hands on her knees. "You could cut the friction between you and your father with a knife. Why the dislike?"

Releasing an audible breath, Zach glanced away, and she thought he wouldn't answer. Finally, he focused his attention on her again. "I have memories of him holding me and playing ball with me. When my mother and brother died, he changed. He couldn't stand to be near me."

"Zach, I'm so sorry. You don't look like your dad. Do you look like your mom?"

"I favor my mom, but I've got my dad's build. I've wondered if my dad loved her so much that looking at me reminded him of all he lost. My brother looked exactly like Dad. Harper was sixteen when he died. Dad adored him. Harper was the golden boy. I wasn't."

"Have you ever been to therapy?"

"No. Are you saying I need it?"

"Probably, but most of us could use a few sessions with a good therapist. Have you tried to talk to your dad about the way he treats you?"

"Let it go, Kate."

She settled back. "All right. Down to business. How do you want me to handle your dad?"

"Be cordial and don't let his attitude get to you."

"I can do cordial. I appreciate your telling me this and also filling me in about Ava." Kate studied him. "Surprising you didn't stay with her. I would think she'd be perfect for you. She's tall, blonde, beautiful, sophisticated, wealthy. Just your type."

He flinched. "Is that how you see me?"

"Isn't that how everyone sees you?"

He smoothed fingers over his short hair. "I guess." His features tight, he leaned closer. "Things aren't always what they seem."

"What does that mean?"

"Forget it. Let's get dressed. I'll be with my dad and the other men all morning in Morgan's office. It may be the holidays but business goes on."

"One more thing. Tell me about Tripp and Missy Hunter."

"He's a first-class asshole. Grew up with money. Thinks the world owes him. He and I started at Star Ventures at the same time. We've been competing ever since. He and Morgan have pretty much edged me out."

"What about Missy?" Kate asked.

"Grew up with money, too. She's as ruthless as he is and will do anything to push her husband along." Disgust reflected in Zach's eyes. "Missy will do anything, including overlooking his dalliances with other women."

Kate shivered. "Thanks for the skinny on everyone. I get why you want to save your dad's company. What I don't get is why a guy who looks like you, with your money, couldn't find a woman to marry you without having to pay her."

He grinned, showing even white teeth and a faint dimple in his cheek. "You think I'm hot?"

"I didn't say that."

His grin got wider. "I know that's what you meant. We'll talk about how hot you think I am later." His grass-green eyes darkened and he touched a finger to her lips. "As for the contract marriage, I have my reasons."

CHAPTER TEN

*J*uliette threaded her arm through Kate's as the women strolled the sprawling grounds after lunch. Kate hadn't seen Zach since breakfast. The men, still closeted in Morgan's office, had taken their noon meal there. Missy and Ava had gone shopping that morning and hadn't returned. Not seeing those two was fine with Kate. She enjoyed Juliette's continual chatter. The young woman's exuberance was catching.

The Morgan estate covered several acres landscaped with lush greenery, maintained by a sprinkler system that could rival a medium-sized city's water supply. Cactus gardens provided little pops of real desert life. In the distance, brown mountains reached for the horizon.

They passed an Olympic-sized pool, sparkling blue in the sun, and surrounded by a grouping of chaises covered in colorful geometric prints.

"When it's not so chilly, we'll go swimming," Juliette said.

With a shiver, Kate pulled her sweater closer around her. She wore a new pink silk top, a hand-knit white sweater, jeans ripped just so by the designer, and kitten-heeled navy shoes. She missed her high-top sneakers, a better choice to traipse around the uneven terrain.

The faint whinny of a horse carried over the clear air. Both women stopped. Juliette slipped her arm from Kate's.

"Are we near the stables?" Kate asked.

"The stables are at the other end of the property. We're going to the garage now to ask Sky to drive us into the city."

"Sky? Oh, the chauffer Skylar who picked us up at the airport."

A dreamy look softened Juliette's face. "Sky's a great guy, so talented with cars. And sexy." She leaned closer. "I trust you, Kate. Can I share a secret?"

"Uh—sure."

"Sky and I are in love."

"That's sweet. Why is it a secret?"

Juliette chewed her lip. "If my father finds out, he'll fire Sky and ship me off to a convent in Italy." She rolled her eyes. "And Ava will be such a bitch."

Kate frowned. "Why would your father object? You're not a child. How old are you?"

"Twenty-one. I'm in my last year at college. My parents hope I'll marry some rich guy who will keep me in the luxury I'm used to." She scrunched up her face. "Rather keep them in the luxury *they're* used to. They keep throwing guys at me who are sons of their wealthy friends. Yuck."

"Don't be too harsh on your parents. They want you to have a comfortable life." Kate didn't want to get involved with any battle Juliette had with Gloria and Carlisle, but if Zach's assessment of the Morgans' financial situation was correct, their younger daughter had a good grasp of her parents' motives.

"Ava is actively on the hunt to marry money." Juliette's lips slanted in a sly smile. "She had her sights set on Zach. I'm glad he married you. Zach deserves someone as nice as you."

Warmed by Juliette's compliment, Kate smiled. "Thanks. I'll be sure to remind Zach how lucky he is to get me."

Juliette laughed. "You're both blessed."

Kate touched a finger to the corner of her mouth. "Let me get this straight. Your dad doesn't want you to be with Sky because he hasn't any money?"

"You got it. Sky isn't rich, not yet, but he's a genius at restoring cars, especially vintage ones. He's saving to buy his own place where he can work on them. There are lots of old cars here in the desert. I'm going to put my business degree to good use, helping him run things."

"Sounds like a solid plan."

"We've worked it all out. I helped him write up a business strategy."

They walked a little more and came to the garage, a wood and stucco building with five bays. Steps led up to the second floor, probably to an apartment where Kate assumed Sky lived.

A handsome young man, his dark hair cut short, was busy shining the black limo with a shammy. Kate recognized him as the chauffeur who'd driven Zach and her from the airport. He glanced up at their approach. His blue eyes lit and he dropped the cloth.

Juliette ran up to him, and he grabbed her in a hug, lifting her off the ground. The couple kissed as if they wanted to devour each other. Kate looked away in embarrassment but also with a pang of yearning. She'd always wanted that kind of passion with a man.

The couple drew apart, but Sky kept his arm around Juliette's waist. The love shining from their eyes ratcheted up the craving that tugged at Kate's heart. She pushed aside her own wants and let her matchmaking mode kick in. This couple deserved to be together, and she'd do all she could to help them.

"Kate, you remember Sky."

Kate held out her hand to shake his. "Nice to see you again."

"You also," he said in a deep voice with a trace of New England accent.

"My parents and sister call him Skylar, and I do, too, when they're around," Juliette said.

Kate smiled. "I'll call you Skylar when the others are near."

Juliette stretched to kiss Sky lightly on the lips. "Can you take us into the city, babe?"

"Anything for you."

"Kate and I need to change. We'll be ready in thirty minutes." Juliette jiggled her hips in a little dance. "We're going to party tonight."

Sky pulled her close again. "Remember who loves you."

"I could never forget."

For sure, Kate would help these two lovers. Although her own happy-ever-after seemed unlikely, she still loved a heart-warming romance.

CHAPTER ELEVEN

"Twenty-two wins," the croupier at the Augustus Casino announced as the roulette wheel stopped. He slid a stack of chips to Juliette.

Kate and Juliette high-fived each other. Kate put two chips, her winnings from an earlier game of blackjack, on Red 22 and let them ride. She took two glasses of wine from the cocktail waitress and handed one to Juliette.

Kate hadn't had this much fun since Graceann and Jake's wedding. Zach had been at the wedding, ignoring her when he wasn't teasing. His date, a Grace Kelly lookalike, was stunning, but he hadn't acted happy, and Kate wondered about it at the time. Since she'd gotten to know Zach better over the past few days, she now realized he'd probably been miserable keeping up the persona of a tabloid favorite.

Juliette put chips on Red 22 again. Her gaming expertise made Kate rethink her view of the young woman. Juliette was a shrewd gambler who knew how to keep her face blank. She'd had a successful run at blackjack, too, winning much more than Kate.

Kate shifted from foot to foot to relieve her screaming feet and calves. Walking and standing on stilettos made her crave a soothing foot soak. The only reason she'd played blackjack earlier was so she could sit. She pulled at the short skirt of her body-hugging beige sheath. Graceann had made her buy the dress, saying the color brought out the gold in Kate's eyes.

Juliette had insisted they dress sexy, to "get more respect and fool people into thinking we're a couple of ditzy broads." The gambit appeared to be working. The expressions on the faces of the dealers and other players when they realized Juliette's shrewdness made Kate smile over the rim of her wine glass.

Cheers went up from the others crowding around them on the casino floor when Juliette's number won again. She and Kate raked in their winnings. Kate's feet shrieked louder. Finally, after two rare non-winning spins, Juliette gathered up her chips and declared her wagering over for the night. Kate had lost the little amount she'd played. She'd never appreciated why people loved gambling, being of the mind she'd rather have something tangible, like a designer bag, to show for her money.

"Let's cash these in," Juliette said. "Then we'll treat ourselves to an expensive meal and a bottle of this joint's best wine. I'll call Sky and invite him to have dinner with us. He must be tired of waiting in that parking garage with only the other drivers for company."

"That's fine with me. He should have been with us this whole time."

"He didn't want to intrude on our girls' night out. Is he the best, or what?"

"He's a cool guy." Kate slipped her arm through the other woman's. "How did you learn to gamble like that? You'd give James Bond a run for his money."

Juliette laughed. "I am pretty good, aren't I? I grew up here in Vegas. We had a driver I called Uncle Louie. Uncle Louie was into a lot of unsavory things. I don't think Dad knew. Louie taught me poker, blackjack, and roulette. He said I was a natural."

Her throbbing calves forgotten, Kate burst out laughing. "You have the face of an angel and the soul of a backroom card shark."

"Thanks for the compliment."

After a meal of steak, shrimp, and more wine, the women and Sky, who hadn't had any alcohol, headed to the casino's garage and the limo. A while later, they pulled up to the Morgan house. Sky dropped Kate off at the front door, while the two lovers stayed in the car and kissed goodnight. Kate entered the house on unsteady, too-much-wine legs. Gripping the black wrought iron railing, she climbed the stairs to the room she shared with Zach.

He set down the book he'd been reading and stood when she came into the room. Wearing faded jeans, worn low on his hips, and a black T-shirt that stretched across his muscled chest, he was swoon-worthy for sure.

Her attention on his scrumptiousness, she tripped on the area rug. She would have fallen if he hadn't caught her.

"Steady there." His low voice rumbled in her ears. "I don't have to ask if you had a good time. I can see you did." Still holding onto her, he scanned her, then let out a low whistle. "You are really sexy in that dress. How many men hit on you?"

A thrill shot through her at the edginess in his voice. "A few. You jealous?"

"You *are* my wife."

"Don't worry. None of the men were as luscious as you."

Surprise flashed across Zach's features and he took a half-step back. "How much did you drink anyway?"

Kate curled her arms around his neck. "Enough to know you're yummy." She pressed closer and kissed him.

Zach slanted his lips over hers, hungry and urgent, consuming her in his heat. Groaning softly, she opened her mouth to his hot invasion. Electricity zinged through her at his deliciousness. He tasted like mint and something sugary. This was one sugar rush she wanted to go on forever.

After several passion-filled minutes, he pulled away and rested his forehead on hers, their ragged breathing the only sounds in the room.

Grasping her shoulders, he gently pushed away. "I'd better get you to bed."

"You coming with me?"

"Not tonight."

"Zach." She released his name on a breathless sigh. "I wanna make love with you."

His eyes teased. "Hold that thought. We'll see what the morning brings."

* * *

KATE BLINKED against the onslaught of sunlight and turned away from the brightness. Nausea made bile rise in her throat. Her head pounded. With slow, deliberate movements, she pulled herself up and leaned against the bed's headboard. Rubbing her temples, she glanced around. The clothes she'd worn to the casino were folded neatly on a chair. She was clad in only her white lace bra and panties.

"Oh, God," she whimpered. Memories of the night before raced at her. Gambling, drinking, falling into Zach's arms. Begging him to make love to her. And that kiss. The man could kiss.

Moaning, she closed her eyes. She'd initiated the kiss, and had wanted more. She wiped sweat from her brow.

The creak of the door made her turn quickly. Bad idea. The room spun. She pressed a hand to her head. Zach, in jeans and a gray T-shirt, entered, carrying a tray with a carafe, a cup, a covered plate, and a pitcher of ice water with a glass.

"'Morning, sunshine," he said.

"Ugh. Stop being so cheerful."

Laughing, he set the tray on the nightstand next to the bed. "I forgot you're not a morning person."

If she had the energy, she'd throw a pillow at him to wipe away his mischievous grin.

"I brought coffee, toast, and aspirin." He held up a bottle of the pills. "I didn't think you'd be up to anything more."

"The thought of food makes me sick."

"Try to get something down. Do you want me to pour you some coffee?"

Kate clutched the sheet closer. "I can do it."

His sexy grin made her skin tingle. "It's not like I haven't seen you almost naked."

She squeezed her eyes shut. "Oh, God." Slowly, she opened her eyes again. "You're still here."

Chuckling, he poured a glass of water from the pitcher and set it on the tray. "You want some aspirin before I go downstairs for breakfast?"

"I'll take some if I need it."

"I'll check in on you in a little while. You sure you're okay by yourself?"

She nodded, then pressed a palm to her head. "I want to die."

He brushed hair back from her face and placed a tender kiss on her forehead. "No one dies on my watch."

Turning, he walked out, closing the door quietly behind him.

She pressed against the headboard and closed her eyes. Zach Lyon, her arch enemy, had undressed her and taken care of her. If she let up her guard around him, she feared he'd suck her into his rarefied orbit. She did fine without all these trappings of wealth, thank you very much.

CHAPTER TWELVE

*Z*ach walked into the dining room and suppressed a groan when he saw Ava, the only one in the room, having breakfast. He pivoted on his heel, anxious to escape.

"Zach! Come have breakfast with me."

He plastered a smile on his face and entered the room.

Smiling, she gestured for him to join her at the long white-clothed table. This early in the morning, she was expertly made up with her blonde hair falling in perfect waves past her shoulders. Her white sweater stretched over her surgically improved breasts. At one time, he'd thought her beautiful.

"Sit next to me, Zach. We have lots of catching up to do," she purred.

"'Morning, Ava."

He grabbed a plate from the buffet server and filled it with scrambled eggs, bacon, sausage, and fried potatoes.

The Morgans' cook, Florence, came into the room. "Toast or bagel, Mr. Lyon?"

"Toast, but I'll get it."

"You sit and enjoy your meal." She picked up the coffee pot and filled a mug, then handed it to Zach.

He took a seat at the other end of the table and set his food and drink down, then stirred cream into his coffee, spending more time than needed.

"You are sexier than ever," Ava said. "Life has been treating you well."

"You could say that," he managed between forkfuls of egg.

"I've missed you. I thought we were friends, but when you didn't stop by my SoHo apartment last month, I figured you were too busy with your *model du jour*." Her blue eyes turned frosty. "Guess I was wrong."

"Guess so." He sipped coffee and tried to enjoy his breakfast.

"You surprised us all by getting married. Awfully sudden, wasn't it?"

"When you find the *one*, why wait?"

Ava's collagen-enlarged lips tightened into a straight line. "I didn't think you were a *one*-woman man. Kate doesn't look like your type."

He put down his fork. "What's my type?"

She gave a toss of her golden hair. "Tall, blonde, sophisticated."

"Like you? We tried dating. It didn't work out. We both moved on."

"How did you and Kate meet?"

Ava's softly-spoken words didn't hide the belligerent edge to her tone. The fine hair on his arms stood up. He would have to watch Ava. He'd seen her vindictive side when they were a couple. He had no doubt she'd undermine his plans and hurt Kate if she could.

Forcing a pleasant smile, he used the story he and Kate had concocted. "We met at a gallery opening in Manhattan. Kate's interested in art, especially silkscreens." They'd agreed they wouldn't reveal she was an actor. When she'd mentioned she had an interest in silkscreens, they'd decided to go with that.

Ava shrugged. "Art bores me. What does Kate do for a living?"

He sipped coffee before answering. "She has a lot of charitable projects. Her grandmother's trust fund is plenty to live on."

Hiding his grin, he bit into a piece of toast. Kate had liked the idea of being a trust-fund baby and thought she could have fun with the role. By the way Ava's face paled, she swallowed their little lie.

"I hear Kate and Juliette spent yesterday at the casinos," Ava said.

He nodded and concentrated on his food.

"I would think Kate would want to spend more time with her new husband rather than traipsing around the Strip with my little sister."

The venom in Ava's voice froze him with his coffee mug halfway to his mouth. He calmly finished his drink, gathering his thoughts. "Kate is an independent woman, and your sister is a charmer. Kate's here for me when I need her."

Laying aside his napkin, he stood, gave Ava a curt nod, and left.

* * *

By lunchtime, Kate felt human enough to face the world and the other party guests. Dressed in skinny jeans, torn in all the right places, and a hand knitted red sweater, and wearing a pair of red Converse sneakers, Zach and everyone be damned, she needed to make an appearance for lunch but doubted she'd eat much.

She reached for the doorknob when the door opened. She backpedaled. Zach stood in the doorway, his face registering the same surprise she knew must be on hers. His gaze skimmed her, slowly, deliberately. She understood the cliché of undressing a person with one's eyes. A rush of pleasure surged through her.

"You're better? You look amazing," he rasped.

"Almost normal." She swallowed in a vain effort to still her racing heart. "You were gone awhile. That was a long breakfast. I was on my way to lunch." She was babbling.

He grimaced and stepped into the room, shutting the door. "Tripp cornered me as I left the dining room. He and Carlisle wanted to run something business related by me. They really think I'll fall for their pretense of caring my opinion counts."

"I'm glad you're on to them. Are we going to lunch? I don't have much of an appetite, but I should go."

He nodded. "In a minute. We need to talk."

"Why does that sound ominous?"

"It's not. Let's sit." He headed toward the sitting area.

Kate followed and sat on the sofa, with Zach in the upholstered chair facing her.

"What's up?" she asked.

"I had breakfast with Ava."

"That must have been fun." Kate chewed her lip. She hadn't meant to sound so smart-ass.

He laughed. "It was as much fun as you can imagine." He sat forward, his palms on his thighs. "Ava mentioned she thought it odd you, a newlywed, would spend the day with her sister rather than your new husband."

"Wait a minute." Kate held up a hand. "First, it's none of Ava's business, and second, you were working all day. What was I supposed to do? Stand outside the office and look forlorn?"

"Of course not."

He ran his hand over his hair, provoking a sudden urge in her to touch his hair and see if it was as soft as it looked.

"Ava made me realize something," he said. "We're putting on this charade to help my dad and his company. You and I have to put on a better show of being in love."

"And that means…?"

"We need to act like two people who can't stand being apart. No more going off with Juliette, or anyone, unless I'm with you."

She started to protest then stopped. "Ordinarily I wouldn't like being told whom I can and cannot see, but this isn't an ordinary time. We have a deal, and I'm playing a role. I'll do whatever it takes to convince the others we're for real."

He smiled. "Thanks for understanding. It's only for a little while. I want you to enjoy yourself, as much as possible with this crowd, for the short time we're here. I have to convince my dad we're in love and I've changed. I don't want people to suspect anything."

She recognized the pain and the trace of fear in Zach's eyes. This man had complexities she'd yet to understand. "I know my lines. I'll be a perfect little wife, so in love with my husband."

He leveled his gaze at her. "Why do I get the feeling I may be sorry I brought this up?"

She laughed to hide her inner confusion. "Let's go to lunch. Time to raise the curtain on Act Two."

CHAPTER THIRTEEN

"There she is now." Juliette's voice carried through the quiet dining room when Kate and Zach entered. Everyone turned. A slow burn began at Kate's neck and spread to her face. She might be an actor, but she hated making an entrance like this, with all eyes on her, and some hostile.

Zach held her hand and led her to the two empty chairs, pulling one out for her. She sat gingerly, not wanting to upset her not-so-stable stomach.

Juliette gave Kate a sympathetic smile. "You okay? I was a little hung over myself."

Sitting nearby, Missy and Ava snickered.

"Too much partying on the Strip will do that," Ava said. "Are you trying to corrupt my little sister, Kate?"

"Grow up, Ava." Juliette, seated next to Kate, touched her hand. "We had a fun time together yesterday shopping and eating. And drinking."

Juliette's eyes held a warning. Kate nodded slightly, letting the other woman know she wouldn't give away her secret that Juliette could gamble like a professional on a Mississippi riverboat.

Kate accepted a bowl of mixed salad from Florence and

grabbed a warm roll from the basket in front of her. The others were on the second course of baked pasta. Kate nibbled on the bread and ignored the salad.

"I had fun yesterday," Kate said. "But I missed my Zachary." She rested her head on Zach's shoulder and gave him what she hoped was an adoring look.

Shock flashed over his features before he composed himself. "I missed you too, *pumpkin*."

Pumpkin? She rubbed his arm. "I don't care how much work you have to do, I'm not leaving your side again. I can't abide it when we're apart."

He patted her hand where it rested on his arm. "I can't stand being apart from you, *pumpkin*."

"That's all you girls did? Shopping?" Gloria's words broke up Zach and Kate's little act.

Juliette waved her fork. "Don't forget the eating and drinking."

"Sounds too touristy to me." Ava went back to her meal.

"Me, too," Missy said, her brown eyes hard as a lump of coal.

"Whatever." Juliette shrugged.

Shivers ran up Kate's arms. She set down her fork and looked across the table to find Zach's father watching her, a challenge in his pale blue eyes. A smart man, he may have seen through Zach and Kate's performance.

Kate declined anything else to eat and sipped her iced tea. Conversations swirled around her, but she tried to tune them out. The other women gossiped while the men talked business. Elle sat quietly beside Greg Lyon. Kate studied the older woman. Occasionally Elle would respond to something Zach's dad said. Each time she looked at him with the adoration Kate had faked with Zach. Interesting. Zach said Elle was in love with his dad. Observant of Zach.

Near her, Zach and Tripp were talking business. She recognized the controlled anger in Zach's voice. Having met Tripp and Missy, Kate better understood Zach's worries.

"Tell us a little about yourself, Kate."

Ava's voice startled Kate out of her reverie. The room grew silent. The whole table focused on her.

She smiled, gathering her lines, the way her acting coaches had taught her. "I was raised on the Main Line, outside Philadelphia." She repeated the story she and Zach had come up with. They wanted the others to believe she'd been brought up in the rarified world of old money. If they knew the truth—that she was from a small town in the Pocono Mountains, they'd look down on her. She loved Spirit Lake and didn't care what the others might think, but Zach hired her to play a part and she'd earn her money.

Elle's eyes softened. "Oh, the Main Line. Beautiful place. I went to college near there." Kate instinctively knew she could trust Elle.

"You must know the Vanderkellans," Gloria said. "I've known them for years."

Kate fought to keep her expression blank. "The name's familiar, but I don't personally know them. Maybe my parents do."

Zach squeezed her knee. Encouragement?

Carlisle turned his attention to Kate, his calculating eyes putting her on guard.

"Strange you don't know the Vanderkellans," he said. "They're active in charitable projects in the Philadelphia area."

"I've been away at school and traveling."

"You don't have a Main Line accent," Ava said.

Missy snickered.

"Ava, you wouldn't know a Main Line accent if it bit you on the ass," Juliette said.

Gloria glared at her daughter. "Juliette, watch your mouth."

Missy leaned forward, her face displaying more animation than Kate had seen. "How did you and Zach meet?"

"I'd like to know that myself," Greg said, his expression tight.

"Cute story." Kate got into her role. "We met at a gallery opening several years ago. Silkscreens, an obsession of mine." She sighed and gave Zach another adoring look. "It was raining and I didn't have an umbrella. I stepped out of a cab and my Zachary was there with an umbrella, shielding me from the rain, and we'd never met before. Such a gentleman."

Zach kissed the top of her head. "I'm not stupid. I saw a beautiful woman who needed to stay dry. I took advantage of that fact to meet her. We were between relationships, and neither of us was ready for another one, but after that first meet, we'd run into each other at different social events and we became friends. A few months ago, we realized our friendship had evolved into love. We couldn't wait any longer to get married. Isn't that right, sweetheart?"

"Right, honey." Kate batted her eyelashes at him. Playing the adoring wife was more fun than she'd imagined.

"Sounds like the plot of one of those sappy Hallmark movies." Disdain dripped from Ava's voice.

Kate placed her hand over Zach's on the table. "Our love isn't sappy, is it?"

"How about dessert?" Gloria signaled Florence to take the plates away.

Kate, on sugar overload from her saccharin posturing toward Zach, didn't know if she could handle dessert.

"Do you ride, Kate?" Ava asked.

"Of course." She'd been on a horse once, and it hadn't ended well, but weren't people from the Main Line part of the horsey set?

"We plan to go riding after lunch," Juliette said.

Missy patted her belly. "I can't go."

"Obviously," Ava said.

"My wife's a talented rider." Zach brought Kate's hand to his lips for a tender kiss. "I think Kate might be too tired after the exhausting day she had yesterday, right, sweetheart?"

Kate yawned. "I am a little tired."

"Me, too," Juliette said. "I'll stay here."

"You don't have to stay for me." Kate snuggled against Zach. "My wonderful husband will keep me company."

He bent and touched her lips in a whisper-soft kiss. "Of course, darling."

Zach's dad cleared his throat. "Zach, we need to come to a decision on the Greenwald contract. We planned to discuss it while we rode. I guess you're more interested in your *wife* than the company."

Alarm bells went off in Kate's head. Maybe they'd poured on the love act a little too thick. She turned to Zach. "Your dad needs you. You should go riding with the others. I'll be fine here."

* * *

"*ZACHARY*?"

"*Pumpkin*?"

Alone in the library, Kate and Zach squared off.

He'd told the others he'd be along shortly, but wanted to help Kate pick out a book.

Zach studied her as she stood before him, arms folded across her chest. Her stylish jeans hugged her curves in all the right places, and her red sweater showed off her perfect breasts. He wanted to kiss her senseless.

"We piled it on a little thick in there," he said.

"Ya think?" She shot him a saucy grin. "You wanted me to be a lovesick newlywed. Just acting my part."

"You're very convincing, if a little over-the-top." He stepped closer to her as a wave of sadness washed over him. "No one has called me Zachary since my mom."

Kate put a hand to her throat. "I'm sorry. I didn't know. I

remembered seeing your full name on the marriage certificate and wanted to use it. I hope I didn't open old wounds for you and your father."

"Don't worry about it." To lighten the mood, he gave her a teasing grin. "I'd rather stay here with you than go riding with that group of stuffed shirts. I can think of lots of things we can do to pass the time. Married people things."

With a hand on his chest, she pushed him away. "Not on your life."

When she looked at him with those big brown eyes, like melted chocolate and caramel, he wanted to pull her into his arms and make wild love to her. *Down, boy. Kate is right.*

She tapped her foot. "*Pumpkin?* Seriously? Honey. Sweetheart. They're fine, but much as I love pumpkin lattes, I don't want to be called one."

He laughed. "Duly noted."

Kate tilted her head toward him. "I have the suspicion your dad saw through our wretched little performance."

"Wouldn't surprise me. He's sharp. Pick out a book. I don't want to keep the others waiting, although I'm not looking forward to discussing business from the back of a horse."

"Your dad wanted to include you. A hopeful sign."

"That surprised me. My plan is working already."

She grinned. "Score one for my acting chops. Maybe we weren't so pathetic after all." Still smiling, she perused the shelves.

"If there's a book you want on a higher shelf, I can get it for you." Zach folded his arms across his chest and enjoyed the way Kate's firm butt filled out her jeans. The concentration on her expressive face made him want to grab her to him and kiss those inviting lips. His own jeans got a little tighter.

"I found a cozy mystery on the third shelf. I can reach it." She stretched her arm toward the book and lost her balance.

Zach grabbed her, steadying her. She turned in his arms. She blinked her big brown eyes and licked her lips. He suppressed a groan. He ran his palms down her arms to her fingertips.

"Why are you looking at me like that?" Her voice was unsteady.

"You're so damn sexy, especially when you're concentrating hard to find a book."

"You don't have to perform when we're alone." She didn't move away.

"This is no performance." He skimmed a finger over her lips. Her eyes darkened. He bent toward her.

She pulled back and held up her hand. "Can you please get that book for me?"

* * *

KATE STRETCHED on a chaise by the pool and absorbed the Las Vegas sunshine, her unopened book beside her. She wore her jeans and a sweater, but held her face to the sun. Born and bred in the mountains of the East, no matter how many winters she'd spent with Graceann in California, she still marveled at having warmth in December.

She breathed in the flower-scented air, grateful she hadn't had to go riding with Zach and the others. Jealousy, surprising and swift, zapped her. Ava was in the riding group. No doubt the scheming blonde wanted to dig her claws into Zach again.

Kate touched her lips. Zach had wanted to kiss her when they were in the library. She'd wanted his kiss. She had to be careful not to let her guard down when they were alone.

"Mind if I join you?"

Kate sat up and shaded her eyes. Elle, in loose-fitting jeans and a boxy long-sleeved top, her feet in moccasins, and wearing sunglasses that might have been trendy in 1950, stood looking down at her.

Kate smiled. "Please do."

Elle settled into a chaise beside Kate.

"Save room for me." Juliette bounced onto the patio, wearing huge designer sunglasses, shorts, and a T-shirt, and plopped down on a lounge on Kate's other side.

Kate glanced toward the doorway. "Is Missy coming?"

Juliette scrunched up her nose. "I invited her although she always looks like she's sucking on a lemon, but she said she wanted to watch TV."

Kate turned to the older woman. "I thought you went riding with the others, Elle."

"Oh, no, I had work to do for Greg. I'm not usually invited to social gatherings unless I'm needed to take notes."

The wistfulness in Elle's voice tugged at Kate. "We're glad you're here."

Henry came out to the patio. "Would you ladies like something to drink?"

"Iced tea would be good," Elle said.

Juliette waved a finger at Elle. "A girls' party needs something more potent than iced tea. Margaritas, please, Henry."

"Of course, miss." He turned and left.

Elle fidgeted. "I don't drink a lot of alcohol. I get silly when I do."

"You deserve to be silly once in a while," Juliette said.

An hour later, sunbathing forgotten, the women sat at a table on the patio, a striped umbrella shading them. A second pitcher of margaritas sat before them. Kate sipped from her glass, her first. She had no stomach for alcohol today.

Elle, on her third glass of the sweet drink, had let down her rigid guard with each swallow. She licked her lips. "I never knew margaritas could be so delicious."

Juliette laughed. "Stick with us and we'll show you a crazy time."

"I don't remember the last time I had fun," Elle answered softly.

Kate pushed her glass away and focused on Elle. She hoped this kind woman could help her better understand the dynamics between Zach and his dad. Kate ignored the little voice that whispered she wanted to know more about Zach. Period. "Elle, Zach says you've worked for his dad for a lot of years."

Elle slipped off her sunglasses and met Kate's gaze. "Almost thirty years. I started right out of college."

Kate studied her. Elle's flawless skin would be the envy of many younger women. Her gray eyes held intelligence and warmth. Her pale blonde hair, cut short in no discernable style, did little to highlight her amazing cheekbones.

"I guess you like working for Greg," Juliette said.

Elle stared into the distance. "I do."

"You started working for him before Zach's mother died, right?" Kate said.

Elle nodded.

Kate ran a finger over the rivulets on her glass. "What was she like?"

"Mimi Lyon was a great beauty. I understand many wealthy and prominent men pursued her. Mr. Lyon's business hadn't taken off yet, and he couldn't compete with those successful men, but he and Mimi were crazy about each other. When she died, he was devastated."

Sadness shadowed Elle's eyes. "Their older son, Harper, died with her in the skiing accident. Greg worshipped that boy. He was only sixteen. Greg changed after that."

"He still had one son, and Zach was eight," Kate said. "I'm sure he needed his dad."

Elle shook her head and looked down at the table. "Greg shipped Zach away to boarding school soon after it happened. I think looking at Zach reminded him of all he'd lost. Zach is the image of Mimi." She glanced up and pressed a hand to her throat. "Please don't repeat anything I've said."

"Don't worry. We won't say anything." Kate leaned closer.

"Zach was an eight-year-old boy whose mother just died, and his father sent him away?"

"Yes."

The image of Zach, a frightened little boy mourning his mother and older brother, and rejected by his father filled Kate's eyes with tears.

Elle frowned. "Zach never told you?"

"Just a little. He doesn't like to talk about himself. The day his mom and brother died, he lost his dad, too."

Juliette shook her head. "That's sad. Greg never remarried?"

Elle's features tightened. "No, but he's had lots of girlfriends, never anyone serious. He's got a new girlfriend, a redhead about Zach's age. I'm surprised he didn't bring her on this trip." Resentment colored Elle's voice. She tossed back her drink and poured another.

Kate pushed aside the pitcher. "Margaritas go down too easy. I'm taking a break."

Elle snorted. "I've spent my whole life going easy, doing the right thing. And where has it gotten me?"

Juliette and Kate exchanged glances.

Henry came out to the pool, and Elle signaled him for more.

"You're in love with Mr. Lyon, aren't you?" Kate touched Elle's arm.

Elle's eyes widened. "I fell in love with him the day I came to work for him. I'm only his assistant. His wife and his mistresses have all been beautiful, glamorous women. I'm so plain, I'm invisible to him."

Kate grabbed Elle's hand and squeezed. "You're not plain at all. Don't put yourself down. Your hair is very pretty, you have cheekbones most women would die for, and you're tall, slim, and elegant."

"If you love him, go get him," Juliette said.

"What do you mean?" Elle asked.

Juliette chewed her lip. "You said you aren't invited to social gatherings. Does that mean you're not going to the big gala tomorrow at Mel Ableman's?"

"I'm going for a little while. Greg and Mr. Morgan plan to meet with Mr. Ableman during the party about a joint business venture. I have to take notes."

Juliette tilted her head, studying Elle. "What do you plan to wear?"

Kate frowned at Juliette. "What are you thinking?"

With a sly smile, Juliette said, "Wait for it."

Giving the other women a confused look, Elle said, "My usual black dress, the one I wear to all black-tie affairs."

"And this dress is conservative?" Kate asked.

"Same as all my clothes."

Grinning, Kate met Juliette's gaze. "Elle looks to be about your size."

Juliette snapped her fingers. "You got where I'm going. I have something that will be perfect for Elle."

Excitement gathered in Kate's stomach. "I'll apply her makeup and fix her hair."

Elle waved her hand in front of the others. "I'm right here, ladies. I can guess at what you're planning, and no, I can't do that."

"You'll be Cinderella at the ball," Kate said. "I've got a rep as a matchmaker. Mr. Lyon will really see you for the first time. Some men need a nudge."

Fear raced over Elle's face. "I couldn't."

"Don't worry about a thing," Kate said. "Juliette and I will make you the belle of the ball."

Juliette chuckled. "Elle the Belle."

Elle's eyes widened. "You think so?"

"Definitely." Invigorated with her new matchmaking mission, Kate slipped on her sunglasses and leaned back. Maybe if Mr. Lyon found happiness, he'd be kinder to Zach. A win-win.

CHAPTER FOURTEEN

*I*n Elle's room the night of the Ableman ball, Kate put the finishing touches on the older woman's makeup. Not an easy task with a fidgeting Elle.

"This is a mistake. I can't do this. It's not me." Elle wiggled in her chair.

"Elle, you are beautiful, and I'm finished." Kate stood back to admire her work. "I did a terrific job, if I do say so, but then I had your fabulous bone structure to work with." Kate swung the chair around so Elle could see her reflection in the vanity mirror.

"Wow!" Juliette came into the room with several dresses over her arm. "You have a classic, elegant beauty, Elle. Every man at the ball will salivate over you."

"I only want one man," Elle said softly.

Juliette turned to Kate. "You're a genius with hair and makeup."

"Thanks." Kate had become adept at doing her own hair and makeup because the small dinner theaters where she played couldn't afford professional hairdressers or makeup artists.

Elle put up a hand to gently touch her hair. "So different, but stylish."

Kate had swept it back from Elle's face into a sophisticated short style that would pass muster in Manhattan's trendiest clubs.

"Time for the dress," Juliette said. "Come see what I have."

Elle selected a sapphire blue beaded ankle-skimming number. Kate and Juliette helped her into the dress. Juliette zipped it up the back, then she and Kate stepped away.

Kate took Elle by the shoulders. "Turn around. Look in the full-length mirror."

Turning slowly to ooh's and aah's from the other women, Elle's eyes widened when she saw her reflection. "I can't believe that's me."

"You are stunning," Kate said. "That color makes your eyes blue. Mr. Lyon won't know what hit him."

Elle smoothed a hand down her dress. "Are you sure I look okay? Maybe he won't like it."

"What's not to like?" Juliette asked.

"What if he fires me?"

Kate waved a hand. "He needs you too much to let you go." *If Zach isn't successful in helping his dad keep the business, you may not have a job anyway.* The thought interrupted Kate's happy mood. She glanced at the bedside clock. "I need to get dressed. The cars will be here soon."

Good thing she'd showered and done everything other than put on her gown, she thought as she hurried down the hall to the room she shared with Zach.

When she slipped through the door, he stood there, dressed in a tux. He looked down at his Rolex and back to her. "Where were you?"

"I was with Juliette and Elle."

"You're up to something. What is it?"

"Nothing."

"Don't flash those innocent big browns at me. I want you to enjoy yourself, but don't forget why we're here."

"I might have found a way to help you, among other things."

"What? Never mind. The cars will be here in fifteen minutes."

"I just have to put on my dress." Although rushed, she couldn't stop herself from checking him out. He looked hot in his tux, like someone who'd stepped out of a fashion magazine. The suit fit him perfectly and enhanced the width of his shoulders and his trim waist. His blond hair, longer now, was combed back, emphasizing his sculpted features.

He frowned. "What? Do you need help getting dressed?"

"No, I'm good." Kate went into the bedroom and shut the door behind her. She quickly undressed down to her red lace bra and panties, then went to the walk-in closet, pulled out the red silk gown, and slipped it over her head.

The soft fabric against her flesh sent warmth spiraling through her, almost orgasmic in its sensuality. For sure, she'd been too long without a man. She stretched out her right leg, exposed to the thigh through the slit in the gown. She'd never worn anything so racy in her life.

Touching her bare neck, she sighed. Her gold drama masks necklace would be perfect nestled between her cleavage. Her parents had given her the jewelry on her eighteenth birthday. She'd sold the heavy chain with the theatre masks charms to a pawn shop in Manhattan to help pay for the caterers for her cancelled wedding reception.

She had no time now to muse over the past. They had a ball to attend, and she had to hurry. She struggled with her dress's back zipper and gave up. "Zach, could you help me, please?"

Strolling into the room, he froze when he saw her and let out a low whistle. "You are sexy as hell. I'll have to fight off the men at the party."

"Zip me up. Please." She bit down on her lip, fighting the erotic pleasure his words provoked.

As he fastened the zipper, his fingers lightly brushed the bare skin of her back, sending thrills of excitement over her nerve endings. "I like the red bra." His soft breath tickled her ear. "We should stay in tonight."

When he settled his hands on her shoulders, she inhaled his unique scent. Her body, boneless and pliable, swayed closer, wanting to lean into him, to feel his arms wrapped around her. This was Zach, she reminded herself. Not her lover, not her boyfriend, her husband in name only.

Freeing herself from him and her own desires, she turned. "Don't get any ideas."

His eyes teased. "I have lots of ideas. We're newlyweds. If we don't show up tonight, the others will understand."

"I'm a talented actor, and you're paying me a ton of money. I know my role, in public. In private, keep your hands to yourself."

Grinning, he leaned closer. "I think you like me more than you want to admit."

"Let's go. The others are waiting."

He stared down at her feet. "Forget something?"

"My shoes." She put her hand over her mouth.

"I'll get them. Where are they?"

"In the closet. The gold sandals."

"Sit on the loveseat. I'll help you with them."

He retrieved the sandals and brought them to Kate. She lifted one leg to allow him to strap on a shoe.

With gentleness, Zach ran his hand down her calf, then slipped on the shoe. His sensual touch burned a slow heat through her. After he secured the first shoe, he repeated the process with the second, slowly skimming his hand down her other calf.

Kate dug her nails into the nubby fabric of the loveseat to keep from crying out with pleasure. If Zach could turn her on with a few touches, she could imagine what making love with him would be like. Pure bliss.

When both shoes were on, he held out a hand to her. The

intensity in his eyes told her he knew exactly what he'd done to her. The louse.

She took his hand and allowed him to help her stand. Pulling free, she snatched her gold beaded purse from the bed. "Let's go." Brushing past him, she marched out. His soft chuckle followed her.

The others were gathered in the marble-floored vestibule when Kate and Zach came down the stairs. Missy and Ava narrowed their eyes as they scanned Kate. She ignored them. Tripp's lecherous gaze trailed over her, fixing on the deep cleavage of her gown, then continued to her leg peeking from the slit. He licked his lips. Kate wanted to gag. She threaded her arm through Zach's.

Zach's dad barely glanced at them. He paced, looking at his watch. "The cars are here. Where is Elle?"

"She'll be right down." Juliette winked at Kate. "Maybe she wants to make a grand entrance."

"She doesn't need a grand—" Greg stopped in mid-sentence.

All eyes turned toward the stairs. Elle, one manicured hand brushing the railing, walked slowly down, a queen meeting her subjects. A collective gasp went up from the others. Kate looked at Zach's father. He stared open-mouthed at his assistant seconds before he advanced toward her and put out his hand.

CHAPTER FIFTEEN

*W*ith the rest of their party, Zach and Kate crossed the threshold of the elegant Calliope Hotel and Casino. Faux marble walls of white and gold were edged in gilt. Greek gods, in various stages of undress, and surrounded by clouds, danced across the floor in colorful mosaics. A Christmas tree, sparkling with pink lights, stretched toward the domed ceiling, reaching for the goddess Calliope painted on its surface. Fat cherubs flew around the goddess.

Zach patted Kate's hand where it rested on his arm. Smiling, he bent close. "Stay near me. We're supposed to be madly in love."

She gave him her sweetest smile. "I know my part."

"Of course you do, *pumpkin*."

She kicked his calf, then smiled up at him.

He winced. "That hurt."

"I meant it to, *Zachary*."

A smile played around the corners of his mouth. "You're something else."

The group headed to the grand ballroom, where the embellished bronze doors ushered them into a fairyland. Kate inhaled the perfumed air and gazed with wonder at the ornate room. Pink marble threaded with gold covered the walls and floor. Tables draped with shimmering gold cloth were set strategically throughout. Heavy crystal chandeliers hung from the ceiling on ornate medallions. A marble topped bar took up one side of the room.

Over-the-top luxury like this made Kate want to hyperventilate. *Deep breath, Kate. This gig will up your acting creds.* Not comfortable with all this ostentatious splendor, she preferred casual clothes, down-to-Earth real people, and nights in front of the TV eating popcorn, propping her feet up, and cuddling with Brewster, her parents' cat. Tonight would test her performance skills.

"Wow!" she said. "Marble much?"

Zach drew her closer. "Little too vulgar for me."

"Same here."

Juliette sidled up to them. "This place is amazing. Every year they outdo what they did before."

Zach and Kate rolled their eyes at one another and laughed.

Ava, Missy, and Tripp stood behind them. The Morgans, along with Greg and Elle, had walked away, heading toward the bar.

"You come to this party every year?" Kate asked Juliette.

Ava stepped forward and flipped her long blonde waves back with her hand. "Of course, we're always invited to Mel's Christmas gala. Why wouldn't we be? The cream of Las Vegas and New York society are on his permanent guest list."

Kate drew heavy breaths to settle her nerves and suppress her snarky reply. Main Line sophisticates didn't get angry.

Zach took Kate's hand. "Let's get a drink."

They strolled toward the bar.

"Kate! Zach! Didn't expect to see you here. And together."

Kate stopped mid-step and turned slowly to find the screenwriter Everett Hayes and his spouse, actor Brad Jeffrey, bearing down on them, huge smiles on their faces. Kate's friends from her days at acting school in New York, the duo were frequent visitors to Graceann and Jake's house. Kate liked the men, but they could blow her cover. Swallowing her apprehension, she returned their smiles.

"Ev! Brad!" She accepted their kisses on her cheek.

They shook hands with Zach.

Brad slid his gaze from Kate to Zach. "We saw Graceann and Jake a few days ago at an L.A. benefit and they didn't mention you'd both be here, together."

Kate shrugged. "They probably forgot. They lead a busy life."

Ev focused on Kate. "I planned to call you. I have a new project I'd like you to consider."

"I'm on board," Brad said. "Jake says you're perfect for it."

A rush of fear slammed into Kate. She hoped the others hadn't heard the men, and she didn't want a reminder of her anxiety about her acting career. "No business talk tonight."

"Let's have some drinks and catch up." Zach took her arm and led her away. The men followed.

While they waited at the bar for their champagne, Ev studied Zach. "I've said this to you before, with your looks, I could get you parts with no problem."

Zach ran his finger around the rim of his shirt collar. "Uh, thanks. I'm not interested."

Brad leaned closer to Zach and Kate. "Give us the deets. Why are you here together at old man Ableman's annual Bacchanalia?"

Kate laughed. "I'm surprised to see the both of you here, too."

Brad waved a finger at Kate. "You first."

Ev held up his flute of champagne. "To friends."

They toasted. The cold champagne slid easily down Kate's throat, calming her nerves. "Zach and I are playing roles."

Ev chuckled. "Acting as if you like each other?"

Zach put his arm around Kate's shoulder. "We're married, sort of."

Brad choked on the champagne he'd just sipped. Ev patted him on the back.

"It's complicated," Kate said. "Please don't say anything. We don't want to blow our cover."

Ev's eyes widened. "You're spies?"

"No!" Zach and Kate said in unison.

"We want all the dirty details," Brad said.

Zach glanced away. "The others are coming over. You three stay here and I'll head them off."

Drink in hand, he ambled over to Juliette and the group. He motioned toward a table and they all headed there.

Kate released a breath and returned her attention to the two men. "Here's the scoop."

* * *

ZACH, his gaze fixed on Kate and her friends, sat at the table with the others and sipped his champagne.

"You know Brad Jeffery?" Juliette asked.

Missy sighed. "He's gorgeous."

"What's the big deal?" Ava said in bored tones. "Zach is much better looking."

Zach's glance rounded the table. "Can we talk about something else please?"

Tripp sneered. "Kate seems close to them. Real close."

"I've never seen her smile so much." Ava raised her champagne flute to her mouth, her hard eyes riveted on Zach.

"Kate smiles a lot when she's with me," Juliette said. "I'm glad her friends are here."

Zach downed his drink in one gulp and plunked down his empty glass. Immediately, a waiter replaced it with a full glass. It was going to be a long night.

Zach turned his attention back to the bar. He'd never seen Kate so animated. He closed his eyes for a second, fighting the longing that overwhelmed him. He wanted to make her as happy and vibrant as she was now. God, she was gorgeous when she laughed. She was beautiful, period, especially wearing that sexy red gown that hugged her curves and showed her perfectly formed legs. He ached to make love to her and give her pleasure no other man could. He wanted her to smile for him.

She had lost her smile and stiffened when Ev and Brad mentioned a part for her. He expected her to worry the others might have overheard, but the fear that flitted over her face told him there was more to her story. She had secrets. He hoped someday she'd trust him enough to tell him why she wasted her talent in small regional theaters, why she didn't want to test herself in New York City or Hollywood.

Zach grabbed his drink and sauntered to the bar. When he reached the trio, he snaked his arm around Kate and drew her close. He needed to share in her warmth. He'd never felt that way about another woman. The thought froze him.

"Kate told me about your little charade, but seeing you together, I'd never believe you were playacting." Brad's words brought Zach back to reality.

"Kate is a talented actor, but she won't give the rest of the world a chance to see it," Ev said.

Kate shook her head. "I'm not ready for Hollywood."

"What are you afraid of?" Brad asked.

Kate's face turned a pretty shade of pink and she looked away.

Ev swung his attention to Zach. "My offer stands. Any time you're interested in changing careers, let me know."

"I can't act," Zach said.

Brad laughed. "You wouldn't need acting skills with that face and body."

Zach shifted uncomfortably. He liked the two men, but he disliked all the focus on him.

"You've teased my husband enough." Kate slipped her arm through Zach's. "Let's go mingle. See you guys later."

Brad put his finger to his lips. "Your secret is safe."

As they walked off, Zach smiled. It shouldn't feel this right to have Kate to himself, but it did.

* * *

"DANCE WITH ME?" Zach rose from the table where they'd had dinner and held out his hand to Kate.

Nodding, she stood and took his hand, letting him lead her to the small area set aside for dancing. She went into Zach's arms and inhaled deeply of his scent of spice and male. His warmth enveloped her. She stared into his green eyes.

Without a word, he pulled her closer.

Held in the comfort of his arms, they danced to the romantic ballad. His heart beat steady against her cheek. Contentment filled Kate, sealing the empty places in her heart. For the first time, she knew she was healing after Brian's betrayal.

She slid a glance to their table. Ava stared at Zach and Kate, ice shooting from her eyes. Juliette and Missy were talking. Tripp was in conversation with the Morgans. Greg and Elle sat stiff and silent. Not a positive sign for her matchmaking skills. She had her work cut out for her.

Zach kissed the top of her head. "You're quiet. You okay?"

Kate met his gaze. "I don't think things are going too well with your dad and Elle." Uh-oh, busted. As soon as the words were out, Kate wanted to bite them back.

Zach stopped, forcing other couples to go around them. "What are you talking about?"

The music ended. Holding her elbow, Zach led her to a corner of the room. Turning her to face him, he narrowed his eyes. "What have you done?"

"Trying to make Greg happy, and hopefully you."

"What does that mean?"

"You were right. Elle is in love with your dad. He takes her for granted. Juliette and I made her over tonight to force him to take notice. He noticed all right, but now they're both sitting like wax figures."

"Please stay out of their business, Kate. We're here on a mission."

"If your dad finds love, he'll be more kindly disposed to you, which will help you. And he'll be happier, too."

Zach gripped her upper arms. "I don't want anything to jeopardize our plan. Promise you'll let it be."

She pulled free. "I can't." She marched back to the table. Zach was right. He was paying her for a specific job. A hopeless romantic, she wanted to bring happiness to two couples. The push and pull knotted her stomach. She grabbed a glass of wine off a tray held by a passing waiter.

She couldn't be wrong about Elle and Greg. They belonged together. So did Juliette and Sky. And her and Zach.

The surprising revelation stopped her. Another guest plowed into Kate. Wine splashed on her hand. She looked over her shoulder to find Zach watching her.

Zach, along with Carlisle, his dad, Tripp, and Elle assembled in Carlisle's office the day after the holiday gala. For most of the meeting, Zach had been ignored, but he refused to let the others cow him into silence.

He struggled to control his annoyance. "Why limit ourselves to the usual government contracts? We have top-notch products. I think we can expand to other countries and some corporations. France has put out feelers about our products."

Tripp and Carlisle exchanged looks that made Zach clench his hand at his side. They'd shot down all his dad's suggestions, and now they did everything but roll their eyes at Zach.

"Our contracts are extremely lucrative." Tripp's voice held a mocking note. Zach wanted to smash him in his grinning face.

"They are lucrative," Zach said, his tone measured. "Why not branch out? We need to keep this company relevant."

His dad nodded. "Zach might be right."

Zach fought to keep surprise from registering on his face. His dad had actually defended him.

Carlisle nodded to Zach's father. "Greg, we've discussed this before. We're better off doing business as usual."

Zach expected his dad to fight back at the other man's condescending attitude, but he kept quiet.

Carlisle gathered papers from the desk and stuffed them in a drawer. "I guess the meeting is over."

Elle closed her laptop and caught Zach's attention. Her eyes conveyed her exasperation, and he guessed she'd figured out what Carlisle and Tripp were up to. Zach had an ally.

The two men filed out. Greg grabbed Zach's arm as he was leaving. "Stay here and let's have a drink."

Zach jerked his head back in surprise. "Okay."

Greg nodded to Elle. "Type up those notes and email them to me today."

Although his dad barked out the order, his tone toward Elle was softer than usual. Zach frowned. Something was going on here. Maybe Kate had a point.

"Of course, Greg." Blushing, Elle slipped out of the room.

Interesting, Zach thought.

When they were alone, Zach poured his dad and himself bourbon from the decanter on the sideboard and handed his dad a glass. Drink in hand, he held his glass aloft. "To your health."

"My health is fine," Greg snapped. He sipped his drink, his attention riveted on Zach standing before him. "Your marriage surprised me. It would have been thoughtful if you'd prepared me before springing it on me with no warning here in front of the others."

"Would you have cared?" Zach blurted the words.

His dad tossed back his drink and marched to the sideboard to pour himself another before turning to Zach. "When my only child gets married, yes I care."

"That would be the first time you ever cared about anything I've done."

Greg had the grace to look embarrassed. "You said you and Kate have known each other several years?"

Zach nodded and lowered himself onto the armrest of one of the club chairs arranged before the fireplace.

"I had someone investigate this marriage of yours," Greg said. "We found your marriage certificate. And Kate's last name."

"You what?" Zach stood. "You had no right. I'm your son." Despite Zach's outrage, some of it feigned, he wasn't surprised. He'd known his dad would dig into his marriage, which was why he and Kate had to marry and not merely pretend.

"I got rich by hard work and due diligence. Why wouldn't I have my son's new wife checked out? I hope you got a pre-nup."

Zach shrugged. "Nope. I trust Kate. I want her to be part of my life forever." He did trust her. Part of him wanted her to be in his life forever. He'd think about that later.

Greg fixed Zach with a hard stare. "I hate to break it to you, son, but your wife has lied to you. There is no Carluccio family on the Main Line. However, this is a Kate Carluccio, actor, from a small town in the Poconos. Not a very good actor at that."

Zach resisted the urge to lash out at his dad's slur on Kate's acting abilities. He wouldn't let the old man goad him into losing his cool. He sat down again. "I know where Kate is from. I should have told you the truth. We concocted a story to help Kate fit in better with this snobby crowd. It was all my idea."

Sweat beaded on Zach's brow. He hoped his dad bought his half lies and didn't pursue it further.

Greg's lips formed a thin smile. "I'm glad you're honest with me now."

Zach swallowed around his guilt and finished his drink.

His dad's eyes drifted to a spot above Zach. "I married your mother after knowing her only a month," he said softly.

Blowing out a breath, Zach relaxed. "Time you thought about remarrying."

Greg lowered his gaze to Zach. "I'll never find another woman who would put up with me."

Zach grinned. "The one woman who understands you best just walked out of here."

"Elle?"

"Kate thinks she has feelings for you. So do I."

"My personal life isn't up for discussion." Greg perched on the edge of the desk and sipped his drink.

Zach gulped a deep breath, shoring up his courage. "I need to talk to you about something. I think Tripp and Carlisle are conspiring against you to take over Star Ventures."

"What? That's crazy."

"You're not old enough to retire, but they're pushing you. Do you ever ask why?"

His dad waved a hand in dismissal. "I'm sixty years old. They want what's best for the company."

"Sixty's not old, not nowadays. I don't trust them. They'll use the company as their personal bank account, emptying it and putting everyone out of a job. That's not what you want."

Greg's features tightened. "Partying with my money and those floozies you dated has warped your mind."

"You've had your share of girlfriends, Dad."

"That's different. I worked hard building my company. I'm no playboy. My picture is seldom in the tabloids, like yours."

"I'm married now," Zach said quietly. "My party days are behind me. I want to be a bigger part of this company."

"Star Ventures is in capable hands with Carlisle and Tripp." Greg slammed his empty glass on the desk and stalked to the door. Turning, his eyes cold, he said, "Why do you care what happens to me?"

"You're my dad."

Without another word, Greg walked out.

"That went well," Zach said to the silent room. He hoped he'd put doubt in his dad's head. At least his dad bought the legitimacy of his marriage to Kate.

Her image popped into his mind. He wanted to share his dad's conversation with her. She'd understand.

He found her in the sunroom with Missy and Ava. The women ignored Kate while they gossiped. The viciousness in their voices halted him. Narrowing his eyes, he stood in the doorway, unnoticed.

*　*　*

I'M IN HELL. Kate fidgeted in her chair in the sunroom, gazing out the Palladian windows to the gardens with the mountains in the distance. She sipped her iced tea and tried to tune out Missy and Ava. The women giggled together and dished dirt on some couples they knew. Their biting comments about the others made Kate wonder what they said about Zach and her behind their backs.

The women finished their gossip and stared at Kate. *Crap.*

Ava, a self-satisfied smile on her expertly made-up face, raised one eyebrow as she perused Kate. "Are women on the Main Line wearing ripped jeans and yellow Converse high-tops now?"

Missy giggled.

Kate narrowed her eyes to slits. "I don't care what they wear on the Main Line. This is what I wear."

"Excuse us." Missy held her nose in the air in a bad imitation of a society woman.

Giving them a disgusted look, Kate lifted her face to the sun streaming through the skylights. Sunshine always calmed her. This morning her parents had texted with the news that back home in Spirit Lake, it was snowing heavily. They'd have a white Christmas. As much as Kate loved Spirit Lake and a white Christmas, she loved the warmth of Los Angeles and Las Vegas, too.

With the money Zach was paying her, she could move to Los Angeles to pursue acting opportunities. If she could find the confidence.

As if she'd conjured him up, Zach's soft voice calling her name took her from her musings. Twisting in her chair, she found him standing in the doorway. Wearing jeans slung low on his hips, a blue button-down shirt, with his blond hair slightly mussed, he looked endearingly sexy. Her pulse did a little jig.

He held out a hand. "Let's go for a walk."

She stood and faced the other women. "It's been real, Ava and Missy. See you later."

Kate sauntered to Zach when she really wanted to sprint into his arms. She took his hand. "I could use a little exercise."

They left the sunroom and closed the door behind them. Kate grinned. "Thanks for rescuing me from those two."

"I heard a little." His gaze trailed her. "For the record, I think a T-shirt, ripped jeans, and yellow sneakers are sexy. At least on you."

"Uh—thanks." Warmth settled in her stomach. Strange to think of Zach as her rescuer. One more thing that had gone topsy-turvy in their relationship since their marriage.

CHAPTER SEVENTEEN

*K*ate and Zach exited the house through the back door to walk around the lushly landscaped property. Nearby, gardeners pruned, planted, and watered. In the dry desert, it took a team to cultivate all the greenery surrounding them.

Zach put his hands into his jeans pockets. "I know Ava and Missy are gossipy and mean, but we need to stay on their good side."

Kate pressed her lips together. Releasing a breath, she said, "I admit I got a little testy with them. I have a hard time keeping my mouth from saying what I want when I'm with those two."

He stopped and cupped her elbow, forcing her to stop, too. She looked up into his eyes. Damn, but he had beautiful eyes. She swallowed in a failed effort to dissolve her traitorous thoughts about Zach's hotness.

"You're a good actor," he said. "You handle yourself well, even in dealing with Missy and Ava."

"Thank you for noticing. It's my job."

His gaze lingered on her.

She looked down rather than risk losing herself in the seduction of Zach's eyes.

"Can we sit and talk?" he asked. "The pool is up ahead."

Lifting her head, she nodded and followed him.

They strolled side-by-side in silence to the pool, where they settled on chaise lounges. No one swam today but two men cleaned the pool.

Kate twisted toward Zach. "What did you want to talk about?"

Frustration etched his features. "I spoke to my dad after the meeting, a meeting that made it clear Carlisle and Tripp are conspiring against him." Zach's intense gaze held her. "Dad knows the truth about you."

Blinking, she shaded her eyes against the sun and frowned at him. "Me? That's disturbing. What did he find out?"

"Remember I told you Dad would check us out?"

"Yes, that's why our marriage had to be real."

"He hired someone to investigate us. They found our marriage certificate with your name and learned you're from the Poconos and not Philadelphia's Main Line."

Dread made Kate's stomach drop. "Wow! He doesn't leave anything to chance. What happens now? Is the gig over? Maybe we shouldn't have actually gotten married. There wouldn't have been a certificate for him to find."

Zach held up a hand. "Don't worry. I knew he would dig until he found something, and if there was no marriage, things would be a lot worse. He thought you'd lied to me about your background, but I told him we invented the story of your being from the Main Line to fit in better with this crowd."

Kate blew out a relieved breath. "Good thinking. Did he buy it?"

"For now. Dad asked if we had a pre-nup."

"No pre-nup, but a contract."

"Let's hope he doesn't find out about that. Then the gig *will* be up."

"Fingers crossed he'll never know."

Zach's jaw tightened. "I assured Dad I trusted you, then I told him my suspicions about Tripp and Carlisle. He didn't believe me and stormed out."

"Real mature of him." As soon as the words were out, she clamped a hand over her mouth and widened her eyes. Lowering her hand, she said, "Sorry. He is your dad and I shouldn't have said that."

Zach laughed. "Don't worry. I expected as much from him."

"At least you put the thought in his head about those schemers."

"That's what I'm hoping. I'm not the only one who doesn't trust them."

"Who else suspects their motives?"

"I believe Elle does."

"She's one smart lady. If your dad ever acknowledges he cares for her, it will help your cause."

"You might be right. I told Dad I believe Elle has feelings for him."

Kate dropped her feet off the chaise and sat on the edge, closer to Zach. "You did? What did he say?"

"Said his personal life isn't up for discussion."

"He didn't say he doesn't care for her. I told you I'm a first-rate matchmaker."

"That remains to be seen."

"Trust me. I know what I'm doing."

He laughed. "Why does that not make me feel better?" His features sobered. "I think you're onto something but don't push it. Dad doesn't like pressure."

She held up three fingers in the Scouts Honor salute. "No pressure. Promise."

He slid his feet off the chaise and moved closer until their knees touched. "Don't flash those big browns. Your charm will only get so far with me."

"I'm charming?" Her thoughts jumbled by his closeness, she blurted the words.

"Don't let it go to your head."

"Never." She'd always liked bantering with Zach, even when their banter was edgier, as it had been at times in the past. Being with him, fighting with him, excited her. She and Brian rarely fought because, as she'd learned, he didn't care enough about her to fight.

While Zach watched the guys cleaning the pool, Kate studied him. For all his playboy ways and his privileged upbringing, she'd discovered a core of decency in him that appealed to her more than she wanted to admit.

"Zach, can I ask you something? Don't answer if it makes you uncomfortable."

He turned back to her. "Sure. Fire away."

Looking down, she fingered the hem of her shirt, gathering her thoughts, then raised her eyes to his. "I know your dad changed after your mom and brother died. It had to have been hard for him. It was hard for you, too. Their deaths are the reason for the strain between you and him, right?"

Zach's features tensed and he drew harsh breaths. She thought he wouldn't answer. His eyes hooded and he slid his attention from her.

"For a long time, I blamed myself for what happened to them. I thought Dad blamed me too." Zach spoke so low, Kate struggled to hear him.

"Blame yourself? Why? And why would he blame you? You were only eight."

"I was supposed to go with Mom and Harper on that skiing vacation to Aspen, but I came down with a cold. Dad was somewhere in Europe on a business trip. I stayed home with my nanny."

Kate touched his arm. "Zach, how could any of that be your fault?"

He turned to her with haunted eyes. "I thought if I'd been with them, they wouldn't have skied on that high mountain. They would have used the smaller slopes with me. They wouldn't have died and Dad wouldn't have been angry with me."

"Did you tell your dad how you felt? He should have comforted you, not sent you away."

Zach's eyes locked with hers. "How did you know he sent me away?"

Heat crept up Kate's face. She'd promised Elle she wouldn't repeat what she'd told her. Too late. "Elle may have mentioned it."

"I realize now I had nothing to do with the accident, but it took a lot of years to let it go."

Kate rubbed his arm. "I'm glad you could let it go." She shifted in her seat. "You told me your brother was the golden boy. What did you mean?"

"My dad adored Harper. He was a top athlete at his private school. The Ivys were courting him. He was perfect in Dad's eyes. Me, not so much. Dad wishes I'd been the one to die on that mountain."

Bitterness had crept into Zach's voice.

Kate grabbed Zach's hand where it clenched on his thigh. "Zach, no. Your father doesn't think that."

"He did. At the funeral, I overheard Dad tell Elle the wrong son died."

"My God." Kate slipped off her chaise and knelt next to Zach. She grabbed him to her and enveloped him in a hug. "How awful for you. You were a little boy who'd just lost his mom. You needed your dad. I'm so sorry."

He gently pulled away from her. "You mean well, Kate, but I'm all right now. I've learned to live with it."

She shook her head. "No one should live with that."

Smiling, he stood and held out a hand to help her up. "Let's walk some more."

In silence, they strolled along the paved paths. Kate breathed in the scent of flowers that grew in abundance under the loving care of the gardeners. She took Zach's hand in hers. His sharing his past had touched her heart. It was apparent he'd said enough for now. They'd opened a new act in this play of theirs. If this was a romance movie, music would swell around them and they'd embrace. Then walk off into the sunset, happy-ever-after.

She dismissed her fantasies. She had to focus on reality.

They came to the garage and Kate waved to Sky who was waxing a red sports car. He smiled and waved back.

Zach stopped and frowned down at her. "Since when are you friends with the chauffeur?"

The roughness in his voice made her drop his hand and take a step back. If she didn't know better, she'd say Zach was jealous of Sky. The thought sent a frisson of excitement up her spine. "Juliette and Sky are in love. She confided to me the other day."

"He's Juliette's guy?"

When Kate nodded, relief swept over Zach's face. Interesting. He reached for her hand again, holding her tightly.

"Carlisle will never go for his daughter with a chauffeur," Zach said. "He told us he's got the son of one of his wealthy friends lined up for Juliette."

"How medieval."

"Kate, I'm warning you, for your sake. Stay out of it. What happens with Carlisle's family doesn't concern us. I only want to keep him from hurting Dad. I don't care who Juliette or Ava love."

"I can't help wanting to advance the cause of true love." She gave him a playful grin. "I know who Ava wants. You."

"That'll never happen. Please, focus on why we're here, and not on everyone's love life."

"Yes, sir. Whatever you say."

He shook his head. "You're incorrigible."

"You got that right."

Kate's mind muddled with Zach's reaction to Sky. Zach jealous of her with another man? Excitement tingled through her.

CHAPTER EIGHTEEN

*Z*ach wished he were somewhere alone with Kate. Seated with the others that night around the dining room table to enjoy pizza made by the cook, the frenzied air belied the casualness of the food. With the Morgans' annual Christmas Eve party in three days, the household staff buzzed around like bees on steroids, waxing furniture, cleaning the hardwood floors, and whatever else it took to make the massive house shine.

He slid a glance to Kate, across from him, then grabbed his glass of wine and sipped to hide his smile. Dressed in a pair of pricey jeans and one of the expensive sweaters from her L.A. shopping spree, Kate appeared the sophisticated socialite, but she proclaimed her independence by wearing her yellow high-top sneakers. He liked her *in your face* attitude.

Her gaze met his. Her eyes sparked gold fire, mesmerizing him. If he weren't careful, he'd fall under her spell. A small part of him exhilarated at the thought.

Laughter from the other end of the table broke his contact with Kate, and he looked over. Ava laughed at something Tripp said and rubbed her hand along Tripp's arm, staring up at him with a come-hither smile. Across from Tripp, Missy flared her nostrils, the only sign of her annoyance at her husband and Ava flirting.

Tripp's reputation as a serial cheater was common knowledge around the corporation, with rumors he kept a girlfriend in Manhattan. The detectives Zach hired had found the woman's identity and address, but hadn't gotten any compromising pictures yet of her and Tripp. Surprisingly, the girlfriend didn't post photos of Tripp on social media. His dad didn't listen to gossip, so Zach had to find proof Tripp wasn't the family man he pretended. Then, maybe his dad would believe Zach about the conspiracy against him from Carlisle and Tripp.

Zach had noticed Tripp checking out Kate earlier. Zach gripped the stem of his wine glass tighter. If Tripp tried anything with Kate....

"This pizza is to die for," Kate said.

Her words diffused the anxiety knotting Zach's stomach at the thought of Tripp's hands on her. If he were honest with himself, he didn't want any other man's hands on her either.

"Best pizza I've ever had." Elle nodded toward Zach's father. "Don't you think so, Greg?"

His dad grunted. "Pizza is pizza."

The comment landed in the room like a ball of uncooked pizza dough. Couldn't his father be happy about anything? Since they'd sat down to dinner, his father hadn't made eye contact with him. Zach tried to not let his dad's dismissive attitude bother him. He wondered why he cared his dad might lose the business he loved.

Kate exchanged glances with Zach and gave him a sympathetic smile. "Too bad Juliette isn't here to enjoy this meal," Kate said.

Ava snickered. "Juliette's been in the city all day with a friend. Skylar went to pick her up. She and Skylar are probably sitting in the limo making out."

Kate gasped, her eyes wide.

"Ava! Why would you say such a thing?" Gloria asked.

"Juliette thinks she's in love with Skylar." Ava calmly picked up her pizza and took a dainty bite.

Carlisle puffed up his chest. "No daughter of mine will consort with a chauffeur. She's meant for better things."

Tripp laughed. "Don't worry about it, Carlisle. Juliette is young. She'll come around and do what's right."

"And what is right?" Zach asked quietly.

Carlisle leaned his palms on the table. "My daughter will marry someone who can afford to keep her in the style she's accustomed to."

You mean in the style you're accustomed to. Zach clenched his jaw to keep from saying the words out loud.

He looked across at Kate. The way she chewed her lip, he guessed she wanted to say exactly what she thought of Morgan's statement. He shook his head, warning her to stay quiet.

She arched a brow, but made no comment.

"I'll fire Skylar if he so much as touches my daughter."

Gloria put a hand on her husband's arm. "Calm down, Carlisle. Remember your blood pressure. If Juliette has a crush on Skylar, it'll go away naturally. If you fire him, she could latch onto him even more."

"That's solid advice," Greg said. "Let's enjoy this meal. Christmas will be here soon. Time enough later to iron out any problems."

Zach froze with his wine glass halfway to his mouth. His father never cared about Christmas. On the holidays he'd allowed Zach home from boarding school, he'd been off to the islands with one of his girlfriends, leaving Zach with the servants. As a child, Zach had cried himself to sleep many nights. When he reached his teens, he stopped caring.

CHAPTER NINETEEN

*a*fter dinner, the men closeted themselves in the office to go over some business matters. The other women went to their rooms, but Kate headed to the library to wait for Juliette. She had to catch the young woman when she came in and warn her about the bombshell Ava had exploded at dinner.

Kate left the library doors open a crack to listen for the front door. Her pulse quickened when she spied the set of striking, colorful silkscreens hanging by brass rods on the far wall. Antoine Boulanger's work? She'd noticed them the other day, but didn't have time to examine them. She hurried over. Her excitement grew when she saw they were indeed the work of the famous artist. She loved silkscreens and had made a few, but had no hope of being an expert.

With gentleness, she ran her fingers over the soft silk of one of the prints. Exquisite. If she could make ones like these, she'd be a renowned artist rather than an actor. And she wouldn't have to worry about comparisons to her beautiful mother, a well-known model who'd done some acting. Kate loved her mother dearly, but remained in her shadow.

Pushing aside her insecurities, Kate admired the silkscreens a while longer, then perused the bookshelves until she found a mystery to read while she waited. Thirty minutes later, her eyes drooped and the book lay open on her lap. She shook herself awake. As much as she needed to see Juliette before the others, she had to go up to bed. Zach must still be in his meeting or he would have come looking for her.

Yawning, she marked her page with a bookmark she found on the shelf. The sound of the front door opening jerked her out of her lethargy. She stood, dropped her book on a table, and hurried to the entrance hall.

Juliette strolled in. Her mussed hair and flushed face shouted she'd been with a man. She stopped and frowned. "Kate! What are you doing up?"

"Waiting for you."

"Why?"

"Come into the library."

Juliette followed her, and Kate closed the doors. She touched the young woman's arm. "You have to be careful. Ava let it out to everyone, including your dad, that you're seeing Sky."

"Holy crap! I was in the city with some friends earlier, but after they left, Sky drove me back to his place. My dad will fire him. So unfair. Sky's almost saved up what he needs to start his business."

"I wanted to tell you before your dad got to you," Kate said.

"Thanks. You're a good friend." Anger flitted across Juliette's face. "Ava is my sister but she's evil. Why would she try to hurt Sky and me like this?"

"Some people don't like to see other people happy."

Juliette fished inside her purse and pulled out her phone. "I need to call Sky and warn him. Kate, what will I do if he's fired and Dad ships me off somewhere far away?"

"This is the twenty-first century. Fathers don't ship their daughters away from temptation."

"You don't know my dad."

"Don't worry about something that might never happen." Kate hugged the other woman. "Get some rest. You and Sky will figure things out. I'll help any way I can."

"Thanks."

The women drew apart as the library doors opened. Zach, confusion on his face, stood in the doorway.

"I wondered where you were, Kate." He acknowledged Juliette with a nod of his head. "All right if I steal my wife?"

Juliette yawned. "Sure. I'm on my way to my room."

The three of them walked out together. Zach put his hand on the small of Kate's back. His closeness sent heat spiraling through her. She knew he put on a show of being the loving husband, but she liked it, to her dismay.

If she weren't careful, her pretend feelings for Zach Lyon could become real.

* * *

ZACH REACHED for Kate's hand as they climbed the stairs with Juliette. He needed to be close to Kate, to touch her. They said goodnight to Juliette, and he and Kate went to their room. Disappointment had settled in his chest when he'd gone to their room after the meeting and found it empty. It hadn't taken long to find her when he heard voices from the library.

He released her when they entered the bedroom. "Want to explain what's going on?" Her wide-eyed innocence didn't fool him. "Don't pretend. I'm wise to you now."

"Really?" she glared at him.

"Yes, really. You told me about Juliette and Sky. I saw what happened at dinner. Did you stay up to warn her?"

"Of course."

He stepped closer. Wrong move. Her scent of lavender wafted over him, filling him with an ache to take her into his arms and never let her go. He backed away.

266

"I don't want to cause problems while we're here," he said. "If you interfere with the Morgan family dynamics, my dad will never forgive me. He refuses to listen to me now, but I still have a chance. I may lose even that hope."

Sighing, she folded her arms across her chest. "I understand, and I'll try to keep out of the Morgans' business, but if Juliette and Sky need my help, how can I refuse?"

He gripped her by the shoulders. "Don't get involved. Please."

She looked away, not meeting his eyes.

"You are so frustrating," he said.

Her delectable lips lifted in a sassy smile and she met his gaze. "I try hard to make you crazy."

"You're doing a good job. You make me crazier than you can guess."

Her face flushed a pretty shade of pink.

Unable to resist her any longer, he pulled her to him and kissed her, breathing in her lavender scent and reveling in her soft body pressed against his. He nudged the seam of her lips until she opened to him. Cupping the back of her head, he drew her closer. Her silky hair fell over his hands, sensuous and welcoming. His hard erection wanted release from the restriction of his jeans.

He nibbled on her lips, inciting small, needy cries from her. Leaving her delicious mouth, he feasted on her neck, kissing a trail down to her collarbone. She wrapped her arms about his waist and gave herself over to him.

Slipping a hand under her sweater, he massaged the smooth flesh of her midriff and trailed his fingers to her breasts. When he caressed one of her full breasts covered in delicate lace, she moaned softly and threw back her head.

"Kate," he whispered against her throat. Every lust-filled cell in his body needed her, wanted her.

Her breathing heavy, she pushed away. They stared at each other. Desire glazed her eyes, and her lips were red from his kisses.

She put up a hand. "No. We can't. That's not part of the bargain."

Zach took a half-step back and ran a frustrated hand over his hair. "I'm sorry. Things got out of control."

"Let's forget it happened."

"No way will I forget that."

Regret in her eyes, she pivoted on her heel and headed to the bedroom. "Good night, Zach."

Taking measured breaths to tamp down his libido, Zach went into the sitting room and his bed. His lonely bed. Sleep wouldn't come easy this night.

CHAPTER TWENTY

Kate, seated across from Zach at the small table their suite, pulled the sash on her silk robe tighter. Protection from him or from her own growing feelings for him? After a fitful night, she was relieved to have a light breakfast in their room. She sipped her coffee and tried to forget the erotic dreams in which he'd had a starring role. Not an easy task with him looking sexy as hell in dark-washed jeans and a white T-shirt that accentuated his broad chest.

Images of him and that kiss spiced her dreams. She'd wanted more then, wanted it now. She raised her eyes to his.

He studied her. "We should talk about that kiss."

She swallowed and set down her cup. "No, we shouldn't."

Leaning closer, he said, "But we have to. This spark, or whatever you call it, has been circling us for years, and has gotten more intense. We can't ignore it."

His lopsided smile made her hand tremble as she poured herself more coffee. She stirred cream into it, then gulped a huge sip, ignoring the burn as it slid down her throat. The hot liquid couldn't compete with the slow heat of desire building in her.

"We've been snapping at each other since the day we met," he continued. "I won't deny I'm attracted to you, have always been. I think you're the same toward me. Despite that, or maybe because of it, we got off on the wrong foot."

Blood rushing through her head, Kate set her cup on the table and looked down. Zach had given voice to what she'd tried to deny.

"Kate?"

She lifted her head, seeing the truth of his words in his eyes. Pressing her lips together, she organized her words. He stared at her, patient, quiet, waiting.

She inhaled deeply, then exhaled. "I acknowledge the pull between us. Lots of people are attracted to each other and it doesn't mean anything, or go anywhere."

"You're right about that, but most times the attraction dies. Ours hasn't."

Fear of losing her heart slammed into her chest. Uncomfortable at the turn the conversation had taken, she twisted away from him and focused on a print hanging on the far wall. Her thoughts were as prickly as the cactus in the painting.

"You seem to have a stronger dislike of me than I do you," Zach said softly. "I think I know why, but I'd like to hear it from you."

She couldn't run away. Pulling her attention back to him, she ran her fingers over the cool tablecloth. "I always found you shallow and arrogant, a playboy I had no time for." There, it was out.

His green eyes darkened. "That's what I figured. I told you before things aren't always what they seem. After these days together, do you still see me that way?"

"No." She averted her eyes. The gentleness and patience in his voice prompted her to give him an honest answer. He deserved that from her.

"What did you say?"

She slid her gaze back to him. "You're not what I thought.

You're a caring and decent man who loves his dad despite how he treats you. I'm sorry I misjudged you."

Zach reached for her hand across the table and held it. "I don't want an apology from you. We're friends now, and that's all that matters."

His words shot straight to her heart and she smiled. "You haven't been exactly fond of me either."

He laughed. "Guilty. I thought you were flighty because of the way you dressed, and that you weren't very ambitious in pursuing an acting career."

Hurt and fear coalesced in her stomach. She stiffened and tried to pull her hand away.

He held her tighter. "Hear me out. I'm sorry I misjudged you, too. You're none of those things. You've shown me how generous you are. I know there's a story behind why you don't try to have more of a career, but that's your business. I hope someday you'll tell me."

Their eyes locked and held. Words couldn't douse the fire burning between them. She had to lighten the mood before she confessed how close he'd come to tapping into her deepest insecurities.

She pulled free. "I'm getting a rush from all the sweetness we're flinging around. I like it better when we fight."

He laughed. "If you want a fight…"

She held up her hands. "Nope. That's okay." She forced her thoughts into a more businesslike mode. "We've got an agreement which I fully intend to honor. That's all that matters." Leaning closer, she said, "No sex. That's part of the deal."

"You're doing me a big favor, for which I'll always be grateful." He reached out and skimmed a finger over her lips. "I'll keep to the contract, but it won't stop me from wanting you."

It won't stop me from wanting you either. The thought came unbidden.

He held out his hand. "Friends? Now, and hopefully for always."

Kate took his hand and shook it. At the touch of his warm flesh, fires ignited her insides.

"We should do something together today. Something fun," he said, releasing her. "Everyone's busy with preparations for the party tomorrow, and they won't miss us. My dad is no doubt closeted in the office with Elle going over contracts or whatever business deals he's got going."

Relieved to talk about something other than themselves, Kate smiled. "It would do your dad a world of good if he'd acknowledge his feelings for Elle."

"What makes you think he shares her feelings?"

"I've seen the way he looks at her. He's a stubborn guy. We should give him another nudge."

Zach stood. "No more nudging. Let's get dressed and go have some fun on the Strip." He scanned her. "Wear something dressy and hot."

"Why? Most people dress casually on the Strip."

"We're not most people. Where we're going, we need to make an impression."

CHAPTER TWENTY-ONE

*Z*ach's searing gaze trailed Kate when she walked out of the bedroom wearing an above-the-knee black sheath and peep-toe red stilettos. "Wow! You pulled out all the stops on hot."

She suppressed the urge to pull on the hemline. She liked the dress and the way it showed off her figure, but she felt exposed.

"Thanks, I think," she said.

His sensual grin incited a desire in her to tear off their clothes until they were both naked. *Get a grip, Kate.*

"I don't give empty compliments," he said. "I'd better keep you close today or some other guy will try to steal you."

His words threw cold water on her libido. "Seriously? I can take care of myself."

"You're too much fun to tease." Zach looked at his phone. "Our driver is here."

"Isn't Sky driving us?"

"I hired a car. I don't feel right using the Morgans' chauffeur."

"I hope Carlisle doesn't punish Sky because he's in love with Juliette."

"I hope so too, but it's not our problem."

The car dropped them off at the elegant and upscale Augustus Hotel and Casino with its marble-floored lobby and world-renowned glass sculpture that stretched to the ornate gilded ceiling. At one end of the lobby stood the entrance to the hotel's famous botanical gardens. Through the arched trellis, Christmas lights and ornaments glittered.

Kate sighed at the beauty and looked up at Zach. "I love this hotel. I was here with Juliette the other day. When Graceann and I came to Vegas on spring break during our junior year of college, we stayed at some dumpy motel. We walked around the Augustus and ooh'd and aah'd everything, wishing we were staying here."

Zach took her hand in his and pulled her closer. "You can afford to stay here now. Any time you want."

The spark in his eyes ignited a fire in her. She looked away. At the concierge desk, near the casino floor, a beautiful young woman smiled at them and picked up a phone. Within minutes, a man wearing an elegant suit rushed from the gaming area toward them.

"Mr. Lyon," the man said. "Welcome."

He and Zach shook hands, then Zach turned to Kate. "Bruno, this is my wife Kate."

"My pleasure to meet you, Mrs. Lyon." Bruno held out his hand to shake Kate's.

"Nice to meet you, too, Bruno."

Bruno gestured toward the casino. "Come, we have your table set up."

Kate shot Zach a questioning look, but he didn't seem to notice. They followed the other man past rows of slot machines and gaming tables. Young men holding beer bottles brushed by them. Groups of women with drinks laughed as they passed. A few players at the tables and the slots glanced at them as they walked by, but most were too intent on their games to pay Zach and her much attention.

Bruno led them to a room off the main area. The guards who

stood nearby unlatched the velvet ropes to let them through. Zach took all this preferential treatment in stride, while she wanted to stand still and absorb the feeling of being treated like royalty.

The room, tastefully decorated in shades of gray and white, held four oval tables covered in dark blue felt. Chairs in navy velvet were arranged around the tables. A thick rug in a geometric print of blue, white, and gray carpeted the floors. Well-dressed men and women occupied the tables. Some played while others watched. A small bar manned by two bartenders took up a corner of the room.

"What are they playing?" Kate whispered to Zach.

"Baccarat."

Bruno took them to a table where a man and woman sat. He held out a chair for Kate. Smiling at the others, she sat. Zach settled next to her.

Bruno signaled one of the bartenders, who hurried over. "What would you like to drink, Mrs. Lyon?" Bruno asked.

She started to order wine, but Zach put his hand over hers, stopping her. "I recommend one of their special cocktails designed for this room."

Her protest died on her lips. She had to play her role of the young socialite wife and not the casual woman who preferred a glass of wine while wearing jeans and sneakers.

Kate touched Zach's arm and stayed in role, giving him what she hoped was a worshipful smile. "What would you recommend for me, darling?"

He blinked his eyes in surprise. "Do you like tequila?"

"Of course." She gave him a coquettish smile.

He swallowed, then looked at the bartender. "Mescal for me and the lady."

"Yes, sir."

"What is mescal?" Kate asked when the bartender walked away.

"Mescal is similar to tequila, but better," Zach said. "Once you experience it, you'll never want tequila again."

Bruno puffed up. "The Augustus mescal is made from wild mountain Magueys grown in the high regions of Oaxaca. It's unlike any other spirit in the world."

"How interesting." Kate didn't understand what Bruno said, but if mescal was a form of tequila, she's was in.

"If you don't need anything else, I'll leave you to your game," Bruno said. "The croupier and dealers will be with you shortly."

Zach slipped some bills into the other man's hand. "Thanks, Bruno."

While they waited for their drinks, they introduced themselves to the others at the table.

The man, Haruto, from Japan, was in Las Vegas on business. Kate guessed his age around sixty. Very polished, and wearing a beautifully tailored dark blue suit, gold cufflinks on his white shirt, and a gold Cartier watch, he presented a picture of the wealthy international businessman. The woman, Marian, who looked to be in her fifties, wore a pale blue silk blouse that brought out her blue eyes. Her understated, unique gold jewelry further proclaimed her a woman of wealth and style. Marian told the others she owned several small fashion boutiques in Atlanta and was in Vegas for pleasure.

Zach held Kate's hand and drew her closer. "I'm Zach Lyon and this lovely woman is my bride, Kate."

The croupier came to the table then, accompanied by two women in black suits, the dealers. The croupier set up the decks of cards and shuffled them. After Zach, Haruto, and Marian placed their bets, one of the dealers dealt the cards.

The bartender arrived with their drinks, and Kate settled back to enjoy the game. She sipped the smooth, delicious drink and had to agree with Zach. After tasting mescal, she wouldn't want tequila again. Who was she fooling? Even with the money Zach was paying her, her she'd still be a tequila kind of girl.

CHAPTER TWENTY-TWO

$\mathcal{B}$y Kate's reckoning, Zach won thousands at baccarat. Seeming psyched and energized with winning, Zach snatched her hand and moved to another room to play poker. A little too relaxed from the mescal, Kate switched to club soda with lime. She sat behind Zach at the poker table as the other players took their seats.

Zach turned to her and bent close. "You must be bored watching me. If you want to play roulette or the slots, I'll have Bruno give you a line of credit. I want you to have fun today."

She inhaled his subtle scent of citrus that would always remind her of him, and felt the overwhelming urge to kiss his full lips, so close to her. "I am having fun. I love watching you and the others play. I've gone past these rooms and wondered about them. It's a whole new world in here." She grinned. "You should play baccarat or poker with Juliette. She'd give you a run for your money."

"Juliette?"

"The woman could wager a riverboat gambler out of his clothes."

He shook his head. "You think you know people. You're sure you're not bored?"

"I'm sure." Zach's intensity when he'd played baccarat, his sharp mind, and his calm demeanor helped him win big. He'd handed her several chips which she'd tucked into her bag. She entertained the idea his gambling augmented his lavish lifestyle and all the models and actresses he dated, then worried he could have a gambling addiction. But she'd never seen evidence of that. Watching him, she dismissed her thoughts.

Kate sipped her club soda and relaxed during the intense and long poker games. She enjoyed the reactions of the players, especially those who couldn't successfully hide their expressions when they had a winning or losing hand.

Tired of sitting, she strolled to the bar for another drink and stayed there to observe the game. Seated behind Zach, she hadn't been able to see his face. Fascinated by his concentration, she focused all her attention on him. His blond hair was slightly mussed from the times he'd raked fingers through it, making him look delectably sexy. He held the cards close with long, elegant fingers, his only emotion an occasional small frown between his brows.

Erotic images of those talented fingers and hands bringing her to heights of pleasure, inflamed Kate. She sensed Zach would be a lover who would take his time, who would please his partner in ways she could only imagine. She waved her hand in front of her face to cool herself off, and chewed on an ice cube.

Intent on his game, Zach never looked her way. After the third game, several of the players threw their cards on the table in disgust and declared themselves out. A grinning Zach raked in the chips for another win.

Zach handed the dealer several chips, then stood. "Great games, everyone. Thanks."

"You would think they were great, Lyon," one of the men mumbled. "You won every hand."

"I'm lucky." Zach looked over at Kate. "Or my new wife brought me luck."

He strolled to Kate, slid his arm around her waist, and kissed her gently on the lips. "Ready to go, babe?"

Babe?

"Sure, *babe*," she said, provoking raised eyebrows from him.

Bruno and two guards appeared, seemingly out of nowhere. Bruno handed Zach a canvas bag. Zach dropped his chips into the bag, and the guards accompanied them out of the room.

"What's going on?" Kate asked.

"I need to cash these first, then we can eat," he said.

They cashed in the chips for more than Kate had imagined, and Zach signed papers to have the money transferred to his bank as Kate stood wide-eyed.

"Let's eat." Taking her hand, he led her to an elevator tucked away from the ones used by the hotel guests. With a key card, he unlocked the elevator doors. They exited on the top floor to face double doors which he opened with his card. Zach ushered her into a suite of rooms tastefully furnished in muted shades of green and beige.

"Wow!" Kate wandered to the floor-to-ceiling windows. Las Vegas spread before her in all its garish, bright, exciting glory. Dusk had settled over Sin City. In the distance, the *faux* Eiffel Tower of the Paris Hotel and Casino, brilliantly lit, thrust into the darkening sky. Beyond that, the lights of the High Roller beckoned. "This view is amazing."

Zach moved behind her and placed his hands on her shoulders. His flesh warmed her through the thin silk of her dress. It took all her willpower not to lean into his taut frame. Her body tingled with need for him. With her self-imposed celibacy, any attractive man would set her juices flowing.

Liar, a little voice whispered. Zach was the only man she wanted. She drew in a breath.

"You okay?" he asked.

Unable to speak, she nodded.

"It is quite a sight," he said.

She turned in his arms. They were inches apart. Her breath quickened. Zach's eyes darkened. He bent closer.

A loud knock on the door startled them to jump back from each other.

"Damn bad timing." Zach strode toward the door.

Two men wheeled in a round table covered in a white cloth, with glass cloche covers over plates of food. A sommelier followed with two bottles of champagne nestled in a bucket of ice.

The waiters put the table in front of the windows and positioned two nearby velvet-tufted chairs to flank the table. One waiter held out a chair to Kate and nodded. "Madam."

Feeling like royalty, Kate sat. Zach sat across from her.

With a flourish, the waiters removed the cloche tops. The sommelier popped the cork on the champagne and poured a small amount into a flute. He held the glass out to Zach, who took a sip and nodded it was acceptable.

After pouring champagne for Zach and Kate, one of the waiters nodded at Zach. "Do you need anything else, sir?"

"No, everything is fine." Zach pressed his hand into the man's, and Kate glimpsed several hundred-dollar bills.

"Thank you." With smiles on their faces, the men left the room.

Kate's eyes met Zach's. "I've never been in a penthouse before or been treated with such deference. This must be what royalty feels like."

He laughed and held his champagne flute aloft. "To Kate, my princess."

He'd called her "*my* princess." Her insides trembled with excitement. She lifted her glass to his.

"Save room for dessert," he said. "We have chocolate covered strawberries and butter cake."

"I'm going to be big as a house if I keep eating like this."

His scorching gaze scanned her. "You're perfect now, and you'll still be perfect with a few more pounds."

"Right answer."

She grabbed her glass and downed her drink, hoping the cool slide of it would wash away her rising libido. Zach was trying to seduce her. Excitement swept up her spine.

CHAPTER TWENTY-THREE

*Z*ach sat back and sipped his champagne, his attention riveted on the beautiful, intriguing woman across from him. "Up for dessert?" The hell with chocolate covered strawberries and cake. He wanted Kate for dessert.

"Give me time to savor that amazing meal." Kate closed her eyes and released a low moan.

Zach gripped the stem of his glass to keep from grabbing her to him and devouring her with all the passion and enthusiasm she'd used to consume her meal. Her full, pink lips were ripe for his kisses. His fingers itched to peel off her stunning dress and expose her womanly curves to his greedy eyes and hands. His mind conjured images of her thick black hair spread over his pillow, of her panting for him, and only him. He tossed back his champagne, then poured himself another.

Kate's sexiness reached out to him on a visceral level, but her warmth and caring touched his heart. None of the models, actresses, and socialites he'd dated had ever made him feel good about himself. No woman had given him warm feelings like the one across from him.

He'd never wanted any woman the way he wanted Kate

Carluccio Lyon. They had a contract he would honor. He couldn't, wouldn't take advantage of their situation to seduce her. He closed his eyes for a second, willing his raging hormones to settle.

"Is this penthouse yours?" Kate's question brought Zach to Earth with a thud.

"I use it whenever I'm in Vegas. I drop enough money at this casino, they should give me the perks."

She twisted the stem of her flute between her fingers. "I've never understood the lore of gambling. A waste of money. I'd rather use my money for something I can hold, like clothes or jewelry."

"Winning is a rush, almost as exciting as sex."

"I doubt that." Her face turned rosy.

Zach threw back his head and laughed.

Looking into his eyes, she said, "Do you have a gambling addiction?"

"No."

She tilted her head to study him. "You're sure?"

"Yes. I only gamble when I come to Vegas, once a year. I have no desire for it at any other time. When I'm at the casinos, I drop a lot of money, hence the special treatment. And they know about my family money and my reputation. It doesn't hurt their image to have me play at their tables. I lose sometimes, but not often. I'm very good."

His mind drifted to Rosina and the others. "I've put my winnings to better use than you can imagine."

"Other than models and actresses?" Her face pinked. "I'm sorry. That was mean."

He waved a hand. "Don't worry about it." It suited his sense of decency and guilt to have the world believe the stories about him in the gossip columns.

"How did you learn the games?" she asked.

"I told you I stayed at boarding school during the holidays."

She nodded.

"Some of the staff stayed behind. I played card games with the kitchen team and the drivers. The headmaster taught me baccarat."

Kate laughed. "You and Juliette and your gambling staffs."

"What?"

"Never mind."

His phone, face down on the table, rang. He picked it up and looked at the screen.

"I have to take this." He jumped up.

Kate stood and waved him back down. "Stay. I need to use the bathroom."

Zach swiped his finger across the screen to connect the call, then waited until Kate walked into the other room. "Did you get the money?" he said into the phone.

"Yup," Brent said. "Just like clockwork. That was quite a haul you had today. The guys are happy."

"I got lucky."

"Not just luck with you. Skill and smarts, too. Everyone thanks you. Things are rolling along. We'll be up and running in no time."

"You got the permits?"

Brent sighed. "Finally. Had to grease some hands, but we're ready to start. If the locals don't shake us down for more."

"God, I hope not. We've already paid out more than we should have in bribes. I'll call you tomorrow. How's Rosina?"

"She misses you."

"I miss her too. Tell her I love her."

Zach hung up, and glanced over to see Kate in the doorway, her face white and her features, so relaxed a few minutes ago, tight.

Dread pounded in his chest. She'd heard his conversation.

"How about some dessert?" he asked.

"I'm not hungry. I think we should leave."

He walked toward her, to take her in his arms until she smiled again. The rigidity of her body stopped him. He should explain, but he couldn't. He'd held his secret too long, and he wasn't at liberty yet to expose the plans. The words wouldn't come.

"I'll call for the car."

CHAPTER TWENTY-FOUR

*T*ension, thick as the butter cake Kate didn't eat, filled the car on the ride back to the Morgans. She'd forgotten her purse, and went back into the living room for it when she overheard Zach on the phone. Her appetite had fled. Who was this Rosina he loved and missed? Kate's warm fuzzies toward Zach dissolved into the cooled air.

He loved another woman, yet he'd paid Kate to marry him. None of it made sense, but she had a contract and would keep to the terms. Once their deal was over he could go back to Rosina. A stab of jealousy tinged with sadness slashed her at the thought.

He'd sounded so secretive on the call, and he'd said the word *bribes*. Suspicion rose in her. She wanted no part of anything illegal.

"Everything okay?" He touched her hand.

She jerked away. Regret flitted across his face, the unexpected emotion confusing her.

"I'm fine, just tired." She needed a relaxing bath, an exciting book, and bed. She didn't need Zach, despite the desire for him that flamed in her, even now.

The car slid up to the circular drive and stopped. Kate alighted from the car, Zach behind her. The front door to the house flew open. Light spilled out onto the driveway as the hired vehicle pulled away. Juliette, wheeling a small suitcase, ran out, followed by her parents.

"Juliette, get back here," her dad yelled.

The young woman whirled on him. "I'm twenty-one years old. I can make up my own mind. I'm sorry, Mom and Dad, but I know what I want. I'm going to Sky."

Gloria Morgan put her hand on her husband's arm, but he knocked it away.

"If you leave now," Morgan said, "I'll stop paying your tuition. I'll disown you."

"I'll find a job to earn my tuition. You can't threaten me."

"You think love will put a roof over your heads?" her dad shouted.

"Carlisle, please," Gloria said.

Zach and Kate stared up at the fighting family. The others finally noticed them.

Gloria shook her head. "I'm sorry you had to see this."

"Just a little family disagreement," Carlisle said.

Juliette turned to Kate. "Dad fired Sky. I'm leaving."

"I had every right to fire him," Carlisle yelled again. "Get in the house now, Juliette."

Kate grabbed Juliette's arm. "Let's talk about this."

Carlisle pointed a finger at Kate. "You, stay out of it."

Gloria wrung her hands. "Everyone settle down."

Zach put a hand on Kate's shoulder. "Keep quiet," he whispered.

Kate brushed him away. "Come in the house with me, Juliette. We'll go to my room and talk."

"Fine, but I won't change my mind. I'm going to Sky."

Both Morgans glared at Kate as she put her arm around Juliette's waist and guided her into the house, Zach following.

At the stairs, Zach said, "I'll go into the library and search for a book while you take care of Juliette."

In the suite she shared with Zach, Kate changed into comfortable yoga pants and a long-sleeved top while Juliette refreshed herself in the bathroom. Hearing a knock at the door, Kate hurried to open it.

Elle, holding a wooden tray with a ceramic pot and three mugs, stood there. Widening her eyes, Kate stepped back to allow the other woman into the room.

"This is a surprise, Elle."

"I heard what happened. I thought you could use some hot tea." Elle set the tray on the table in the sitting area and wiped her hands down the sides of her navy-blue tailored pants. Her pale hair was fashioned in the same mousy style as always.

Kate's matchmaking skills were taking a hit all over, first Juliette and Sky's rocky road, and now Elle going back to the shy, quiet person Mr. Lyon ignored.

"Thank you," Kate said. "How thoughtful of you."

Juliette came out of the bathroom. Kate put an arm around her shoulders. "Come have some tea. We'll talk."

The women sat at the table, and Elle poured tea into the mugs. Silence filled the room as they fixed their drinks.

Her hands wrapped around the steaming mug, Kate forced herself to relax. "Juliette, tell us what happened."

The younger woman sniffled, then sipped from her mug. With a heavy sigh, she set down her drink and slid her attention between Kate and Elle. "Today was Sky's day off. I told my mom I was going out with my friend Beth. I drove to Beth's house where Sky met me. We went to Valley of the Sun to do some hiking, then we had something to eat. When we got back to Beth's, my father was waiting."

"He followed you?" Elle asked.

Nodding, Juliette pulled a tissue from her purse and blew her nose. "He hired a PI to follow me. He suspected I'd gone to Sky.

The guy followed us the whole day and we didn't notice. How could my own father do that?"

"I agree that wasn't right," Kate said. "You're a grown woman. So, your dad fired Sky on the spot?"

"Yes."

Elle poured Juliette more tea. "You poor thing. You must feel betrayed."

"I do. Sky texted me. He came back here, under guard of the PI, packed his clothes, and now he's staying with friends. He wants me to meet him there. We'll get married. I love him and I want to marry him."

"Let's consider this calmly," Kate said. "You love each other, but you're both very young. You need time to think things through. If your love is strong, it will survive. Why don't you go back to school, see what happens? When you graduate, if you and Sky still want to be together, then you can marry. In time, your dad will change his mind."

With a sad smile, Juliette shook her head. "I know my father. He's stubborn, and he can't stand the thought of his daughter marrying a chauffeur. Sky is a good man."

Kate smiled, trying to lessen the other woman's agitation. "I like Sky, and he loves you, but I don't want you making a mistake."

"Kate is right," Elle said. "Don't do anything you might regret."

Juliette turned to Elle. "Elle, you're sweet and thoughtful, but look at you, in love with old Mr. Lyon, a man who treats you like a rug under his feet. You're too afraid to show him you love him or to fight for him. Are you happy with your life?"

Her face stricken, Elle sank back into her chair.

Kate frowned at Juliette. "That was harsh, and not like you."

"I'm sorry." Juliette wiped tears from her eyes. "Elle, forgive me. I didn't mean to hurt you. I'm too upset to think rationally. I believe when you find love, you need to grab it and never let go. I don't want to spend the rest of my life wishing I'd taken a chance on Sky."

Juliette nodded at Kate. "You and Zach are madly in love. It's so romantic you didn't wait to be married. You knew what you wanted and you went for it."

Kate's mug slipped out of her hand. It landed on the floor with a thud, splashing tea over the sides. Grabbing a napkin, she set the mug on the table and blotted the floor. She and Zach madly in love? They deserved an Oscar if they'd made Juliette believe that.

"Zach and I are at least ten years older than you and Sky," Kate said, grateful her voice was calm.

Elle stood and looked down at Juliette. "I know you didn't intend to hurt my feelings. Why don't you go to bed, sleep on it, and things might not seem so bleak in the morning?"

"I'll try to sleep." Juliette grabbed her purse and stood, too. She hugged both women, snatched up her suitcase, and left.

Kate and Elle looked at each other.

"I'm sorry she said that to you," Kate said.

Elle brushed a hand over her short hair. "Out of the mouths of babes. I've got some thinking to do, too."

"We could all use a decent night's sleep," Kate said, standing. "I need to think about some things of my own."

"I'll have someone pick up the tea stuff tomorrow. Good night."

"Good night, Elle."

Kate walked to the bedroom and closed the door behind her. Her empty bed beckoned. She suspected sleep would elude her tonight.

CHAPTER TWENTY-FIVE

*K*ate opened her eyes and winced. A headache pounded her temples. The events of yesterday and last night jabbed her consciousness. She rubbed her eyes and sank farther into the mattress. Her day and evening with Zach had been wonderful, a fantasy. His mysterious phone call had ruined it all. She might be married to a drug lord who loved another woman. She should have followed her first instinct and not agreed to his crazy scheme.

The Zach she'd come to know couldn't be into anything nefarious. It didn't add up. A man she trusted had scammed her once before. It couldn't be happening again. She chased the thought away for another time.

Juliette and Sky. *Crap.* Kate groaned. Hopefully, a night's sleep had helped the young couple realize the importance of not doing anything rash. Kate sat up and stretched, then slid out of bed. Silence from the other room told her Zach had already left. Her stomach rumbled. She wished Zach's call yesterday had come after dessert.

In the bathroom, she turned on the small radio and was greeted with Christmas music. Tomorrow was Christmas Eve and the Morgans' holiday bash. Kate so did not want to celebrate the holiday with the Morgans and their guests. Homesickness punched her in the stomach. She'd call her parents today and again on Christmas. Her brothers and their families would be spending Christmas at the family home in Spirit Lake. She missed them, especially her nieces and nephews.

Dressed in black jeans and a beige sweater with silver sequins scattered tastefully throughout, and wearing silver flats, she headed to breakfast. In the entry hall, a woman dressed in a suit and holding a clipboard, directed workers who were setting up sawhorses and tools. Boxes of silver and blue metallic fabric, along with greenery and small lights were set in one corner of the spacious hall. Apparently the Morgans went all out on their party decorations.

She continued to the dining room where Zach sat alone at the table finishing his meal. He looked up when she entered. "'Morning."

Nodding to him, Kate filled a plate from the food on the server and took a seat opposite Zach. A pot of coffee rested in front of her. Without a word, she poured herself a cup and tackled her breakfast. She knew Zach watched her, but she felt in no mood to talk to him yet.

The worst of her hunger satisfied, she picked up her mug and said, "Quiet this morning."

"You slept through the drama earlier."

Dread pressed against her chest, and she set down her coffee. "What drama?" But she knew.

"Juliette ran off during the night. She texted Gloria that she'd gone to Sky and they were getting married. Gloria was in hysterics when I came down ninety minutes ago. Carlisle was so red-faced with anger, I feared he'd have a heart attack."

"I didn't want her to do that, Zach. Believe me."

"Good luck convincing Gloria and Carlisle. They blame you. I'm sure Tripp and Missy are gloating, no doubt thinking you and I are out of favor now." His lips formed a wry grin. "Like we were ever in favor."

She stood. "Where are Gloria and Carlisle? I'll talk to them."

He put his hands out. "Don't know."

"I'll find them and assure them you and I aren't responsible for Juliette running off."

"I'm not sure any of it matters anymore."

At the despondency in his voice and the tightness of his features, some of her unease toward him dissipated. They still had to talk about Rosina and that phone call. For now, she had a contract to fulfill. She'd try to make things right between him and the others, especially his dad.

Kate didn't find the Morgans in the living room or sunroom. She passed the open door of the study and spotted Elle and Greg working at the small table. She tapped lightly on the door and they both looked up.

Elle smiled. "Hi, Kate."

Greg didn't acknowledge Kate and went back to the papers on his desk.

"Have you seen Gloria or Carlisle?" Kate asked.

"Not since breakfast." Elle slipped off her glasses. "They were so upset about Juliette. What a shame for the whole family."

Greg pushed aside the papers he'd been reading and turned his attention to the women. "If you two want to gossip, do it on your own time, not while I'm working. I don't give a whit about the Morgan family problems. I only care if it affects my business." His cold gaze caught Kate's. "It had better not interfere with business."

His arrogance and subtle threat made Kate clench and unclench her hands.

He removed his glasses and stood, his eyes narrowed at Kate. "I understand you're behind this mess. What kind of woman did my son marry? I'm sorry Carlisle invited you and Zach here. You've caused too much trouble."

Elle jumped up from her chair. "Greg! What a terrible thing to say."

"Sit down, Elle." He waved a hand but Elle continued to stand, glaring at him.

Kate took deep breaths and counted to ten, steeling herself not to tell this egotistical, infuriating man what she thought of him. "I haven't upset anything and neither has Zach. He's your son, your only child. He came here to spend the holidays with the only family he has, and he wanted you to meet his wife."

She swallowed and summoned all her acting ability. If this were a movie scene, her Oscar nomination would be in the bag. "Zach and I are in love. We're starting our life together. He wants a relationship with you. So do I." She fought the urge to retch on that last sentence.

He sat down. "Family is overrated. Zach is a disappointment to me. Does he really think marrying someone like you will convince me he's changed his playboy ways?"

Red-hot anger propelled Kate from the door to stand in front of the table. "What do you mean—someone like me?"

"Zach must have told you I checked you out. Saw your marriage license, had someone investigate your background."

"How dare you investigate me?" She didn't need to act angry. Her body flushed with heat, and her heart pounded.

"Zach will inherit millions from my estate. You don't think I wouldn't check out the woman he marries? How did you, a no-account actress from some crappy little town in the Poconos, convince my son to marry you?"

Elle gasped and sat down.

Kate drew in slow, steady breaths to keep from slapping the top of the table, or punching Lyon in the face. She willed peace to flow through her veins. Any way she answered, she might implicate herself and Zach in their little deception. She couldn't let this offensive man get away with his rudeness.

"You are the most unlikeable man I've ever met. It's a wonder

Zach turned out as good as he has. Zach's told me what a terrible father you've been to him, shipping him off to boarding school after his mom died, abandoning him to spend lonely holidays there with the staff while you were gallivanting around the world with your latest girlfriend."

Leaving him staring open-mouthed, she whirled around and stomped to the door, then turned back. "You should thank the universe you have a son like Zach, a man who cares for you and about you. I intend to give him the happiness and love he deserves and could never get from you."

Kate stepped into the hall and slammed the door shut. She'd made a bigger mess. But it sure felt liberating to get that off her chest.

CHAPTER TWENTY-SIX

Zach knew Kate entered the game room before he saw her. Her lavender cologne, soft and gentle like her, enveloped him. He concentrated on knocking the ball into the corner pocket before turning to her.

"You got me," Tripp said. "I owe you a bottle of bourbon."

Zach ignored him, his attention on Kate.

She strolled toward him, her hips swaying suggestively. The woman could wear a baggy housedress and she'd set his pulse to double time. Her tight black jeans and sparkly sweater enhanced her natural beauty and threatened to set off a series of erotic fantasies in his head. *Down, boy.*

With Tripp in the room, Zach had to put on the performance of a man totally in love with his wife. He'd begun to wonder if it was an act.

He reached for Kate when she got near, and grabbed her to him, half bending her over to plant a hungry kiss on her full, inviting lips. Her luscious taste incited him to throw self-control out the Palladian windows.

"I'll leave you two to whatever is going on here."

Tripp's words brought Zach from his sensual haze. He ended the kiss, but held Kate close with his arm around her waist.

The other man left the room and closed the door behind him.

Kate pulled free of Zach. "What was that about?" She brushed her hands down the sides of her jeans.

"Pool. Tripp and I played several games. I won them all."

Her eyes glinted with gold fire. He wanted to tell her she looked beautiful and sexy when angry, but he valued his nose too much to have her break it.

"I'm not talking about a pool game," she said. "What was that kiss about?"

He leaned closer. "Playing my part of a besotted newlywed."

"Besotted? What is this, the Middle Ages?"

"Checking to see if you were paying attention." He grinned. "Tell me you didn't like the kiss."

"I didn't like it."

"You're a terrible liar."

Her features tightened and she drew an audible breath. "After what I just did, our little gig here might be over."

"What did you do?"

She gathered her hair into a ponytail, then let it fall softly around her face and over her shoulders. The temptation to run his hands through her silky hair made Zach take a step forward. The anxiety on her face stopped him.

"I couldn't find Gloria and Carlisle but I saw your dad and Elle in the office," she said. "I went in to ask if they'd seen the others, and I had an altercation with Greg."

"About what?"

Kate looked down and kicked the edge of the rug with her toe. "He said he wished the Morgans had never invited us, that I'd caused trouble, and he accused me of being a gold-digger."

"He had no right. I'm sorry Kate. I'll speak to him."

She chewed her lip and lifted her head. He had an insane urge to grab her to him and suck on that alluring bottom lip.

"I doubt it would help for you to talk to him. I called him a lousy father. I said he didn't treat you right."

"You don't need to defend me," Zach said softly, warmed by her defense of him.

"Someone should call him out on what a terrible father he's been."

Zach leaned against the pool table and massaged the bridge of his nose. His entire plan had drifted away like a sandstorm in the desert. Disappointment clogged his chest. His dad would lose everything, and along with it any hope of mending their relationship.

Kate stared intently at him. Agony reflected in her eyes. She might have ruined his plans but at that moment, he'd never admired anyone more. Kate had courage.

"What's done is done," he said. "The final curtain call. We'll make some excuse and leave." He stepped closer and touched the pads of his fingers to her lips. She stiffened and pulled away. Regret swept him. Whatever had upset her last night stood between them like a prickly cactus. He had to make things right for her. "I want you to have a happy Christmas. If we stay here, you'll be miserable. Let's try to salvage what we can of the holiday."

Unshed tears sparkled in her eyes. "I understand if you don't want to pay me."

"The plan was for us to present a united front, to convince him I'd changed my ways and settled down. It was probably a bad strategy to begin with. You did your part. I don't blame you for Juliette or for what you said to Dad. I'll pay you what we agreed on."

She chewed her lip again, looking adorable.

He took her hand and held it tight. "Let's pack, make our excuses, and get the hell out of here."

The door opened and Tripp swaggered in, a bottle of bourbon in one hand and a glass of the liquor in the other. "Here's your prize, Zach, old man. You'll need it. I talked to Carlisle." Tripp leered at Kate.

Zach took a step forward, ready to knock out the other man's lights. Kate squeezed his hand, stopping him.

Tripp nodded to Zach. "You beat me at pool, but I'm winning the long game. Carlisle is mad as hell at the two of you. I'm looking more golden by the minute. After this, you won't have any say at all in the company. You'll never be a match for me."

Kate gripped Zach's hand harder.

Tripp laughed and ogled Kate again. Zach's muscles tightened. He balled his free hand at his side and took a fighting stance.

Kate yanked on his arm and stood on tiptoe to whisper in his ear. "He's not worth it. You're not leaving the field to him. We're staying."

"You're sure?"

She nodded.

He put his hand on her back and led her out of the room, ignoring Tripp.

* * *

AWAY FROM THE closed doors of the game room, Zach looked down at Kate. "You're okay with staying?"

She touched his arm. His muscles tensed under her fingers. "I'm up to the challenge." Despite whatever secrets he held, they were in this together.

"Thanks for stopping me from beating the crap out of that jerk." A hard edge of anger filled his voice.

"If you had hit him, it would be one more reason for the Morgans and your dad to show us the door."

They climbed the stairs from the bottom level. When they reached the main floor, Zach kissed her lightly on the lips. "Go up to the room. I'll meet you there a little later and we'll go for a walk. We could use it. I want to find my dad, see what damage has been done."

Her mind a confused mess, Kate watched him march away. Like an acting part that spoke to her, the realization struck that as much as she needed the money Zach had promised, she wanted to help him. He might be into something illicit, but every cell in her body denied that. Maybe he loved another woman, which hurt Kate more than she cared to acknowledge, but Zach needed her. If she could help him repair his relationship with Greg and live the life he truly wanted, with no subterfuge, her work here would be complete.

She started up the stairs to their suite on the upper floor. Voices from the living room reached her. Curious, she headed there. Staff, under the direction of Gloria and Ava, were moving furniture around in preparation for the guests expected for the party tomorrow night. Mother and daughter turned when she entered. Ava sneered and Gloria studied her with cold eyes.

"Gloria, can I help with anything?" Kate couldn't talk to Gloria about Juliette in front of the staff and Ava, but she could get on the woman's good side by helping out.

The older woman's eyes shot ice picks at her. "Haven't you done enough?"

Kate retreated a half-step. "I'm sorry, but what are you talking about?"

"Don't play innocent," Ava said. "It's your fault Juliette ran off with that—that driver."

A lump formed in Kate's stomach. "I counseled her to sleep on it and not make any rash decisions. I suggested she finish school and get her degree, and if she and Sky were still in love, they could discuss their future then."

Ava rolled her eyes. "Yeah, right."

"I have no time to waste on my younger daughter," Gloria

said. "My mind and my energies are focused on the Christmas party." She turned away, a clear dismissal.

The women went back to directing the staff, leaving Kate standing there.

Her steps slow, Kate went up to her room. Sadness pulsed through her. Poor Juliette. No wonder the young woman wanted to run away. She, Kate, would leave too if she had parents and a sibling who didn't seem to care about her. Kate's parents loved her and her brothers unconditionally, and would support them regardless of what they did.

Kate blinked back tears. She missed her family. She snatched her phone off the night table. Holding it to her chest, she fought guilt. Her parents thought she planned to spend the holidays with Graceann. They didn't know about her contract marriage. When it was over and she handed them the money, she'd tell them everything. They didn't blame her for Brian's scam, but she'd never forgive herself if she didn't make some attempt to get back their savings.

Settling on the loveseat, she punched in her parents' number. "Hi, Mom," she said when her mom answered. Tears streamed down Kate's face. After this, she'd never again lie to her parents.

CHAPTER TWENTY-SEVEN

A little before dawn the next morning, Kate, dressed in workout clothes, tiptoed out of the room so as not to waken Zach. She left the house by the back door to go for a run, hoping to clear her head. She needed to make sense of the past few days. She also wanted to get in some exercise before things got crazy busy around here with the party tonight.

She shivered in the cool desert air, glad she'd worn long sleeves. The sun hadn't fully risen yet, and the night birds and insects sang their goodbyes in a concert that rang through the clear morning. Small clouds scudded across a sky streaked in purple and gold.

She'd been raised in the Pocono Mountains, which she loved. In the summer, those mountains were covered in carpets of lush green; and in the winter, snow glistened on their tops, diamonds put there by nature. The mountains surrounding Las Vegas possessed a different grandeur, smoky colored and pushing up from the desert floor to dominate the horizon.

After about three miles, she stopped to catch her breath. Ahead of her loomed the garage, the doors closed, and no one around. Kate leaned against a palm tree, breathing deeply, and remembered the day she'd walked here with Juliette. Sky had been detailing one of the cars, but when he looked up and spotted Juliette, his face had lit, love shining from his eyes. If the young couple loved each other, they'd be okay.

Painful memories surfaced. Brian's lies and deceit. The hurt he'd inflicted on her and her family. She squeezed her eyes shut and rubbed a hand down her face. She'd survived.

After that humiliating ordeal, Kate had toughened. No man would ever hurt her again. Zach's image intruded into her thoughts. She wondered if his Mr. Nice Guy was an act. It didn't matter. She'd contracted to do a job, for which she'd be well-paid. Whatever Zach did after that wasn't her concern. Her stomach cramped at the thought of parting ways with him.

With a sigh, Kate continued her run. Her head throbbed with all the unanswered questions. She would do her job, she would get through this.

With the sun high in the sky and her exercise over, she entered the house through the back door and headed to their suite. Zach, dressed in jeans and a T-shirt, sat on the sofa and turned at her approach.

"'Morning, sunshine," he said. "Why didn't you wake me? I would have gone with you."

She tightened her ponytail and wiped sweat from her brow with the back of her hand. "I needed to be alone, to think things through."

He frowned. "What things?"

"Nothing important."

He gestured toward the small table. "Help yourself to coffee and toast. The maid brought them up."

"Thanks. I'll eat after I get out of these sweaty clothes." She strolled toward the bedroom.

"We should talk about the elephant in the room."

Zach's words stopped her and she whirled around. "What elephant?"

"You're upset, thinking you made a mess of things with my dad and the Morgans. I don't want you to worry. I can handle whatever happens. Anything you did was out of kindness and wanting to help."

She blinked, digesting his words. Warmth spread over her neck to her face. "That's probably the nicest thing you've ever said to me."

"I mean it. We have a contract, which you've more than lived up to. You didn't need to defend me to Dad, but you did. I'm grateful."

"I don't like the way he treats you. I didn't want Juliette to run away, but her family sure isn't very understanding. I'm sorry for her. She needed a friend."

He smiled, showing even white teeth. Kate had always loved his smile.

"Another thing," he said.

Warning bells went off in her head. "What?"

"Our day together in Vegas was great. I thought you felt the same, but you turned cold. If I did something to upset you, please tell me so I can make it right."

She could no longer ignore that phone call. "I need to know something. The truth, please. Are you into anything illegal?"

He jerked his head. "You heard the call. I'd hoped you hadn't."

"I heard enough to make me wonder if you're into some sort of illicit activity."

"I promise you everything I'm doing is aboveboard. I'm not at liberty yet to divulge. It's all good, but there are others involved and we agreed to stay quiet for a while longer. It involves some delicate negotiations and we don't want to mess things up. Please trust me."

Kate wanted to believe him. He'd never done anything to make her suspect he had his hands in unlawful activities. She wondered if he'd tell her if she was his "real" wife.

She wouldn't ask him about Rosina. The other woman didn't concern her, and truth be told, Kate didn't want to confirm he loved another woman.

"I want to believe you. I'll give you the benefit of the doubt for a time but I need the truth of what you've got going."

He released a breath. "Thank you for that. Can you tell me what things you had to think through on your run?"

"Personal stuff."

"If you ever want to talk about anything, I'm here."

His kindness brought a lump to her throat and opened a little door in her heart.

CHAPTER TWENTY-EIGHT

*T*hat evening, Kate sat at the vanity applying her makeup. A pivotal act in her real-life drama would start soon. She clutched her blush compact, fighting the anxiety that roiled her stomach. She could do this. At the black-tie party tonight, she had to give a convincing performance as the loving newlywed and contrite houseguest. She'd do all she could to make amends with Gloria and Carlisle, and Zach's dad.

She rested her chin on her hands and stared at herself in the mirror. She looked more glamorous than she ever had, except when on stage. The secret marriage contract, the scene in the study between Greg and her, the rift between Juliette and her family, all would make a great Lifetime or Hallmark movie in which she and Zach were the stars.

Smiling at her fanciful thoughts, she went to the closet and pulled out the green silk gown she'd found at a trendy boutique in Santa Monica. Paired with red stiletto sandals and a necklace and earrings with stones that looked like rubies, her outfit shouted Christmas. But in a classy way, she hoped.

She slipped on the dress and smoothed her palms down the soft fabric, then pirouetted in front of the long mirror, giving her hair a toss. It curled gently and framed her face. She fastened the pendant, then, for luck, rubbed her finger over the marquis-shaped stone nestled in her cleavage. She missed her gold drama mask necklace. Sighing, she added the chandelier style earrings. Moving her head back and forth, she admired the way the earrings caught the light and sparkled. The sensual movement of her hair gliding over her shoulders, bared by the thin straps of her gown, made her think of Zach. She felt beautiful and confident, almost like she wasn't playing a part at all. She hoped Zach liked the way she looked.

With one last appraisal of her reflection, she said, "Any more sparkles and I'll shine like the tree at the Augustus."

When she opened the bedroom door, Zach spun to face her. Their eyes locked. The man rocked a tux. His blindingly white shirt dazzled. Her gaze trailed over him. She appreciated the superb fit of his tuxedo that she knew had to be custom made. Even his black shoes were polished to a high shine. The man had it going on.

He let out a low whistle. "Wow! You're gorgeous."

"Thanks. You're pretty hot yourself."

His green eyes lit, and his lips tilted in one of his signature sexy grins. She'd swoon, if she were prone to swooning.

"You think I'm hot?" he asked.

"Puhleez. You know you are."

Laughing, he held out his arm. "Ready for the show, Mrs. Lyon?"

She slid her arm through his. "Let's go break a leg."

The railing of the staircase was festooned with fresh greens. White fairy lights twinkled from the branches. The scents of evergreen and cinnamon reminded Kate of Christmas in Spirit Lake. Filled anew with homesickness, she stumbled on the hall carpet.

Zach held her, pulling her close. "You okay?"

"I'd rather wear my Chucks than these high heels."

He leaned toward her. "But they're so much sexier than those high-top Chucks you wear."

"I prefer my high-tops, thank you very much."

His deep, throaty laugh almost made her stumble again. She really needed to get hold of herself.

Frowning, Zach stopped and released her. He reached into his inside jacket pocket to pull out his phone. "A text."

He looked down at the screen, then swiped. Pictures flashed past. He raised his head, disgust written on his face.

"What is it?" she asked.

"Tripp's girlfriend posted sexually explicit shots of her and Tripp. My PI sent them."

Kate grabbed Zach's arm. "You have your ammunition for your father."

Shaking his head, he slid the phone back into his pocket. "I'm not going to use them."

"Why not?"

"Too sleazy. Whatever Tripp is doing with another woman is between him and Missy. She'll be hurt by this. I can't do it. My dad has to believe me and open his eyes to the way Tripp and Carlisle treat him. He'll trust me on my merits, or not at all."

Kate slipped her arm through his again. "A classy decision."

"You understand?"

She kissed his cheek. "You're a good man, Lyon."

He laughed. "You'll ruin my reputation. I'm no Boy Scout."

When they descended to the entry hall, Kate gasped. All day yesterday and earlier today, sounds of hammering had echoed through the house as teams of workers put up the decorations and trees and built sets to rival any movie's. She'd glimpsed the décor throughout the day, but hadn't seen the finished product until now. The hall had been transformed into a glistening scene out of the movie, *Frozen*. A giant white Christmas tree, lit with blue and silver and decked with the same color balls, dominated the area. Translucent lights sparkled from the ceiling. Pots of white poinsettias set strategically throughout continued the theme.

"Hard to believe we're in the desert," she said.

"Where the temperature outside is sixty degrees."

"They do this every year?"

"Sure do, but this is the first time I've accepted their invitation."

"Why is that?"

He squeezed her hand where it rested in his arm. "I never had you to go with me."

"You're full of it."

"Newlyweds. Remember."

"You're right, *darling.*"

He grinned down at her. "That's better, *pumpkin.* Let's make our entrance."

Arm-in-arm, they ambled toward the living room, along with other arriving guests, all dressed to the nines. Henry and an assistant stood ready to take coats and other outerwear from the attendees. Some of the women wore furs. *Gotta show off their money no matter the temperature.* Contrite for her snarky thoughts, Kate bit her lip. It was none of her business how others showed their wealth.

A Douglas fir, the elaborately gowned angel on top reaching for the ceiling, stood in a corner of the cavernous living room. Multi-colored lights shone from its branches. Large glass balls in shades of red and green adorned the festive tree. Antique children's toys were set up in a creative display along one wall. *Frozen* in the entry hall, and *Babes in Toyland* in the living room.

"They sure go all out," Kate said.

Zach's mouth twisted in a wry smile. "I suspect they're in competition with their wealthy friends."

A uniformed waiter holding a tray of champagne flutes approached them. Zach took two glasses and handed one to Kate.

"To Christmas." He touched his glass to hers.

"To Christmas with my family." Another round of homesickness grabbed Kate.

"You miss them?"

"I do."

"It must be nice to have a close family." His features tightened. "I wouldn't know."

"Maybe you'll have a family of your own someday."

He shrugged. "Not on my bucket list."

The vulnerability on his chiseled features arrowed to her heart, cutting another chink in the wall around it. Zach Lyon, her sort-of husband, had a gentleness to him she wouldn't have guessed. She didn't believe he was into anything shady.

"Zach, you look amazing."

Kate whirled to face Ava. The blonde wore a shimmering gold gown with a neckline that displayed most of her assets.

The woman sidled closer to Zach, ignoring Kate.

"Ava," he said, his voice strained.

Ava slid her hand along his arm. "You fill out a tux better than any man has a right to."

"Thanks." He sipped his drink, not looking at her.

Kate gripped the stem of her glass and fought the urge to slap the woman's hand away from *her husband*. For Zach's sake, she couldn't afford to offend any more members of the Morgan family.

Zach extricated himself from the blonde python and grabbed Kate's hand, squeezing tightly.

Ava pressed her lips together and swiped a glass of champagne from a waiter.

"Your parents have done a wonderful job on the decorations." Kate's voice dripped with enough sugar to give her a rush. "Your house rivals the display at the Augustus."

Ava lifted her chin, the haughty lady of the manor. "We use the same firm that decorates their botanical gardens."

"How marvelous," Kate said.

Next to her, Zach coughed.

Ava waved her fingers. "I must mingle."

When she'd moved away, Zach laughed and looked down at Kate. "Marvelous? What is this, a 1920's movie set?"

"It just came out. Everything here is too over the top. We're actors in a play, or passengers on the deck of the Titanic."

"Let's hope we don't have the same outcome as the Titanic."

Kate held her glass aloft. "I'll drink to that."

He clinked his glass with hers. "Your humor makes it easier to deal with this crowd."

His words warmed her more than the rich champagne.

CHAPTER TWENTY-NINE

*Z*ach and Kate circulated among the guests, nibbling on tasty appetizers of crab cakes, grilled shrimp, mini tacos, and other delicacies she didn't recognize. They said their hellos to Gloria and Carlisle, but the hosts, bustling around, barely acknowledged them. Kate hoped they weren't still angry over her perceived role in Juliette's leaving.

She spotted Zach's father with Elle, and tugged on Zach's sleeve, getting his attention from the tray of scallops wrapped in bacon a waiter held out to him.

"What is it?" He popped the treat into his mouth.

"Your dad and Elle are over there. She looks incredible, better than she did at the Ableman's, and she looked terrific then."

Zach followed her gaze. "Elle really is a beautiful woman. I don't think any of us realized it."

"You men can be clueless sometimes. Even dressed in her mousy clothes, I could see her beauty."

He chuckled. "We men are a bunch of Philistines."

Her laugh joined his. "You said it, not me. Let's go over and talk to them."

They threaded their way around the guests and waitstaff until they reached the other couple.

Determined to make things better with Greg, Kate gave him and Elle her biggest smile. "Merry Christmas."

Elle smiled. "Merry Christmas, Kate, Zach."

Greg grunted and sipped his drink.

Jerk. Kate turned to Elle. "You, wow. That dress is gorgeous."

Elle's gown of dark blue velvet skimmed her slim body, hugging her curves. The deep neckline showed off her impressive cleavage. A pendant with a large sapphire-colored stone peeked from between her breasts. Matching earrings dangled from her ears.

Elle's blush brightened her face and made her seem years younger. "Thanks. I bought the dress and jewelry yesterday at a trendy boutique at the Calliope. I went to a salon there today for my hair and makeup. I didn't want to bother you again because I knew you'd be busy getting ready for tonight. I'm glad you like it."

"You look wonderful, Elle," Zach said. "Are you having a good time?"

"Thanks. I'm having a wonderful time."

Greg ignored them to talk to another guest.

Elle touched Kate's arm. "I'm sorry for the way Greg treated you yesterday in the study. He was rude and out of line."

"Don't worry. These things happen. I'm over it."

"You're a generous person, Kate."

The man talking with Greg walked away, but Greg continued to snub the small group around him.

"I hope you're enjoying yourself, Dad, and not worrying too much about business."

Zach's words forced his dad's attention back to him. Greg scowled. "Business is always on my mind."

"The Morgans can sure throw a party, don't you think, Greg?" Kate said. The older man finally made eye contact with her.

"Waste of money if you ask me. The Morgans live high. Don't know how they do it," he added in a softer tone.

Despite his "bah humbug" attitude, Greg was civil to her, a promising sign.

"I'm starving," Elle said. "I'm going to find something to eat." She nodded to Greg. "You coming?"

"No, I'm fine." He stared at Elle as if seeing her for the first time.

She shrugged and sauntered away, hips swaying.

Greg's eyes followed Elle through the crowd. Other men watched her, too. Kate sipped her drink to hide her smile.

Zach raised an eyebrow to Kate.

Greg focused on a man who'd stopped Elle to talk. "I'd better make sure she's all right. Elle's a soft touch."

When he strode away, Zach looked at Kate with a huge grin. "She's a lot savvier than Dad thinks. I suspect he doesn't know what hit him."

"Let's hope this matchmaking works out better than Juliette and Sky. Thanks for being understanding about all of it."

"You didn't tell Juliette to run away, and I don't think Elle's going anywhere."

"She's got your dad right where she wants him."

Kate gave her empty glass to a waiter and turned to Zach. "I need to go to our room to use the bathroom."

"I'll mix a little more, talk to my dad, see if I can get him to smile."

"Good luck."

Tripp paced the wide hall when Kate exited her suite a short time later. Foreboding pushed her to hurry past him toward the stairs.

He grabbed her arm and pulled her around to face him.

Red-hot anger ratcheted up her pulse. "What are you doing? Let go."

He pushed her against the wall, using his powerful body to

hold her there. He touched strands of her hair that fell over her bare shoulders and brushed his fingers along the tops of her breasts.

"Let me go." She tried to raise her leg to knee him in the groin but he had her pinned against him.

"You are one sexy woman. You need a real man, like me, not some no-good playboy like that man you're married to. My wife and I haven't had sex in seven in months, since she got pregnant. My girlfriend is back in New York. I want a little, and you're just the woman to give it to me."

"Whatever the hell are you on? I'm happily married, and even if I weren't, you'd be the last guy I'd be interested in."

"I love a feisty woman." He took her lips in a harsh kiss, forcing his tongue into her mouth.

Kate gagged and bit his tongue.

Tripp jumped away. "You bitch!"

Suddenly Zach had Tripp against the wall, holding him by his shirt collar. Zach's free arm went back and his hand formed a fist, prepared to hit Tripp.

Kate grabbed Zach's arm. "No, he's not worth it. Don't."

Breathing heavily, Zach looked at her. "Let me at him. He's got it coming."

"Let him go. I'm not hurt, and everything will be ruined. He won't bother me again."

Zach released Tripp and pushed him. Tripp fell, then picked himself up and rubbed his hand over his mouth.

"Don't you ever touch my wife again," Zach ground out.

Tripp smirked. "She was asking for it."

Zach pulled back his arm again, ready to strike.

Kate hauled Zach away and glared at Tripp. "Better get out of here before I let him go at you."

Tripp hurried down the stairs.

Zach threw the other man an angry look, then followed Kate into their room.

He closed the door and leaned against it, anger etched on his face. "That SOB. If I hadn't come up to check on you…"

"He's a jerk."

"Did he hurt you?" He pushed away from the door and pulled her to him. Holding her close, he rubbed his hand up and down her back.

"He didn't hurt me. But his tongue will be sore for a while. Poor Missy. She's stuck with him. He admitted he has a girlfriend in New York."

"I may rethink showing those pictures to my dad."

"Don't. Tripp will get what he deserves. I stopped you from punching out his lights because your dad would think you were still the wild playboy who can't settle down. Tripp would have found a way to blame you and make himself some sort of hero. I couldn't let you fall into that trap."

Zach took her face between his big hands and kissed her, his lips moving tenderly over hers. He pulled away and held her at arms' length. "Keeping you safe is more important than my dad's company. If Tripp tries anything else with you, you won't be able to keep me from beating the crap out of him."

"I wouldn't try." Kate's adrenaline began to wear off and she started shaking.

Zach grabbed her in a fierce hug. "Sweetheart, it's okay. Let it all out. I won't let anything happen to you."

She wound her arms around his waist and held tight. "I'm strong." Her voice was muffled against his hard chest. "I can handle myself but I've never been attacked like that before."

"I know you're strong, but no woman should have to put up with what Tripp did." Zach pushed gently away and put his fingers under her chin until their gazes met. "If you want to leave, we will."

"I'll be okay." She stood on tiptoe and kissed him, pouring out her fears and her blossoming need for him. She ended the kiss and breathed in a calming breath. "Let's go back to the party and schmooze."

"Schmooze?"

"I'm a world-class schmoozer."

They left the room and walked down the stairs, arm-in-arm. Warmth settled over Kate. She and Zach had started a new act in their relationship.

CHAPTER THIRTY

Back in their room after an evening of sumptuous food, fine wine, and entertainment provided by a trio singing Christmas carols, Zach closed the door and rested against it, loosening his tie.

Kate toed off her shoes and flung herself on the sofa. "I may never eat again."

"Me, neither." Slipping off his jacket, he dropped it on a chair and plopped down next to her.

"I enjoyed the party, but I miss Christmas Eve with my family," she said.

The melancholy in Kate's voice tugged at Zach's heart. He took her hand and held it. Longing filled him for the family and love Kate knew, two things denied him growing up. Rosina had tried to fill the void left by his mother, but it hadn't been enough. He had needed his father, too.

"Tell me about your Christmases in Spirit Lake." He slid his arm around her shoulders. When she snuggled against him, contentment coursed through him, and his breath came slow and easy. He never wanted the feeling to end.

Her sigh settled over him like the promise of dreams realized.

"I'm the only girl, with two older brothers," she said. "At times, they made my life rough, teasing me, daring me to do things that would get me into trouble."

The love in her voice made Zach draw her closer. "Now I understand why you can't refuse a dare."

She laughed. "I almost refused yours."

"But you didn't. And I'm grateful. Tell me more about you and your brothers."

"No matter how many fights we kids had all year, when Christmas came, we presented a united front to make sure Santa brought us everything we wanted."

"That sounds like fun." He couldn't hide the wistfulness in his voice.

"It was. Christmas Eve, we barely slept. When we were teens, we went to Midnight Mass with our friends. We all went back to our house where Mom had put out food, and we'd party. We didn't go to bed until the wee hours."

Kate settled more comfortably against him. "My godfather would visit all his godchildren on Christmas, starting with me. He usually knocked on our door at eight in the morning. I'd stumble downstairs to see him. And of course, to receive my gift. I remember always being tired Christmas Day, but I wouldn't have it any other way."

Zach rested his chin on the top of Kate's head, scenes from her Christmases playing in his head like a movie. "I would have liked that."

Kate twisted to meet his gaze. The softness in her gold-brown eyes touched the lonely places in his heart. "You said you spent most holidays at boarding school. Did you spend any with your dad or other relatives?"

He shook his head. "My dad was an only child. My mom had a sister but they were estranged and I never met her." He stared across the room, seeing the lonesome little boy spending the holidays without a family. "The staff at the school did everything they could to give me a loving Christmas, but I always knew my dad didn't want me."

"Oh, Zach." Kate sat up and cupped his face between her hands. "I'm so sorry."

"I've dealt with it. When I got older, I spent my holidays with Rosina and her large clan. I saw what a close family was all about."

Kate stiffened and released him. "And you're in love with this Rosina."

"What? Love? Rosina was my nanny, and when I went to boarding school, she took a position as a maid in my dad's household. She did it to stay in touch with me any way she could. She managed to convince Dad to let me spend the holidays with her family."

"Rosina was your nanny?" Kate asked.

"Why?"

She massaged her forehead and stood. "There is something I should tell you."

Dread wound through him, and he pushed up from the sofa and faced her. "What is it?"

She looked down, then back to him. "When I overheard your phone call that day in Vegas, you mentioned Rosina and said to tell her you missed her and loved her. I-uh thought she was a woman you were in love with."

Relief bubbled to the surface and he smiled. "You thought that?"

She nodded.

"You were jealous?" That thought made him happier than he had a right to be.

"Don't get too full of yourself." She tapped a finger to his chest. "I like to think we're friends now. You said you're not into anything illicit. Please come clean with me now. I want the truth."

His mind spun. Kate had been a trouper through everything.

The others would understand. He gripped her shoulders and looked deeply into her eyes. He saw the confusion, and the hope. "You deserve the truth. Here it is. A few friends and I, with help from the local church, started a foundation in Nicaragua. Rosina is from that country, and I spent the best summers of my life in her little village during breaks from college. Since retiring, she lives there. Our foundation is building a shelter for women and children. My gambling winnings go there, and I send money on a regular basis."

He touched her chin with his fingers. "Okay now? I'm not into anything illegal. Please don't tell anyone about Nicaragua. We don't want anything leaked until the plans are finalized."

Kate drew a deep breath, and her eyes locked with his. "Thank you for telling me. That relieves my mind. Why keep it a secret? You're doing a great thing."

"I'm not special. Others without my resources do a lot more. Our group has had to grease a lot of palms for the building permits needed. We don't want to mess anything up so close to the end."

"I understand."

He took both her hands in his. "Merry Christmas, Kate."

"Merry Christmas, Zach."

Holding hands, they stared at each other.

With a groan, Zach gathered her into his arms and kissed her waiting lips. She opened to him, pressing closer, giving herself freely.

He palmed her nape and slanted his mouth over hers. Their tongues danced to an erotic tune. Her muted whimpers fueled his hunger for her.

They dropped to the sofa together. Kate lay back, and he positioned himself over her. He watched the play of emotions on her expressive face—desire, warmth, wonder. Her full lips begged for more. Her golden eyes, dark with need, searched his.

"Kate." He took her lips again. He wanted to devour her, to claim her as his. Forever.

He left her mouth to trail kisses down her throat to her collarbone. Soft and pliant, she linked her arms around his neck. He kissed her deep cleavage, flicking his tongue out to feast on her smooth flesh. She moaned softly and squirmed under him. His erection threatened to break free from his pants.

Zach slipped her thin straps off her shoulders, exposing more of her chest. He kissed and caressed her breasts under the soft silk. Tremors shook her and she uttered small cries. He pushed her gown farther down and released one perfect breast straining against the lace of her bra.

He freed her other breast and reached behind her to unhook her bra. Flinging the piece of lace away, he sat back on his heels and worshipped her beauty, a feast waiting for him. His pulse raced and his breathing grew shallow.

He bent to trace her pebbled nipples with his tongue. His penis ached to plunge into Kate's heat and never let her go.

"Zach, please, please, I want you," she said on a ragged breath.

"You're sure?" he asked. "I won't do anything you don't want."

Squirming free of him, she stood and let her gown pool at her feet. Clad only in her red lace panties, she was a goddess. His goddess. Only his. She took his hand and looked into his eyes.

The trust in her golden-brown eyes crumbled the last of the chains around his heart. He belonged to her now.

"I'm very sure," she said on a breath.

Hand-in-hand, they went into the bedroom.

CHAPTER THIRTY-ONE

Suddenly shy when they entered the other room, Kate dropped Zach's hand and marched to the night table to turn off the lamp.

He put his hand over hers, stopping her. "Don't."

Her insides trembling, she turned to him. With wonderment on his face, Zach skimmed his fingers over the swell of her breasts. Molten heat uncoiled in her stomach, and her nipples pebbled, aching for him.

He gathered her into his arms. His mouth descended on hers, consuming her with a hunger that matched the fierce need that weakened her knees. He backed her up to the bed, then released her.

He kissed his way down to her midriff. His hands skimmed her ribcage, searing her flesh. His hair shone golden in the dim light. She dug her fingers into the firm skin of his shoulders and drew in harsh, too-fast breaths. He kneeled and removed her panties. Shivers danced along her nerve endings at the sensual slide of the delicate lace on her sensitized flesh.

Zach straightened, and his vivid green gaze roamed over her, burning her flesh as surely as if he touched her.

"You are more beautiful than I imagined," he said, his tone reverent.

"Please, Zach," she rasped on a breath.

His arm around her waist, he pulled back the comforter and top sheet, then tenderly laid her on the bed.

He quickly undressed and stood before her, golden, his muscles rippling in his chest. She let her gaze wander down his perfect body and gasped at his erection, so hard and ready for her.

Joining her, he took her into his arms as his lips sought hers. She opened eagerly to him. His tongue filled her mouth, exploring. She wrapped her arms around his neck and pressed him closer, reveling in the warmth of his taut, sculpted flesh.

He positioned his body over her and leaned his weight on his forearms, on either side of her head. The wicked spark in his eyes fired her blood.

He kissed her, his lips demanding, urgent. Passion exploded around them.

The male scent of him enveloped her, and the heat of his body scorched her. Her insides flipped and begged for more. Zach didn't merely kiss her, he claimed her. Somehow, she'd always known it would be like this with him, a fiery need that branded her with heat. Maybe that was why she'd told herself she disliked him. Her desire for him scared her.

He kissed his way to her throat, then her breasts, swirling his tongue over her nipples. He buried his face between her breasts, eliciting guttural moans from her. Filled with an aching need, she clawed the sheet.

Zach pulled away and looked down at her. Sexual urgency hardened his face. His eyes glimmered with yearning and another emotion that charged her with hope, and a little bit of fear. She brushed fingers over his face, stamping every chiseled feature into her heart.

"We have all night," he said. "But I have to have you now."

"Yes."

He left the bed to pull a condom out of his pants pocket. Sitting on the edge of the bed, he rolled on protection, then turned back to her.

Kate opened her legs, welcoming him. He slid in easily, as if he belonged there. On some level, she knew she'd waited for him her whole life.

Gentle at first, his thrusts increased. She lifted her hips and met his every push. He hammered into her, taking her higher and higher until she came apart in his arms, her orgasm ripping through her with the force of a raging fire.

He shuddered his own climax.

Wrapped in each other, their harsh breathing the only sounds in the room, they lay for long minutes. Finally, Zach sat up and pulled the top sheet and comforter over them. Gathering her into his arms again, he feathered her lips with a soft kiss.

She snuggled against him, inhaling his unique scent mingled with the musk of their lovemaking.

"That was amazing," she breathed.

"I always knew it would be like this between us."

Kate raised up on one elbow to stare down at him. "You had a funny way of showing it, acting like you couldn't stand me."

His features sobered. "A defense mechanism."

"What do you mean?"

"You talk too much." He pulled her head down to his and silenced her with a kiss, feasting on her lips.

Her insides trembled, and she was wet again, needing him. She felt his answering desire in the rock-hard length of him against her thigh.

CHAPTER THIRTY-TWO

*K*ate opened her eyes to pale gold sunlight peeking through the drapes. Happy and languid, she snuggled into the covers, enjoying the warmth and her half-awake state. The memory of the night before, and of the early morning hours, pushed through her consciousness. Fully awake, she reached out to the pillow next to her. Empty. She sat up. Zach was gone.

Anxiety sparred with her happiness. Their lovemaking altered their relationship permanently. More than the physical had changed between them. She'd seen into his soul to his hurt, to the lonely little boy and the lonely man who wore a mask.

They still had a contract. Would they go their separate ways when they completed the mission?

She wanted Zach more than ever. She couldn't resist him, and wouldn't try. The future be damned. She'd take whatever happiness she found. If they split, he'd take a little piece of her heart with him. Hell, he'd take a whole chunk of it.

When she heard the shower, calmness settled over her again, knowing he was near. Resting her head on his pillow, she inhaled his scent and drifted off to sleep.

Later, Kate blinked her eyes to clear the sleep from them and glanced at the bedside clock. Eight. Time to face the day.

Her heart beat faster at the sounds of Zach moving around in the other room. She wondered what surprises this day would bring.

Showered and dressed in a black pencil skirt, dark stockings, black kitten-heeled shoes, and a pale green silk blouse, with her hair in a high ponytail, she was ready to face Zach and the world. Not wanting to go completely conventional, she wore whimsical earrings in the shape of tiny red Christmas balls.

She stepped into the other room and stopped when she saw Zach.

The sexual tension in the room covered them like the twinkling lights that decorated the downstairs. Unable to help herself, her ravenous gaze consumed him. Wearing black tailored pants that emphasized his slim hips and long legs, a fitted beige button-down shirt, and black leather dress shoes, his beauty made her breath hitch and her stomach flutter.

His lips curved in a smile and he walked slowly toward her, a graceful lion claiming his mate. "Good morning." He kissed her tenderly on the lips. "Did you sleep well?"

"I didn't get much sleep, but I feel better than I have in a long time."

He grinned. "Wonder why."

She smacked him on the arm. "You know why, and don't puff up like a proud rooster."

Still grinning, he kissed her again, then pulled away to scan her, his gaze hot. "You're beautiful. Very Christmassy. The earrings are a nice touch. Very Kate."

"Thanks. You look good, too. I like the longer hair. Much better than the buttoned-down executive you portray."

"You're influencing me to change my ways."

"I hope so."

He took one of her hands in his. "Last night and this

morning were amazing." His eyes searched hers. "Are you okay with everything?"

She nodded. "No regrets."

He stared at her for long moments before he released her. "I want to make love to you all day."

Stretching on her toes, she kissed his cheek. "That sounds perfect, but we can't. The others are expecting us."

"The hell with them."

Laughing, she grabbed his hand. "We have a mission to complete. Time to go."

His lips tilted in a teasing grin. "Last chance. We'd have more fun here."

Tempted, she met his gaze. She shook her head and smiled. "We need to get downstairs."

Chattering voices from the dining room greeted them when they stepped into the entry hall. Holding hands, they went into the dining room where the others were having breakfast, the atmosphere festive. Kate looked up at Zach and squeezed his hand. He smiled at her and squeezed her hand in return. Their new closeness lent a layer of warmth between them. They were in this together.

She searched the long table, not seeing Greg and Elle. Probably working in the study. Nothing seemed to take Greg away from business. His loss.

"Merry Christmas, everyone," Zach said.

"Merry Christmas," Kate echoed.

Gloria and Carlisle voiced their holiday greetings. Ava barely looked at them. Kate and Zach took their places at the table while Florence served them breakfast.

Zach held out a coffee carafe to Kate. At her nod, he filled her delicate china cup. Kate added cream to her drink and sipped the life-saving brew.

"You look pretty, Kate," Gloria said, all animosity of the day before gone.

"Thanks," Kate said.

Ava rolled her eyes. "Love the earrings."

Ignoring Ava, Kate concentrated on the delicious meal before her, surprised at her voracious appetite after all they'd eaten the night before. She suppressed a smile. A few fervent rounds of lovemaking sure increased her hunger.

"Where's my dad?" Zach asked.

"Don't know." Carlisle smirked. "Probably sleeping off all the champagne he drank."

"Dad's usually awake early. I've never seen him drink to excess."

The talk around the table turned to opening gifts after breakfast, then dinner plans at the home of Marissa, one of Las Vegas's major singing stars. Kate tamped down her excitement at meeting her idol.

The others, including Zach, seemed to take it in stride they'd have dinner with a world-famous, much-loved pop singer. What a whole new world she found herself in.

Heavy footsteps coming their way drew everyone's attention toward the door. Greg, his features tense and his shirt half tucked into his pants, stomped into the room.

Zach threw down his linen napkin and pushed his chair back, almost toppling it. "Dad! What's wrong?"

"She left me," Greg said, his eyes tortured. "After last night..." He ran a shaking hand over his gray hair. "I woke up and she was gone. How could she do that?" He leveled a harsh glare at Kate and pointed to her. "You! It's all your fault."

CHAPTER THIRTY-THREE

"*D*ad, what are you talking about?" Zach asked. "Why are you accusing my wife of whatever it is that's got you riled up?"

His breathing heavy, Greg stared at Kate.

She fidgeted and took calming breaths. She couldn't let the others know her insides recoiled at the anger shooting from Greg's eyes.

Zach placed his hand on her shoulder. She touched his hand, telling him how much she appreciated his support. No matter what happened, she was comforted in the knowledge Zach had her back.

"Greg, settle down," Carlisle said. "Have some coffee and breakfast. I'm sure we can resolve the problem."

"What's going on, Dad?" Zach asked.

Greg pointed at Kate again. "That woman is responsible for Juliette leaving. Now she's made Elle leave me." His face reddened. "Elle's gone."

Kate pushed back her chair and stood to face Greg. "Gone? Wow! I didn't have anything to do with Elle or Juliette leaving. Why are you accusing me?"

Greg's nostrils flared. "Elle said you gave her the courage. She told me she's loved me for years, and she's tired of waiting for me. Even after last night... She left me a note." His voice cracked. "She's going out into the world to see if she can find a man who appreciates her."

Stifling a grin, Kate rubbed her hand over her mouth. *Way to go, Elle.* "Mr. Lyon, Elle is a grown woman, free to do what she wants."

"You did it," he said. "You fixed her up so she's beautiful. You filled her head with nonsense. I can't run my business without her. I want her back." He looked down at the floor, then back to Kate. "I can't live without her."

Kate widened her eyes at Greg's confession. Some of her animosity toward him began to peel away at the hurt in his eyes and voice.

"Sit, please, Greg." Gloria motioned Florence to bring Greg a plate of food. "Eat, and we'll discuss."

Stony-faced, he sat and folded his arms across his chest, like a toddler, pointedly ignoring the food placed in front of him.

Zach and Kate sat. Kate grabbed her coffee cup and finished her drink, in a vain attempt to settle her nerves.

"Dad, whatever's happened between you and Elle, I'm glad you realize how important she is to you, and I don't mean just to your business," Zach said.

"You knew?" Greg poured cream into his coffee and stirred, but he made no move to drink.

Kate leaned toward him. "Elle confessed to me that she loves you. I helped her change her dress and hair so you would really see her." She twisted her mouth into a wry smile. "Did it work?"

At his stony silence, Kate continued. "Elle is a beautiful, loving woman. She deserves a man who loves her. If you're not that man, let her go. But if you are, then go after her. That's all I have to say."

"You've said more than enough," Greg shot back. He threw

his napkin on the table and jumped up, knocking down his chair. Without a backward glance, he stamped out of the room.

Kate and Zach stared at each other. Kate shrugged. Her matchmaking skills needed refinement.

Dressing for dinner that evening, Kate tried to tamp down the butterflies that had taken up residence in her stomach and were having a holiday party of their own.

"Do not act like a groupie tonight, Kate," she told her reflection in the dresser mirror. "Marissa is a person, like everyone else. You're supposed to be a socialite. A real socialite wouldn't go all fangirl on meeting a celebrity."

Convinced she had control over her fangirl tendencies, Kate sauntered to the closet and pulled out the long-sleeved short black dress with the scoop neckline. The dress skimmed Kate's hips and settled just above her knees. Sheer stockings and her kitten heels completed her look of hip elegance.

She put on gold hoop earrings, then ran her fingers over her bare neckline, once again missing her drama masks necklace. She shrugged. Water under the bridge now.

Zach, dressed and ready, waited for her in the other room. Earlier, he'd invited her to share his shower. The sheer eroticism of making love with him as warm water rained on them seared her with heat. Weak-kneed from the memory, she pressed a palm to her stomach and leaned her hip against the dresser. She'd never craved a man with an insatiable hunger like she did Zach Lyon.

Counting to ten, she drew deep breaths, forcing the sensual thoughts away, and snatched up her red silk clutch from the bed. She and Zach had to finish the terms of their contract, then they could talk about this thing between them.

He whirled to face her when she walked into the other room. His appreciative gaze roamed over her before returning to her face. "You're beautiful."

"Thanks. So are you."

He wore a dark blue suit that fit as if it had been made for him, which she guessed it had. His white shirt and patterned tie perfectly complemented the suit.

She shaded her eyes. "Your shirt is so white, I need my sunglasses."

He laughed and shook his head.

"I guess we'd better head downstairs," she said.

"Before we go, I want to give you your Christmas gift. I didn't want to do it earlier in front of the others."

She put a hand to her throat. "You got me a gift? We agreed no gift exchange."

"I lied." With a teasing grin, he dipped his hand into his jacket pocket and pulled out a piece of jewelry.

"What is that?"

Stepping closer, he held out the necklace. "I think you'll need this."

Tears sprang to her eyes. She reached out and touched the heavy gold chain with the theatre mask charms. "It looks like the necklace...".

"It is."

"How? When?"

"Graceann told me you'd had to pawn this, and how much it meant to you. I bought it the next day. I remembered you always wearing it. I planned for Graceann to gift it to you and say it was from her. I flew out to California with it, and when this whole marriage thing came up between us, I figured I'd give it to you."

"My parents gave me that necklace on my eighteenth birthday." Her insides shook. "I never told them I'd pawned it. When they asked about it, I said the clasp had broken."

"Turn around and I'll put it on you."

She swallowed and swiped at a tear. "Glad my mascara is waterproof." She tried to make light of her emotions, but she was afraid her tears told Zach how much his gesture meant.

She swept her hair away while he fastened the necklace. He

rubbed her shoulders and planted a gentle kiss on the back of her neck.

Kate rubbed the smooth gold masks. "I wore this every day for sixteen years, and felt like a part of me was torn away when I sold it."

She turned and curled her hands over his shoulders. "Thank you. This is the nicest thing anyone has done for me in a long time."

"You're doing something important for me. I wanted to show my appreciation."

She stared into his eyes, soft and kind, and felt herself falling. For him. Zach Lyon. Who would have thought it?

She pulled away before she begged him to make love to her. "Let's get going."

* * *

AT THE PRE-DINNER cocktail party at the singer Marissa's elegant house in a gated community outside Las Vegas, Zach sipped the exquisite Cristal champagne and watched Kate across the room, in animated conversation with a well-dressed elderly woman.

His Kate could charm an apple off a tree. *His* Kate? She'd charmed *him* with her generosity and depth. He tossed back the rest of his drink and set the glass on a nearby table.

He'd judged her by her unorthodox wardrobe choices and her reluctance to leave her comfort zone of Spirit Lake to pursue a real acting career. He'd never let himself know the real Kate, the woman who made him laugh, who made him believe in himself again. And the woman who could make him forget his name with one touch.

The image of her in the shower earlier, pressed against the tile, water pouring over her lush body as he drove into her heat provoked a fierce, desperate need for her again. He didn't want to lose her when the contract ended. Jarred by the admission, he grabbed another drink from a passing waiter and finished half in one gulp.

Thoughts jumbled through his mind. To convince his dad Tripp and Carlisle were planning to dismantle the company, he'd come up with his cockamamie scheme to marry someone, anyone who was game to play a role. Now, he couldn't imagine any woman other than Kate in that part. She'd altered the plot by getting involved in others' love lives, but that was Kate, kind-hearted and ready to dive into a new script where emotions dictated. He didn't regret for one minute she'd agreed to this marriage.

"Great party, huh?" Ava said, coming up to him.

"It is."

"Have you met our hostess before?"

"No, but she's charming and real."

Ava tossed her head back, letting her long blonde waves swish over her shoulders.

Zach guessed she practiced that movement in front of the mirror for hours.

"My family has known Marissa for years," Ava said. "The movie star Cole Lassiter was married here not long ago."

"Didn't he have some sort of contract marriage that turned into the real thing?" Kate and their contract marriage popped into Zach's mind. Maybe he and Kate... Not wanting to go there, he let the thought drop.

Ava waved a hand. "That's the story. Lassiter married some Latina bartender. The whole thing is sappy if you ask me." She glanced around. "Have you seen Tripp and Missy?"

"Not since we got here."

"Tripp is awfully quiet. So are you. Anything happen between you two?"

"Nope." If Ava learned about Tripp's assault on Kate, the blonde would find a way to use it against Kate.

Ava took a step closer and stared up at him with heavily made-up blue eyes. Zach compared her icy stare to Kate's warm gold-brown eyes. Ava came up wanting.

"Later, Ava." He started to walk away.

She put a hand on his arm, stopping him. "You're sexy as hell. Maybe afterwards we could meet, share a drink, and more. For old times' sake." She flicked her tongue over her full, red lips.

"I'm married, Ava, and definitely not in the market."

"That's never stopped Tripp." She pouted. "Why should you be so high and mighty?"

He shrugged off her hand and strolled away. He needed Kate, his wife.

CHAPTER THIRTY-FOUR

Seated in the back of the limo on the way home from Marissa's, Kate leaned her head on Zach's shoulder. Past midnight, sated from food and drink, and from Zach's attentiveness all day, she rubbed a finger over her necklace. His kindness in buying the jewelry back from the pawn shop melted her insides with a warm glow.

Before their contract, he hadn't paid her much attention except to growl at her whenever they were together. Yet, he'd bought the necklace that had meant so much to her.

Photos of him with various long-legged blondes flashed into her mind like a B movie. The tabloids and gossip shows loved Zach. Breathtakingly handsome, super rich, and sophisticated with a bad boy vibe, he helped sell papers and upped TV ratings. Zach wasn't anything like that image. Smiling, she snuggled closer to him.

Closing her heavy eyelids, she began to drift off to sleep when her phone signaled a text. Frowning, she straightened and dug into her purse for her phone.

Need to talk. Meet me noon Capri Bar at Augustus. Juliette.
Okay.

Kate slipped the phone back into her purse. She felt Zach's stare and looked up into his questioning eyes. She put a finger to her lips and shook her head. She didn't want the Morgans, who also rode in the limo, to know Juliette had contacted her.

After "good-nights," everyone headed to their rooms. Pulling off his tie, Zach walked toward the sofa and dropped the tie on the arm. Turning to Kate, he said, "It's none of my business, but do you want to share the text you got?"

She flopped on the upholstered chair. "I don't mind sharing. It was from Juliette. She wants me to meet her later today."

Zach sat on the sofa facing her. "Do you think that's a good idea? I understand you want to help, but this is something between Juliette and her parents. The Morgans appear to be over their anger at you." He shook his head. "I don't want to tell you what to do, but I'll never get Dad to listen to me if he thinks the Morgans are against you. Although I don't know what's going on now with him and Elle. You were right all along about them."

"But will your dad see the truth about his feelings for her?"

"I sure hope so." Zach grabbed the carafe of water from the small table and held out the carafe to Kate.

"No, thanks," she said.

He poured himself a glass and settled back. "Strange we haven't seen Dad since breakfast. It's not like him to miss dinner. Wonder where he went."

"Probably stewing in his room." Kate pushed up from her chair. "I don't want to make things harder for you. Juliette is young and troubled. I can't ignore her. I have to meet her. I promise I'll be discreet. I'll call for a car to drive me, and I'll tell the others I'm meeting a friend who's in Vegas for the holiday."

He stood too and brushed a hand over his hair. The tiredness on his face and the vulnerability in his eyes propelled Kate to go to him and rest her head on his chest. He massaged her back.

"That might work," he said. "I'll cover for you if I need to."

She pulled away to look up at him. "Thanks."

"It's been a long day and we're tired. Let's turn in." He kissed her tenderly. "I'm not too tired to make love to you."

* * *

KATE alighted from the hired car in front of the Augustus. She smoothed a hand down the side of her dark jeans, paired with a pale pink sweater that hugged her chest, and a khaki jacket. On her feet she wore her favorite navy-blue high-top sneakers.

Along with a group of tourists, she pushed her way into the world-famous hotel. On her left off the lobby, she spotted the Capri Bar and Grill and headed there. Her rubber soles squeaked on the polished marble floor. When she entered the intimate bistro, Juliette waved to her from a table in the far corner. Kate threaded through the lunch crowd to the young woman. They hugged and Kate sat.

Juliette held a glass of white wine. She signaled to the waitress to bring a glass for Kate.

"Lunch and drinks are on me," Juliette said.

"Thanks." Kate accepted her wine and sipped. "What's going on?"

Tears filled the younger woman's eyes.

Kate reached across the table and placed her hand over Juliette's. "Did you and Sky break up?"

"No. We're still very in love."

"What's the matter?"

Juliette rubbed a finger down the condensation on her glass. "Too much stress all around. We've been staying with Sky's friends and their two kids in their small house in Henderson."

"Okay."

"Sky's in talks with a production company to do a cable show about restoring classic cars."

"That's terrific."

Juliette finished her wine, and the waitress brought over a

fresh glass. "I'm happy for Sky. He's been so busy I barely see him. His friends think I'm their free babysitter. The children are darling, but I miss my family." She looked down. "I really missed them yesterday. I've never spent Christmas away from them."

"I miss seeing my family on Christmas too."

Juliette raised her head. "You were right."

"About what?"

"I want to go back to school. I hope I'm with Sky forever, but I think it best I finish school and give him the space he needs to develop his show. He and I talked, and he wants to support me financially and show my parents we can make our relationship work."

The tightness in Kate's stomach eased. "That's very mature of you. I think you're making the right decision. Anytime you need to talk, I'm here for you."

"Thanks. You're a true friend. I'm going to stay with Sky through the New Year, then go home."

"You should call your mom."

"I called her Christmas Eve to wish her Merry Christmas. We didn't talk long, but at least she took my call." Juliette's eyes met Kate's. "She wanted to know where I was. I told her I'm with Sky and I'm safe. Please don't tell her we met today. She'll be hurt I called you to meet me and not her."

"Zach is the only one who knows I'm here. Our secret is safe with him. What will you do if your parents demand you give up Sky?"

"I don't want to think about that now. I'm hoping if they see we're still in love after I've finished school, they'll be more under-standing." She picked up her menu, then set it down. "I almost forgot." She pulled a newspaper from her oversized purse and slid it to Kate. "Look what I found."

Staring from the front page was a picture of Zach and Kate the day they'd come to the casino together. Her arm through his, she smiled up at him, the portrait of a woman in love. Kate read the caption. *Sorry, ladies, but playboy and model magnet Zach Lyon is off the market. Rumor has it he and this petite cutie tied the knot in a secret ceremony. Can the new wife keep him away from all those leggy blondes?*

Kate reread the caption, then looked at Juliette. "I didn't realize anyone had taken our picture."

Juliette laughed. "You're famous." She touched Kate's hand. "Don't let what they say bother you. You and Zach are obviously meant for each other."

She deserved an Oscar for her performance as a woman in love. *Maybe it's not an act.* The errant thought came unbidden, and she shoved it away to think about another day. "The tabloids don't bother me, but I don't want to be famous." She snatched up the menu and pretended to read.

"Too late," Juliette said.

The words on the menu swam before Kate's eyes. She, Kate Carluccio, tabloid fodder. What if her parents saw the photo? She didn't want them to find out about her marriage this way. She'd never wanted to hurt them, but if they saw the picture, they'd be confused and heartbroken. She couldn't do that to them. She'd call them as soon as she had the chance.

Over lunch, Kate tried to focus on Juliette and not on the tangled web she'd woven. Wanting more time to figure out how to tell her parents about the marriage contract, she agreed to go shopping with Juliette.

Lunch over, the women left the grill and headed to the escalators and the lower level where the boutiques were located.

Shouts of, "That's her. Wait, Mrs. Lyon, we want your picture and a statement," reverberated through the lobby.

Kate spun around to face a herd of reporters, flashbulbs going off, some holding their phones up, running toward her. Fear she'd be trampled to death had her clutching her chest. "Go away. Leave me alone."

Juliette grabbed her arm. "Ignore them."

She let Juliette lead her away and tried to tune out the shouted questions.

"How long have you and Lyon known each other?"

"Why were you married in secret?"

"How did *you* catch him when supermodels couldn't get him to settle down?"

At that last question, Kate stumbled. She started to turn, to tell the reporter what she thought of her snarky comment.

Juliette pulled at her arm. Hotel security guards surrounded the reporters, allowing the women to hurry toward the escalators and safety.

CHAPTER THIRTY-FIVE

*W*omen's voices floated from the living room when Kate arrived back at the Morgans' house after lunch. She quietly climbed the stairs to her suite, intent on warning Zach about the paparazzi. Silence greeted her when she stepped into the room. She called his name. Nothing. Disappointment tugged at her. She missed him.

The bed beckoned. She unlaced her shoes and pulled them off, loosened her jeans, and removed her bra but left on her sweater. Comfortable, she lay down, intending to close her eyes for a few minutes.

"Wake up, Sleeping Beauty."

Kate opened sleep-blurred eyes to find Zach leaning over her. She pushed hair away from her face. "What time is it?"

The mattress dipped as he sat next to her. "Six o'clock. Dinner is in an hour."

"I need to freshen up." She couldn't persuade her languid body to move. The small lamp on the night table bathed the room in a pale golden light. Zach's body heat reached out and enveloped her. His eyes were shuttered, provoking her to wonder what he was thinking.

The sleeves of his dark green shirt were rolled up, exposing a smattering of gold hairs on his muscled forearms. His blond hair was mussed, tempting her to run her fingers through its softness.

He lowered his head toward her. Desire shimmered through her, and her heart pounded. She opened her mouth, inviting him. His lips pressed hard on hers, hot and intense. Spirals of excitement curled in her abdomen and shot through her body.

With a soft murmur, he pulled away and caressed her face. "We have time before dinner."

Much later, happier than she'd been in a long time, Kate whistled softly as she pulled on dark-washed jeans, a blue and white striped shirt, and navy flats. She fluffed her hair and smiled at her reflection in the mirror. A woman in love, her face glowing, stared back at her.

Kate gripped the edge of the dresser. No. Passionate love-making gave her skin its glow. Not love. *Liar*, a tiny voice taunted. She hurried into the other room.

Zach stood when she approached. His lips curved in a sexy smile, and he bent to give her a whisper-soft kiss. "We were so busy with other things, I didn't get a chance to ask about your lunch with Juliette."

Worry over the reporters chasing Juliette and her diffused some of Kate's joy. "We had a great time. Afterwards, we went shopping. And good news! Juliette is coming home. She's taking my advice to go back to school and graduate before getting married. She agrees she's too young and both she and Sky need more time."

"Good for her, and you."

Kate took one of his hands in hers. "I have some not-so-good news."

"What?"

"A picture of you and me the day we went to the Augustus was in one of the tabloids. Juliette showed it to me."

He grinned and waved his free hand. "That's not a big deal. I'm a tabloid regular."

She shot him a wry smile. "That's not all."

He nodded, waiting.

"Paparazzi chased us today when we came out from the restaurant. They wanted a statement from me. They snapped photos."

"Don't worry about it."

"If the Morgans find out, they'll be furious I saw Juliette without telling them."

"I hadn't thought of that." He rubbed the back of his neck.

"I doubt they read the tabloids or watch those gossip shows. We're probably safe."

"Let's go with that."

Despite her assurances, a premonition of dread wrapped around Kate as she headed toward the door. She stopped and turned, almost colliding with Zach, close behind her. "I hated leaving you here alone all day. Did you find something to keep you occupied?"

"I met with Tripp and Carlisle about some business, nothing major. Dad didn't show so I went to his room and he wasn't there. I called him and he said he's fine and was handling some personal matter. He was cagey when I asked where he was."

"Strange. I have a feeling his 'personal matter' might have to do with Elle."

* * *

PARTIED OUT, Kate was glad dinner that night was a casual affair. Two friends of Ava's, interchangeable blondes named Nikki and Amber, joined them. Missy, a morose expression on her face, barely ate. Each time she stole glances at Tripp, her face grew more sullen. Kate wondered if Missy had seen the incriminating pictures Tripp's girlfriend posted on social media.

Kate put her hand out to touch Missy's to offer her support, but pulled back. Missy would rebuff any overtures.

Ava's friends snubbed Kate, but flirted outrageously with Zach. Annoyance knotted Kate's stomach, and she gripped her wine glass. Engrossed in a conversation with Carlisle, Zach ignored the women's flirting. As with most great-looking men, he was used to women coming on to him and knew how to tune them out.

Zach's attentiveness toward her helped ease the knot in Kate's stomach.

"I'm surprised Greg's not here," Gloria said when Florence served the sandwiches and soup.

Carlisle filled his wine glass from the carafe on the table. "Haven't seen Greg since he ran out of here yesterday morning."

"I'm sure he's okay," Zach said. "I wouldn't worry about him."

Zach and Kate exchanged looks. She hoped her intuition was right and Greg was with Elle.

Dinner over, Gloria stood. "Let's have dessert and coffee in the library."

Kate would rather not spend any more time than necessary with this gang, but she had to keep up appearances, for Zach.

They trooped into the library, where warm apple pie and coffee laced with Irish whiskey waited. Her pie and coffee on the low table in front of her, Kate settled onto the sofa. She sipped her drink and inhaled the scent of books and leather. She could spend all day in this room. Alone.

Ava plucked the TV remote off a chair. "I'm bored. Let's watch TV."

"Let's," her friends said in unison.

Kate would rather sit quietly and enjoy her dessert and coffee. Being near all these books calmed her. She felt someone staring and looked over to find Zach, seated opposite, watching her.

He smiled, and her world brightened. The room, the others, faded until there was only Zach and her.

"*Hollywood Report.* They always have the juiciest gossip," Ava said.

Kate froze and widened her eyes, her attention on the TV as the logo for the popular show flashed on the screen. The sensual tension crackling between her and Zach morphed to anxiety. The worried expression on Zach's face told Kate he felt it too.

Ava sat straighter and grabbed the remote to turn up the volume. "Oh, my God. Is that Juliette. And Kate?"

CHAPTER THIRTY-SIX

*T*he room quieted. Video of Kate and Juliette strolling out of the Capri Bar and Grill, laughing, filled the screen. Then, holding up their hands to ward off the paparazzi. The announcer identified Kate as Zach Lyon's secret wife.

Bile rose in Kate's throat. Crap!

With a smug grin, Ava muted the TV when the segment ended. Kate's phone vibrated. She glanced down at the phone where it lay next to her. Texts from Graceann, from Ev and Brad. And from her mom. Could things get any worse?

Everyone in the room turned to Kate. Her face flamed, and she knew she blushed.

"You saw Juliette, and you didn't tell us?" Gloria spoke through clenched teeth.

Zach jumped from his seat to stand behind Kate. He put his hands on her shoulders, squeezing his support.

Kate swallowed and took calming breaths. "Juliette asked me not to tell anyone. She asked to meet, and I wanted to help her in any way I could."

Carlisle's face contorted in anger. "We are her parents. You owed it to us to tell us she contacted you."

"Juliette is an adult," Kate said. "She's not in trouble, and she's not hurt. She came to a decision that will make you happy. She plans to call you."

Gloria pushed up from her chair and put a hand on her hip. "And that's supposed to make everything better?"

"Zach," Carlisle said, his tone harsh. "We've put up with your wife's meddling, but no more. If you can't control her, she has to leave. You can stay, but we want her gone."

"Kate is my wife and I stand with her. We'll both be gone today."

Kate set down her coffee mug and gave the warm pie a wistful look. She took Zach's proffered hand and allowed him to help her stand.

"Good riddance." Tripp, seated on the sofa facing them, attempted to pull Missy closer, but she slid away, causing him to frown at her.

Ava's enhanced lips formed a cold grin.

"No one is going anywhere." The booming voice cut through the tension.

Everyone turned and stared at the doorway. Greg and Elle stood there, arms around each other's waists.

Ava's carbon-copy friends jumped up from their chairs and ran to the door, sliding out.

"Dad!" Zach said.

"Where the hell have you been?" Carlisle asked.

Greg pulled Elle closer. "Doing something I should have done long ago. Elle and I were married today at one of those Elvis chapels off-Strip."

"Married?" everyone said.

Elle's smile lit her face. "Greg found me at the airport yesterday, in the security line for my flight back to New York. He proposed, and here we are." She laughed. "It was like a movie, with him shouting my name and security guards running up to him."

Zach and Kate moved toward the couple.

"Congratulations to both of you." Zach shook his dad's hand and hugged Elle.

"I'm so happy for you," Kate said, hugging Elle.

Elle held Kate at arm's length. "Thank you. Without your help this would never have happened."

Kate exhaled a tense breath. She wasn't a total disaster as a matchmaker.

"You all belong in a hokey Hallmark movie," Ava said.

"Greg, have you lost your mind?" Carlisle asked. "Wait until the board hears of your rash action."

"You'd like to make me seem incompetent, wouldn't you, Carlisle." Greg's icy gaze swung to Tripp. "You, too."

Tripp stood. "Greg, you're not making any sense."

Greg gave a dismissive wave. "I had an interesting conversation with Zach, which spurred me to talk with some of my board members, the ones loyal to me. I'll have my say with both of you later. Right now, I want to speak privately with my son and daughter-in-law."

Excitement made Kate's insides shake. Greg had called her daughter-in-law. Zach's father had accepted her into the family. She was Zach's wife in name only, she reminded herself. Regret reared up, tightening her chest.

"You'll be sorry, Greg." Tripp tried to grab Missy's hand but she slapped him away and jumped up.

"Don't touch me, Tripp!" Missy yelled. "Our marriage, everything, is over. I saw the pictures. I've had enough of your cheating. I'm filing for divorce. I'm tired of playing the good little wife while you screw any woman who comes along." Head high, she marched out, leaving a confused Tripp behind, his face mottled in anger.

"Ava, let's go. We need to call Juliette. She'd better come home now." Gloria stalked to the door, Ava following.

Worry etched on his face, Carlisle glanced around the room before his gaze landed on Greg. "We'll talk later." His strides heavy, he left the room, slamming the door shut behind him.

CHAPTER THIRTY-SEVEN

*K*ate stared at the closed door, then met the surprised faces of Elle, Greg, and Zach.

"Wow, I did not see that coming from Missy, although I suspected she might know about the pictures."

Greg frowned. "Pictures?"

"Tell you later." Zach smiled at his dad and turned to Elle. "Welcome to the family. About time."

"Thanks, Zach."

Greg gestured toward the sofas and chairs. "Let's sit."

Kate snatched up the remote and flicked off the TV, then sat on a chair, turning her phone face-down on the cushion so she wouldn't have to see the text notifications, glaring and accusing. She curled a knuckle against her mouth, curbing her apprehension. She'd call her mom as soon as this meeting with Greg was over. Zach settled into a chair next to her.

Folding her hands on her lap, she forced her muscles to relax. She hoped Juliette straightened things out with her family. Greg and Zach had their own family matters to deal with.

Elle and Greg sat on the sofa holding hands. Greg slid his attention to Zach.

"Zach, son, I owe you an apology and an explanation. I haven't been much of a father. I'm sorry for all the years I used my anger and pain against you."

"They were rough years. Thankfully, I had Rosina and my teachers at school."

Greg rubbed a hand over his eyes. "I'm grateful to the others for stepping in when I shirked my duties."

Zach stayed silent, his focus riveted on his dad.

"I can't excuse my behavior, but I had reasons, selfish ones," Greg continued. "You're so much like your mother it hurt to look at you. Selfishly, I shut you out and didn't think what that would do to you."

"I barely remember Mom now," Zach said, regret coloring his voice. "I missed her when she died. I needed you, Dad, but you weren't there for me."

The pain in Zach's voice pierced Kate's heart. Fighting tears, she reached over and grabbed his hand, holding it tightly.

"I was grieving too," Greg said. "I was also angrier than I'd ever been in my life. Two of the three people I loved most in the world had been taken from me."

"And you wished I'd died instead of Harper." Zach's quiet words hung in the room.

Kate and Elle gasped. Kate's insides shook.

Tears glistened in Greg's eyes. "That's not true, son."

"Dad, I heard you."

"Forgive me. In my grief, I said things I shouldn't have. I've been unfair to you. I'm glad you've found Kate. She's what you need. She makes you happy."

Zach raised Kate's hand to his lips. He placed a gentle kiss on her palm. "Kate makes me very happy."

Kate's heart beat double-time.

"Kate." Greg pulled her attention from Zach. She met Greg's gaze.

"I'm sorry for the way I treated you," he said. "Can you forgive me?"

Greg aged in front of them. Kate assumed dredging up the old memories hit him hard. Swallowing around the lump in her throat, she nodded. "I forgive you."

Greg's features relaxed, and he released an audible sigh.

Elle skimmed fingers down Greg's face. "I've forgiven him, too." She turned to Zach. "All the girlfriends and pushing you away were your dad's way of coping."

Greg kissed Elle's hand, then looked at Zach. "Can you forgive me, son?"

Zach released Kate's hand and stood. "I have so much hurt inside me. I do love you, Dad. Give me time."

Greg's face seemed to shatter as Zach and Kate walked out.

CHAPTER THIRTY-EIGHT

*Z*ach and Kate trudged silently up to their room. When they entered, Zach shuffled to the sofa and sank down, putting his head in his hands.

Kate shut the door softly. Unsure what to do, she leaned against it. The dim lights bathed the room in shadows. Weak moonlight filtered through the open drapes. The door between the rooms was ajar, and she could see the staff had turned down the covers on the bed.

Her heart broke for Zach. She went to the sofa and sat next to him. He gathered her close and buried his face in her neck. She inhaled his fresh soap scent and wrapped her arms around him.

"I'm so sorry, Zach. I'm here to help if you need me."

Without answering, he held her more tightly. Finally, he pulled away.

"Thanks, Kate. I need a few minutes alone."

"I'll go in the other room. Come in when you want to talk." She brushed her hand over his hair and kissed away the single tear that slid down his face.

Closing the bedroom door, she fought her own tears. Her

phone vibrated with another text. She slipped her phone from her pocket and looked at the screen. Her mom.

With a hand that shook, Kate punched in her mother's number. Her mom answered immediately.

"Hi, Mom."

"What is going on, Kate? We saw *Hollywood Report*. Your father and brothers and their families are in shock. Our only daughter and their sister is married and she doesn't think to tell her family."

Her mom's voice had risen against the voices in the background. "Mom, settle down. It's not like it looks."

"Really? It looks like you married Zach Lyon, a man you've disliked for years."

She couldn't tell her mom the truth over the phone, not when her mom was so upset and the entire family clamored behind her wanting to know what Kate had to say.

"Mom, please trust me on this. What Zach and I have is complicated. I'll be home in a few days and I'll explain everything. I promise."

"Are you or are you not married to Zach Lyon?"

"I am."

"Where are you now?"

Kate gulped deep breaths. "I'm in Las Vegas at the home of one of the officers in Zach's company. We'd planned to stay through the New Year, but we'll be out of here soon."

"Vegas? And not California with Graceann? Another lie, Kate?"

"Please, Mom. I'll tell you everything when I see you."

"Come home now."

Kate glanced around the room. Like the sun peeking through clouds, her mind opened to the truth. "Zach needs me."

"Do you love him?" her mom asked quietly.

"Yes." Kate had denied what was in her heart for so long. "I'll see you in a few days, Mom. I need to go now."

Kate dropped the phone on the bed. Maybe Zach didn't return her love, but she wouldn't abandon him. She went into the other room. He hadn't moved. Kate sat next to him and took his hand in hers.

He turned to her, his eyes haunted. "I'm glad Dad bared his soul. The hurt has been part of me for a long time, it'll take me a while to forgive him."

"I know, but you love him. If you didn't, you wouldn't want to help him keep his company. You're not a person who holds a grudge."

She searched his eyes. "Your father took girlfriends to cover his pain. All those models and actresses you dated. Was that a farce to hide your true feelings?"

His slight smile warmed her. "What do you think?"

"The Zach I've come to know isn't anything like Tabloid Zach."

"Thanks for that. I childishly lashed out at my dad by disappointing him, making him think I was no more than a shallow player. Most of those women meant nothing to me. I had something they wanted—a chance to get publicity."

"You've never loved any of them?"

"No. I had strong feelings for some, but never love."

He leaned toward her. "I never met a woman as kind and loving as you." He took her lips in a tender kiss. She wound her arms around his neck and deepened the kiss, opening to him.

His tongue explored her mouth, eliciting small cries from her. Desire burned through her. Zach wasn't just any man. She'd gotten to know the real man behind the playboy façade. And she liked what she saw. She loved him.

He trailed kisses down her throat and along her collarbone. Boneless and melting, she threw back her head. He kissed his way to her chest, kissing her breasts through the thin fabric of her shirt. On fire, she moaned.

Drawing back, he gripped her shoulders. "I need you, Kate, more than I've ever needed any woman."

"I need you, too."

"No pity."

"None."

CHAPTER THIRTY-NINE

Zach slowly opened his eyes, breathing in the honied scent of the woman nestled against him. Raising himself on his elbow, he glanced down at his sleeping beauty. Kate's thick black lashes brushed her face like gossamer wings. Her raven hair spread over the pillow, and her soft pink lips invited him to feast on them again.

He flopped onto his back and stared at the ceiling. Kate was everything he knew she'd be, and all he'd feared. From the first time he met her, the day Graceann moved next door to him in Manhattan, Kate stirred him with feelings he refused to acknowledge. He convinced himself there was no attraction—she was flighty, lacked ambition, was unsophisticated. She didn't like him either, he'd told himself. Shame washed over him now. Digging deep, he recognized the true reason he pushed Kate away—his feelings for her scared him. Witnessing the hurt his father suffered when he lost his wife, Zach had vowed to never love anyone so much his life would shatter if she left.

He and Kate had butted heads constantly, as if both fought the sensual tension that always hovered over them. They'd grated Graceann's patience on more than one occasion. He wondered if she'd figured out their attraction and that was why she'd suggested he hire Kate as his temporary wife.

Zach turned to his side to watch his wife again. She slept peacefully, an angel with kitten claws who'd shredded the barrier he'd built around his heart.

Their contract marriage had worked. His dad had believed him enough about Carlisle and Tripp's manipulations to do his own investigation. He and his dad still had hurts to resolve, but Zach didn't doubt he'd take his rightful place at the company. His agreement with Kate provided he'd pay her and they'd go their separate ways. They had no reason to divorce right away.

He needed her now. He caressed the satiny skin of her face. She opened her beautiful golden-brown eyes.

"'Morning, Sleeping Beauty."

She held out her arms to him. "'Morning."

He gathered her to him. He'd come home.

* * *

THEIR LOVEMAKING OVER, Kate snuggled with Zach under the covers. Regret and sadness nibbled away at her peacefulness. Things were working out. Zach and his dad would heal. She'd reimburse her parents what they'd lost, and Zach would fade from her life. Fighting the pain, she squeezed her eyes shut.

He pulled himself up to lean against the headboard, taking her with him. When she settled into the crook of his arm, he kissed the top of her head.

"Kate, tell me something. Please."

She looked up at him. "What is it?"

"We've become friends." He smiled. "More than friends. You're one of the few people who know about Nicaragua. I hope you know you can tell me anything."

"Ookay." Anxiety formed a lump in her chest.

"Why did you become an actor?"

She shifted more comfortably and smiled, seeing herself as a toddler dressed up like a fairytale princess or a Ninja warrior. "Since I was very little, I've loved dressing up in costumes and pretending I'm someone else. As I grew older, I put on skits for my family. I starred in my high school plays. Acting is a compulsion. I can't imagine not doing it. The day I received my acceptance to the Tisch School of the Arts at NYU was one of the happiest of my life."

"I'm impressed. You have to be an extraordinary talent to get accepted there."

She inhaled, feeling the pride of that long-ago day swell her chest. "I'm very lucky."

"I doubt luck had anything to do with it. You're gifted, trained at one of the top schools in the country. Yet, you stay in your small town and perform in dinner theaters and regional theater. Nothing wrong with them, but you're young and talented. You have connections in Hollywood. I don't understand why you don't want to pursue other acting options, try to make a name for yourself, to use your skill."

She lowered her head and smoothed a hand over the comforter, her thoughts tumbling over each other. Zach had confided in her about his foundation and his hurts. Surely, she could trust him to understand her deepest fears.

Not looking at him, she said, "Despite everything, I lack confidence in my acting ability. I'm afraid I'll fail and others will compare me to my mother. I hide in Spirit Lake. I'm not proud of myself."

He touched her chin with his fingers, gently lifting her face to his. "Compare you to your mother?"

"You know who my mother is."

"Kirsten Baker, supermodel and actress. I had a crush on her when I was a teen."

Kate smiled. "You and most of the male population. Can you understand what it was like in high school when guys asked me out just to get invited to my house so they could meet my mom?"

"I can't imagine." He pulled her closer and held her against him for a heartbeat.

Kate met his gaze again. "My mom is wonderful, the best. I wanted to be like her in every way. Growing up, I hated the way I looked. I desperately wished I had her blonde hair and big blue eyes. She's tall, too. My brothers are the images of Mom, but I favor my dad's mother. My parents did everything they could to instill me with a solid sense of self-esteem. I love acting, but I've always felt in Mom's shadow."

Zach kissed her tenderly. "If you favor your grandmother, then she was a beautiful woman."

"Thanks." Kate focused across the room, not seeing the dresser or the photo of a Southwestern canyon, but her insecurities. "Mom acted in a few movies and TV shows before she married Dad. She's a good actor. She gave up everything for Dad, and the two of them are still very much in love. I could never be a model because I'm not tall enough, but I'm an actor. I'm afraid people will compare me to her. I can't handle that."

Zach gripped her shoulders and forced her to look at him. "You, Kate Carluccio Lyon, are beautiful in your own right. Don't ever sell yourself short. I've been attracted to you since I met you. Your beautiful dark hair, those big brown eyes flecked with gold, and your sexy body have given me erotic fantasies for years. You don't realize your own power. But more than your beauty, you care about others. Celebrate the special woman you are. Go to Hollywood or New York City. Put your heart into your craft. And if you fail, so what? At least you tried."

Tears rolled down Kate's face and words clogged in her throat.

"Come here," Zach whispered. He gathered her close and stroked her hair while she cried, releasing the hurt and pain she'd held in for so long.

CHAPTER FORTY

*D*ressed and hungry, Zach and Kate went downstairs in search of something to eat before they left the Morgans and Las Vegas. If Kate didn't urgently need a cup of strong coffee, they'd already be on their way. Thankfully, all was quiet when they got to the main floor.

Her body hurt in places she'd forgotten about, but it was a good hurt. She wanted to dance and proclaim to the world she'd had her sexual fantasies, and a few new ones, satisfied in ways she'd never imagined. She wanted to shout her love for Zach. That secret would stay between her and her mother. He couldn't know she'd fallen deeply in love with him. She didn't want his pity that he couldn't return her love.

She stole a glance at him. The caring side he'd exposed to her warmed her heart. His kind words and understanding about her fears gave her renewed confidence to put herself out there to succeed or fail.

Loud voices from the office threw water on her thoughts. She and Zach exchanged glances and headed there to stand outside the door and listen.

"Greg, hear us. You aren't capable of running this company." Carlisle's voice.

"Look at these invoices," Tripp said. "You've approved expenditures that are way over the top for supplies we don't need."

"Stop it, both of you!" Greg shouted. "The gig is up. I didn't sign those. My signature was forged. Zach told me you're trying to wrest the company from me for your own gain. And that you're embezzling. I hired a new and trusted accountant to audit the books, and I fired those board members loyal to you."

"That's bogus," Tripp said. "Zach is jealous because you trust us more than him. And you had no right to fire board members."

"I had every right. I still own controlling interest."

"We're only doing this for you," Carlisle added, his voice as smooth as a snake oil salesman. "Take your pension and your stock options and enjoy your life. You'll still have a small stake in the company. We'll take care of everything."

Zach touched Kate's arm. "Go find yourself coffee and something to eat. I need to help Dad."

* * *

ZACH ENTERED the office and slammed the door shut behind him. The three men turned, surprise on their faces.

Tripp sneered. "What are you doing here, Lyon? Don't you have a supermodel or two to screw? I'll make sure your wife is satisfied."

"Don't worry about my wife," Zach said. "Handle your own problems."

"Zach, this doesn't concern you," Carlisle said.

"It sure as hell does." He wouldn't let these vipers walk all over him or his dad. "My dad built the company from scratch. He lost his family while he devoted all his time and energy to his business. He wanted only to make a decent living and do some good."

Greg moved to where Zach stood and put his hand on Zach's shoulder, squeezing his encouragement.

Zach continued. "I've known for a long time you two were conspiring to take the company out from under him, that you'd been embezzling for years. Whatever pension or stock options you'll give him will be gone by the time you're finished your looting."

Tripp, his chin jutting out and his posture menacing, moved closer. "You have a hell of a nerve. You have no proof."

Zach chuckled, an ugly sound even to him. "I hired people months ago to investigate you both. You heard my dad that he hired someone trustworthy to review the books, not the accountant you've been paying off. You've quietly planted rumors with the board about Dad's mental state."

Zach looked over at Carlisle. "And I know how close to bankruptcy you are."

Carlisle's face reddened. "You lie!"

Greg stepped away from Zach and nodded toward the other men. "My son doesn't lie. He warned me about you two, and he was right. Moreover, he's turned a new leaf. He's married to a woman who is good for him. He's ready to take his rightful place at the company, if he wants it. What do you say, son?"

Zach's gaze met his father's. "It's what I want, Dad." Emotion thickened Zach's throat. He'd waited his whole life for his dad to accept him and love him.

Greg turned back to Carlisle and Tripp. "On my orders, the remaining board members will begin separation proceedings for you both. I want you out of my company."

"My wife is due to have a baby soon," Tripp said. "I need the money. Divorce isn't cheap either." Anger tightened his features. "At least we deserve a severance package."

Greg waved a hand in dismissal. "You should have thought about that before you and Carlisle conspired against me. You've embezzled enough funds. That's your severance." He chuckled.

"If I decide to press charges, you won't need money where you'll go."

"Why, you—you," Carlisle sputtered. "I want you both out of my house now. That includes your wives."

"With pleasure," Greg said.

Shoulder-to-shoulder, Zach and Greg left the office.

CHAPTER FORTY-ONE

*H*ugging herself, Kate stood at the floor-to-ceilings windows in Zach's new Manhattan apartment, on the top floor of a renovated historic building. The lights of the city spread before her, sparkling and festive, ready to celebrate the New Year. The TV behind her broadcast nonstop coverage of New Year's celebrations around the world. All day, people crowded together in Times Square to watch the crystal ball drop hours from now. She shivered. No way would she be in that crowd, braving the rowdiness and the cold. And the lack of bathroom facilities.

For the past three days, since arriving back in New York, she and Zach had explored the city like tourists. As much time as she'd spent in the city, at school, then visiting Graceann, sightseeing with Zach made her see everything in a new light, romantic and exciting, all her senses heightened. She'd remember these days for the rest of her life. Sadness crept into her musings. She would not be sad tonight, her last with Zach. She alone knew it was their last time together as a couple.

They planned a quiet evening in the apartment. Zach's part-time chef had prepared a meal they only needed to heat up.

Tomorrow, she would leave for Spirit Lake. She hadn't told Zach, but with the success of his plan to help his dad, there was no reason for them to stay married.

Leaving him would be like ripping off a Band-Aid. She wanted the initial pain over. The ache in her heart might never heal. She'd never loved any man the way she loved Zach, which is why she had to leave. Loving him hurt so much she couldn't stay. She was strong. She'd handle whatever unhappiness waited.

Thanks to Zach, she'd grown and found new self-assurance. She would step out of her comfort zone and move from Sprit Lake to try acting in New York or Hollywood.

Soft footsteps on the polished wooden floors told her he approached. He put his arms around her waist and drew her against him. Kate breathed in his familiar scent and rested her head on his shoulder, determined to make the most of these last few hours they had together.

"Beautiful, isn't it?" he asked.

"It is, but I'm glad to be here, indoors, away from the crowds and the forced gaiety."

"I've never liked the forced gaiety of New Year's Eve either."

She turned in his arms and looked up at him, skimming his face with her fingers, imprinting his features onto her mind forever. "Everyone tries so hard to have a good time this night. Fun should be spontaneous."

"I agree." He brushed hair back from her face. "Speaking of fun, I can think of a few spontaneous and entertaining things we can do right now."

"Really?" She clutched his shoulders and kissed him lightly on the lips. "I can't imagine what you mean. Are you talking about dinner?"

"I'm hungry for you. I'll teach you some exercises to build up an appetite."

"What are you waiting for."

Without another word, he put his arm around her waist and

led her to the bedroom. Her insides tingled and trembled with anticipation mixed with sorrow.

* * *

THE SCRUMPTIOUS DINNER OVER, they sat on the sofa listening to classical music while enjoying dessert and Kahlua-laced coffee. Kate slid closer to Zach, needing his heat. She wanted to remember everything about tonight to warm the lonely nights ahead.

"That was a great meal," she said. "Compliments to your chef." She swallowed a forkful of pie and moaned at its deliciousness. "This coconut custard pie is to die for."

Zach bent toward her and licked the corner of her mouth, firing up her insatiable hunger for him.

"You had some pie there," he said. "Thought I'd save you from having to use a napkin."

"You're much sexier than any napkin." She set down her empty plate and lifted her coffee cup, taking a sip before placing it on the low table in front of them. Zach put his arm around her shoulders, drawing her nearer.

"What will you do now that Tripp and Carlisle are out and your dad has full control of the company again?" she asked.

He leaned his head back. "My player days are over. I'm going to help Dad run it."

"I'm glad things worked out."

Zach pushed away and faced her. "I doubt the outcome would have been the same without you."

"You mean the contract?"

"That too. I gave you a hard time about your matchmaking, but without it, I wonder if I would have been able to get through to Dad."

"Elle is a calming influence on him."

"I've never seen him this content. Between you and Elle, you softened him, made him open his mind to what was around him."

"I'm happy I could bring them together." She widened her eyes. "I forgot. I got a text from Juliette. She's made peace with her family. She loves Sky as much as ever, and they plan to marry when she graduates, regardless of her parents' objections."

Zach planted a gentle kiss on Kate's lips. "You are something else. Wanting to help others. Why did you and I fight all those years?"

She shrugged. "I felt the attraction but refused to admit it."

"Same here. We had our issues, and we were afraid."

"That's behind us now." She pulled the sash on her silk robe tighter, then met his eyes. "What...?" She wanted to ask him about their divorce, but the words wouldn't come.

"What were you going to say?"

"Nothing important." She skimmed a finger down his face to his lips. "Kiss me."

CHAPTER FORTY-TWO

"*I* made you hot chocolate."

Holding two steaming mugs, Kate's mother entered the sunroom of their house at Spirit Lake. Kate set aside the book she'd tried to read for the past thirty minutes. Unable to concentrate, she'd read the same page three times. Brewster, the family cat, curled up next to her.

"Thanks, Mom. I love your cocoa. I haven't seen Dad this morning. I thought he was taking off all this week."

"One of his clients called with an emergency. Your dad likes to be available to his clients. He doesn't want to let anyone down or lose any business either."

Kate accepted a mug from her mom and laughed. "As only one of two lawyers in the town, I doubt he's in danger of losing business."

Her mom lowered herself onto a bright print-covered wicker chair opposite the loveseat where Kate sat.

Sipping her hot drink, Kate studied her mom. Kirsten Baker Carluccio retained her California Girl sunny beauty and disposition. Her deep blue eyes behind the stylish glasses shone with intelligence. A top Manhattan hairdresser saw that her mom's thick, long hair was as luxurious and blonde as it had always been. With her smooth skin and slim figure, she appeared decades younger than her sixty years.

Kate loved her to death.

Her mother glanced at the doorway, then back to Kate. "Want to talk about Zach?"

"What do you mean?"

Kirsten smiled, that dazzling smile with the bright white teeth that had made her famous. "You love him. What are you going to do about that?"

"What can I do? He doesn't love me. I'll endure and get on with my life." Despite her bravado, Kate wasn't sure she'd survive the heartbreak.

"What makes you think he doesn't love you?"

"He's never said the words."

"A man doesn't need to say the words to show his love."

"I need the words, Mom." Glad to finally talk to someone about her feelings for Zach, Kate settled more comfortably on the loveseat. "I've been in love with him for a long time but refused to see it. Our contract benefited us both, and now it's over. After our divorce, we'll see each other a few times a year in California at Graceann's." She shrugged. "That's that."

"Put aside your father and I are still angry with you about that contract, why don't you tell Zach how you feel?"

"I can't. I don't want him to pity me."

Her mom slid her gaze toward the doorway and back again, then gave Kate a wry smile. "He hasn't told you he loves you, but you haven't said anything either. I suspect you're both too stubborn for your own good."

"Why do you keep looking at the door?"

"Wondering when your dad will be back." Her mom's face pinked and she concentrated on drinking her hot chocolate.

In the silence, Kate glanced out the sunroom windows. Heavy snow fell, blanketing the world in glimmering white. She'd arrived in Spirit Lake last evening after a long drive with a hired car and driver.

Before dawn yesterday, she'd left Zach's bed, packed a few things, and walked out, leaving him a note and her gold wedding band. Fighting tears, she bit her lip. She'd never told Zach good-bye. She trusted him to make good on their agreement and pay her.

I don't want his money. I want him.

The contract was over. She and Zach were over. She had to accept that. She'd run home to the welcoming arms of her parents. She could have gone to her own apartment, but she needed her family.

When she told her parents of her contract marriage, they were furious with her for doing something so radical, something that could have hurt her. They said again she wasn't to blame for them losing their money.

"What will you do now?" her mom asked, drawing her attention. "A new dinner theater opened in Lake Harmony. You could try for parts there."

"No more dinner theaters for me. I've decided to use my share of the money to rent a place in California. I'll look for an agent and acting jobs. I'll give it my all, and if I fail, at least I tried."

She remembered Zach's words. He'd cared enough to make her face what she'd denied for years. She was afraid of failing at the very thing that gave her joy. Tears welled. She blinked them away and concentrated on her rich chocolaty drink.

Her mom glanced toward the doorway again, then set her empty mug on the table between them. "I'm glad you're going to pursue your career more fully. Your dad and I will miss you so far away, but you're a talented actor. You need to try. You'll be successful. I believe in you."

Kate laughed. "Mom, you would think I'd be successful in anything I do."

"Of course. You're my daughter, my beautiful, kind, brilliant daughter. In California, you'll be closer to my family in San Francisco."

"I can visit Grandmom more often."

The sound of the front door opening and closing made the women look at each other. Brewster jumped off the loveseat, and tail high, headed out of the room. Probably to find a quieter place to sleep.

Kirsten stood and smoothed a hand down the side of her jeans. "That must be your father. I'll go see if he wants some hot chocolate."

The nervousness in her mom's voice made Kate frown. Wrapped up in her own problems, she sipped the remainder of her drink and continued to stare out the windows to the softly falling snow. Heavy footsteps sounded, coming closer.

"Hey, Dad."

Smiling, she turned to the doorway. She pressed a palm to her stomach and slowly set her empty mug onto the table.

Not her dad, but Zach, stood there.

"Zach, what are you doing here?" Her voice trembled.

"I couldn't let you go."

"What?"

He closed the distance between them in two strides and slid next to her on the loveseat. He took both her hands in his. His intense green eyes captured hers.

"When you left you took a piece of me with you. The loneliness and regret were almost too much to bear. Please don't do that to me again. At first, I told myself it was for the best. I'd start divorce proceedings, and we'd go our separate ways. I called my accountant this morning and had him deposit the money into your bank account. I figured that was that."

He smiled, that sexy smile that made her insides shake.

His gaze searched hers. "I lied to myself. I've been lying to myself for years."

"Lying?" The word squeaked out of her.

With a gentle touch, he smoothed hair back from her face. "I need to tell you something."

Unable to speak, she could only nod.

"You know those stories about me and all the women were a cover to hide from my true motives, a vow to punish my dad."

"Oh, Zach." She grabbed his hand and kissed it, then held it tightly.

"I couldn't let anyone guess the aloneness I felt, the certainty I wasn't worthy of happiness. My mother abandoned me by dying, and Dad rejected me."

Tears rolled down Kate's cheeks. "Zach, your mother didn't abandon you."

"Try telling that to an eight-year-old."

"I'm sorry. I always thought you were self-confident and arrogant, that you had everything a person could want."

"I didn't have you." His eyes darkened. "I didn't want to ever fall in love, to have my heart crushed, to end up like my dad. I pushed you away, refusing to grasp what was right in front of me."

"What was that?" Her words came out on a breath.

He smiled. "Kate Carluccio Lyon, I've loved you for years, but I was too blinded by self-pity and fear to see it. Do you think you could learn to love me?"

Her racing heart drummed in her chest. "I already love you. I have for a long time."

His eyes glistening, he got down on one knee, reached into his pocket, and pulled out a ring. He held up a large pear-shaped sapphire surrounded by diamonds.

"Marry me again? Please. This time forever."

The love shining from his eyes touched all the hidden places of her heart where she'd stored her deepest wishes.

Tears blinded her. "Yes," she managed.

He slipped the ring on her finger, then helped her stand.

She rolled her hand back and forth, letting the lights from the Christmas tree in the corner reflect off the facets of the gem. "It's exquisite."

"It was my mother's. She would have loved you."

"I wish I could have met her. I know I would have loved her." Kate placed her hands on his shoulders.

Zach pulled her close and kissed her, showing her without words how much he loved her. With a small moan, she returned his kiss, pouring out her love and hope.

"Can we come in now?"

Zach and Kate turned toward the doorway. Kate's parents stood there grinning. Her dad held a silver bucket holding a bottle of champagne resting in ice. Her mom carried a tray with four flutes on it.

Kate swiped at tears. "Yes, please. Dad, I'm glad you're back from your appointment."

He laughed. "The emergency I had was Zach wanting to meet with me and ask for your hand."

Her mother grinned. "And he was only too glad to give it. I can't believe you didn't see my nervousness, Kate, waiting for your dad and Zach."

"I noticed, but I was too involved in my little pity party."

Her dad held up the bottle of champagne. "Time for a real party. Let's celebrate."

While her parents opened the champagne and poured them each a drink, Zach took Kate into his arms again. "We'll have a big church wedding this time."

She put her arms around his waist and laid her head against his firm chest. His heart beat a steady, comforting rhythm.

"Ours will be a contract of love," she said.

EPILOGUE

F our months later

Sunlight spilled through the stained-glass windows in the small church in Spirit Lake, bathing the vestibule in blues and golds. The colors shimmered on Kate's ivory silk gown, a slim column that skimmed her body. Seed pearls trimmed the sweetheart neckline and bordered the long train. Kate clutched her bouquet of white and pink roses to her waist, fighting the nerves that made her knees wobble.

A harpist played "At Last," a tune made famous by Etta James. The song perfectly described her and Zach. An usher walked Kate's mother down the aisle. In the second row of pews, on the bride's side, Kate's brothers waited with their families. On the groom's side, Elle and Greg occupied the first row. Behind them, Rosina sat with her husband. Kate smiled. She'd met Rosina last night at the rehearsal dinner and liked her immediately. The love between Rosina and Zach shone brightly. Kate was grateful Zach had had Rosina in his life.

"You okay?" Graceann, Kate's matron of honor, touched Kate's arm. Graceann's pale green gown brought out the green of her eyes, bright now with love and happiness.

"I'm a little nervous."

"You've never been more beautiful," Graceann said.

"I agree," Kate's dad said, standing next to her. He leaned in to kiss Kate's cheek. "Remember that picture you loved of your grandmother on her wedding day? You're as beautiful as she was. You have her beauty and her strength."

Tears filled Kate's eyes. "Thanks, Dad."

The harpist, joined by the guitarist, began playing, "Don't Stop Believing," the bridal party's cue to begin their procession.

"Here we go," Kate said. "All those people there waiting."

Graceann laughed. "When you walk down that aisle, you won't see anyone but Zach." She waited for her note, then began slowly walking along the white runner.

Kate put her arm through her father's as Zach and his best man, Jake, took their places near the altar.

Her dad patted her hand. "Zach is a good man, and he loves you deeply. He'll make you happy." He laughed. "If he doesn't, he'll answer to me."

Kate stood on her toes and kissed him on the cheek.

Then it was their turn to walk the white runner. Calmness descended over Kate. Today was her true wedding day.

Her eyes met Zach's. His smile lit her heart. Everything in the church faded. She saw only the man she loved above all else.

When she joined him at the altar, he bent to whisper in her ear.

"You're beautiful, and I'll cherish you forever. That's a contract I'll never break."

Kate kissed him lightly on the lips, sealing the deal on their love.

THE END

*THANK you for reading *Wedded On a Dare (Love On a Dare Book 2)*. I really appreciate your purchase. Please turn the page for an excerpt from *Wedded in Vegas (Gambling On Love Book 1)*, the story of the marriage-of-convenience between a major movie star and a Las Vegas bartender. *

WEDDED IN VEGAS

WEDDED IN VEGAS EXCERPT

CHAPTER ONE

"*A*nalisa, look sharp. He's here."

Analisa Barbero glanced sideways at her co-worker, Patti, and finished pouring the glass of wine for her customer. After acknowledging the customer's thanks, she turned to Patti. "Who's here?"

Patti moved close to whisper. "That hot guy who's been coming in here the past five days, the one who's sweet on you."

Like fine champagne, excitement bubbled through Analisa. She looked toward the entrance of the Capri Bar and Grille, one of the elegant bars in the Augustus Hotel and Casino. The five-star Las Vegas hotel boasted an eclectic clientele of celebrities and millionaires, many of them sexy, polished men who frequented the Capri. Analisa was used to them coming on to her. She took her job as bartender seriously and always fended off their advances with a smile. Her smiles helped get her nice tips too. She sure needed the money.

Despite the beautiful people who came in and out of her bar, none had affected her like Cody Lamont, who stood in the doorway until their eyes met, then sauntered toward her, his full lips tilted in a smile. She liked his friendly smile, his easy-going manner, his humor, the respectful way he treated her. She'd had customers treat her as their servant, but never Cody.

His looks weren't bad either. She thought of him as a sexy nerd, with his short black hair, and his intelligent brown eyes behind black-framed geek glasses. The ruggedness of his chiseled cheekbones and square jaw hinted at hidden depths of strength.

Her pulse jumped a notch when he sat at the bar in front of her. "Hey, Analisa, how's it going?"

My day just got better now that you're here. "It's been busy," she said instead.

"That's good, right?"

"Sure is. The usual?"

When he nodded, she pulled down a Pilsner glass from the overhead rack and filled it with the draught lager he always ordered.

"Thanks," he said with a smile when she slid his drink in front of him.

His smile dazzled as always, his teeth perfect and white in his tanned face. He'd told her he was a medical supplies salesman from Ohio, in Vegas for a conference. Considering the cloudy March weather in Vegas, and that it probably wasn't sunny now in Ohio, his tan surprised her. The blackness of his hair made her wonder if he dyed it, but he didn't strike her as a guy who would dye his hair or go to a tanning salon.

Analisa returned his smile as she scanned him. His white, button-down shirt, opened at the neck to reveal a scattering of fine light-colored hair, stretched across broad shoulders. She'd checked him out many times and knew the dark jeans he favored showcased his tight butt and his long legs that went on forever.

"You look nice," he said. "But then you always do. I like your hair down."

"Thanks." She resisted the urge to flip aside strands of her long hair that lay over her shoulders. She usually wore it pinned up, but this morning, running late, she hadn't bothered to style it.

Another customer sat at the bar, and she reluctantly left Cody to wait on the other man. She couldn't allow herself to get too close to Cody. When his conference ended, he'd go back to Ohio and she'd never see him again. Years ago she'd fallen deeply in love with a man whose work took him to Las Vegas on a regular basis. His betrayal had torn a hole in her heart. She would not let that happen again.

Busy with the crush of customers who'd come in for the bar's Happy Hour, Analisa couldn't spare more time to talk to Cody. Friday night in Vegas, the workers poured out of their buildings and casinos, and the tourists finished their sightseeing or were taking a break from gambling. Everyone wanted to party in Sin City. Everyone except her. She'd go home to the small house she shared with her mom, have dinner, then hit the books. In about eighteen months, she'd have her degree, and she could do what she'd always wanted—teach.

She snuck a glance at Cody. He'd finished his second beer and signaled her over. "Another?" she asked when she reached him.

"No. I'm fine." He drew a deep breath, then met her gaze. "What time do you get off work?"

"Six."

He cleared his throat. "Analisa, I was wondering. Would you have dinner with me tonight?"

She smoothed a hand down her black pants. The Augustus frowned on employees becoming involved with hotel guests, but Cody had told her he was staying at the MGM. She wanted to go out with him, and her mom would be glad to see her enjoy herself for a change. But if she went to dinner with him and they had a great time, his leaving would be harder on her. She didn't want to like him enough to miss him when he left.

"Analisa?"

He watched her, waiting.

Her trepidation warred with her desire to see more of him. She was overthinking, as Patti always told her. "I'd like that," she finally said.

Cody seemed like a genuine guy, but she had to be careful. She made it a rule not to get into cars with guys she didn't know well. If they stayed on the crowded Strip and she didn't get into a car with him, she'd be okay. "I have to go home to change. How about if we meet back here at seven-thirty?"

His smile kicked up butterflies in her stomach.

"Great! It's a date." He stood and placed several bills on the bar. "See you at seven-thirty."

She watched him as he walked away.

"He finally ask you out?" Patti said, coming up to her.

"Yes."

"You go, girl."

"Patti, I don't know. He seems really nice, but I have studying to do, and I'm scheduled to work all weekend. I don't want to get to know him better when he won't be here long."

"Overthinking again, girl. You'll fit in the studying. Go out and have some fun."

"I guess you're right." Analisa scooped up the bills Cody had put on the bar. As usual, he over-tipped. Way over.

ALL ABOUT CARA MARSI

An award-winning and eclectic author, Cara Marsi is published in romantic suspense, paranormal romance, and contemporary romance. She loves a good love story, and believes that everyone deserves a second chance at love. Sexy, sweet, thrilling, or magical, Cara's stories are first and foremost about the love. Treat yourself today, with a taste of romance.

When not traveling or dreaming of traveling, Cara and her husband live on the East Coast of the United States in a house ruled by two spoiled cats who compete for attention.

Read more about Cara's books and sign up for her newsletter at her website CaraMarsi.com. She's on Goodreads, Facebook, Instagram, and Pinterest and is always interested in meeting new friends.

BOOKS BY CARA MARSI

A Catered Romance

A Cat's Tale & Other Love Stories

(All stories in this anthology are available separately)

A Cinderella Christmas

A Groom for Christmas (Love On a Dare Book 1)

Wedded On a Dare (Love On a Dare Book 2)

Love On a Dare Duet Boxed Set

Accidental Love

Capri Nights

Cursed Mates

Her Forever Husband

Her Snow White Christmas (Snow Globe Magic Book 1)

Her Frog Prince Holiday (Snow Globe Magic Book 2)

Her Red Riding Hood Valentine (Snow Globe Magic Book 3)

Snow Globe Magic Holiday Boxed Set

Logan's Redemption (Redemption Book 1)

Franco's Fortune (Redemption Book 2)

Luke's Temptation (Redemption Book 3)

Josh's Salvation (Redemption Book 4)

The Redemption Series Boxed Set

Love Potion

Loving Or Nothing

Murder, Mi Amore

Storm of Desire

Sweet Temptations

Sweet Temptations Boxed Set

The One Who Got Away

The Ring

Wedded in Vegas (Gambling on Love Book 1)

Love by Chance (Gambling on Love Book 2)

A Very Vegas Christmas (Gambling on Love Book 3)

The Gambling on Love Trilogy

Multi-Author Boxed Sets

Wedding Dreams Boxed Set

Brandywine Brides: A Blackwood Legacy Anthology

Sizzling Summer Boxed Set

The Marriage Coin Boxed Set

Read excerpts at www.caramarsi.com

All books available at online booksellers

A Catered Romance, A Groom for Christmas, Brandywine Brides: A Blackwood Legacy Anthology, Capri Nights, Cursed Mates, Franco's Fortune, Logan's Redemption, Love On a Dare Duet, Loving Or Nothing, Luke's Temptation, Murder, Mi Amore, Snow Globe Magic, The Gambling on Love Trilogy, The Marriage Coin, and Wedded On a Dare, are available in print

www.ingramcontent.com/pod-product-compliance
Lightning Source LLC
Chambersburg PA
CBHW020509260626
47156CB00006B/1935